overthrown

by

strangers

also by ronan bennett

THE SECOND PRISON
THE CATASTROPHIST

ronan bennett

overthrown
by strangers

review

Copyright © 1992 Ronan Bennett

The right of Ronan Bennett to be identified as the Author of
the Work has been asserted by him in accordance with the
Copyright, Designs and Patents Act 1988.

First published in 1992 by Hamish Hamilton

First published in this edition in 2001 by REVIEW

An imprint of Headline Book Publishing

10 9 8 7 6 5 4 3 2 1

ISBN 0 7472 6820 7

Typeset by
Letterpart Ltd, Reigate, Surrey

Printed and bound in Great Britain by
Clays Ltd, St Ives plc.

Headline Book Publishing
A division of Hodder Headline
338 Euston Road
London NW1 3BH

www.reviewbooks.co.uk
www.hodderheadline.com

For Eithne

CONTENTS

Your country is desolate, your cities are burned with fire: your land, strangers devour it in your presence, and it is desolate, as overthrown by strangers.

Isaiah, 1.7

p a r t   o n e

Overthrown by Strangers

ONE

The soldier, twenty-one years old, thirty-six hours into his first tour, had a sense of humour, and it stopped him killing Quinn. Ten minutes before Quinn had come into his sights, his sergeant had sent him to the backs of the houses. He had gone to the corner of the entry, where he crouched, shivering from the cold and damp. He had squinted into the dark and tried to concentrate. But he was bored. It was unlikely there would be an escape. There was still an hour before dawn: the raiding party would find the wanted man, probably still in bed. The soldier's attention had wandered.

Behind him, slightly to the right, a building was on fire, and the soldier had turned to look at it. The building, a bakery, had three large, long windows, through which the soldier could see flames slithering around doors and corners in search of a way out. The flames found the windows, and the panes vibrated as the fire sucked its breath. The soldier wanted to smash the windows to free them. How wrong, he thought, that something as fragile as glass should hold back the flames. Called by the light and colour and play, he had begun to get up from the damp pavement.

As he did so, he became aware of a figure in the entry hurrying towards him. It was, the soldier knew at once, Quinn, the man they had come to take. The soldier raised his rifle and put the sight on Quinn's chest. It brought Quinn to a halt; he lifted his arms and said something the soldier did not understand.

The soldier and Quinn were fifteen feet apart. The soldier increased by a fraction the pressure on the trigger; it brought him a feeling of intense satisfaction, of pleasure. He

3

tightened his trigger finger and imagined the gun's straining mechanism. The moon was full and bright. Behind him he heard the fire's roar and crackle and felt its delicious heat. To kill in such a setting.

It was then the soldier's sense of humour intervened. He had not noticed – at first – but he saw now that the man before him was naked. The soldier raised his chin half an inch from the stock, his eye from the sight. In the moonlight Quinn's skin was a corpse blue, licked by the yellow and orange of the flames. The soldier noticed the long vertical lines of Quinn's stomach muscles, lines that deepened and faded with his heavy breaths. The soldier's eye could see the beating of Quinn's heart.

He could have shot Quinn; instead (he could not help himself) he began to chuckle. As the squad's humorist and story-teller, the comedy of Quinn's nakedness would provide a tale. Already the soldier was thinking of how to play it. He decided it would work best played down. 'Down,' he whispered.

Hearing his own whisper startled him, and he realized that although Quinn had surrendered, he had yet to make him prisoner. For ten seconds he had neither said nor done anything to bring the man fully into his power. He saw that Quinn, having recovered from his shock, was eyeing him carefully. In the distance he could hear his comrades' voices, rushed and panicky, and, to call to them, the soldier moved his cheek further from the stock and shouted.

The word that came from his mouth was the last word he had formed. It was the word 'down', and it was followed, after a grimace, by 'shit'.

Behind the soldier the flames had gathered at the three windows into balled fists. They exploded through the glass. The soldier was knocked sideways to the wall by fire and heat.

Quinn was gone. 'Shit,' the soldier hissed; and he thought, What a miserable soldier am I. He shouted to his comrades, but the sound of his voice, thin and high, embarrassed him. Disconsolate, he fired a shot into the darkness of the entry, and in the echoes of the explosion found a shelter from his suffering. So powerful was the feeling of well-being it brought him, so instant the gratification, he could not stop himself firing again.

The glass confetti reminded Quinn of a time, many years before, on a farm when he had followed a tractor at harvest and had gazed at the spray of straw and dust, a shower that glinted in the sun and pricked his face and bare chest. It seemed to him now as if he were staring at the same sun, and, aware that his eyes must be deceiving him, he squinted until he grasped that what he was looking at was a naked light bulb. He heard a shot, and remembered there had been another, a second earlier.

He lay on his back. He knew he was no longer in the entry: he was in a house, in a room, a kitchen. He looked at his body and saw blood and thought he must have been hit. But where? No part of his body registered any pain. He stared at his chest and there was blood, on his legs, too, there was blood; but nowhere was there an obvious source.

He decided to get up. It was hard work. Now that he was standing he could find out where he was, what was going on. He screwed up his eyes in an effort to make sense of the shapes around him. The effort was too much and his vision suddenly faded, as if someone had turned on a powerful spotlight whose effect was to bleach everything of colour, dimension and depth. His head spun and he put out his hands in a blind search for support. He found nothing. He had the presence of mind to put out a hand to break his fall. His open palm hit the floor hard and struck something sharp. His hand slid along the floor and, clownishly, his body followed. He lost consciousness for a moment.

When he came to, he inspected his hand and found a long shard of glass had pierced the fatty part below the ball of the thumb. Quinn smiled, unconcerned. There was no pain, and (although he could not be certain) he was fairly sure the bloody hand belonged to someone else.

He saw a woman. She stood by an ironing board. She

wore a crimson nylon housecoat and had rich auburn hair.
At her feet was a plastic basket full of newly washed shirts
and blouses. Quinn squinted; the woman was Monica. He
strained to make out an expression on her face, but it
seemed blank, and for a moment he was not sure if it was
Monica at all. Although made anxious by her lack of
warmth, Quinn still thought, This is my luck. To find
Monica when my enemies have come for me. He got to his
feet to go to her and meant to say her name, but it came
out 'Ma'. He laughed and started to apologize, but his
words were making no sense. She continued to watch him,
her expression changing, becoming frightened. His confusion rose. The harder he strained to see her, the more
distant she became.

Then she screamed.

'Monica, darlin',' Quinn said, and he staggered closer to
her. 'Monica, are you doing the smoothing?'

The woman said nothing. She shrank back in alarm and
raised the iron. Quinn felt the heat against his chest, sharp
and stinging. His vision blurred. He passed a hand in front
of his face, trying to wipe away the fog in front of his eyes as
he might swipe at troublesome midges. His vision cleared.
He saw the woman was not Monica, but an older, stouter
woman. The hair, Monica's glinting dark red hair, was not
hair, but a coloured scarf that sat high over thin, damp,
roller-wrapped strands.

'Get away from me!' the woman screamed. She pushed
the iron into Quinn's chest. The pain made Quinn cry out,
and he had to grip a sideboard to keep himself from
falling.

But the pain focused his mind. He now knew where he was
and how he came to be there. He remembered the soldiers
breaking into Monica's house, their house, and his escape
into the entry, where the soldier had surprised him. He had
put his hands up and said, 'Don't shoot me, for the love of
God,' and had waited for the soldier to do something; and
waited. Until the fire overcame its glass guards and
exploded. On impulse, without time to evaluate his chances,

Quinn had leapt sideways and crashed through a window to end up lying on a torn back.

He was in the kitchen of someone's house and he had to hide.

His gaze fell on his blood on the floor, and he filled with panic: the blood would lead his pursuers straight to him. He would have to clean it up. His eyes picked out a mop, and, with a burst of energy, he lifted it. He said to the woman, forgetting she was not Monica, 'Monica, I must wipe away my blood. If they find me, they will kill me.' He worked frantically, passing the mop back and forth in wide, careless arcs. But, like a worn wiper on a windscreen, the mop merely left a grimy smear. Seeing this, Quinn worked more furiously. The effort exhausted him.

Outside he heard an engine roar, a radio, voices, angry and animated. He pressed the mophead to the floor, but could not find the strength to continue. He rested against the handle and watched, hardly aware that he was involved, as the blood from his wounds worried its way over the knots and the grain in the wood. Quinn stepped forward to erase the smears. Then he checked behind him, only to see that he had leaked yet more blood. He turned to deal with it. The trickle of blood had thickened; the handle was slippery and painful to hold. He lost his grip and the mop fell to the floor.

A face, camouflaged with black streaks, appeared at the broken window and the woman screamed again. The soldier, who wore a paratrooper's red beret, raised his rifle. Quinn dived for the door. There was another shot, and this time, for the first time, Quinn became aware of smell, of the cordite in the round; he wanted to be sick.

He was in the hallway. To his left were the stairs that led on to the landing, where a small window framed the moon. To his right, six feet away, was the front door. He made for it, thinking to escape on to the street. Before he had taken two steps the door crashed inwards. A soldier, very large, his rifle across his chest, momentarily off-balance, stumbled into the hallway. Quinn punched him in the face, with

7

terror-strength, and the soldier fell backwards. Quinn turned and made for the stairs. The first strides quenched his strength. Gripping the banister, he steadied himself and fixed on the window before him. He thought if he could only reach the window he could escape for ever. He would fly through the glass and be free. He let his head fall back, drew breath. He dived for the window.

There was a shot. He fell awkwardly on the landing. His ears rang and his nostrils filled with gun smoke. He was on his stomach and, feeling defenceless, made to turn on his side. As he did so, he noticed a dark, meaty hole in his thigh, just below the groin.

He looked up and saw a number of men coming quickly up the stairs. He squinted to make them out. With joy he saw that one of them was Denis. He again felt favoured by luck. Denis stood over him and grinned.

'I'm so happy to see you,' Quinn said.

Denis looked puzzled and turned to the other men. 'What did he say?'

'Denis,' Quinn said, 'I'm glad you have come, for I am in trouble.'

Denis bent down and, looking at Quinn's wounds, said in an urgent voice to the man behind him, 'Get the medic.'

Denis was talking strangely. Quinn's ears still buzzed with the gunshot, and the memory of the shooting brought back a recollection of the smell. It made Quinn want to vomit and he heaved. Blood came to his mouth and Denis caught the back of his head. He soothed Quinn. 'Hold on, cock, hold on.' Denis's accent was so strange Quinn could not understand what he was saying.

Denis. Denis was shouting to him across a smoky, noisy bar. He was saying, 'Hold on, hold on.' And Quinn watched as Denis pushed past the drinkers and approached him. Where were they? When was this from, this memory of a night in a bar? There were English voices around them. And Denis had a young face; it was long ago, then. 'You don't know how to handle that girl,' Denis was saying. 'She's after you.' Quinn said nothing and Denis turned to inspect the girl, a few feet from them. He said, 'If you don't want her, I do.'

Quinn had not liked it in England. They had arrived at Heysham on the night ferry, caught the train from Lime Street to Euston, and went to live in Kilburn in a hostel run by priests. They spent nine weeks in London. They worked mending roads and digging holes, eleven hours a day, sometimes more, and Saturdays and Sundays. They were up at five-thirty and on site by six. At night, they came home with their newspaper-wrapped suppers and cartons of milk. In nine weeks they went out only twice. The first time was to see a James Bond film in Leicester Square. They had planned it for a week. Before the film they had a Chinese meal in Soho. They ordered Sweet and Sour and the waiters were rude to them, which made Quinn angry but made Denis laugh. 'Paddy in Chinatown,' Denis had said, pointing at Quinn, red-faced with rage and humiliation.

After the film they had walked to the tube. As they were buying their tickets, Denis saw a photo booth. They combed their hair with Denis's comb before squeezing into it. They sent a photograph each to their mothers and kept the other two for themselves. Denis carried his in a wallet, and, in later years, would occasionally take it out to show to Quinn. Denis's face in the photograph was thin, shiny and clean-shaven. His eyes, which were light blue, came up in the half-tone as a shade of the palest grey. By contrast, Quinn's face was fuller; over the years he had lost weight and his face had hardened. The day Monica found Quinn's copy of the picture in a drawer of the dresser in their bedroom she studied it, then became angry. 'We've been married six years,' she said, 'and you never told me about this.' He said it was a photograph, nothing more. She said he was selfish. Quinn never saw the photograph again.

The young Denis was next to Quinn in the bar, the girl near by. This was their second night out. Denis had wanted to go for a drink. It was Saturday night and the bar was full of young people. There was music. They fell into company and the girl had started talking to Quinn. She drank a lager and lime. She stood next to the jukebox and pointed out the names of the bands and told Quinn which were her favourites. She was fifteen and sentimental, and she favoured songs about impossible love. She had run away from home after her mother had started sleeping with the lodger, she lived in a squat, did not work, did not go to school and had not one thought in her head about the future. To Quinn, who was little more than a year older, she was a child. As last orders were called, she pressed herself close to him and Quinn felt her breasts against his ribs. She said her friends were having a party and invited him back to the squat. Quinn said no. They parted, and as she left she gave Quinn a lost smile. Denis mocked Quinn. He said, 'I told you you didn't know how to handle that girl.'

'She was a child,' he said sharply.

'A child with big tits,' Denis said.

In bed that night Quinn was sure he had done the right thing, although later there were to be many nights when he wished he had gone with her. On these nights, in his dreams, Denis would come to him and taunt him.

Denis. In front of Quinn's eyes, by magic, Denis transformed himself into a uniformed soldier with a red beret. Quinn tried to speak, but found his mouth full of blood. The soldier who had been Denis shouted, 'Get that fucking medic.'

Quinn began to feel cold. The cold told him to be afraid, for Quinn understood about gunshot wounds; he knew there was a difference between fatal and non-fatal injuries, and generally the wounded were aware of the distinction. Until the cold had laid itself upon him, Quinn had almost forgotten that he had been shot, he had simply been waiting for the men around him to take him somewhere. With the cold he began to think about being shot. Years before, after his return from London, eighteen years old and working again as a road-mender, on a misty autumn morning, he and the men he worked with laid their drills and shovels to one side and went to the tin hut, where they sat and drank tea. One man opened a tabloid newspaper at the naked woman and exhibited her to the others. She was blonde, had high, round buttocks and dark dots of nipples. Her back was arched and she clasped her hands behind her head. The men admired her and made jokes. They were laughing when the shooting started.

A gunman at the entrance of the hut fired three shots into the grubby huddle of working men. He fired only three shots because, on the third, the magazine dropped out. The gunman, unaware of this, aware only that his gun would no longer shoot, fled. He was gone before Quinn had the chance even to move to defend himself or to hide. Quinn looked at the floor and saw the newspaper, saw the model's breasts and saw blood drip on to them, drops darker than the nipples. The picture became splattered and then soggy with Quinn's blood. He had been hit in the neck but knew then, as he knew now, that at least until the terrible cold had begun to crawl over him, the wound would not kill him. One of his workmates put a handkerchief against his neck and told him to be still until the ambulance arrived.

Quinn continued to stare at the model until she dissolved in his blood.

Monica appeared from nowhere and she stood beside Denis. She looked tired and disappointed; she leaned against Denis's shoulder, and Denis put his hand on her head. Quinn would have liked to have reached out to her, and to have said something to explain; but he knew before trying that it was useless. He had neither the strength nor the words. Nor the will. He had lost Monica a lifetime ago. When she had married him, she had been fascinated by him. That was how Quinn remembered their first two years together. And then, one day, the fascination stopped. Quinn said nothing and could only watch. Her loving words changed; they were no longer careless, fantastic expressions of her passion for him. They turned into considered statements; she was a woman weighing up the advantages and disadvantages, the past and the future; she would not trust love.

Quinn did not press her, and there was no way he could tell what effect this had on her, how she interpreted his silence – as acquiescence in her withdrawal from him? He did not know. Quinn knew only that love could not be cajoled or bullied or bribed back. He watched Monica, silently but without resentment, slip loose from him; although they continued to live together (when they could, for Quinn was usually wanted for something), their life shrank and shrivelled like paper scorched by flame. From time to time Quinn would catch the look of disappointment he saw now in Monica's eyes as she stood with Denis on the landing.

Quinn shivered with the cold. Denis, but in a voice that was not Denis's, and in words that neither were his, said, 'Hold on, lad. The medic's on his way.'

Quinn, withered by Monica's disappointment, could not care about the medic. Anything to be out of this cold, he thought. He said, 'Oh, this is the end of me.' The words came out in a splutter of blood. The man who was Denis seemed to think this faintly comic, and laughed gently, and stroked Quinn's forehead with thick, heavy fingers.

At his touch, at human touch, Quinn grew afraid of death. His resignation turned into panic; he did not want to die before Denis and Monica. He had seen the dead. They had always looked stupid. Death was neither tragic nor heroic; it was just stupid. It would be embarrassing to die before his wife and best friend, to be so weak before them. He struggled against the cold, trying to cast it off, as if it could physically be lifted and flung aside. But the cold would not go.

Quinn concentrated on Monica before him, and on Denis. He could see them clearly now, Monica leaning on his friend. He saw Denis turn to kiss her. He kissed her fore-head, her eyes were shut to receive the pleasures that came with the kisses. He stroked her hair and gently lifted her face up. He kissed her on the mouth and she bit his lower lip and sucked it. With sudden excitement Denis pulled her to him. She took his head in her hands and kissed him. When she stopped, she turned to look at Quinn. Denis pushed his nose and mouth into her thick hair. There was blood on Monica's lips.

Blood ran into Quinn's eyes. What he saw was a still image of his friend and his wife. Monica, her eyes expressionless, looking out at Quinn. Quinn's blood trickled over the top of the photograph. The first fat bead made a line between Denis and Monica; the second went through Denis's face; the third, the thickest, which thickened with every second, ran across Monica until it obliterated her. Quinn blinked to get the blood out of his eyes. The harder he blinked the more quickly the photograph dissolved. When the picture became so drenched and soggy that the images of Denis and Monica were wiped out, his love and jealousy having at last bled away, Quinn was able to feel relief.

Denis, wearing the paratrooper's beret, in a voice bearing the sympathy of one comrade for another, said, 'Hold on, lad.' Then he shouted to the other men, 'Where's that fucking medic?'

One of the men shouted, 'He's coming now, Sergeant.'

The medic pushed his way up the stairs and through the throng of soldiers. On reaching Quinn, he said, 'Well, what's this?' He peered at the bloody hole in Quinn's inner thigh and gasped admiringly.

He said, 'I'd fuck that, wouldn't you?'

When Monica opened the door to Quinn, it was as to a stranger. She regarded him, abstractedly, from another and distant shore. Quinn, uneasy, searched her face and eyes; he searched and found nothing there for him.

Quinn indicated the telephone and said, 'I tried to call from the airport . . .'

She interrupted him. She said, 'I didn't answer.'

At the same time he said, 'There was no answer.'

They watched each other in silence.

Then she said, 'I knew it was you. I heard it on the radio.'

She spoke, Quinn thought, from a faraway place, and for a moment he believed she must be sad, and he imagined himself as the bringer of relief from her sadness. He was about to say, 'Monica . . .' but stopped; for Monica gave a brief, harsh laugh. A rush of sentiment and nostalgia took hold of him and squeezed until he shook. Monica moved away and left him alone in the doorway.

After a moment he followed her to the kitchen, where he found her leaning against the fridge. She held a cigarette nervously in her long fingers. The two dark lines that started at the corners of her eyes gave her a tired, vulnerable look, and Quinn was touched. In spite of the hardness Quinn saw, he still thought he could be the bringer of joy to her; he would soften her with his kisses and transport them back to the happy time and place they had once occupied together. He stepped towards her.

Monica reacted as if it were an assault. She pressed herself against the fridge and tightened. Quinn froze. She would scream, she would strike him, he knew, if he tried to touch her. He felt a surge of anger; he wanted to hit her, to beat her to the floor. Monica, who could read his thoughts, was not cowed. She stood her ground, trembling only a little. The shore she stood on was a floating island, carried further away from Quinn by currents he could not fight.

From behind came a deep voice, genial and concerned. Quinn turned and, eyes closed, clasped Denis to him, his head resting on Denis's shoulder. Denis slapped his back and let Quinn rest there.

Denis said, 'You've lost weight, you poor fucker.'

Quinn laughed. He was aware of Monica moving around them, taking advantage of Denis's arrival. From over Denis's shoulder Quinn caught a glimpse of her, her back to him, in the kitchen doorway. She stopped. She drew deeply on the cigarette, stubbed the butt into an ashtray, and, her head slightly tilted back, exhaled. She turned her head, not to look at Quinn or Denis, but to a mirror. She stared at herself with stern eyes. What she was thinking Quinn could only guess. She moved on through the door and into the other room. Quinn heard an angry swish as Monica pulled the curtains.

'How's the form?' Denis asked.

'Your name got mentioned,' Quinn said, disentangling himself and not looking Denis in the eye.

'It was in the papers,' Denis replied, unconcerned.

'Once or twice.'

Denis said, 'Everything for me was sound.'

Quinn nodded and leaned back while Denis regarded him. 'You need fattening up, boy, and I know just the thing for you. Let's go.'

'I have to talk to Monica.'

Denis put his warm hand behind Quinn's neck and said quietly, 'Let's leave her a while.'

Quinn felt Denis take his arm and gently lead him into the hall. It was the first time in his life that Quinn had allowed himself, or wanted, to be led.

Denis opened the door. He called out cheerily to Monica in the front room. 'I'm taking the man out to get a bit of meat on his bones. We won't be long.'

The room was in darkness but for a violent blade of sunlight which slashed through the curtains. Quinn could see Monica seated in a high-sided armchair; cigarette smoke, silvery and airy, drifted up from her. Denis said again that they would not be long. Monica said nothing, and Denis pulled the door behind them.

Outside in the street there was a new saloon car, deep red and highly polished. Denis took out the keys and Quinn frowned. Denis, uncomfortable, grimaced. He indicated the car with an anxious wave of his hand.

'Times have changed,' he said.

Quinn got in and they drove to a bar. Denis parked in a side street and they walked to the high wire fence surrounding the bar. Denis pressed a buzzer on the intercom and a voice came back, 'Who is it?'

Denis said, 'Have a guess, Shot-in-the-head.'

Inside there was a clock that said it was ten to three. There were two barmen and four drinkers: men, there were no women. There were Formica-topped tables, scored with ring stains; there were hard chairs; the floor was lino-covered. Sunlight squeezed through two narrow and heavily grilled windows.

Denis said to the barman, 'What about you, Shot-in-the-head?'

'What'll you have, Denis?' The man's tone was neutral.

Denis ordered and brought the glasses to the table. 'We're going to get you a right feed of drink,' he said to Quinn.

Quinn said, 'I have to talk to Monica.'

Denis drained a third of his pint. With the back of his hand, he wiped the froth from his mouth. He said, 'Give her a minute to adjust. She thought you were going to get life. She needs to come to terms with it, with you.'

'She had two years,' Quinn said.

Denis nodded.

They finished their beers and Denis ordered another two pints. The barman, whom Denis again addressed as Shot-in-the-head, served the drinks.

'Isn't that Pat Coogan?' Quinn asked.

'Shot-in-the-head,' Denis said. 'Pat was in here the night the UFF came in – you were in jail in England. The Yuff shot the place up, and Pat, he wasn't behind the bar – he was by the back door. On the way out one of the Yuff men whacked him over the head with the rod, it was an old Grease gun. It turned out three people got hit. Old Liam Clarke was worst, he got hit in the back and got paralysed. Pat was running around, a bit of blood, you would hardly see it, on his head, screaming, "I'm shot in the head." It was where they'd clocked him with the Greaser.'

'He doesn't like it.'

'Would you? I mean, there was people seriously hurted, and all he had was a cut in the head – hardly fucking heroic.'

Denis drank. He sat down his glass and looked closely at Quinn. 'Speaking of bullet wounds, what about your own?'

'I was hit only the once,' Quinn said. 'The doctors said I did more damage to myself jumping through the window of your woman's house.'

'Aggie Fitzgerald. I heard she ironed your chest.'

'She was frightened.'

Denis shook his head. 'She was never sympathetic. I went round to have a word with her after. Told her did she not know how to show a bit more hospitality to her neighbours.'

'If I'd known I was going to beat the charges, I'd have surrendered when they broke in.'

They drank, and the bar began to fill up. Some of the new arrivals, recognizing Quinn, came over to congratulate him. Good to see you out, they said, slapping him on the back. Good to be out, Quinn replied.

Denis, more drinks on the table, said, 'You probably wouldn't have heard. Jim Kerr beat that murder charge he was in on.'

'Murder of who?'

'A peeler. It went back to '83. You remember Jim? He was in the cages with us.'

'Yes.'

'He beat the murder – when was it? – about six or seven

weeks ago,' Denis said. 'But then the Garda wanted to talk to him about – do you remember that tout, Macmillan, got hisself killed in Dublin a few years ago? They wanted to talk to Jim about that. But, like, Jim didn't want to discuss it, so he blew. He's supposed to be in New York.'

A man brought drinks to the table. 'Make up for lost time,' he said. Quinn and Denis thanked him.

Quinn told Denis that Monica had not come to see him in jail and had written only once. When Denis tried to say that Monica had a point of view, Quinn cut him short. 'I don't want to hear it,' he said. Denis shrugged and went to get more drinks, pints with chasers of vodka and Coke.

Quinn, never a big drinker and getting drunker, began to lose interest in the conversation. His thoughts reached for Monica. Warmed by the company of Denis and by the greetings of old acquaintances, he assumed that Monica, too, would now be warm to him. Into his mind came pictures of them together when they had been happy. He remembered a time early in their marriage on a hot summer's afternoon when they had lain on the bed, the covers on the floor. Quinn, his head on Monica's stomach, had been dozing. He woke and dreamily started to kiss her belly. Monica pushed her fingers into his hair and he felt her nails on his scalp. He buried his face in her stomach, one hand under the small of her back, the other on her thigh. They lay still and then Monica began to laugh, a laugh from deep in her throat. 'Sean,' she said, 'you have the most powerful heartbeat of any man I've known. You're going to have to move from there.'

He wanted to talk to Monica.

'Have you change for the phone?' he asked Denis.

Denis did not answer at first. He put his hand on Quinn's forearm and said, with concern in his voice, 'Give her a little time.'

Quinn had a sudden flash of the image of Denis and Monica he had had in his head when he was lying wounded on the stairs. He replied coldly, 'She's my wife.'

Denis shrugged.

'Have you got change – or not?'

Quinn got to his feet and leaned over Denis. Reluctantly, Denis handed him some coins. Quinn made his way, a little unsteadily, to the phone on the far end of the bar. He selected a coin and dialled. He let the phone ring twenty times before hanging up and trying again. This time he counted thirty-five rings. He returned to the table, where Denis had set up another round.

Denis was looking expectantly at him. 'Not in,' Quinn said.

A woman's voice, loud and friendly, calling his name, startled Quinn.

'You look like you need a big Ulster fry, child.' The woman came up and kissed him on both cheeks. 'And how are you keeping, you old rogue?' she enquired of Denis.

'Sound, Bridie. Would you have a drink?'

'You're awful good, Denis. A Norwegian, to celebrate Sean getting out.'

'Ano'her wee gin,' Denis said, going to the bar.

Bridie turned to Quinn and said, 'When are you going to call in for a bit of crack with your Aunt Maire and me?'

'Soon. How have you been keeping, the two of you?'

'No complaints.'

Denis returned with the drinks, then spotted someone he knew. He hailed him, and to Quinn and Bridie he said, 'I'll only be a minute.'

Denis made his way through the drinkers and caught the man by the arm.

'That's Brendan Doyle,' Bridie said.

Quinn looked over; he knew the man.

'Wait till I tell you something,' Bridie was saying.

Denis, Quinn saw, appeared anxious, Brendan subdued. He barely heard Bridie and her story, but, instead, drawn by Denis's manner, strained to catch the men's conversation above the chatter in the bar, now bustling with early-evening drinkers. Denis pointed a finger at Brendan; Brendan shook his head. Denis gave Brendan a hard look and then, chin trembling with anger, moved off in the direction of the toilets.

Bridie's story was winding down and Quinn laughed appreciatively. She was already aware that his mind was elsewhere when he said, 'Bridie, excuse me a minute. I want to have a word with Brendan.' Bridie looked at her watch and said she had to be going. She finished her drink and stood up with Quinn.

'Watch yourself now,' she said, kissing him. 'And come and see us soon.'

'I will, of course.'

Quinn went over to Brendan. 'Sean, good to see you out,' Brendan said.

'I saw you having a word with Denis there.' Brendan said nothing. 'Is there anything I can help with?' Quinn asked.

Brendan shrugged. He looked towards the door to the toilets, watching, Quinn assumed, for Denis.

'You know how Denis is, always cutting corners, you know?' Brendan said quickly.

'I know,' Quinn replied with a laugh and a broad smile intended to encourage Brendan. It did not come easily to Quinn, this false heartiness. He thought he must look like a spiv, and he cancelled the smile.

'He has his faults,' Quinn said.

Brendan said, 'He's desperate with money.'

'Is there anything I can do?'

'I don't know.' Brendan glanced at the door to the toilets. 'There's a row over some things that have gone missing.'

'What?'

'A gun, for one thing.' Brendan paused before continuing. 'Denis and me dumped it and now it's vanished. There's a Court of Inquiry and Denis wants to say he didn't know where the rod was. He says with the other trouble he's got—'

'What other trouble?'

'There's some money that went missing.'

'How much?'

'I heard twelve hundred pound. Denis says that he can argue one thing, but two and it's looking bad for him – no smoke without fire, you know? The thing is, I can't do what he wants.'

Denis, Denis. 'I'll talk to Denis,' Quinn said. 'Then I'll talk to them. Don't worry.' He put a hand on Brendan's arm. 'It'll be all right.'

Brendan did not seem convinced, but he said, 'Sound.'

Denis came up. He was unable to conceal his surprise at seeing Quinn and Brendan together. He scrutinized Brendan's face. It made Brendan nervous. Denis slapped him on the back, then turned to Quinn.

'Bridie's a good soul.'

'Yes,' Quinn replied.

'Let's move on,' Denis said, glancing at Brendan.

Quinn drained his glass and said goodbye to Brendan, making sure there was nothing in his tone that implied a confidence had been exchanged.

Outside it was dark and Quinn felt depressed. He thought about Monica: he wanted to be with her.

'Where are we headed?' he asked Denis.

'Andytown.'

'Have they got a phone where we're going?'

'Yes,' Denis said. There was impatience in his voice, which he quickly tried to cover with a smile. Quinn pretended not to have noticed.

Fifteen minutes later they were outside the bar. Denis locked the car doors, dropped the keys on the pavement and hiccuped loudly as he bent to retrieve them.

'Looks like we'll be needing a taxi from here on,' he said.

Quinn was surprised. Denis normally held his drink well.

In the bar they drank two rounds more. Quinn talked with the customers, men he had not seen for two years. But they could not take Monica out of his thoughts. He wanted to phone her; his heart began to pound. He looked to see if his shirt was moving with the beat of his chest. He turned over in his mind memories of the times Monica had laid her head against his heart and of the times she had squirmed and laughed as the blows of his heart had fallen between her legs. The memories excited and encouraged him. A feeling of optimism was awakening within him, and to nourish it he selected the memory of the time when they had argued and

Monica had thrown cups and plates at him, and overturned a table and smashed a lamp. They stood in the wreckage, and Quinn, who had been unable to soothe her, could say nothing and just stayed still. And, at last, Monica, exhausted, came over to him and unbuttoned his shirt and kissed his breast. Then she laid her ear against his heart and seemed at peace.

As Quinn got up to use the phone, Denis took hold of his arm.

'Are you calling Monica?'

Angrily, Quinn shook him off and Denis said, 'Sorry.'

Quinn went to the phone. As he dialled, he watched Denis at the table, head bowed. Quinn felt sorry for him. Denis had troubles. They came from his disregard for rules, his liking for sailing close to the wind. Denis was a chancer. But he was also warm and generous. Quinn would sort out Denis's problems later; now he had to attend to his own.

Heart thumping, unsteady from the drink, he leaned sideways into the wall and pressed the receiver to his ear. On the last digit Quinn's finger slipped. He cursed and began again. Looking up, he saw two men staring at him from across the bar. They whispered to each other and one nodded while the other turned and went outside. Quinn finished dialling while keeping an eye on the man, whom he was sure he knew from somewhere. The ringing tone snatched his attention and he jerked up from the wall. He heard the phone ring two, three, four times. On the fifth ring Monica answered.

'Hello?' she said.

The man was approaching.

Quinn leaned over the mouthpiece and was about to speak when a hand fell on his shoulder.

'There's someone wants to see you outside,' the man said.

Monica said urgently, 'Sean, Sean, is that you?'

'He's sort of in a hurry.'

'Sean?'

Reluctantly Quinn replaced the receiver. The man indicated the door.

As they were leaving, Denis came over.

'Denis, how's the form?' Quinn's escort said. His attitude to Denis was not friendly.

'Sound, Sammy,' Denis replied, going through the formalities. He glanced at Quinn.

'Sean's with us for a minute. There's no bother.'

'No problem,' Quinn said.

Denis, after a moment's hesitation, moved aside and Quinn and Sammy left. Sammy pointed to a car across the street. 'In the back,' he said.

The car smelt of cigarettes and hair tonic. A tubby, middle-aged man with horn-rimmed spectacles and thin, slicked-back hair sat in the corner of the back seat. He put out his hand as the car moved off.

'Sean, a bit of justice for a change. How are you?'

'Sound, Seamus. Yourself?'

'You know, the usual. Nothing ever changes.'

The car turned right. Seamus said, 'I'm not going to take up your time. I just wanted to see you, see you were all right. But, once you've got settled and sorted yourself out, I'd like for you to come and see me.'

'Tomorrow?'

Seamus laughed. He put his arm around Quinn. The car turned right again, then again a little further on. 'You've been missed, Sean. I'm going to send someone to your house. They'll tell you where and when.'

'Fine.'

'A word. I know Denis is your friend.'

'He is,' Quinn said to make sure Seamus understood before he went on.

'Sometimes friends can do more harm than strangers. Sometimes friends, even lovers, turn out to be strangers to you.' Seamus stared at his hands and twisted the wedding band on his stubby finger. 'Denis,' he began slowly, 'has some problems . . .' – he paused to select the right words – 'which are considerable. These problems that he has might not get resolved in his favour. Don't get caught up in any of his troubles.'

23

The car took another right and came to a stop. They were outside the bar again. Quinn opened the door and said, 'Tomorrow.' He was thinking he had been foolish in having talked to Brendan. Brendan had got word to Seamus. He was about to get out when Seamus beckoned him to close the door.

'I ask you to come to see me. You say, tomorrow. You're just out of jail. You need time. But I know if I had asked you to come now, you would have said yes. Why?'

Quinn shrugged. 'I don't know what to tell you. There is nothing else.'

Seamus gazed directly at him and did not speak for some moments. 'Well,' he said at last, and with a certain disappointment in his voice, 'it's always harder to put these things into words. It's easier just to do, though there are those who would say that's an excuse not to think.'

'You don't have to think when there's nothing else: no options, no dilemmas.'

Seamus said, 'Tell me, what's the main thing that makes Denis different from you and me, and the people we work with?'

Quinn shrugged.

'It's this. He is an individual. He does not understand – he can't grasp – what it means to be part of something, thinks it's absurd, thinks it restricts him. Now where does that take you, if you're like Denis? It means you will do whatever you have to to get what you want. The individual is greedy, cowardly, mean. The individual has nothing behind him, no strength, no direction.'

Quinn wanted to defend Denis, but before he could say anything Seamus reached across and opened the door. The smell of the hair tonic was strong; Quinn's eyes smarted.

'He'll do whatever he has to,' Seamus said, 'if he has the balls.'

The door closed and the car pulled away. As Quinn made for the bar, Sammy approached him. 'That's a chancer in there. The man is a hollow big bastard.'

'You're talking about a friend of mine,' Quinn replied coldly.

'You remember Eddie Stilges, the hood? You remember Stilges, the one who raped his own half-sister and beat her near to death? Ask Denis, ask your friend about that.'

Quinn pushed Sammy out of the way. Inside he found Denis at the table. 'What did Sammy want?' Denis asked.

'Nothing.'

'Did you talk to Monica?'

Quinn suddenly remembered Monica's voice on the phone, the way she had said his name. The night had softened her, as it had softened him. He did not answer for some time, until he became aware of Denis's gaze on his face. At last, he said, 'Yes.'

'And?'

Quinn looked past Denis, a warmth creeping into his heart. He said, 'It's going to be all right. She said it's going to be all right.'

They had two more drinks before Denis suggested moving on again, to another bar. Quinn sensed that Denis needed him, and, though he desperately wanted to return to Monica, did not protest. Denis got to his feet and said that as he was too drunk to drive he would call a friend of his who worked in the evenings as a taxi driver.

'Taxi'll be here in ten minutes,' Denis said on his return. 'Time for another round.'

They gulped down the last of the drinks when the taxi driver entered. Denis said to Quinn, 'You know Pat, don't you? From Albert Street.'

Quinn vaguely remembered the family.

Denis gave Pat directions to a club, where they served after hours. Quinn did not know it. The journey took about fifteen minutes.

As they were entering the club, Quinn said, 'This'll be the last one. I want to get back to Monica.'

Denis said, 'You're making a mistake.'

Quinn stopped abruptly. 'Denis, I have come back from the dead. I am back and I want my wife.'

It's not that easy,' Denis replied, staring blearily into Quinn's eyes.

Quinn grabbed Denis and shook him. 'I have come back.'

He was so angry that he almost confronted Denis with the things he had been told. But he held back: he would not speak now; he would need his senses about him for that. He forced his anger down. He let Denis go and entered the club.

Denis said in a whisper, to himself, 'You have come back.'

Denis bought a round, which they drank in silence. There was no one in the club Quinn knew, and he felt uncomfortable among the strangers. After half an hour Quinn said he wanted to leave. Reluctantly Denis went to phone for a taxi. The call took a long time and Quinn was becoming agitated by the time Denis returned.

'What took you so long?'

'I couldn't get Pat so I had to ask for another one I know that drives. You have to be careful with these taxis, with all the assassinations. He'll be here in twenty minutes. We'll meet him across the road so he can miss the one-way.'

Denis ordered more drinks, which Quinn only accepted after some hesitation. He was not drunk, his head ached and he felt nauseous. He took deep breaths to try to sober up. They did no good.

Denis drained his glass, checked his watch and got up. Together they left the club. Denis put his arm around Quinn and said, 'I'm jealous of you.'

For a moment Quinn thought he meant Monica. He said suspiciously, 'What?'

'Your name.'

Quinn was relieved. He laughed.

'Me, on the other hand, what do people say about me? There's a couple have told you tonight what they think about me, isn't that right?'

Quinn became uncomfortable. 'You're sound, Denis.'

'People think I'm some sort of fool.'

'No.'

'But there's one thing I'm not a fool about. I know the

difference between what's important and what's not important.'

It was to be, Quinn realized, one of those drunken talks. Funny, no matter how drunk he got, when the talk took this turn he was always conscious of it; he knew it was mawkish and still he accepted his part in it; he repeated the lines for the occasion, even though, drunk as he was, he could always hear his speech with sober and embarrassed ears. But, after their sharp exchange on entering the club, he was happy enough to go on with it.

In the dark they walked, unsteadily, across the main road, Denis still with an arm around Quinn. It was early in the morning, there was no traffic and there was no one in sight.

'You know what I mean?' Denis continued stubbornly.

'Yes,' Quinn replied. 'Yes, I do.' He had no idea what Denis was referring to; they were the words for the occasion and as such should have been accepted without question, as he had accepted Denis's words. But Denis stopped. He knew Quinn had lied, that he did not understand, and he pushed Quinn away from him and gave him an angry look.

'That's not what I mean. You don't know what I mean.'

'You're right,' Quinn conceded with a laugh, hoping his jocular honesty would calm Denis.

'Ah, fuck it!' Denis exhaled heavily and regarded Quinn. 'What is important,' he said with bitter impatience, 'you take what's important, and what's not important – what's important is what you fucking leave behind.'

Quinn stared at him.

'You get what I'm saying to you?' Denis said belligerently.

'Yes,' Quinn said vaguely. He wanted to get home. He was tired, desperately sleepy. He wanted to be with Monica.

Denis looked around. 'Where's Eddie with that fucking car?'

Quinn came out of his sleepiness. 'Eddie? Eddie Stilges?'

Denis's head weaved on his shoulders. He mumbled, 'Eddie? How the fuck would I know? Eddie the cunt is what I know.'

Stilges's name reminded Quinn of the serious talk he

would have to have with Denis. He thought about Denis's troubles. *Which are considerable*, Seamus had said.

Denis spotted a car, a dark four-door saloon parked in a side street about thirty yards from where they stood. 'That's probably it,' he said. Quinn could just make out the driver; he was watching them.

'Wait there a minute,' Denis said, 'and I'll see if it's for us.' He stumbled towards the car. He bent down to talk to the driver through the passenger window, and came back to Quinn.

'It's ours,' he announced. 'I need a leak first. Come on over here.' Quinn, who also wanted to piss, followed Denis to an entry between two rows of houses. There was no moon; the stars were bright in the cold night sky. Quinn and Denis took opposite walls.

As he urinated, Denis said, 'When there's something important, at stake, that's when I stop being somebody's fool. That's when I take what I want.'

Denis, Quinn thought, had sobered up. His voice was sharp, it had an edge. Quinn looked up at the stars as he buttoned his fly. He turned around.

The impact kicked Quinn back against the wall, and he folded, slowly, to a sitting position, his legs stretched out before him. He raised his eyes and saw Denis, the gun at his side, take two steps towards him. Denis was breathing heavily, almost panting, the vapour visible in the cold air. Quinn looked up at the stars, they had turned red and were growing in size. They were big red holes in the black sky. Quinn now understood that, in reality, the sky beyond the black cover was a blood red. Good God, what a discovery. He would tell Denis, once he got to his feet. He put his hands on the ground by his hips and pressed. Nothing happened.

Denis stood beside him. He raised the pistol until it was pointing into Quinn's face and fired. Quinn's head rocked back as though it had been punched, and then fell forward. Denis crouched to peer into Quinn's face. Dissatisfied with the poor light, he stood back and lifted Quinn's head by putting his shoe under the chin. The head rolled back against the wall. Denis bent down for a closer look.

There was a lot of blood. Some of it was on his shoe. He cursed, then walked, unhurried, to the car.

The engine was running. Denis got in the front passenger seat. The driver put the car in gear and pulled smoothly away from the kerb.

'What was that about?' Eddie Stilges asked.

part two

The Captain of Fifty

THREE

It was just before sunset and in the heart of the city, as the hot air cooled to give the people their rest, the four labourers cast away their trowels and shovels, and made their way along the wide boulevards. The labourers were dirty, hands cut and aching; they passed palm trees, policemen and small children. The long route that they took was where no buses went, where the streets became alleys, and the people were silent. A police car went by; a drunk vomited in the gutter; a prostitute laughed; a bitch suckled her litter. A child sat in despotic silence atop his throne of a burnt-out car to review his sad kingdom and subjects. The labourers passed on.

In a clearing of waste ground stood a group of musicians. A dozen girls, their black hair swept back and held by clips, strummed banjos. The twanging was softened by the chords of guitars strummed by a dozen young men so carefully groomed they looked as though they had been scrubbed by their mothers. The musicians sang hymns to the greater glory of God. The labourers, embarrassed, not wanting to be there, leaned against the wall of an abandoned building.

Some people had gathered, twenty people or so. They stood in twos and threes and pawed the dusty ground; the women outnumbered the men, the children out numbered the women. A couple were junkies or winos. A scarred white man staggered to a telephone pole, leaned against it and opened his mouth wide to take in deep breaths. His chest heaved, he spluttered as he received each shock of air.

A woman, Spanish white, was different from the rest. She

stood, slightly apart, by a mail box. Her dark glasses hid most of her small face. She wore a short, fawn-coloured jacket with wide shoulders, and high-waisted, tight black pants. Her hips were slim, her finger nails painted red. Some of the poor people stared at her, but she affected not to notice. She gazed ahead, severe and arrogant.

Nick Zenga, in smart casual clothes, moved around taking photographs of the gathering. Most of the people turned away shyly or put their hands up to their mouths, grinning sheepishly like children. Zenga finished the roll and strolled across the street to join Pastor Victor Jank.

'Not a bad turnout,' Jank said, 'considering.' He spoke softly and slowly, his manner that of a mild and humourless university professor.

'Maritza Dorfmann should be bringing some of her people, I suppose,' Zenga said.

'How many people does she have over there?' Jank asked.

'Maybe twenty. Right now there's more. She got men doing construction, hired another seven or eight to put up another building beside the factory.'

'So, twenty-five, thirty?'

'Yeah. But not that many will come, even though Maritza gave them time off. They are all mostly illegal also, afraid of *la Migra.*'

Jank checked his watch. 'The bus should be here any minute.' He put up his hand for shade against the setting sun and gazed down the long street. There was little traffic and no bus in sight.

'Here comes Maritza,' said Zenga, staring in the opposite direction.

A car, bright red with a white roof, pulled up across the street. The two men went over. Zenga opened the door. An overweight middle-aged woman, wearing large tinted glasses, got out. She had short, thin hair set in a perm. Her bust was large and heavy, the breasts did not appear to be separate but part of a roll of fat on her chest. She had no waist and was a foot shorter than Jank.

She took Jank's outstretched hand. 'Pastor Jank,' she said.

'Nice to see you again, Maritza,' Jank replied. 'I'm glad you could make it.'

'Any of your people here yet, Maritza?' Zenga asked.

Mrs Dorfmann pushed her glasses with her middle finger. She lighted on the labourers. 'Yes. Those men, they work for me.'

'How many? Three? Four? Those four?' Zenga asked. 'You think any more will show?'

Mrs Dorfmann pressed her thin lips together, pushed out her chin and turned up the palms of her hands. 'You know what they're like.'

Jank looked at her as she spoke. Her lipstick was smeared around her slack mouth.

'Well,' he said, 'that's what we're here for.'

'Is Andrew here?' Mrs Dorfmann asked.

'Any minute now. He's coming with the bus from Phoenix. He's in charge of the missionaries specially recruited for this programme. They're mostly pretty green, but Andrew's licking them into shape.'

Zenga, looking up the street, said, 'This could be the bus.'

He pointed to a bus which had pulled in off the main road and was coming towards them.

'Okay,' Jank said, smacking his hands together and casting an eye over the people. Not many, and bewildered-looking, except for the woman by the mail box; she was not one of them.

When the bus pulled to a halt, Zenga got the musicians to form a reception line. They sang louder, and quickened their playing. Zenga made a signal, the door opened with the noise of air being expelled, and the first passenger, a middle-aged woman, stepped carefully down. Zenga started to clap and, showmanlike, turned to the people to encourage them. Mrs Dorfmann clapped loudest.

The passenger blushed at the attention and whispered indiscriminate thank-yous. Jank, at the far end of the reception line, beckoned her forward and the woman hurried down between the musicians to be embraced by him. 'God loves you,' he said warmly. 'God loves you.' He shepherded the woman to one side and prepared to greet the next passenger.

Some of the people, curious, had taken a few steps towards the bus and were watching to see what it would disgorge next.

A fresh-faced, tall, broad-shouldered young man came into view. He exuded an air of easy confidence and was comfortable with the scrutiny. He waved to the small crowd and strode forward to meet Victor, who embraced him with great affection and said, 'Andrew, it's good to have you here.'

Andrew said, 'I'm here to do the work that has to be done, Uncle Victor.'

Andrew noticed Mrs Dorfmann smiling at him. He hugged her, and Mrs Dorfmann said, 'You must tell me later what you've been doing this last year.'

'It would be my great pleasure,' he replied.

Mrs Dorfmann reddened.

In all, twenty-seven men and women alighted and passed down the line of musicians to be embraced by Pastor Victor Jank. Zenga, carrying a microphone in each hand, corralled the missionaries into a semi-circle facing the people, and arranged the musicians in a second semi-circle behind.

Zenga handed Jank one of the microphones. Jank wound the lead around his wrist and stepped forward to address the people. He spoke to them in fluent and only lightly accented Spanish.

'My friends, I am Pastor Victor Jank. I am Field Director of the New Era Mission of Christ, and I am here to tell you about something wonderful that is going to happen in your lives.'

Jank paused and drew in his breath. When he spoke again it was in a hushed voice. 'Sometimes, it seems that God has turned his back on a people. There is so much evil, so much drunkenness, so much drugs. But God never abandons his people. Sometimes, it seems that God has a time, a special time, for a people. Sometimes it seems God has opened a door. That door is here. That door is now.

'When God has set that special time for a people, when he has opened that door, no one can turn our Saviour, the Lord Jesus Christ, away. And that's why we're here, to help you open the door to Jesus Christ, to let him in, to let him help you. Together we can change our lives. Poverty, loneliness, unhappiness, everything bad will be thrown away when Jesus steps in the door.'

Jank paused and the seconds filled with the half-silence of the corners of cities where the traffic sounds are far off and muffled. Then he raised his head and turned to indicate the new arrivals.

'My friends,' Jank said, 'I want to introduce you. These men and women have come from all over the United States to speed the Word. They will be with us here in Los Angeles for six weeks. They have come, at their own expense, as missionaries. Because here there is a need for God, like there is a need in the jungles of South America and Africa and New Guinea, or wherever the Word is still to be heard.

'On Garfield,' Jank continued, 'about half a block down from the San Bernadino Freeway, you'll find our head-quarters, a building that was once used for the sale of liquor. Now, we want to turn that building into the focus point of a mission to this community. Wednesday night – that's not tomorrow night but the night after – there'll be a prayer meeting at seven-thirty. That is when the work of the New Era Mission of Christ officially opens in Los Angeles. We invite you to come along, bring your brothers and sisters, your wives, husbands, children, bring your neighbours and friends, bring everybody – because the Lord spurns no one.

'God is holding a key for you to open up a better life. We will teach you how to take that key, and how to use it for your social and spiritual betterment.'

Jank paused to let the words reach the people. He surveyed his audience of uncomprehending faces, but he was used to this and there was no trace of disappointment when he continued. 'I will talk to you again the night after tomorrow, but right now, one of our young missionaries – Andrew, who despite his young years, has a vast experience of doing God's work in all kinds of places – he's going to say a few words. So I'm going to hand you over to Andrew and I look forward to seeing you again soon. God bless you all.'

Andrew stepped forward and accepted the microphone. With tremendous enthusiasm he shouted, '*Hola!*', pronouncing the *h*.

Jank, Zenga, Mrs Dorfmann and all the musicians responded with a loud, chorused '*Hola!*'

A few of the people murmured, and two of the labourers stiffened slightly. One flicked his eyes over to a companion, then back to the speaker.

Andrew was smiling. He was used to being liked, his confidence that of a puppy. He spoke in English. 'My friends, we have waited a long time to come here . . .'

Behind him, Zenga raised his microphone and translated. '*Hemos esperado largo tiempo para venir acá . . .*'

'We have come to bring you God's Word. We have come to build His church . . .'

'*Hemos venido para traer la Palabra de Dios. Hemos venido para edificar Su Templo, la iglesia de Dios.*'

'We're real happy to be here, and real proud too. We're going to be here for six weeks and our slogan will be "Reaching Out for the Unreached", that is, bringing the Word to the abandoned. We aim to establish a centre for the Lord's work in Los Angeles that, with your help, will grow and become strong and spread so that you, all of you, will find a betterment beyond your wildest dreams. This is, my friends, Power Evangelism. Power Evangelism. The New Era Mission of Christ is the world's premier missionary organization, global, the biggest, most successful anywhere in the world. If we can't help you to improve your lives, nothing can. There is nothing we cannot do for you if you will only have faith. We're going to be looking forward to seeing you all at the mission Wednesday night. So be there.'

Zenga finished the translation and shouted into his microphone, '*Gloria al Señor! Gloria al Señor!*'

The chorus was taken up by the missionaries. The musicians struck up and began to sing a hymn. Zenga and Jank passed out small bundles of leaflets and copies of a religious magazine, *Simple Truth*, to the missionaries, who, some more confident that others, went in among the people to hand them out. '*Hola!*' the missionaries said when they approached the people. '*Hola!*' and '*Gloria al Señor!*' A young blonde woman came up to one of the labourers, a tall man with a wide mouth and dark eyes.

'*Hola!*' she said brightly, offering him a leaflet and a magazine. 'And what's your name?'

The man seemed to consider something before answering. 'Agustín,' he said at length.

'Augustine. That's such a lovely name,' the woman said. 'We hope to see you Wednesday night.'

'Yes,' he said, accepting the literature. The blonde girl started to hand leaflets to Agustín's companions. Sabino, humble and timid, in awe of the girl's whiteness, grinned uncertainly as he received his. Pascualito, the youngest, stared directly into the girl's eyes, unnerving her as she tried to pinch and separate a leaflet from the bundle. When she said '*hola*', the bright word had lost some of its shine. She blushed, dropped her head and hurried on. Pascualito hissed after her, two short thin hisses. '*Mamacita*,' he said crudely, 'I see you Wednesday night, *all right.*'

Agustín turned to see Pascualito squaring up to the drunken-looking white man. The man was having difficulty standing up and he lurched into Pascualito, who swore at him again and pushed him roughly back. Agustín addressed the man in Spanish, telling him to be more careful. The man did not respond, but raised his stubbled bony face as if searching for the source of a sound he had only half-heard. He tried to straighten. The effort cost him his balance, and he would have fallen had Agustín not reached out and pushed him harshly against the wall behind. The man was a mess. He smelt stale, his hair and clothes were dirty, his skin blotchy. On his chin was a scar the shape of a teacup handle, and there were other scars, thick, livid vines snaking up from the collar of his shirt. His right cheekbone looked like the imperfectly panel-beaten wing of a car, and on one temple there was a dent that reminded Agustín of a bruised apple.

Agustín took away his hand and the white man collapsed to the ground. Pascualito gave a bitter laugh, kicked at the man's sprawled legs and told him not to take up so much space. He flicked a ball of yellow spittle from his tongue; it landed on the man's cheek. Agustín watched as the white man struggled to get her up, then lost interest.

The musicians were singing a hymn Agustín had first heard many years before in Peru, and the memories it conjured up caused him to shudder. Behind them, the white man, using the wall as a prop, raised himself and stumbled off to go his own way.

Agustín became aware of someone else standing by him. It was Mrs Dorfmann; Andrew was at her shoulder, grinning.

Agustín's heart thumped with shock. He felt the kind of fear that fills so much space it leaves no room for thought or reason. He felt light-headed, and the only sense left to him was that of sight. For several long moments all he was aware of was the face of Andrew Jank, looking expectantly at him, almost disembodied, without context.

At last, he recovered to say, '*Señora Dorfmann, cómo está usted?*' He noticed another of the labourers, Dulio, taking steps backward. Dulio's face was expressionless, but Agustín, who knew him well, could tell he was also unnerved.

'Mrs Dorfmann said, '*Habla inglés?*'

'*Sí, señora.*'

In English she said, 'Do you know who this man is?' She indicated Andrew.

Agustín looked at the man. There was a pause before he said, his words deliberate and slow, 'No, señora.'

'He is Mr Andrew Jank. He is Field Leader of the New Era Mission of Christ.'

'Field Leader?'

'Oh,' Andrew said, 'the title means nothing. It's the work that counts, and there are a lot of us that are trying our best to do God's work.' He put out his hand and Agustín pressed it. Agustín looked for Dulio; he was not in sight.

Andrew asked, 'Do you work for Mrs Dorfmann?'

'Since almost two weeks, sir. I don't work in the factory. I work on the new building.'

'We're expanding,' Mrs Dorfmann explained to Andrew.

'You have a very good, very caring employer. She is held in high regard in this community,' Andrew said.

'Yes, sir.'

'Where are you from?'

'From near Nogales, sir.'

'I've been to Mexico. And to Chile, and Peru. A lot of God-fearing people down there.'

Agustín nodded.

'Where did you learn your English? You speak very well.'

'In night school, sir.'

'You study, that's great. Well, Mr . . .?'

There was a long silence.

'*Cómo se llama usted? Dígale al señor,*' Mrs Dorfmann commanded quickly.

'I am Agustín Romero Arce.'

'Well, Mr Ar-say,' Andrew said, extending his hand, 'it is a pleasure to see you here. I hope we'll be seeing you at the mission Wednesday night.'

'Yes, sir.'

Andrew moved on to talk to another of the people. Mrs Dorfmann took a look at Agustín and said, in Spanish, her voice heavy with suspicion, 'What are you doing here?'

Agustín said evenly, 'You told us to come, señora.'

'You don't look the type. Have you a green card?'

'Yes, señora.'

'Of course,' Mrs Dorfmann said. She looked at him carefully, and then left him. Agustín watched her as she went; and he watched Andrew, and Nick Zenga, and Victor Jank. He watched them all.

'Now you have seen him.' It was Dulio, who had reappeared.

Agustín nodded.

'Did he recognize you?' Dulio asked.

Agustín shook his head.

'Do you know what you're going to do?'

41

'No,' Agustín said, without taking his eyes off the missionaries.

'One person can do nothing.'

'So you say.'

'Nothing that counts.'

The new arrivals were preparing to leave and were gathering by the bus. They waved goodbye to their small audience. As they boarded, Victor Jank embraced each of them. Some had tears of happiness in their eyes.

Agustín looked around for the woman in the dark glasses. She was nowhere in sight.

Agustín and Dulio spent the evening drinking. At first they drank slowly, and they said little. Dulio was not a talkative man: he was gruff, that was his way. The two had known each other many years, and each recognized the boundaries of the other's temperament as clearly as if they had been drawn on a map; and, knowing them, understanding the inviolability, they made no incursions of any sort. Yet later that night they argued.

It had to do with seeing Andrew Jank. Dulio pressed, but all Agustín could say was that he still did not know what to do. After an angry silence Dulio said that whatever Agustín did, he would stay with him. 'We walk on thin ice,' Dulio said, 'there's no one keeps us from sinking, except each other.'

The bar closed at one. They walked four blocks together before separating. Not one person was on the street.

Agustín turned west on Garfield and found himself in front of the old liquor store that was now the New Era Mission of Christ's Los Angeles headquarters. It was a drab, one-storey building, the stucco painted a mid-green; but it had been decked out with flags and ribbons and now resembled some medieval king's war tent. A banner stretched over the entrance: REACHING OUT FOR THE UNREACHED. Agustín stood and gazed at the building and allowed his anger to rise, to empty him of thought and block out what Dulio had said.

After five minutes he moved on, cut through the old tyre factory and went south. He walked with his hands in his pockets, only slightly drunk. The night sky circled and wheeled above him.

The tenements and projects in this area were dangerous. Thieves were everywhere. They attacked people walking on the street, ambushing them from the cavernous mouths of the alleys, dragging their victims into the darkness to knife and rob them.

He was two blocks from home when he saw something moving in an alleyway, some dark form. He squinted into the gloom. There was a movement. Agustín heard something fall, a heavy, dull thud, and he stopped to listen. He was trembling as he approached the alley and listened again for some clue. Just as he decided that it was probably a cat or a dog, there came a human noise, a groan.

Agustín's initial impulse was to go on his way. But then, for some tangled reason which was bound up with Dulio, he decided to enter.

Agustín peered around the corner into the alley. He took a knife from his pocket. Its weight in the palm of his hand was reassuring. He pressed the button and the blade unsheathed itself with a clean click. He held the knife before him. He went lightly and silently, pausing to listen and give meaning to the shapes he saw. The light was poor, but he could make out the usual rubbish: old packing cases, rotting fruit, beer cans, broken bricks and ash. He continued on into the gloom. Then stopped. He could make out a dark form spread among the litter. A discarded coat, he thought at first, for it seemed to lack the bulk that would make it human. He kept his eyes fixed on it, however, for something told him this was what he had entered to find.

As he got nearer, he could see it was human, the form of a man, slumped with his shoulders against the wall, his head hanging listlessly to one side, legs outstretched.

Standing over him, Agustín tapped the man's leg with his foot. There was no response. He hooked his foot under the man's knee, raised it a couple of inches and let it fall.

Nothing. Agustín bent down slowly. He was conscious of a bad smell. Beside the man he saw what looked like a short length of sodden grey rope. There was more of it on the man's chest. Agustín wanted to vomit himself.

A noise like a sick laugh made him jump with fright. He swivelled and pressed his back against the wall, holding the knife before him. He heard the laugh again but could see nothing.

'What do you want?' Agustín said.

He heard a sigh, then a man's voice, harsh, rasping. 'What do *you* want?' the voice demanded.

Agustín thought he could make out a shape, something, someone deformed, very short – a dwarf. Or a man, full-grown but misshapen.

'I want nothing,' Agustín said.

'Then why are you here?' The words were bitter and hoarse, they scraped their way over the man's coarse tongue.

The unconscious man at Agustín's feet groaned, and again Agustín thought of Dulio. *We walk on thin ice.* Agustín thought now he could see his dwarf, or at least some misshapen thing. *There's no one keeps us from sinking, except each other.*

'I said, why are you here?' The words scraped their way out of the thing's sandpaper mouth.

Agustín said nothing, but snapped his knife shut and returned it to his pocket. He bent down and found a piece of newspaper to wipe the vomit from the man's chest. He hoisted the man on to his shoulders. It was no burden. Agustín could feel the bones on the back of his neck.

The dwarf was laughing sourly. Agustín heard him from the mouth of the alley, as he emerged into the street; and in his mind he heard the laugh follow him home. So near, so real did it sound that twice he stopped and turned his head to listen.

Agustín only managed to get the door to his room open after accidentally banging the man's head against the jamb. He got inside and dumped him on the single bed. The bare light bulb gave out an inexact light, but Agustín recognized the face. He went to the sink and ran the water. He took a handkerchief and soaked it.

The man was feverish and struggled against the wet rag. Agustín looked at his watch. It was two-twenty. He ran his hands through his hair and muttered a curse. Then he left the room.

He walked three blocks until he came to a run-down wood-framed house with a wide porch. Through the window of the darkened front room Agustín saw the ghostly blue light of a television set playing against the wall. He rang the bell. No one answered. He rang again. A woman opened the door. She held a T-shirt to her naked breasts.

'Yeah?' she said.

'Is Roy here? Roy Jones?'

'Who are you?'

'Agustín.'

The woman – she was about forty and had dyed blonde hair – hesitated. She took a close look at Agustín before disappearing into a room on the right of the hall.

Agustín waited about five minutes before Roy Jones emerged. Roy was wearing a dirty vest, stained shorts and black socks. He was six feet five, thin, about forty-five, and wore his hair – dark brown turning grey – in a pony-tail. He also wore a bandit moustache. The skin from his high cheekbones to his chin was pitted and scarred by acne. There were tiny red spots in the craters.

'Agustín, how are you?' Roy spoke with a trace of a country accent, a little slow.

'I need you to look at something, someone.'

'Old Dr Inconvenience, huh? Sick?'

'Yes.'

'I'll get my bag. Better come in, though. I'm going to need a minute to get my stuff together.'

In the living room, Roy stroked his moustache and thought about where to start. He looked behind a chair and pulled out a battered beach bag. The woman lay on the couch watching the television. She held the T-shirt to her front and, when she saw Agustín, pushed the tails between her legs. They did not cover much; the effect was something like that of a modern, high-cut bathing costume. Agustín could see the side of her buttocks, and where her breasts fell to the sides; he could see the pubic hair at the tops of her legs. Her upper arms seemed to be bruised, and there were other bruises on her thighs.

'This is Alice,' Roy said.

Alice looked at Agustín and smiled, 'Hi,' she said.

'How do you do?'

'You going out, honey?' Alice said to Roy.

'Agustín's got a problem.'

Alice inspected Agustín. 'He looks okay to me.'

'It's a friend of mine,' Agustín explained.

The woman grunted and turned back to the television.

'Yup,' Roy said. He was filling the beach bag with various things. 'I think that's it,' he said absently. 'Better put some clothes on, I guess.'

Approaching the hotel from the west, they cut right and went through the alley between the pawnbroker's and the Chi-Chi Club.

'You still do this much?' Agustín asked Roy as they entered.

'Not so much. Did a gunshot wound Friday night – first one in a long time. Took me right back.'

'The one I got for you has no gunshot wounds.'

'Knife?'

'Fever.'

'Junkie?'

'Could be.'

They were at the bedside. Roy put his hand on the man's forehead. 'Wow. Hot, hot, hot.' He pushed up the patient's sleeves. 'You got another light here? A better one?'

'No.'

'Shit.' Roy looked up at the dim light bulb. 'See if you can move that fucking thing a bit closer. I want to look see what's on his arms.'

Agustín climbed on to the narrow bed, placing one foot

either side of the metal frame. He manipulated the bulb by holding the fitting at the top, and moved it to where it threw what little light it possessed on to Roy and his patient. Roy moved to one side to let the light on to the man's arms.

'No tracks I can see,' Roy pronounced. He rubbed his hands together and, as if suddenly remembering something, sniffed them. 'Shit,' he said. 'I should have washed my hands.'

'What?'

'Before I started. It's one of the rules they teach you.' He held up his palms for Agustín, who was still holding the light, to see. There were long shadows in Roy's rough face. 'I was eating pizza when you came. Didn't get a chance to wash up.'

'I don't think he's going to be worried for pizza, the way he is,' Agustín said, jumping down from the bed. The light bulb swung in slow arcs.

'I was doing some pretty unspeakable things to Alice also.'

'Use the sink.'

'You're right, I don't suppose it matters now.'

'What's wrong with him?'

Roy looked down at the man. 'Hey, hey, wake up now,' he said, slapping him on the face. The man's eyes flickered, then, reluctantly, came open.

'That's it,' Roy said gently. 'Your chest hurt? Just here?' Roy put his hand on the bottom right side.

The man nodded slowly, then burst into a coughing fit. The phlegm was green.

'Uh-huh,' Roy said, taking a stethoscope from the beach bag. 'Pleuritic pain.' He unbuttoned the man's shirt and, when the coughing subsided, put the instrument to his chest. He listened for a few moments. The man slipped back into unconsciousness.

'How long's he been like this?' Roy asked.

'I don't know. I found him on the street about an hour ago. I saw him earlier, about five o'clock, and he wasn't so good then, either.'

'He been sick?'

47

'Yes. Where I found him. I thought he was a drunk, but there's no smell of liquor.'

'Smells of everything else, though.'

'So what's he got?'

'Looks like pneumonia. We ought to get him to hospital. Maybe Cedar Sinai'd take him. He got any ID?'

'No. I already looked through his stuff. There's nothing with his name on it.'

'Nothing?'

'*Nada.* I don't like to take him to Cedar's. The police would be there to ask him questions when he wakes up.'

Roy looked closely at his patient. 'His face is pretty bashed up. And look at this,' he said, pointing at the man's chest.

Agustín bent closer. 'What?'

The light bulb above swung back and forth.

'Scars, man. Look at the scars.'

'What are they?'

Roy took his time about answering. 'I'd say that' – he pointed to the man's upper chest and waited for the light – 'is definitely gunshot. And these' – he indicated the criss-crosses that went up his neck – 'are . . . I don't know, auto accident maybe. Pretty damn unlucky to get so many scars. But where did he pick them up? He doesn't look old enough to be a vet.'

Roy looked into the man's mouth, manipulating the lips as he would those of a horse. 'You know, these don't look like American teeth to me. Some interesting dentistry has gone on in here.'

'I didn't know you were a dentist.'

'I was a paramedic and I did teeth just like I did dysentery and clap, and I would stake my professional reputation on it, this sick sucker is not a true American.'

'I can't keep him here long.'

'He needs antibiotics. Penicillin. I'll pick some up tomorrow morning. I got a source down in the *centro médico*. In a week he'll be on his feet. At least enough to move on.'

Roy gathered his things. 'I gotta get back to my little Alice. She don't like me staying out late.'

'She didn't seem to mind when you left.'

'That's because her sexual needs had just been fulfilled.' He looked at his watch. 'She'll be needing more fulfilling any moment now. She kind of gets bad-tempered she misses out.'

'What do I owe you for this?'

'Pay me tomorrow, or whenever. I'll be round in the morning to have a look at him.'

'I leave at six.'

'I wasn't planning on getting up much before eleven. What time it is now?'

'Three-fifteen. You can take my key. I'll call for it when I get back from work. Thanks for coming.'

'Glad to be of service.'

Roy let himself out.

Agustín looked at the unconscious man and shook his head. He stood up and went to the sink and splashed water over his head. He looked in the mirror. His brown face was solemn and tense, his eyes grave. He did not like his reflection and turned his back on it. The reflection did not disappear.

He went and sat on the edge of the bed and gazed out the window into the street below. He was just in time to see Roy Jones, Dr Inconvenience as they called him, lope off towards the Chi-Chi Club, turn the corner and vanish.

Agustín had lied, about everything. He had told Mrs Dorfmann and Andrew that his name was Agustín Romero Arce; it was not. It was Agustín Cienfuegos de la Cruz. Nor was he from near Nogales, but from Ayacucho, a city in the high Andes of Peru, whose Quechua name means Corner of the Dead. He did not, of course, have a green card, but Mrs Dorfmann knew that, in the same way she knew that his answers about his name and origin were also false. But one thing Mrs Dorfmann did not know: Agustín had not learned his English in night school, but in the Lurigancho Prison on the dusty outskirts of Lima.

Agustín's father was Adolfo Cienfuegos, a morose and violent man who worked as a day labourer with decreasing regularity as the years wore on. When Agustín was seven, Adolfo joined the wave of ragged refugees to the capital in search of something better. Agustín, his brother and two sisters, his mother and father lived first in a shanty where the houses were of straw matting and cardboard. After two years Agustín's mother, Silvia, had saved enough money to move to a squalid *callejón* on Jirón Ica in the dangerous, dirty centre of the city. Silvia hated the capital and its beggared people and the deformities they carried: limps, lumps, twisted hands, cataract-fastened eyes, feet growing out at right angles where the knee should be. In summer Lima was airless and hot, in winter cold and damp, and the *neblina*, the sea-mist, both chilled and frightened her. She would gaze into the haze and see old ghosts from Ayacucho. The ghosts followed her, she told Adolfo between sobs; but he would give her no reassurance.

Silvia sold chocolates and cigarettes from a tray. She sat in the doorway of a cheap restaurant in a street that ran off the Plaza de Armas towards Tacna; day-in, day-out she offered her pathetic and overpriced goods to passers-by. In winter she sat with her cardigan pulled over her knees and her hands dug into her armpits. Adolfo bought liquor.

Agustín was nine when he entered the world of work. He was about to leave for school one morning when his mother stopped him and brought him instead to Polvos Azules, the street market near the Post Office, to buy a shoeshine kit. Agustín polished shoes in the Plaza San Martín from eight in the morning to three or four in the afternoon. Then he would go to keep his mother company until, around eight, they made their way home.

Agustín adjusted quickly to life on the street. The plaza was always interesting. In one corner was what people ironically called the Wall Street of Peru, a narrow street of money-changing shops that ran off the square behind the Hotel Bolívar. Beneath the statue of General San Martín drug-dealers, pimps, lovers, shoeshine boys and vagrants gathered to conduct what business they had. Thieves were numerous, but were neither skilful nor, from what Agustín could see, very successful. They tended to prey on the crowds filing into the cinemas or on newly arrived tourists. From time to time the police arrived and arrested people at random. On one occasion two policemen came up to Agustín and two of his friends – Pepe and Polo, shoeshine boys like Agustín. Agustín was wearing a dirty grey sweatshirt, dark blue tracksuit bottoms with a double white stripe down the outside of each leg, and worn, flapping basketball boots. His hair was shorn. Pepe and Polo looked just like him. The police arrested them and, since they had no car of their own, hailed a taxi – a clanking, rusting Volkswagen Beetle, long since blinded by thieves who had gouged out its headlights. The six travelled to the *comisaría*, where the boys were held until Silvia arrived with Agustín's sisters, Nita and Roxane. Pepe's father arrived at the same time to claim his son, but no one appeared for Polo and he was taken to a juvenile detention centre, where he remained for five weeks.

One summer afternoon, two men approached Agustín for a shine. Their appearance and manner unsettled him and, as he worked the wax and polish into their shoes, he decided not to haggle over the price, as he did with tourists and his more middle-class customers. He scanned the square for a policeman, just in case, but could not see one. Nor were Pepe and Polo around, having decided to go to the beach at Miraflores to try their luck there. Agustín hurried the shine and hoped that nothing bad was going to happen.

He shined the shoes of both men. When he told them the price, the men looked at each other. 'What did the little fucker say, Juan?'

The other replied, 'He said he wants to make you a gift of the shine.'

'Did he?' Juan smiled at Agustín. 'Then it is not true what they say, after all. There is still gratitude in the modern world.'

Out of pride, Agustín insisted on payment. He clutched at Juan's arm. Juan pulled away, grabbed Agustín by the throat and spat in his face. His companion turned out Agustín's pockets and found his day's takings, a little less than a dollar in soles de oro. Agustín tried to cry out, but Juan squeezed his neck so tightly that he began to choke for breath. Juan slapped him in the face and told him to be quiet, then dropped him to the ground.

When the men had gone, Agustín went to find his mother. She was not in her usual spot in the restaurant doorway and the owner told Agustín that she had gone home complaining of stomach pains. Agustín found her lying in bed with Nita and Roxane beside her. His father was not home. Silvia asked him for some water. As Agustín raised her head so she could sip from the cup, she explained that his father had kicked her in the stomach that morning. She sipped the water and then closed her eyes. Agustín left her and went out into the courtyard, where he studied his surroundings. The house had belonged to a rich colonial family. Once, a century and a half before, servants would have washed clothes in the courtyard; there would have been a carriage, horses. Now there was decay and stink, the stink of the drains, of the uncollected rubbish that piled in rat corners, of the piss lying in evil, slimy pools oozing into the fabric of the building, for ever to become part of it. The stink sickened him. There were twenty rooms in the house, a family in each one, a hundred people or more. Some of them Agustín knew, most were strangers.

Agustín watched an infant girl, dressed in only a filthy vest, toddle to a pool of piss and splash in it.

He went out into the street and wandered aimlessly in the dark. He was walking on Colmena when suddenly, all the lights went out. People speculated noisily on the cause of the blackout. There was a muffled bang, then another, and another. In the distance, they heard the pop of rifle shots, and every so often a burst of machine-gun fire. The terrorist war was in the capital.

Three days after their first visit, Juan and his companion returned to demand a shine. Polo and Pepe, whom Agustín had told about the incident, spotted the men first. They shrank back, almost diminishing in size in their effort to be overlooked. Agustín prepared his polishes and waxes as calmly as he could and then shined the shoes slowly, methodically, and when he had finished he did not ask for money. He said quietly that he hoped the gentlemen were pleased with his work. Juan grinned and looked at his partner. Then he asked Agustín how much money he had. Agustín replied that he had just over one dollar in soles. Juan demanded the money and Agustín, with no show of reluctance, handed over the soiled notes. The men went off. Pepe and Polo were too frightened to talk to Agustín for the rest of the day. As they were preparing to leave that afternoon, Agustín broke the silence and asked them to lend him some money. 'I have to buy something,' he said. Pepe and Polo dug out the notes they had concealed in a dozen places around their bodies.

It was a week before Agustín saw the men again. It was a

public holiday, the Feast of the Immaculate Conception. There were few people about, but Agustín had gone to the plaza anyway, calculating that although the office workers would have the day off, the people going to mass and the processions would want their shoes shined. He watched as the procession made its way slowly along Colmena, heading for the cathedral. Four men, dressed in their best clothes, carried the Virgin, who stood under an arc of blue and white flowers arranged in delicate sprays. Before the Virgin went several young girls dressed in white, and they skipped along happily carrying bouquets of flowers. Flanking the procession were men in black leather masks with thick red lips and popping eyes. They wore white trousers and their waistcoats were decorated with military badges and stars and medallions. They represented the black slaves the conquistadores had imported to work the gold and silver mines and to cut the sugar cane, and they danced, holding little bells, like cow bells, from light chains attached to their wrists. Behind them was a band, men in bright football shirts who played trumpets, clarinets, guitars, mandolins and *zampoñas*.

Juan and his partner stopped to admire the procession, then made their way to Agustín. Juan urged his friend, Enrique, to take his turn first. Enrique settled down for his shine, put his foot on the little stand and Agustín went to work. He polished the shoes carefully and shined them with extra spit and effort. Enrique appeared satisfied and he grinned at Juan, whose turn it was next. As Juan took his place, Agustín turned to watch the procession, now just behind them. He liked the music and was enthralled by the dancers impersonating the black slaves; they did delicate little tripping steps. Juan slapped him sharply on the face and Agustín apologized.

When he had finished, Juan expressed himself satisfied and made to get up. Agustín put up his hand. 'No, señor. You cannot go with your shoes in such a poor condition. I have something special for them.'

Juan looked up at Enrique and chuckled as he relaxed back into the bench. 'Okay,' he said, 'shine them up.'

Agustín rummaged around in his box as if he had misplaced something. He grinned apologetically to Juan.

He found what he wanted, a kitchen knife with a five-inch blade. Holding it in both hands above his head, he plunged it into Juan's upper thigh. Before Enrique could decide whether to help Juan or give chase, Agustín had launched himself into the procession and escaped.

Pepe and Polo, when they heard of Agustín's deed, were full of admiration for him. But Agustín did not boast. The truth was that he was frightened, and he would not venture out into the street. Silvia, from whom he kept the news of his troubles, berated him and called him lazy, but he could not be prevailed on to go out. He sat in the courtyard and watched the dreary life of the *callejón*.

Without Agustín shining shoes the family's money problems worsened. One evening Silvia came home to find Agustín in the courtyard.

'Why do you sit here all day doing nothing?' she asked him.

'I don't know,' Agustín said.

'Do you like it here?'

'No.'

'Would you like to leave this place?'

'Of course,' Agustín said.

'We can only leave if you work,' Silvia said.

'Even if I work every day for the rest of my life I will never be able to get out of here.'

Agustín scanned the courtyard. He looked at the infants, dressed in rags, playing in the doorways. He looked up to the wood-framed balconies where the men and women slumped in chairs to wait for the night to come in and close the day that tomorrow they would remember nothing about. He looked at his mother. She was not yet thirty; she was an old woman.

She was an old woman, and ill. The doctor diagnosed tuberculosis but could not give a name to the cause of the pains that clenched her stomach. Silvia herself attributed them to the kick Adolfo had given her. Adolfo stayed less and less at home. He had found another woman and had two children by her. He would return at intervals to spend a couple of days 'resting' before disappearing again. Agustín's brother Luis started work as a shoeshine boy. Nita was an earnest student. Roxane, a year younger than Agustín, was delicate; she was pregnant at fourteen.

One night, during a blackout, Agustín sat in the foul-smelling courtyard. He stared into the darkness and thought about his wrecked family and could see nothing for them. The following day, without telling Silvia, he borrowed some money from Pepe and Polo and caught a bus to Ayacucho, where he went to live with a sister of his father's.

In Ayacucho the war mixed the brutal and the bizarre. Walk among dogs dangling strangled from lamp-posts, placards around their stretched necks proclaiming their betrayal. Wake up at night and hear a woman's pleading before the shots. See half-charred bodies, legs and arms split like grilled sausages, faces distorted by sick grins. Watch in the night a hillside burst into flame, watch as the fires settle into the pattern of a hammer and sickle. 'What is that?' Agustín, gazing at the fiery pattern, asked an old man. The man looked into the hill and said, 'What?', and hurried on. A policeman on leave assassinated; the brother, mother and uncle of a dead terrorist blown up in their house; the mayor of a village executed by rocks dropped on his head; a trade-unionist arrested by the army and five days later found floating in the river.

In this war, dogs are traitors; only men are loyal, unswervingly so.

One day Agustín was travelling on a local bus. The driver, seeing a small crowd gathered at the side of the road, pulled over. Agustín got off the bus with the other passengers to find out what was going on. He saw a group of dazed-looking Indian women standing in a semi-circle. They were silent, even those who were crying. As Agustín got closer, he could see the body of a young man lying by the roadside. The man's shirt-tails were up around his chest, and the belt and zip of his cheap work jeans had been undone, exposing red underwear. There was a dark stain around the man's groin where blood and urine had spilt. The eyes were half-open and grey. His mouth was open, too; a beetle crawled out of it. The people, in silence, got back on the bus and the driver restarted the engine. Before he pulled away to leave the dead to look after the dead, Agustín saw a pick-up stop by the crowd. Three men got out, made their way to the body and lifted it up: it was so stiff it was like a mannequin from a shop window; the arms were set out as if in some action, to signal something, and had frozen there.

This was Ayacucho, the Corner of the Dead.

Agustín continued to live with his aunt and her family for two years. Occasionally he wrote to his mother, and once or twice to Nita. But he had no desire to see them. Shortly after his sixteenth birthday, Pepe and Polo came to visit him. They had no money, but they had a plan, and they had two guns.

Agustín, Pepe and Polo returned together to Lima. Agustín went to visit his mother while Polo set about stealing a car. When Agustín arrived at the *callejón* he almost turned away, so powerful was the stench. He climbed the stairs to the family's room. Silvia was in bed. She was shrunken. Some death thing, some crumbling, wasting disease was sucking from inside her, sucking her flesh and blood so that only her bones and skin were left. Her eyes were going grey and filmy like those of the dead man he had seen by the roadside. When she spoke it was with a death hiss, and it caused coughing fits that turned into vomiting. Only Nita was there. Luis, Nita told Agustín, had run away, and Roxane was living with her baby in a shanty on the outskirts of the city. Adolfo was now living permanently with his other family in a street only two blocks away.

'Who looks after you, Nita?' Agustín asked his sister.

'I do,' she said.

Agustín said, 'I'll be back in a week with money.'

Nita said nothing. When Agustín went to embrace her, she stiffened and turned away. Agustín kissed his mother. She had a smell of decay about her, so strong it almost made him ill.

When Agustín returned a week later with the money he had promised, he found the room occupied by another family. He asked the new tenants where the women had gone, but they knew nothing. He asked the people in the room opposite. They knew nothing, either. He asked everyone he could find; no one could tell him anything.

Strangers, Agustín thought, we are all strangers to each other. He started down the stairs. In the distance he heard a bomb explode, soft like rolling thunder.

Mrs Maritza Dorfmann, in the office of Dorfmann Furnishings (Los Angeles), was yielding to a fantasy. Its advance had taken her by surprise, for she had been think-ing about money and it had gone on from there: pleasures and fancies built on smaller pleasures and fancies until they transported her. Behind her a fan mounted on a filing cabinet swept in crescents, brushing the hair on the nape of her neck like a finger. She moved to let the air touch her skin, wondering at how so little could give so much pleasure, and looked again at the note from her bookkeeper. Dorfmann Furnishings would net $60,000 this year; next year, with the extension they were now building, it might be $180,000.

Mrs Dorfmann detached part of herself from the fantasy to check that it was prudent to proceed. She saw she was alone in the office, by the window that looked out on to the extension; the door was closed. The scout part of her also reported that she was conducting her fantasy in English, and the news was received well. Safe, she closed her eyes and pushed her head back to let the sweep of the fan air fall across the crown. Cat-like, basking in selfish pleasures and giving nothing in return, she let the fantasy progress.

Twenty years ago, in Mexico City, things had come to a stop in her life. Then she met Martin, a slow-talking, slow-thinking, placid man of German-Dutch Oklahoma stock. They married as soon as Mrs Dorfmann's divorce came through.

In Martin Dorfmann Maritza saw a way forward. It was not that Martin himself could take her on. Things had not come together for him. After the navy and the merchant marine, Dorfmann bought a shrimper and worked out of New Orleans, but went broke. He ran into an old navy friend from his Korea days, Victor Jank, who offered him a job as a Bible salesman, salary and commission, for the New Era Mission of Christ travelling in El Salvador, Guatemala and Mexico. Dorfmann was fifty when he married Maritza; she was thirty-two.

She saw that Victor Jank, who maintained a soft spot for her husband, was an influential man. Maritza had been born Catholic, but had come to believe that the way forward was with the Protestants. Protestantism was modern and North American. Victor Jank was the embodiment of successful North American Protestantism. She could not have him, but she could have Martin, a younger brother of Jank's, she liked to imagine, in whom were visible all the traits of the older, more powerful sibling: though they were not so well developed, still they were there, and the new Mrs Dorfmann determined to use them.

She and Dorfmann moved to the United States, first to Chicago, where they set up Dorfmann Furnishings, with the support of Victor Jank. Martin, whose health began to fail, soon bowed out of the day-to-day running of the business to spend most of his time reading the Bible, watching television and playing golf. Mrs Dorfmann filled the gap in the business: for the first time in her life she felt she was approaching her reward.

Mrs Dorfmann's drive had a lot to do with her colour. In Mexico, she used to take pleasure in looking at the dark faces around her and reflecting on her own comparative whiteness. In Chicago, however, with so many real white people around, her colour depressed her. She kept out of the sun as much as possible. At dinner parties or social gatherings she conducted tests, stretching her forearm across the table to make a furtive comparison with that of a white neighbour. She could see she was getting whiter. In her heart she knew brown people were inferior: irreligious, Catholic, lazy, undisciplined. Nor did they speak English.

She was not like other brown people, and there were times when the injustice in the circumstances of her birth took her to depressions so severe she locked herself in her bathroom, where she experimented with make-up she believed made her look whiter.

These thoughts began to spoil the fantasy. She led herself to Victor Jank's nephew Andrew, no stranger to her in these moods. She had first met him two years before and had been smitten instantly. He was handsome, tall, blond and had fair skin, the kind that reddened in the sun. He was twenty-nine but had the freshness and enthusiasm that belonged, so Mrs Dorfmann thought, to a teenager.

Her fantasies did not involve scenes of them as lovers: her common sense was strongly developed and until now had not permitted anything so improbable; even in her dreams she had not been his lover. But still the dreams were sexual. They had to be ambiguous, and allow room for excuses, though the only thing demanding them, as she herself knew, was another part of her own imagination. So, in her fantasies, he was injured, bleeding: he came to her, she treated his wounds, she had to cut away his shirt. She nursed him, held him. She touched him.

That was as far as she had been able to get, but it was enough for Mrs Dorfmann, who, trembling and disturbed could spin the fantasy out for hours while Martin read the Bible or watched television in their bedroom.

Now Andrew was back in Los Angeles. Each time she and Andrew met they arrived at some new stage, a new point beyond the line. How much further would they go this time?

From the office window Mrs Dorfmann noticed her foreman, Rex, talking to Pascualito, one of the labourers Rex had hired on Pino and Main to work on the new extension. She could not hear what he was saying, but from his attitude she knew Rex was angry. Rex would sort it out. He had sorted out other things for them. In Chicago she and Martin had inadvertently hired a couple of troublemakers who tried to organize the factory and make communistic demands. The strain took its toll on Martin, who at the height of the

trouble had his first heart attack. Fortunately for the Dorf-
manns they met Rex, newly arrived from Guatemala, where
he had been a police sergeant. Rex had left Central America
following what Mrs Dorfmann came to call 'his justice
problem', which involved the disappearance of the leader of
an Indian organization notorious for his links with foreign
journalists.

Looking now at Rex as he argued with Pascualito, Mrs
Dorfmann could see why he had made such an effective
foreman. He had been designed to menace. She smiled at
the thought, then compensated for the unkindness of her
assessment by deciding that he looked, she searched for the
word, *traditional*. Rex had a thin, bony head, wore his greying
hair short – sideburns shaved to the temples – and took
pride in his pencil moustache. He had a scar which ran
parallel to his lower lip, and there was another scar, short
and thick, on his right cheekbone which drew attention to a
vicious turn in his eye. It unnerved people, looking into his
face and not knowing which eye to concentrate on, or what
it was telling them. It unnerved the workers. They would see
him standing in the middle of the factory stock still, gazing
around, and they could not tell who Rex was looking at.

A car horn sounded. Mrs Dorfmann felt confused, as if
woken after having drifted off to sleep in an armchair
following a heavy meal. She pushed her glasses up and
rubbed her eyes. Rex signalled a worker to open the gate.
Mrs Dorfmann looked at her watch and saw that it was
two-thirty. Earlier that day, she now recalled, Nick Zenga had
called to say he would be coming over. He had not said why,
but Mrs Dorfmann assumed that it would be to ask for
money. She watched Zenga's BMW pull up between her
Chevy Nova and Rex's pick-up in the space to the left of the
new extension. Rex opened the door for Zenga and the two
men shook hands. Andrew Jank emerged from the passenger side. Mrs Dorfmann, excited at seeing the young
missionary, then aghast, turned on her heels and scanned
the office for her handbag and make-up. She whitened
herself as quickly as she could, pulled in her belly and

stepped out to greet the missionaries. The workmen were watching, though they were pretending not to. Like a thief mixing with honest people, she worried in case they could see through her. She was sweating.

'Mrs Dorfmann,' Andrew said, 'it's a real pleasure to see you again.' He examined her face with a faintly worried look; its colour put him in mind of cinema ghosts and zombies. 'A real pleasure,' he repeated, correcting his expression.

'It's always a pleasure to see you,' Mrs Dorfmann replied, and she glanced at Zenga to check if he had seen what the workers had seen. Zenga was the kind that noticed everything: shrewd, the Calabrian hustler, always alert, always interpreting people's words and actions as springing from the basest of motives. She was pretty sure what he was thinking, so she smiled at him, trying to even out her favours between the two men. Zenga got that, too.

'Nick said he was coming over, so I took the chance to come as well,' Andrew said.

'Of course,' Mrs Dorfmann replied. 'Rex, make some coffee for Mr Jank and Mr Zenga. We'll have it in the office.'

'I've never seen the factory before,' Andrew said.

Mrs Dorfmann said, 'I've got some of the best carpenters in the United States working here. They turn out furniture you wouldn't believe was from LA, you'd think it was from Paris.'

'That's just what Nick was saying. Can we take a look?'

'Of course.'

'It certainly looks impressive.'

The factory was a long, narrow one-storey building of stucco-covered cinder block and wood, and stood alone in a cyclone fence compound. From the street, it was hard to tell whether the building was in use. There was a desolate air to it: the roof was of rusting sheets of corrugated iron which the heat had curled at the corners; the windows, those not broken and covered with plywood, were dirty with greasy dust; the stucco was cracked and in places had completely fallen away to expose large, irregular patches of lathing.

Inside the air was heavy and smelt of sweat and glue.

Mrs Dorfmann called her workers carpenters. The carpenters worked at benches cobbled together from offcuts, discarded doors, old plywood boarding. The older ones operated the lathes and machines cutting shapes from templates, which the younger workers stapled and glued together. The sewing machines were operated mostly by women. A boy of thirteen swept the floor.

'It's like the Golden Gate,' Mrs Dorfmann, pointing to the boy with the broom, told Andrew. 'As soon as he's finished sweeping, he starts again.'

Andrew seemed interested in the operation, which gratified Mrs Dorfmann. He stopped and talked to the workers, sometimes getting Zenga to translate, and he commented on the fine things they were turning out. 'Real impressive,' he said.

'You know what the problem is?' Mrs Dorfmann told him. 'The Government. The thing is that Americans won't do this kind of work. You could offer them twenty dollars an hour, they don't want to do it. Like gardening, they won't do that. My gardener's from Chiapas. So we get these people. Then the Government says, well they're illegal and there's a fine if you get caught giving them work. But what are we supposed to do? We need the labour. It's crazy. They want us to close down? Which is what will happen if things keep going the way they're going.'

'Do you have problems with the authorities?' Andrew asked.

Zenga interrupted: 'You know, a couple of years back the City Council passed a law. It was supposed to stop the police picking people up on suspicion that they're illegal.'

'But it doesn't work,' Mrs Dorfmann continued for Zenga. 'The *Migra* still come round looking for Mexicans. Not so long ago it was so bad I had to shut the factory during the day and run it at night. Can you believe it?'

'Really,' Andrew said.

'It was the only way to keep open. When I tried to open during the day the *Migra* would come. I had people hiding in cupboards, under tables. I found a girl in the filing cabinet.'

'Crazy,' Andrew said.

'Of course.'

Rex appeared and said the coffee was ready. Mrs Dorfmann indicated the way to the office.

'I tell you something,' she said, 'these people, they can't be trusted. They don't value things, they're irresponsible.'

'Well,' Andrew said, 'that's part of the reason we're here. Once they've experienced Power Evangelism, they'll know all about value.' He smiled at her and patted her shoulder.

At his touch Mrs Dorfmann imagined the line she and Andrew were crossing: she could see it, a border, broken, receding. She made an effort to keep herself under control.

'They need to be taught social responsibility,' she said seriously.

'That's why we're here also,' Zenga said.

'Do you take sugar, Andrew?' Mrs Dorfmann asked as she went to the filing cabinet for the cheque book.

She did not mind making investments in the New Era Mission of Christ. It brought stability wherever it went. She thought of it as a tide. You looked at a place, a city or even a whole country, a continent, messed up, the way the sand on a beach temporarily abandoned by the sea gets churned up by people, bikes, horses, dogs. Then the tide comes in and cleanses everything, makes everything ordered. Some people made propaganda against the Mission. But Mrs Dorfmann knew better: the Mission settled things.

The office was a partitioned corner of the factory, functional and not meant to impress. There was a grey metal desk with a telephone, a computer, a three-tier stack of red plastic trays containing correspondence and invoices, and a plastic cube with photographs. The metal filing cabinet, painted a military shade of green, contained invoices, accounts and orders. The petty cash was kept in the bottom drawer. A door at one end led to Mrs Dorfmann's bathroom.

Mrs Dorfmann took Andrew to the window and pointed to the extension.

'How long before it's ready?' Andrew asked.

'Three or four weeks.'

For some moments they stood, side by side, Mrs Dorfmann sharing with Andrew a view that brought her pleasure.

Andrew said, 'You know, Saturday afternoon I have to go to Newport Beach to see old Fred Feddersen. I look him up every time I'm in LA. Maybe you'd like to come?'

'I'd like that very much,' Mrs Dorfmann replied, her heart kicking.

Agustín was sawing wood at one end of the half-finished extension, from where he had watched the arrival of Jank and Zenga. His memory of Jank was so vivid he could not believe the man did not remember him; but he did not. Agustín was trying to think as he cut into the wood, trying to plan, but it was not working. He felt angry and frustrated with himself, with the sense of distance that was blocking him.

From behind a partition wall, Agustín heard Dulio's voice. Something was wrong. He drew the saw into the wood and went to see what the problem was.

Dulio was angry. Nothing very much ever happened in his face and it took someone who had known him for as long as Agustín to realize he was on the point of exploding – a barely perceptible narrowing of eyes already little more than lines, a hint of facial muscles tensed, no more. Pascualito was waving his arms around hysterically. Sabino stood, shoulders hunched, in the corner.

Pascualito was shouting, 'Keep out of my business.'

'*He*,' Dulio indicated Sabino, 'is my business.'

'I'm telling you polite, leave me a-fucking-lone, or I won't be responsible.'

They glared at each other. Before either man could throw the first punch, Agustín stepped between them. As he did so, he noticed Rex standing in the shadows of the back door. Agustín pushed Dulio out of the way. Dulio stumbled and Pascualito started forward to take advantage of his opponent. Agustín put up a hand and caught Pascualito in the chest.

'Hey,' Agustín said fiercely. Pascualito strained forward. Agustín pushed him back. Rex was still watching from the doorway.

'You want to lose your job?' Agustín said to Pascualito. 'Dulio?'

Pascualito said, 'I've had it with him. First I have squint-eyed Rex complaining at me, now him. I'm telling you, man, someone says something to me I don't like I'm not gonna be responsible.'

Dulio and Pascualito, breathing noisily through their noses, eyes wide, fists clenched, gradually began to calm down. Agustín lowered his hands. 'Let's get back to work. Pascualito, go with Sabino and finish cutting the glass.' Agustín jerked a thumb over his shoulder. Pascualito demurred, spat into the ground and turned.

To Dulio, Agustín said, 'You should know better.'

Dulio sucked in his breath. 'He's on something,' he said. 'He took money from Sabino for dope and he hasn't paid it back.'

'If Sabino doesn't like it, let him say so.'

'That's shit. Sabino's so timid, he won't ask for it back.'

'It's his problem,' Agustín said. 'Give me a hand with this wood over here.' He looked over at the back door. Rex had gone. 'You remember that gringo yesterday? The one fell down?'

'What about him?'

'I saw him again. Last night.'

'You want me to finish sawing?' Dulio asked.

'He was in an alley, lying there. Cut the rest of those four-by-twos. I took him back to my room and got Roy to have a look at him.'

'He survived that?' Dulio bent down and blew the dust away before easing the saw out of the cut.

A hot, gritty wind had picked up. Dulio's lips had a grey rim of spittle and grime and Agustín's mouth felt as if it had been coated with sand.

'You think Jank has recognized us?' Dulio asked.

'No.'

'Do you know what you're going to do about him?'

Agustín drew in his breath and pushed the saw into the wood.

'Look at that.' Agustín pointed at the sun, an hour away from setting and already melting into smog that was grey, golden and red at the edges: it was absurdly beautiful. He said, 'I'm going to kill him.'

Dulio did not reply at once; eventually he said, 'It's the wrong thing to do.'

From the back door Rex watched Pascualito and Sabino preparing glass. He waited and watched, defying them to make a mistake in his presence.

Sabino shivered. Pascualito caught it and said, 'What are you afraid of? Him?' Pascualito looked over to where Rex was standing. Sabino dropped his gaze and concentrated on the work in hand. The turn in the foreman's eye deceived Pascualito.

'He tried to act tough with me this morning. Said I fucked up some aluminium frames. I told him fuck his mother.'

Pascualito's words terrified Sabino.

Pascualito said, glancing again at the door, 'Don't worry. He's not looking at us, Sabino.' Sabino refused to look up. 'Sabino. Sabino? Look at me.'

Sabino did what he was told. Pascualito crossed his eyes and rocked his head about, idiot fashion.

Sabino saw Rex before Pascualito did. He lowered his head at the foreman's approach.

Rex said, 'You two can go.'

Pascualito looked up. 'Go where?'

'Go. There's no work here for you any more.'

Agustín and Dulio came over. Agustín said, 'What's the problem here?'

'Get back to work,' Rex said. 'This is nothing to do with you.'

'This fuck has just sacked me,' Pascualito said.

'That's it. Out,' Rex said. 'You too,' he said to Sabino. 'You can collect your money from the office.'

When Rex had gone, Pascualito picked up a brick. 'The fuck,' he said, and he turned in small circles, veins taut in his neck, stamping his feet, repeating the obscenities. He launched the brick.

At the sound of breaking glass Rex turned. He looked at the labourers for a moment, then disappeared inside. Through the office window the labourers could see the shadows of the foreman and their employer and they observed the silent picture show of their movements. There was no dialogue they could hear, but they understood what was going on. They saw Mrs Dorfmann go to the filing cabinet, saw her bend down and go temporarily out of view, saw her rise, cash box in hand, saw her go to the desk.

A few minutes later, Rex came out. He handed Pascualito and Sabino a ten-dollar bill each.

'Ten dollars?' Pascualito said.

For the first time, Rex affected to notice the glass. He pawed some splinters with the toe of his boot.

'Get out,' he said.

Pascualito, barely able to restrain himself, was thinking about lifting a shard of the glass to slice Rex's throat. But Rex frightened him, so he swung his jacket over his shoulder and made for the gate.

Dulio slapped Sabino on the back. 'Don't worry,' he said. 'I'll see you later.'

Rex said to Agustín, 'Clean up that glass.'

From the gate, Pascualito shouted, 'You squint-eyed son of a bitch. Don't think I'm forgetting this. The first thing I'm going to do is I'm going to fuck your daughter. The second is I'm going to fuck your ugly wife. Third, I'm going to fuck your dog. And then,' Pascualito paused, 'then, I'm going to fuck you.'

Pascualito went off, howling with laughter. Sabino trailed in his wake.

Agustín got off a stop early to go to Roy Jones's house. Alice answered the door. She wore a short, dark blue robe; her legs were bare and she had nothing on her feet. 'Come in,' she said.

'Is Roy here?'

She beckoned him inside. She closed the door and led him into the living room. The television was on. 'What'll you have?'

'Is Roy here?' Agustín asked. 'I said I'd call by for the key to my room.'

'He said he'd be right back. Sit down, have a drink while you wait. Got some pretty good vodka here.' She poured out a glass and gave it to him. 'Where do you know Roy from?'

'From Peru.'

'You Peruvian?'

'Yes.'

'You were in prison with Roy, right? Roy told me about all that stuff.' She sat on the couch opposite Agustín and took a sip of her drink. 'We haven't been properly introduced. My name is Alice Marie Washington, from Houston, Texas. How do you do?' She got to her feet, took a step forward and held out her hand.

'Pleased to meet you,' Agustín said, as he shook her hand.

Alice giggled. Agustín's eyes fell on their hands, still joined; her eyes followed his. She giggled again.

'Well,' she said, 'what kind of friend of Roy's are you?' She withdrew her hand and curled up on the couch, arranging the robe over her knees. There was a white scar that ran six inches from above the kneecap to the inner calf. She saw Agustín looking at it. 'They say one day I'm going to have plastic kneecaps put in. When they done this,' she traced the scar, 'it was just before they invented a special kind of surgery that don't leave no scars. I just missed it by a matter of months.' She stretched her leg out. 'But you don't think it looks too awful, do you?'

'No,' Agustín said. He drank.

She refolded her leg and gave him a coy look. 'So, you didn't tell me what kind of friend you are.'

'What do you mean?'

'I mean,' she took a long sip from her glass and giggled, 'I mean, are you the kind of friend that gets friends with your friend's friends? Or don't you follow me?'

'No, I don't.'

'I think you do. You're just teasing me.'

'I thought it was the other way round.'

'See,' she said with a laugh, 'I knew you knew.'

Agustín drained the glass and stood up. The drink hit him hard. 'Is Roy coming or not?'

'What's your hurry?'

'Is he?'

She studied him for a moment, weighing him up. 'He said he was going to your place.' Her voice was truculent, but as Agustín left she called after him brightly, 'Call by again honey, and we can talk some more.'

Roy let Agustín into his room.

'Alice told you I was here? I said to tell you.'

'How is he?' Agustín said, nodding in the direction of the gringo.

'Better,' Roy said, smiling. 'Remember I said he weren't no son of Uncle Sam? Well, he ain't.'

'Where's he from?'

'Irish.'

Agustín looked over at the man, apparently asleep. Roy had cleaned him up, brushed his hair and shaved him. He looked helpless. Agustín stared at the apple-dented forehead, at the smashed cheekbone, at the teacup-shaped scar on his chin. He whispered, 'Is he a junkie?'

Roy shook his head. 'No. Like I said, it's pneumonia.' He took a small brown bottle from his pocket, unscrewed the top and shook out a handful of red and yellow capsules. 'Amoxil,' he explained. 'Penicillin. One of these three times a day for the next week. Okay? After that, he should be all right.'

'And if he isn't?'

'Well, then I'll have probably made the wrong diagnosis and he'll die on us.'

'Oh.'

Roy laughed and said, 'I gotta get going. Don't want Alice feeling lonely.'

'Where'd you meet her?'

'A bar in Hollywood. Great gal, huh?' He pushed a long arm into the sleeve of a baseball jacket. 'You be in tomorrow night?'

'Depends what time. I'm going to the New Era Mission meeting,' Agustín said, and he waited for Roy's reaction.

Roy's movements became hesitating. He took time arranging his jacket, lifting his shoulders to fit it around him. He put some small things into his bag. He put the bag down and pulled at the jacket again. He stooped and lifted the bag. He got to the door, but did not open it. He was like a lover who had said he was leaving but wanted to be stopped and called back.

Agustín went to him and Roy thought for a moment that he would be embraced. They looked at each other closely. Then Agustín opened the door, and Roy stepped out on the walkway.

'I don't have money to pay you for this,' Agustín said with a glance to indicate the sick white man.

Roy shook his head and Agustín closed the door.

Agustín went to the window. He liked to watch Roy when Roy did not know he was being watched. Roy's legs were long and bandy, and he strode along with his body bent slightly backward, head down, always worried-looking. It used to make Agustín laugh. He had first seen Roy from a window in Lurigancho, the strange gringo striding around the exercise yard, always alone.

He went to the bed and looked at the stranger. The man opened his eyes and gazed at him.

'Are you feeling any better?' Agustín asked.

'What time is it?'

The accent was strange. 'Seven-thirty,' Agustín said when he had decoded it. The information did not seem to sink in. 'That's p.m.'

The man smiled. 'I had a dream I was in New York,' he said.

'How was it?'

'I washed dishes in New York. But it was too cold. I went north. It was cold there too.'

'Why did you go to where it's cold?'

'I did stoop labour. They call it stoop labour there.'

'When did you come to LA?'

The man frowned.

'This year? Last year?'

'I don't remember.'

'Where did you pass Christmas? Easter? Do you remember?'

The man was silent.

'What's your name? Do you remember that?'

'Sean.' He spelt it for Agustín, who repeated it and told Quinn his name.

'Hungry? You want something to eat?'

'Coffee.'

Agustín went to the shelf by the sink where he kept a jar of instant coffee. He put the pan on to boil. 'Those scars that you have, they look like they might be political.'

'No,' Quinn said, propping himself up, 'self-inflicted.'

Quinn said it so matter-of-factly that Agustín, for an instant, thought he might not be joking. He said, 'You must bear a big grudge against yourself.'

'No,' Quinn replied, smiling. 'I don't bear grudges. That's part of my trouble. Where are you from?'

'Peru.'

Agustín poured the water into the cup, sprinkled the granules straight from the jar on to the surface of the water and, because he could see no spoon to hand, swirled the liquid around. By the time he had brought the coffee to the bed, Quinn was asleep.

A sense of distance and apartness had always been in Agustín, building up in him until it defined him. But, in the process of its growing, its sources had become blurred, as though by the *neblina* he had grown up in. Only dimly could he now perceive the moments that had created this distance, from others, from himself: standing in the courtyard off the *callejón* in Lima, watching the half-naked children playing in the piss-drenched corners; seeing Silvia on her deathbed; and other moments he cared not to recall. The images were captured for him as if in photographs held up by an unseen hand, and a voice from a mouth out of sight was saying this is why you are what you are, and at the same time the hand holding the photographs was slipping back into the *neblina*, the images becoming distant, blurred, and blurring the reasons for his distance.

Only once, many years before, had his and another's stories touched, and then only for a brief time. And though it was then that Agustín felt a reversal had taken place, that instead of running out of life he was growing deeper into it, things had turned out badly. Still, that time exercised a power over him, reminding him, maliciously, of what might have been. Revenge was the wrong word for what he was about to do: it would be a way of forgetting the only time in his life when he had not moved in and out of others' stories, the occasional visitor, but had truly been involved. He had to forget; to remember was to live with an enormous failure, the failure of a whole life.

He put the coffee on the floor and looked at the man who was in something deeper than sleep, who was sweating and mumbling. Fighting the distance, Agustín sat on the edge of the bed and put a hand on the man's forehead. Quinn seemed relieved by the touch, accepting the hand like an embrace and taking pleasure from it. Quinn's left hand lay across his chest, over the sheet. Agustín took it in his own right hand and squeezed it.

Then he fell asleep and began to dream of the things he never wanted to dream of.

SIX

The vibrations alerted Agustín to the menace. Imperceptible at first, they became tremors of increasing violence. They travelled along the stone floor of the corridor to the iron bedstead. They rose, trembling through the rubber-footed legs, and spread out in the frame, juddering Agustín awake. He raised his head a fraction and listened. The hollow echoes of the footsteps were filling out, becoming clearer, nearer, more real. Agustín was frightened, but he had to see. He propped himself up. The corridor was long and dark. He caught the glinting reds and greens in the dwarf's animal eye-shine, and drew in his breath, his fear swelling. Behind him, dry leaves rusted in a corner under a window that let in no light.

The dwarf continued his advances towards the bed. When he got to Agustín, he leaned over, his head now ten times bigger than his body, the forehead high and sulcated, the eyes tiny stars of light far back in dark space. With a conjurer's flourish the dwarf produced five large cards, like playing-cards but bigger and with pictures. The dwarf's voice was high and squeaky, as though filtered through helium from a lost diving-bell at the bottom of the ocean.

'You're in a dream,' he said.

With these words the dwarf's head shrank, leaving the space above Agustín empty and cold. The dwarf passed the fan of cards in front of Agustín.

'Each card will take you to a different dream. Judge by the pictures,' the dwarf said slowly; and added: 'It's only a dream.'

While Agustín studied the cards, the dwarf muttered to

himself, a disarrangement of words, shuffled out of sequence, invaded by high giggles and sniggers.

'Pick,' the dwarf said with impatience.

Agustín took a card.

The picture was a family portrait. Agustín saw his mother, Silvia, seated on a straight, high-backed wooden chair. She sat with her ankles crossed, legs slanted, hands folded in her lap. She was smiling in a way that suggested unconfessed and private burdens long endured. His father, who was standing behind her, an arm across her shoulder, also smiled. The posture he struck – spine rigid, chin up, head back – gave him the air of the patriarch sniffing with pride in his brood and possessions. Agustín's infant brother and sisters were scattered in the corners of the scene. Luis looked stern, Roxane suspicious. Nita sat on the floor and was holding a rag doll before her in both hands. Only Agustín was near his parents, wedged between his father's legs. The expression on Agustín's face was older than his years properly permitted: anxious, watchful, defensive.

Strange, Agustín thought. He had no memory of such a photograph. When had it been taken? Where? He took a closer look and realized the picture was a fraud. The faces of Silvia and the children began to collapse like melting wax images. Agustín peered at his father, but it was not Adolfo: it was Agustín, and the pride he thought he had seen in the patriarch had already turned and set into conceit and spite and malevolence.

The dwarf chuckled knowingly and snatched the card back before offering another.

It was pornographic. A naked woman lay on her side, one hand supporting her head, the other pushed into her dark hair. So explicitly were her genitals displayed that a wave of disgust crashed over Agustín and he nearly dropped the card. But, almost at once, a jolt of sexual curiosity drew his eyes back to the woman and her pose began to excite him. He inspected her, following the line of a splayed leg from calf to knee to thigh. He looked at the dark hairs between her legs, at the pink and red helices of her vagina. His eyes passed on to her belly, then her breasts and the small, pink nipples. He examined the woman's fine shoulders and long neck, then her face. The skin was fair and flawless. The lips were parted, the teeth small and strong. He wanted to check her expression, to make sure her promise matched his expectation. He looked into her eyes.

They were poisonous; those of a being tortured who, in the last withered moments of life, was staring out her torturers.

Agustín gasped and let the card drop. The dwarf chuckled and pushed up the remaining cards. Agustín brushed them away.

The dwarf, carefully arranging the cards, said in his high squeaking voice, 'You can't go through this dream without making a choice. Don't be afraid, it's only a dream.'

When Agustín looked at what the dwarf was offering he saw there was now only one card. The dwarf repeated in a whisper, as if to himself, 'Only a dream, only a dream.'

Agustín reached for the card with the reluctance of the man who knows he is about to draw the short straw but has no other choice. His fingers brushed the dwarf's hand. It was soft, tiny and hairless, the hand of an infant, and its incongruity astonished Agustín. He looked into the dwarf's face with the expression of a man who has only just realized that a woman he has known all his life and whom he has never noticed has a special, hidden beauty about her. The dwarf dropped his head demurely and looked shyly at Agustín from under his eyes. Agustín was touched. He should not have been suspicious. He took the card.

It was what Agustín had feared it would be. He looked up and saw that the dwarf was laughing, a silent and mirthless laugh.

The picture was of a large prison cell, bare, the concrete stained and scorched. It was full of brown men, most of them stripped to the waist, some in torn jeans, others in ragged shorts, all of them shoeless. They had the marks of beating on their bodies and faces. Some were unconscious and close to death. Those who were able held the dying in comforting embraces. Agustín recognized himself. There was a man's bloody head in his lap.

'I knew it,' the dwarf squeaked triumphantly. 'You picked it.'

'I did not,' Agustín said, jumping out of bed and tossing the card away. A current of air captured it and sailed it into the corner behind him where the dry leaves stirred with a delicate, brittle rustle. The card fell among the leaves and they gathered over and covered it. The dwarf squealed in alarm and waddled over to retrieve the card. He snatched it up. When he spoke, his voice was arch. 'I don't know what you're angry about,' he said in rebuke. He turned and padded into the darkness.

Agustín, exhausted by his fright, by his anger, flopped back on the bed. He was breathing hard, and sweating. He heard the dwarf's voice from some way off. 'I told you it was a dream. All this' – Agustín raised his head to see that the dwarf had stopped halfway up the corridor and was sweeping his arm around to take in the surroundings – 'is an illusion.'

Agustín felt he must be sick. He would never have chosen *that*, not if he had known.

Only two companies ran services to the capital. Buses left at midday and midnight. It had been a last-minute thing, and they would have preferred the other company: its buses were newer and more comfortable; the tickets more expensive; the travellers, and pickings, richer. But the seats for their midnight departure had been sold out by ten that morning. The other company had two seats left. Agustín paid for them. The clerk took the money and began filling in the forms.

Across the street Polo was waiting in the car he had stolen two days earlier. They had time to kill so they drove together to the fishing village five miles from the town. It was sunny and warm, the *neblina* was dissolving and retreating further out to sea. The fishermen, straddling their reed boats like horses, their bare legs and feet in the icy water, were paddling in from the sea. Their wives and children waited on the beach for the nets of crabs, which they emptied while the fishermen hoisted the boats to their shoulders and stacked them against the stone wall on either side of the pier.

Agustín and his companions found a restaurant and ordered *ceviche* and beers. Pepe read aloud from the Government newspaper an account of an ambush the day before in the mountains to the south. Fifty terrorists in two lorries had been surprised. Forty were dead and ten made prisoner. A photograph showed soldiers lifting the dead by the arms and legs, hammock-shaped, their clothes twisted half off, and arranging them in a long straight line. Pepe said he was happy the army had achieved this success and that if the terrorists ever came to power he would leave Peru. 'They would make it intolerable for us,' he said.

Polo and Pepe ordered more beers. Agustín left them and headed for the old pink church on the hill overlooking the village. From the beach the church looked pleasant. Agustín imagined he would find a cool, dark interior and looked forward to sitting by himself. But when he climbed the hill, he found that the church was no longer in use. The pink paint was decayed and the crumbling adobe showed through. It was as if fine skin had been peeled back to reveal rotting flesh.

To the left was another neglected wall, beyond which was the cemetery. Agustín passed through the gateway and stared at the tombs lining the sides of a long rectangle. Most of the dark homes had been opened, and the place had a plundered look; the tombs gaped back at him empty, like rotten, gap-toothed mouths. In the cemetery's centre was a leafless forest of poor crosses planted by the families who could not afford tombs. The crosses leaned this way and that, teetering, trying to hold up. Everything in the cemetery and the church was crumbling. But that was appropriate. This part of the country was crumbling. The mountains here were not of solid rock, but soft and giving out, like exhausted concrete. The roads, too, were weary, their integrity hammered by trunks and buses; great chunks fell away at the verges. Near by, the great adobe ruins of Chan-Chan, the imperial city of the Chimú, were turning to dust.

Agustín sat down on one of the newer, unspoilt tombs and looked over the village. He was not happy about tonight. The last robbery had not gone well. Pepe had almost been overpowered by a passenger and Polo had had to open fire at the man. Although he was less than six feet away when he fired, Polo had managed to miss. The shot secured Pepe's release and Agustín was glad the passenger had come to no harm, but the episode had done nothing for his confidence. Besides, the haul had been miserable: a few hundred thousand useless soles de oro, 'Golden suns', the worthless currency of the Republic.

Agustín had given most of his cut to Nita. He had eventually traced his mother and sister to a slum off the Carretera Central. Finding them had been a nightmare. Wandering, wandering from place to place, asking questions of people he barely knew, walking alone among crowds, hearing in all the babble only his own footfalls and the muffled breaking thunder of the terrorists' bombs, walking, going nowhere, in the dark. Nita and Silvia were sharing a hut with a family of five. The roof and sides were rush-matting, the floor cardboard; there was no electricity, no running water. Silvia lay inert in a corner. How completely their family had disintegrated. Silvia was so weak she could hardly open her eyes, and when she spoke there was no inflexion in her voice.

Nita took the money without a word. Agustín asked about Roxane and Luis. Roxane had been abandoned by the father of her child, Luis hung around with some toughs near San Martín.

'Our father?' Agustín asked.

Nita shrugged. 'He is with his other woman.' She was looking at the money as if it were so much waste paper.

He said, 'Who do you blame for this? Our father?'

Her eyes suddenly brightened. Agustín braced himself for an outpouring of bitterness. But Nita's voice was low and steady. 'Our father is weak,' she said, 'like many men. But if I blamed him, I would have to blame every father in Peru. Look' – she motioned to the infants in the corner – 'they are in the same condition. There are millions like them, like us.'

'The saints do not lay blame,' Agustín said harshly, a rebuke to what he saw as his sister's attempt at martyrdom.

'I do lay blame. I blame . . .' – she paused – 'I blame you and me and everyone, all of us for allowing this to happen.'

'What happened in our family has nothing to do with other people.'

'If we knew what it was to stick together, if we only knew that.'

Agustín grunted. 'We're all to blame, then,' he said in mockery.

'You more than most,' Nita said. 'You could have done so much.'

Agustín burst into anger. 'I've just given you money.'

'All you've done,' she said, 'is perform one act. We need more.'

'I'll be back with more, soon.'

'More? More money? You don't understand my *more*,' she said. 'Perhaps you will be back. But it would still be just another act. A single act. That won't help. Not people like us, in this situation.'

Agustín felt Nita's gaze on him as he walked off. He stopped and turned, expecting her to say she was sorry and had not meant it. When their eyes met, she said, 'I blame you because you are a parasite and because you think only of yourself.' She spoke without reproach or bitterness. She was fifteen, and Agustín knew she was one of the terrorists.

From his vantage point of the cemetery Agustín watched another wave of fishermen come in to receive the welcome of their families. He had not seen or heard from Nita since the day he had given her the money. He had been travelling around the country with Pepe and Polo. He felt a stab of envy when he thought about Nita, but could not find its source. He dug further and dragged out the idea that it was because Nita had hope, to have made the commitment she had made, young as she was, implied hope.

He assumed Silvia was dead, that she had died among strangers. He thought of his mother crouched in Lima's doorways with her tray of overpriced confectionery and cigarettes, staring out into the street, waiting, waiting, then dying. These thoughts brought him something worse than sadness, they brought him nothing. What he felt was worse than pain. The loss of his mother, of his whole family, had been inevitable. He hated this country, the people in it, himself. Nothing good can come of this country, he told himself, or the continent. It was destroyed half a millennium ago, it was its destiny to be overthrown. The church, the cemetery, the mountains, the roads, Chan-Chan, all were in ruins; and the people were ruined. They were like drug addicts or alcoholics, too far gone to want to help themselves. The envy he had experienced subsided. Nita was wrong, wrong to have hope.

Agustín rejoined Pepe and Polo. A little before seven they drove back to Trujillo. They pulled off Avenida España into a dark street and parked the car. Agustín checked the bus tickets. Then he and Pepe took a gun each from a bag concealed under the passenger seat.

'See you at Las Delicias,' Polo said as Agustín and Pepe got out of the car.

They made their way to a bar off Pizarro, a five-minute walk from the bus company's offices, and ordered beers. Pepe bought a Lima newspaper and they settled in to pass the time. Pepe read the latest reports of the ambush. 'They have captured an important leader,' he said. 'He is the nephew of the Archbishop of Lima.' Pepe sipped his beer. 'A rich family.'

'Then he has lost much,' Agustín said.

By eleven-thirty, when Agustín and Pepe got to the office of the bus company, there was already a crush of people. Company officials announced the bus would be late, that it had not yet arrived from the capital. Pepe muttered under his breath. He opened the broadsheet with a disgusted snap and began to read the sports news.

The bus arrived forty-five minutes late. It was after one by the time the incoming passengers had disembarked and the Lima-bound were on board with their luggage. Agustín and Pepe had a seat over the wheel arch, and Pepe made a fuss about the lack of space. They had arranged for Polo to be in Las Delicias, a road-side restaurant halfway between Trujillo and the capital at which the driver always broke the journey and the passengers had half an hour to get something to eat and drink. Once Polo saw the bus arrive, he would leave the restaurant and drive to a pre-arranged spot off the main road to wait for the hijacked bus. He would help Agustín and Pepe rob the passengers and disable the bus, and afterwards they would disappear into the night.

The atmosphere in the bus soon became heavy with smells. The heat made everything sweat, even the metal roof and the glass in the windows. The passengers' brows and upper lips glistened. While Pepe slept, Agustín weighed up the passengers, looking for those who might cause problems. There were a couple of big men, but they appeared slow and stupid. There was a smaller, neat-looking man in the seat behind the driver. He was wiry and alert, and he caused Agustín more concern.

Pepe came awake and said to him, 'You remember the *terruco* leader that was captured?'

'The Archbishop's nephew?' Agustín continued to study the wiry man behind the driver.

'They will kill him.'

'That is his risk.'

'If he had not done what he did that day, if he had not gone with the others, he would live.'

Agustín made no comment.

Pepe continued, 'I mean only that one decision wrong, one mistake, and your life is over.'

The thought was obvious, but Agustín did not think it trite.

Pepe said, 'Even now, we don't have to go through with this. Are you frightened?'

'Always.'

'We can do nothing at Las Delicias,' Pepe said. 'We can say to Polo we have changed our minds. We can go on to Lima, or leave the bus, and it will be as if this fear never existed.'

'What would we do then?'

Pepe shook his head. He had followed this path and knew it led in loops back to what they were doing now. He said nothing more, and Agustín went back to thinking about the wiry man: he would like to know what he did for a living.

At Las Delicias, before the driver had even pulled to a stop, a swarm of children burst in. They pushed down the aisle bearing ice-creams, cold drinks, oranges and chocolates, and called out their wares. The passengers roused themselves and most made for the restaurant; a few remained in their seats and tried to sleep. Agustín nodded to Pepe and together they got off the bus and went into Las Delicias.

The restaurant was a one-storey rectangular building without electricity. Inside the floor was of compacted dirt, the tables were crude and unsteady, the wood of the benches was roughly planed. The *menú* consisted of beans and rice with a little meat. Polo was finishing a cold drink at a table in the corner. He gave Pepe and Agustín a look to say *I thought you were never going to get here*, then left. They had agreed that unless there was some urgent reason, they would not talk.

Neither Agustín nor Pepe was hungry. They had a cola each and went outside to stretch their legs. The minutes passed slowly and maliciously. After half an hour, the driver rounded up the last of the passengers, chased the children away and got the bus back on the road. No one paid any attention when, ten minutes later, Agustín tapped Pepe on the arm and got to his feet, checking, as he did so, the gun's position in the waistband of his trousers. Most of the passengers were sleeping and that suited him. Agustín would do this as quietly as possible. With luck the passengers would not know what was happening until the bus had left the highway and pulled up at the spot where Polo was waiting for them. He took a look at the wiry man behind the driver, asleep now and snoring lightly. He went up and stood on the driver's right in the doorway.

Neither the driver nor his assistant noticed him at first. Agustín, making no sudden movement, took the pistol from his waistband and said to the driver, 'You know what this is?'

'Yes,' the driver said. The bus swerved slightly as the shock reached his arms.

'I do not want to use it. My friends' – Agustín used the plural to give the impression of numbers – 'do not want to use theirs. But we will, unless you do what I tell you to do.'

'Tell me, then.'

As the bus turned off the highway, the wiry man came to. He blinked awake and stiffened when he saw Agustín. Agustín pointed the gun at his head and said, 'Easy, *hermano*.'

The man relaxed, but though he appeared to be under control, Agustín did not like it; he was not frightened enough.

Some of the other passengers had begun to sense something was wrong, and a murmur started up in the bus. People gripped the headrests of the seats in front, waking up the occupants and spreading the alarm. In the end Agustín had to shout to tell everyone to stay seated and to put their heads between their knees. Pepe patrolled the aisle and cursed at those whose heads were not down far enough. Some of the passengers grumbled about the pain in their backs.

'You,' Agustín said to the wiry man, 'what is your profession?'

'I am an engineer,' the man replied evenly.

'Where do you work?'

'In Lima.'

'What business had you in Trujillo?'

'I am from Trujillo. I was visiting my mother.'

The man had too much self-possession. His answers were probably untrue.

'Put your head between your knees, right down,' Agustín told him. There was nothing else he could do.

Fifteen minutes later Agustín saw the flicker of headlights and told the driver to pull up and open the doors. Polo burst on to the bus, eyes wide, movements jerky. Agustín made a calming motion with his free hand. Polo went to the rear of the bus, where Pepe was instructing the passengers, one by one, to empty their pockets. Agustín took the keys from the driver and covered the passengers from the front of the bus.

Some took a long time to part with their possessions, and, with only an hour to go before dawn, Agustín felt time pressing on them. He urged Pepe and Polo to be quick.

When they were about a third of the way along the aisle, Pepe pointed his gun at a fat, middle-aged man wearing a grey suit and a Panama hat. A woman of similar build beside him sobbed. The man, every move a wheezing effort, produced a few sticky notes from his pocket. 'That's it,' he said.

'Give me the rest you fat bastard or I'll cut your balls off and stuff them into the mouth of your fat wife,' Pepe said.

'There are so many robberies on the roads. I now travel with the minimum.'

'You fat *maricón*. Pepe hit him with the gun on the head. The man fell sideways into his wife, who screamed. Some of the other passengers, frightened by the commotion, let out cries. A few got to their feet.

'Sit down and wait your turn,' Agustín said, waving the gun from person to person. The wiry man had not moved, but was watching him intently. Pepe was laying into the fat man.

'Get his money,' Agustín shouted at Pepe, meaning stop wasting time beating the man. Pepe either did not near or misunderstood. He seemed in a frenzy and continued to lash out.

'*Hombre!*' Agustín shouted at Pepe, almost in despair. He had started down the bus when he became aware of a sudden movement behind him. He knew it was the wiry man and spun around to shoot. The man was quick, he had a gun. He swung his free arm under Agustín's gun hand and the shot went into the roof. There were more shots. Agustín felt something, or someone, slicing at his legs, and he went down, losing his gun on the way. He heard more shots, small pops that expanded into booming explosions. He heard screams. He tried to move, but could not. Someone was lying on top of him, someone very heavy. He felt he was being crushed, buried alive, and, in his panic, he clawed until he got his head clear. He was gasping for breath when he saw the wiry man standing over him, pointing the muzzle of a revolver into his eyes.

'Easy, *hermano*,' the wiry man said.

He let Agustín free himself from the corpse, then produced a set of handcuffs from the pocket of his leather jacket and locked Agustín's hands behind his back before dragging him off the floor and into the seat behind the driver. He stood in the aisle and pointed his gun at Agustín's chest.

The driver got back on the Pan-American and drove at high speed to Huarmey, the nearest town. They stopped first at the hospital, where the dead and wounded, six in all, were unloaded. Pepe was still alive, but unconscious and bleeding heavily. Polo was dead from a single wound to the right temple, so small it was scarcely noticeable. The fat man was also dead, as was the man who had fallen on Agustín. Two injured passengers were able, with help, to walk into the hospital.

The wiry man kept Agustín covered. Most of the passengers were silent and did not look at Agustín as they disembarked.

The wife of the fat man came up, supported at the elbows by two men. She stopped and stared at Agustín. There was nothing, not contempt, not hatred, in her face. Agustín turned away. The men shepherded her on. The wiry man said, after she had passed, 'Her husband need not have died. Nor the others. They were alive this morning. Tell me why they had to die.'

Most of the passengers got off at the hospital; a few stayed on to see Agustín delivered to the *comisaría*. As he was frogmarched through the main doors, Agustín heard the wiry man tell the officers he was a detective of the Policía de

Investigaciones del Perú, a PIP, who happened to be travelling to the capital on the bus.

Two uniformed policemen brought Agustín to a room off the main courtyard, pushed him into a wooden chair and chained his hands to the back. To the left, through a barred window, Agustín had a view of the courtyard. There was a great deal of activity. Men and women he recognized from the bus were gathering and talking excitedly among themselves and to the police. Agustín saw the PIP lounging against the far wall, smoking, enjoying an extended joke with uniformed men. A group of soldiers came into view. They escorted a dazed-looking man, a prisoner, and the chatter subsided, only to start up again immediately the party had passed on. Someone said, 'One of the *terrucos*.' A terrorist. The ambush had taken place near here.

Agustín saw the PIP shake hands with a lieutenant of the Guardia Civil. They exchanged a few words, shook hands again and the lieutenant beckoned to a sergeant and another man. The detective leaned back against the wall and watched as the lieutenant and his two men started for the interrogation room. They were followed, hesitatingly, by about a dozen of the passengers.

On entering, the lieutenant drove his fist into the side of Agustín's face. Agustín, his arms chained behind him, toppled over with the chair, falling heavily on his left shoulder. The sergeant righted him, sat down at a desk near the window and ratcheted a sheet of typing paper into his machine. The passengers had gathered around the barred window and were peering in at the scene. Others were at the open door. There was no guard, nothing to prevent them passing into the room, but none dared put a toe across the threshold.

'Name?' the lieutenant demanded. He did not look up.

'Agustín García García.'

'I should tell you,' the lieutenant continued without looking at Agustín, 'that if you give me a single false answer I will have you taken to the back of the building and shot with the *terrucos*. Do you understand?'

'Yes.'

'Name?'

'Agustín García García.'

'Very well. You know the risk you are taking?'

'It's my name.'

'As you wish. Father's name?'

The sergeant was a slow typist, jabbing the keys with rigid fingers, attacking them in a way that reminded Agustín of the pecking of a hen. It took almost an hour to get down what Agustín told them about his background, almost all of it invented. The passengers pressed at the window and door. When the lieutenant began to question Agustín about the details of the robbery, they became agitated and shouted into the room, 'It was not like that, it was like this.' They contradicted each other loudly, and one man acted out, for the lieutenant's benefit, the parts of the three robbers and the detective who captured them. There was a dull pain from the lieutenant's punch throbbing in Agustín's head, a tightness in his temples; the vision in his right eye seemed to be deteriorating. He saw the lieutenant as though the image were an enlarged photograph, a pattern of shaded dots with the dots growing in size until they disrupted the pattern and became more important than the image. Fear was coming to him at intervals, breaking over him, ebbing away, returning. It was a relief when the fear went, but it took with it other things, his strength, his reason, his capacity for logical thought. When the lieutenant asked him for information on his companions, on the guns, on what other offences they had committed, Agustín refused to say anything. The lieutenant, who had still not looked his prisoner directly in the eye, gave no sign of impatience or anger at Agustín's silence.

A second sergeant pushed his way through the throng at the door and broke the news that Pepe had died in hospital. The passengers cheered in approval. The lieutenant seemed not to care one way or the other. And truthfully, Agustín realized, neither did he.

By the early afternoon the crowd had thinned out. A sergeant told the passengers that the bus for Lima was leaving at three and that those who had still not given their statements should do so without delay.

The policeman left the room several times; for meals or for coffee, Agustín assumed. He remained alone, struggling with his thoughts, fighting to overcome his fear. He could not think about Pepe and Polo, could not think about their dead bodies.

At one point the interrogators withdrew. A handful of passengers lingered at the window and door. Two uniformed men walked purposefully into the room, closed the door behind them and pulled the shutters across the window. Agustín heard the people outside whispering and the sound of them slowly backing off. He turned to look at the faces of the men and saw they were wearing black woollen balaclavas. One produced a length of pipe, the other a leather sap. The man with the sap brought it down on Agustín's face.

He thought he had been asleep for a long time, his dreams were of such intricacy and convolution. Yet he was conscious in time to see the men open the shutters and leave, and the flow of their movements suggested only a short time had elapsed. His right eye was closed now. He heard a silence, heard it as a recognizable sound, from the passengers outside. One by one, they gathered again around the window and door. Agustín would have told them he was sorry, but he knew it was pathetic, pleading. The passengers were building a whispered consensus. They withdrew.

He was left alone until after the dark had fallen and the last of the passengers were on their way. The lieutenant entered and sat down at the desk.

'Name?'

'Agustín García García.'

'We have reports of other robberies, similar to the one you committed today, several in the capital. You are a common delinquent and we have more important things to do than waste time on you. My companions will come for you. Last time I told them to treat you with care. This time I will leave it to their discretion.'

The lieutenant gathered some papers and left. He had still

not, as far as Agustín was aware, looked into the face of his prisoner.

Agustín waited for the hooded men. The time passed slowly, for Agustín was visiting and departing from consciousness, and the dreams he had went on for days. When he realized they had not yet come, that there was still a chance for life, he called out to the lieutenant. His name was not Agustín García García. He was Agustín Cienfuegos de la Cruz and he was sorry for what he had done, for everything. No one heard him and he began to cry.

Movement in the dark. He felt himself being unchained and pulled to his feet. A blow to the stomach unbalanced him and he went down. They hauled him up. He saw, through his one working eye, that the men were not hooded, and he became confused, uncertain whether they were bringing life or death to him. They dragged him into the courtyard, around a corner, through a barred door and into a corridor lit by a single low-wattage bulb that hung from the concave ceiling of whitewashed brick. There were six cells to the right, to the left a featureless wall. The jailer approached. There was an exchange of words Agustín did not take in. He could not see much. He could make out the jailer, who looked perplexed. The jailer's fingers rasped over his growth of beard so deafeningly, so jarringly that Agustín shivered. This is what fear does, Agustín said to himself. It jandles all the senses; first levels, then distorts proportion, making small noises loud as tolling bells; it shrinks or dilates time, capriciously, vindictively, so that your speed does not synchronize with others', so that nothing – time, movement, sound – has sense. The jailer's fingers rasped on his throat; his head shook slowly in mockery of time.

One of the escorts said, 'We have to put him somewhere.' The jailer nodded and said, 'The one at the end. It's special, though.'

The door opened and fear brought a metallic taste into Agustín's mouth; his tongue recoiled as though it had touched silver paper. A slash of white moonlight pierced a high window no bigger than the size of a missing brick, but it did not illuminate the cell; rather, it was blinding, like torchlight shone directly into the eyes. Agustín could hear his heart thumping. He groped for the wall and was absurdly happy when he found it; he put his forehead against it and breathed out. Then he turned and, his palms flat on the wall, slipped down to the floor. He fell instantly asleep.

Agustín woke but he did not know why until he heard the second shot. He shivered and let out a soft cry. He drew his knees up to his chest and clasped his hands together in front of his ankles and rocked slowly back and forth. A volley of shots, and men's hushed voices.

He heard the sound of breathing – heavy, deep, painful – from within the cell, from a shadow in the far corner. He did not move, was afraid to move, afraid to speak. In the corridor there were heavy footsteps, scuffing sounds of soles turning on the concrete floor, and whispers. Agustín froze and waited, unaware he was holding his breath until it burst from him. Even though his damaged eyes had adjusted and reached into the darkness, he still could not make out the shadow.

Another volley from the courtyard, more ragged this time, shots spluttering in an ill-defined trail. The door swung open and a guard, framed in a rectangle of dim light, called his name.

'Are you going to shoot me?'

'Are you García?' The guard held a clipboard and pen.

'Yes.'

The guard ticked the clipboard and said, 'There are others before you.' He pulled the door to.

Agustín dropped his head to his knees. He moaned, 'No, no, no.'

From the corner came a voice, from a man controlling pain, bearing up.

Agustín was too frightened to respond. He did not want to establish contact. The prisoner, he knew, would be one of the captured *terrucos*; to survive he had to avoid contamination.

A single shot trailed a dismal echo into the night.

'They are killing the survivors.' The voice was a hoarse whisper. It waited for Agustín to respond. 'Who are you?'

With a bullet just fired, an image came into Agustín's head of the victim – surely blindfolded, half-conscious after interrogation – hands tied behind the back, a gun pressed behind the ear; the executed man collapsing into a heap on the ground. Now Agustín wanted contact, something to remind him of life. He said, 'I am not one of you.'

'Then you'll live.'

Agustín's mind confiscated the words. 'Yes? They won't kill me, only the terrorists?'

'You'll live,' the terrorist said.

Agustín had expected the voice to contain some rebuke, or carry disappointment or anger. But it did not. It loaded shame on to him.

After some moments the terrorist spoke again. 'Why are you here?'

'There was a robbery. My two friends were killed.' Agustín put it this way, passively, to lessen his burden.

'Who did you rob?'

'A bus.' Again, to lessen the burden.

'Travellers on the bus?' the tone was not accusatory, but neither was it matter-of-fact.

'There were businessmen among them.'

'In Peru there are so many men and women of business. The man who washes car windows at the traffic lights, the woman on the street corner who squeezes oranges or sells *chicha* and *anticuchos*. All *comerciantes*. A nation of entrepreneurs.'

Agustín understood the rebuke. There was no reply to make and he dealt with his shame in silence.

Agustín was thinking he must have fallen asleep, for he could make no sense of his surroundings. He felt the way he felt in the mornings, his mind working to build a context around the things his eyes saw. It was still dark, there was still the slash of moonlight.

He was aware of the prisoner making some attempt at

movement. There was another shot from outside, the noise of a diesel engine turning over, another shot. The prisoner made a noise like a small groan. Agustín sensed the man was tensing. Then he seemed to give up, having tried something and failed.

The prisoner whispered, 'I want to ask you to do me a favour.' There was a pause. 'I cannot use my arms.'

'What happened?'

'I need to piss.'

Agustín scrabbled over to the prisoner. He found his armpits and hauled him up. It was a difficult business, even though the prisoner used his legs to propel himself upwards. The man caught his breath as Agustín laid him against the wall, where the sword of moonlight fell across his face. Agustín could see that he was young, in his late twenties or early thirties. His cheeks and jaw were stubbled and bruised, his mouth cut and swollen from blows. The man screwed his eyes shut to receive a wave of pain. When the pain had passed, he opened them slowly, like fists uncurling into open palms.

'They snapped my arms in the interrogation,' the prisoner said. 'There's a tin somewhere.' He nodded into the gloom behind Agustín.

Agustín got down on his hands and knees and waved his right arm in blind semi-circles an inch or two above the floor until he found the tin. He fumbled in the prisoner's trousers and placed the tin under the man's penis. Some of the urine splashed Agustín's hand.

'Are they going to kill you?' Agustín asked after he had helped the man down.

He did not reply at once. 'Sadly,' he said, 'it's looking that way.'

'Do you regret what you have done?'

'I wish I could say no and mean it.' He paused before continuing. 'Still, I think I can say no, in spite of everything, in spite of what's going to happen.'

'If you had not got involved, you would not be here.'

'I wish I could contradict you.'

'And tomorrow you would be alive.'

Agustín was thinking of what Pepe had said just before they reached Las Delicias.

'If you had not joined the terrorists, your life would not have been wasted,' he went on. He wanted the prisoner to admit his error, had to hear him confess it, because he, having no hope, wanted there to be no hope anywhere. He could not accept that Nita was right. He wanted them both to be wrong. Something else tugged at him, irritation at the smugness of the man: the terrorist believed he had unlocked secrets. Like Nita. Agustín understood now why the encounter with his sister had left him so angry. Their certainties irked him. 'Your life is over, a waste,' Agustín insisted.

The terrorist said, 'Believe me, I've failed in a lot of things, and if there was a way of getting out of this – a way I could do it without losing my name and my face – I would do it. But I can't, so I have no alternative but to say to the guards, "More weight," and no alternative but to say to you, "No regrets." What I hate is that, because of my situation, I don't really know if I mean it.'

'So it's pride.'

'Maybe,' the terrorist conceded wearily.

After some minutes Agustín asked, 'Have you been to prison?'

'Many times.'

'What's it like?'

'The world outside. There are those who live in shit, those who live in luxury.'

Agustín knew he would never be among those who live in luxury.

The terrorist read his thoughts. 'You have survived this. You will survive prison.'

'You must be ruthless?'

The terrorist paused. 'The ruthless, some say, survive longer than the rest.'

Agustín felt almost relieved. The words reassured him. He could do what it took to survive. They fell into silence and a sleep of sorts overcame Agustín.

*

Heavy footsteps in the corridor woke him.

'*Hermano*,' the terrorist said in an urgent whisper.

Without thinking, Agustín scrambled over to him. The terrorist said, 'They will take you to Lurigancho. There, contact the Party. Will you do that?'

'Yes,' Agustín said. A key entered the lock.

'Tell them you spoke to Gabriel Jerónimo López, and tell them one word: Abancay.'

The Archbishop's nephew. Agustín said, 'You were the captain of the ambushed terrorists.'

The guards were in the doorway. One turned on a torch and swept the light into the corner of the cell where Agustín was crouched beside the prisoner. His contamination exposed, Agustín became afraid and shrank back, trying, without being noticed, to put as much space as possible between him and the terrorist. He could see that one of the guards was aiming a rifle at them. Agustín shut his eyes and waited.

Another guard kicked Agustín in the face. His head cracked against the wall. He pulled his arms over his face and felt another blow to his lower back, another to his hip. He was aware that they had raised Gabriel to his feet and were dragging him to the door.

Then there was a sudden, momentary lull. Agustín glanced up. The terrorist was looking directly at him.

'I was the captain of fifty,' the terrorist said.

The soldiers pulled him away.

Agustín stretched on the floor and let out a howl. He wanted to understand what Gabriel had been telling him, what Nita had told him. He was outside them and all they possessed and laid claim to, by himself, with nothing. He heard the shuffle of Gabriel's feet in the corridor, the muttering of the guards, the cocking of an automatic weapon. *More weight, more weight.*

Around Lurigancho, where the desert was grey dust, the Guardia Republicana patrolled. The concrete of the prison's main walls was scorched and held the imprint of black flame-shaped stains. Men and women sat on decaying rocks before the gates, in wait for visiting time.

Inside, as Gabriel had told Agustín it would be, there were those who lived in luxury and those who lived in shit. The drug-traffickers retained access to their riches and they spent conspicuously on the things that pleased them: good food, alcohol, cigarettes, newspapers, television sets, drugs and women were brought to them for their use. Then there were the dwellers in shit: they went in rags, barefoot, with unkempt beards and lice-ridden hair. Their eyes were far back in their heads, and they carried on their bodies and faces bruises and abrasions that were not wounds but the mark of the hopeless. They were always hungry, always frightened, for violent death was one of their number, alive beside them in the prison. Here Agustín did not know if he walked among the living or the dead.

The terrorists were housed in a separate block, the *pabellón industrial*; another world, Agustín heard prisoners say, that was neither luxury nor hell. There were no murders there, no screams emanated from it, as they did from the other blocks, day and night.

It took Agustín a week to deliver Gabriel's message. He spent as much time as he could near the *pabellón industrial*, waiting for an opportunity. Eventually, he caught the attention of a surly-looking man with narrow eyes and a neatly trimmed beard. The man turned away as Agustín approached him, but stopped on hearing the name of Gabriel Jerónimo López and the word Abancay. He listened to what Agustín had to say and told him to wait. Five minutes later he returned with another man, who asked Agustín to repeat what he had just said, and to describe as much of what had passed in the cells of the *comisaría* as he could remember. When Agustín had finished, the second man whispered something to his companion, whom he addressed as Dulio. Dulio left at once. To Agustín, the second man said, 'Wait here.' Then he too left. After ten minutes Dulio returned and handed Agustín a paper parcel. It was warm and greasy in Agustín's hands. It was food: rice and beans. He ate where he stood, and, when he had finished, he licked the grease from the paper until the paper disintegrated on his tongue.

On his return to his cell block, a captain of the Guardia with an escort of a dozen armed men entered and ordered the prisoners to line up. He then introduced two men from the United States who had come to the prison to do charitable work. Their names were Hal and Jerry and they were from an organization based in Florida. The New Era Mission of Christ.

The New Era Mission of Christ banner hung listlessly above the mission hall, the flat-roofed former liquor store, now bedecked with broad yellow, white and purple ribbons. It was almost nine o'clock by the time Agustín got off the RTD. He could hear the guitars and banjos from a hundred yards. The music made him shiver. He noticed all at once how cool the night had become. The cold invaded him, his flesh tightened, and, trembling, he pulled up his collar. He had taken a dozen paces when he stopped, and could not move. A man and a woman standing at a table set out by the door watched him curiously. He realized there was nothing in his head: no plan, no memory of how he had got to this point. He was travelling on instinct, not one move ahead was worked out.

The banner, bearing the legend REACHING OUT FOR THE UNREACHED, flapped abruptly, suddenly stricken by the wind, and it stretched out to Agustín like a challenge. He pulled himself together and walked towards the door. The couple by the table smiled encouragingly at his approach.

'Read this,' the woman said, taking a *Simple Truth* from a pile on the table. 'It's the Mission's magazine. Read the truth, for free.'

'And you'll want this.' The man gave him a Xeroxed sheet containing the words to several hymns.

Agustín found a seat at the back. At the far end was a platform, raised two or three feet off the floor, in the middle of which was a lectern of blond wood. To the left, the guitarists and banjo-players stood in four stepped rows, men and women alternating. The hall was full, the people rapt.

Nick Zenga was at the lectern, clutching it tightly at the sides, leaning, head bowed, into the microphone, eyes closed. A television camerawoman crouched beside her sound man to shoot Zenga from below. After some moments of silence, he raised his face. He wore the look of a weight-lifter stretched to the limit. He held his arms out to the congregation. The fingers, then the hands, began to shake, then the arms, shoulders, legs: a tremor working through his body until it possessed him. His head swivelled grotesquely, rocked back and forth, side to side, while the rest of his body shook like a puppet's.

His arms shot to his hips and he became rigid. The camerawoman got up slowly and refocused. Zenga mumbled into the microphone, one word a nonsense word, a child's silly word, then after a pause another, then a stream of mixed-up words gathering in momentum until they sounded like a song sung in some weird tribal language, all the time the pitch and volume getting higher until it became almost like a scream. The people were transfixed, and watched as young children watch television, mouths open, eyes wide, believing.

Zenga, leading up and into the scream, unexpectedly and shockingly, fell silent.

Some people in the audience gasped and Agustín heard the thud of a body falling. Zenga said, in a hoarse whisper, 'Faith.' He paused and looked into the faces of the people.

He said, 'To another faith by the same spirit . . . So then faith cometh by hearing, and hearing by the Word of God . . . While we look not at the things which are seen, but at the things which are not seen: for the things which are seen are temporal; but the things which are not seen are eternal . . .

'Do you see now? That to have faith is total; it is every-thing, it is eternal, it is power. There are no half measures, everything is all the way. Listen to the Word of God: "Is not my word like as a fire? saith the Lord; and like a hammer that breaketh the rock in pieces?"

'*Power.* Together we shall be the fire and the hammer,

breaking the enemies of the Lord, burning them and their corruption, cleansing the world.'

Zenga paused and dropped his head. Then slowly he raised it, neck muscles taut, struggling against the weight. 'Have no fear, have no fear. For the Word of God is total. Did Jesus not say, "All power is given unto me in heaven and in earth"? Power. Power comes from authority and from authority comes power. Jesus said, "Go ye therefore, and teach all nations, baptizing them in the name of the Father, and of the Son, and of the Holy Ghost. Teaching them to observe all things whatsoever I have commanded you: and, lo, I am with you always, even unto the end of the world." *End of the world*. Authority, power right to the end of the world.'

There was another silence. Zenga emitted a low whistle that was like a whisper, and he turned to examine the faces in the congregation one by one. The shaman who sees into a person's soul by looking into the eyes. When he spoke it was slowly but with real force in his voice.

'The Mission calls you to Jesus, because we have power and authority to the end of the world, as Jesus says. But it begins with faith, you need faith. Do not doubt and it will grow. Then it will work. Then all the things will be in your grasp. Help the Mission and Jesus will help you.'

Zenga jerked back from the lectern as though he had received an electric shock. The camerawoman moved closer to the platform to film as Zenga's legs gave way. Two young men – one was Andrew Jank – rushed forward to catch him and they led him, as the dazed survivor of a car crash is led, to one of the dozen or so straight-backed chairs lined against the far wall behind the lectern. Someone out of sight was leading a chorus of alleluias, and the hall filled with noise.

As Andrew and his companion sat Zenga down, Agustín scanned the men and women in the chairs, the Mission's luminaries, as he supposed: Victor Jank sitting next to a middle-aged white woman he took to be Jank's wife; Mrs Dorfmann; to her right a long-legged, lean, grey-haired man Agustín thought must be her husband; a smartly dressed

Hispanic who wore gold rings; some of the missionaries Agustín had seen the day before. Agustín saw Victor Jank go over to Zenga, still collapsed in the chair, bend down to pat him on the shoulder and whisper in his ear.

Agustín examined the congregation and saw in their faces hope gone wild to the point of desperation, trust so perfect it was idiocy. Apart from the sprinkling of white missionaries, the people were all from the *barrio*. They were the mothers of *cholos*, out-of-control children; people looking for something that might lead to something better, looking backwards and wondering if any of it had been worth it. They bore a nowhere look, belonging nowhere, dreams gone, going nowhere; they had the cast of people standing out in the rain looking in.

One middle-aged woman had on a low-cut black evening dress and black hat. She wore gold lamé high-heeled shoes and clutched a matching evening purse. Agustín imagined its contents: with X-ray vision he could see inside, and it made him sad because her possessions were predictable, like everything about her was predictable, her past and future; he felt like a policeman turning over a poor person's home, exposing all the victim's pathetic secrets and failures. He turned away and tried to find someone whose story was better concealed.

And found her, the woman from the street meeting. She was wearing the same high-waisted, tight black pants, but had changed into a light cotton jacket a fashionable size too large. She had the sleeves turned back and pushed up over her elbows. She hugged the jacket around her, crossing the lapels over in front with her folded arms. Her long, dark hair fell in curls in front of her eyes, giving her a reckless look. When he had first seen her, Agustín thought, she had seemed more severe. He watched as she stroked her hair back from her forehead to reveal a *V* of veins: it gave her a different look, one of anxious concentration.

Another missionary was at the lectern. His style was old-fashioned preacher hectoring. He mentioned something about social deprivation and squalor in east Los Angeles.

'Lives are not changed by political action,' he said. 'The poor, it is true, will always be with us. But there is no reason why you have to be among them. What counts is the relationship with God. The closer the relationship, the more you can prosper.'

Agustín ignored him and turned his attention back to the young woman. She was out of place here, as she had been two days before. She was *Latina*, at the least she had Latin blood, Agustín was sure, but she was not from these people.

A chorus of alleluias and *glorias al Señor* sounded as the preacher left the lectern. Victor Jank stood up. The way the luminaries watched him, the attitudes they struck, made it clear that this was the one with the authority. Agustín inspected Jank. He saw a man over six feet tall, grey-haired and thin. He had a wide mouth and a long, straight nose: he looked friendly, the kind you could go and tell your troubles to.

Victor Jank was preaching in a manner as homely and mild as he looked. Agustín scarcely heard. He was thinking of the man's deeds, and those of his nephew, and his thoughts tumbled until he became giddy and had to shake his head to clear his mind. He looked around and saw the people were children again, watching and listening, rapt, mumbling to themselves, sniffing, sobbing. A huge woman in a Mickey Mouse T-shirt fell to her knees, tears streaming down her face. Others, eyes screwed shut, arms lifted and outstretched, turned in small circles, tears falling on the Bibles they clutched. They hymns congested the hall, making it overpoweringly, stiflingly close. Agustín wiped the sweat from his forehead.

He saw the young woman looking at him, such a direct and challenging look, and his unease deepened.

Jank, escorted by his court of missionaries, walked a circuit of the hall, disembodied hands from the amorphous press trailing off his head, shoulders and back. As they returned to the platform, Zenga, recovered from his fit, gestured to the musicians and the tempo slowed, slowed until it came to a natural and graceful stop. All that could be heard were the muffled sobs of the congregation.

Zenga went to the lectern and said, 'It's not over till it's over. Now stay around. We have some refreshments right here.' He did a half-turn to introduce another group of missionaries, who at that moment appeared from the main door and passed up the central aisle bearing paper cups, pitchers of lemonade and trays of sandwiches.

As they circulated, the missionaries talked to the people about ordinary things – prices, jobs, homes, families, babies. Agustín heard the people repeat words and phrases from the preaching in awe. He gulped his lemonade to stop himself from shouting out.

Agustín saw the young woman approach the platform. He followed her. He saw her call to Zenga, stretch out her hand and say something to him. Agustín got nearer and heard Zenga say, 'Nick Zenga. How can I help you?' Zenga, the man who had spoken in tongues and writhed as one possessed, smiled broadly at the woman and looked like a salesman preparing to dip into his box of tricks.

'My name's Judy Mendoza. I'm a comparative religion post-grad at UCLA. I'm doing my dissertation on missionary activity among Hispanic communities in the US.'

'That's a real interesting field. I'll look forward to reading it when you've finished.'

'I'm just starting, really. What I was wondering – I'd be very interested to talk to Pastor Jank about the work of the New Era Mission of Christ.'

'That's the full name,' Zenga said with a smile. 'It's better known as just the Mission. You go anywhere and say, "the Mission", people know who you're talking about. Like the President. Nobody says the president of what or where? They know you're talking about the man in the White House. That's the way it is with the Mission.'

'Interesting,' Judy said. 'As I was saying—'

'Well,' Zenga said, 'it'd be hard, I'd imagine, to write your dissertation without talking to Victor. He's *the* man you'd need to talk to. A very wonderful man.'

'I've certainly heard and read a lot about him,' Judy said.

She opened her copy of *Simple Truth* and pointed to a page. 'I was just reading this profile of Pastor Jank. It says he only recently came back to the States.'

'That's correct. He was in Bolivia, but when the Board – that is the Directory Board, to give it its full name, it's the Mission's governing body in Florida – set up the Home Programme, Pastor Jank was elected to head it.'

'The Home Programme?'

'That's what all this is all about,' Zenga stretched his arms out. 'There was a feeling that people here in America, specially people of Hispanic origin, were neglected. You know, it was the attitude of some churches that, well, these people are illegal and they shouldn't be here, so we're not going to minister to them. And we felt this was wrong, like it was excluding them from the Word of God, which no man has a right to do. So, about six months ago the Home Programme was started to cater for the needs of people who perhaps up until now have been feeling sort of abandoned.'

'I see. And how successful has the programme been?'

'Well, Judy,' Zenga said, 'take a look around. We got people here, cable network, newspaper, radio coverage. What do *you* think?'

Judy inspected the scene. Her gaze fell on Agustín. He was, she saw, watching her and Zenga out of the corner of his eye.

Zenga, his smile firmly fixed, said, 'Judy, just let me talk to Victor and see if he's free.'

He went over to the group milling around Jank and whispered to him. Jank disengaged and he and Zenga walked over to Judy.

'Victor, can I introduce you to Judy Mendoza? Judy is a post-grad at UCLA.'

Jank's eyes were mild and contemplative. He smiled at Judy and said in soft voice, 'I'm delighted to meet you, Judy.'

'A pleasure,' Judy replied, and they shook hands.

'Judy's doing her dissertation on missionary activity among Hispanic communities in America,' Zenga explained.

'How interesting,' Jank said.

'I suppose working here must be very different from Bolivia,' Judy said.

'In the obvious ways, yes. You know, climate, environment, that sort of thing,' Jank replied. 'But the core of the work is pretty much the same, taking the Word of God to the people. We always emphasize that, you know. Living with the people, preaching. Preaching is paramount. Jesus said, "Preach." It's as simple as that.'

'Our missionaries', Zenga interjected, 'are the most thorough-trained of any missionary organization. You know, they go to Bible college – most of ours have been to Minneapolis or North West – then there's a year at the Mission's own college, kind of missionary boot camp we call it.'

'Boot camp? Sounds sort of militaristic,' Judy said, and immediately regretted it. 'Sort of', she added quickly, 'disciplined.'

Zenga made his glassy smile. 'We're evangelical militants, Judy. We make no bones about it.'

Jank took over. 'At boot camp it's mostly language training, training for the jungle or whatever part you're being sent to. Linguistics is very big. Phonetics, syntax, theory, how to take down languages that have never been written before. Then missionaries who have been out in the field come and lecture. There's Bible presentation, preaching, basic medical training.'

'Thorough,' Judy said.

'Like I said,' Zenga smiled at her.

'Is Latin America still the main focus of the New Era Mission's work?'

'We have missions in Asia, West Africa and New Guinea also, but, yes, essentially our work is in South America,' Jank replied.

'What would you say, in a nutshell, is the aim of the Home Programme?'

It was Zenga who answered. 'We are providing a social service to people. The Bible changes the lives of people. People who are drunkards, who are squandering their money. They become useful members of society. They begin to save their money, to put it into things that are helpful. It learns, it teaches them, I mean, to make more of their money, to *stretch* the dollar. It helps their image, their self-betterment.

'My wife' – Zenga turned to indicate a small, neat woman a few feet away – 'she is a beautician. She works with people like that, helping them to improve their self-image of themselves. We try and provide a gospel for the whole man. We help them spiritually, not only that, but we help them socially.'

'Materially?'

'If you like. It's not a dirty word, you know.'

'Where is your accent from, Mr Zenga? Italy?'

'You've got a good ear, Judy. I'm Calabrian, through and through. Call me Nick.'

Judy took a sip from her paper cup of lemonade and said evenly, 'Why is it that in some countries people say the Mission supports dictatorships to win favours from the regimes?'

A look of puzzlement crossed Jank's face, but again it was Zenga who answered. 'Our responsibility is to teach people to be good citizens and to support the government in power. If God wants to put that power down, if God puts a nation up, which the Bible says, and we believe that, we teach the people to be good citizens. It's not our job to go around undermining authority. God puts up a power, only He can take it down.'

'You know,' Jank put in, 'the whole question of authority and the Mission's relationship with government is, as far as we are concerned, a distraction. It gets in the way of the work we have to do. Ideally – we can't choose where we go, after all, we have to go where people need the Word – ideally, it would be nice if these countries were democracies. But they aren't, or at least some of them aren't, by American standards, that is. So what can we do? Abandon the souls in those countries? We can't refuse to bring the Gospel to countries just because the regime there doesn't respect human rights.'

A middle-aged woman tugged at Jank's arm from behind. 'Victor, can you come and say goodbye to Councilman Gonzales? He's leaving in a few minutes. And Ted Morrisey from Cable Network wants that interview.'

'Of course, dear,' Jank said. The woman withdrew a couple of steps and waited. To Judy, Jank said courteously, 'Will you excuse me? It's been very nice meeting you.'

'I was wondering if I could fix up an appointment for a more thorough talk,' Judy said hurriedly. 'It would be so helpful for my dissertation.'

Jank addressed Zenga: 'Nick, can you sort something out?'

'Sure,' Nick said. Jank smiled politely at Judy and withdrew. 'You better leave me a number, Judy. I'll see what I can do.'

She gave him her number and said, 'Nick, it was a privilege to talk to you and Pastor Jank. He is everything they say he is.'

Zenga smiled.

Judy put her hand into the bag that hung from her shoulder and rummaged around. 'I'd like to make a donation to the Mission's work. It's work that's long overdue here.' She sorted out some bills.

'Are your parents from the US, Judy?' Zenga asked.

'They live here now. They came from . . .' – Judy paused as she handed over the bills; fifty dollars should do it – 'Nicaragua.'

He shook his head at the bad news and clucked his tongue. 'Still,' he said, 'things are improving. Maybe you'll be able to go home soon.'

'Wouldn't *that* be great.'

He took the money. 'God bless you, Judy.'

Agustín had heard most of it; he moved away as Zenga shook Judy's hand. Judy Mendoza was here for her own reasons. He wanted to get out of her way.

Agustín saw two men he recognized near by, Mexicans from Dorfmann Furnishings, and he nodded to them. He let his gaze wander, hoping for some distraction. He noticed Rex, who had two thin, timid women next to him, his wife and daughter, talking to Mrs Dorfmann's husband. The man looked frail: his cheeks were laced with blue; his skin had a yellowy colour that for Agustín was always associated with the seeping smells of decay and fetor. He could look at the man no more and turned away, only to find Mrs Dorfmann beside Andrew Jank. Andrew was talking earnestly to the woman in the Mickey Mouse T-shirt and her companion. When Andrew had finished with the women, Mrs Dorfmann followed him. A man brushed against her and she stumbled into Andrew, her fat bust pushing into his elbow. She steadied herself by holding on to Andrew's arm, then smiled at him.

The guitars and banjos started again. Agustín wanted to leave.

Then Andrew Jank was upon him, Mrs Dorfmann just behind. 'Good to see you, Mr Ar-say. Real glad you could come. I see quite a few of Mrs Dorfmann's people here tonight.'

'Yes, señor.'

'I've been talking to Mrs Dorfmann about maybe starting a Bible study group at the factory. I was thinking maybe once or twice a week during lunch. Would you be interested?'

'Of course.'

'That's great,' Andrew said, slapping Agustín on the arm.

Agustín was aware that Judy Mendoza had joined them. He did not dare look at her directly. She introduced herself to Andrew and said that she had been talking to his uncle, what a fine man he was, and that she hoped to get a proper interview with him for her dissertation.

Andrew seemed nervous with Judy, though he tried hard to conceal it. As the group chatted, Agustín saw Mrs Dorfmann brush her wrist for some tick; she was holding it within an inch of Judy Mendoza's forearm, exposed where Judy had pushed the sleeves of the over-sized jacket up to her elbows. Mrs Dorfmann looked petulant.

Andrew was saying, 'We can arrange it next week. I'll call by the factory.'

'Yes,' Agustín said.

A lull came to the conversation. Mrs Dorfmann smiled at Judy.

'I think we better see how the refreshments are going. Nice to have met you, Señorita Mendoza,' Mrs Dorfmann said. The 'Señorita' was an insult, a reminder to this young woman that she had brown blood, that in spite of her perfect English and her North American ways she was no better than Mrs Dorfmann. Mrs Dorfmann took Andrew by the arm and, leaning into him to whisper something, led him away.

'The only way she could make it more obvious would be to take off her clothes and jump him,' Judy said when they had gone. 'What is that make-up? Like something for ghouls?'

Agustín said nothing. Judy assessed him quickly. 'What are you doing here?' She stared into Agustín's eyes.

'To hear the preaching,' Agustín replied.

Judy Mendoza snorted.

'I have to go,' Agustín said. 'I don't want to miss the bus.'

Judy looked at him and seemed to be considering something. 'Where do you live?'

'Not too far.'

'I'll give you a lift.'

The woman was beautiful, that was how it was. Agustín accepted.

On the way out, they passed Victor Jank and Nick Zenga, who were saying goodbye to Councilman Gonzales.

'God bless you, Miss Mendoza,' Jank said, seeing Judy.

'I hope to see you again soon,' Judy said.

Jank smiled, but did not reply.

Judy glanced at Zenga.

'God bless you, Judy. Thank you for coming,' Zenga said.

Judy left with Agustín.

When Gonzales had gone, Zenga said to Jank, 'She tried to buy an interview. Fifty dollars.'

Jank sipped his lemonade and considered. 'Find out who she is.'

They drove in silence. As they crossed El Repetto on Garfield, Agustín pointed out Dorfmann Furnishings. The building was dark, but no more desolate at night than in daylight.

Judy said, 'So you work for Mrs Dorfmann?'

'Yes.'

'You know a man called Rex Maldonado?'

'The foreman.'

Judy said nothing more. Some minutes passed before Agustín said, 'You know LA?'

'Not too well. I live – I used to live – in San Francisco.'

'Turn right on Whittier, it's two blocks.'

He turned to look at her. The lights from an oncoming car swept her face before moving up to illuminate the quilted roof lining, where they seemed to linger for longer than they should. Her lips were full, Agustín saw, the upper as full as the lower. Her chin was small and her eyebrows were a single unbroken gull's wing. She wore red enamelled earrings.

'Where are you from?' she asked him in Spanish. He was trying to guess her age.

'From near Nogales,' he replied, putting on his best Mexican accent. Thirty, perhaps.

She said nothing for a while. Then she said, without looking at him, 'Bullshit.' She made the right turn on Whittier. 'Why do people go for all that stuff? The bullshit in the Mission?'

'You're the student. Don't you know?'

'Why were you there?'

'My employer told me to go.'

'You're not that kind.'

'How do you know?'

'Because before, during and after you were faking it. If you fake it, the least you have to do is put on a face. I watched you.' She turned to look at him. 'Women know all about faking it.'

'Why were you there?' he asked.

'What do you know about Rex?'

'He's the foreman.'

'Americas Watch has evidence that links Rex Maldonado

111

García to a murder in Guatemala City in 1984, when he was part of a police death squad. He's a suspect in several other killings also. Did you know that?'

'No.'

'But you know something about the Mission, don't you?'

'No,' Agustín said.

'Shall I tell you why people go for their bullshit?' she said. 'People are afraid of responsibility. They want to be told they're shit, they're worthless, because then they can just throw their hands up and say, "It's no good, I can't do anything for myself. I'm too bad. Let them do it for me." That way they don't have to think. It's all laid out for them. What better way to live, being led by the hand by Granddaddy Victor and Uncle Nick? Beats taking your chances on the street, wouldn't you say?'

Agustín did not reply and they fell into a silence.

They were on Sixth Street. Agustín said, 'You can drop me here.'

'What's your name?'

'Agustín Romero.'

'I suppose that's bullshit, too.'

Agustín smiled. She said, 'I'm Judy Mendoza.'

As he got out, Agustín nodded his thanks.

'You forgot this,' Judy said, holding out his copy of *Simple Truth*. He took it and as he did so was aware of Judy trying to get him to look at her. His eyes moved up and met hers. What struck him most was the *V* of veins in her forehead, and the slightly worn look it lent her beauty.

She said, 'If you can help me . . .'

He said, suddenly shocked, 'Help you? I can't help anybody.'

She grabbed his arm before he could get away.

'Here.' She took a pen from her jacket and scribbled on the cover of the magazine. 'My number.'

Agustín, angry now, turned without a word and strode to the building's entrance.

Judy watched Agustín emerge from the stairs and on to the walkway. She watched him stop, search for his key, open the door and go inside. Judy clicked on the car's interior light and pulled over her shoulder bag. She opened it up, rummaged through the compact, handkerchief, lipsticks and other junk to get at her notebook. It was beside her gun, the .38 Smith and Wesson she had owned for the last three years. She retrieved the notebook and wrote down Agustín's address.

Quinn was still in bed, breathing in the rhythms of deep sleep, his head hidden in the shadows. Agustín was tired. He needed a good night's sleep. He sat on the bed and thought about getting a blanket to put on the floor. He would get it in a minute. He put his head down on the pillow beside Quinn. Tomorrow he would have to talk to Dulio about finding Sabino another job.

He thought of the Bible study class and laughed out loud, his laughter then stilled by the thought of Judy Mendoza. What did she want?

He was confused by her. The picture he had of her led him back to other women he had known. He would not like to have to put into words, not for anyone, especially not for himself, how he had behaved when he had been in love: with anger, jealousy, spite. And so he had confined himself to visiting women, as he visited the lives of all those he came into contact with, easing selfishly in and out of their existences until they, and he, became anonymous.

He wondered where Judy was going, having dropped him off: it was unlikely a woman with her looks would be alone.

The thought, his thoughts, made him angry. He pulled himself up, jaw clamped, fists clenched. It took half an hour to unlock himself. He fell asleep beside Quinn and returned to his unwanted dreams.

EIGHT

He survived a week, no more. He was of the ragged men when he licked the greasy paper around the food Dulio had given him, licked it and licked it, stroked it with his tongue to absorb the hints of tastes; then, as the tastes became remote, sucked it until the paper collapsed and he was like a dog champing on something inedible, sieving it, spewing the indigestible shreds from the sides of his mouth. The first scabs had already appeared on his face and arms, and his clothes were matted to the skin by fetor; after seven days he bore the mark and smell of the ragged men. It was if he had never had another life, had never known anything but what he now knew.

'How long before trial?' Agustín asked a prisoner as he arranged his blanket. In the cell were eight men: two had beds; at night the others unfurled threadbare blankets and laid them, three inches apart, on the squalid floor. Agustín's stomach was bloated from the terrorists' food. When he spoke, he caught the odour of his meal, and he glanced nervously at the man next to him, momentarily alarmed in case he, too, had sniffed it and had marked him down, like a rich and stupid man astray in a poorer quarter, as prey to be robbed. The man, who was named Miguel, had, in a gruffly tolerant way, been answering questions for Agustín for most of the day. But this question overtaxed his patience. Agustín asked again, 'How long do they take to bring prisoners to court?'

Miguel turned on him and clasped his hand around Agustín's windpipe; then, with a huff of impatience, or contempt, released him.

Miguel said, 'You see that man, the black?' He pointed to a middle-aged negro playing cards with two others. 'He doesn't exist.'

Agustín looked at the man; then, for an explanation, at Miguel.

'He doesn't exist,' Miguel repeated. Agustín watched as Miguel spread his blanket, casually picking off the lice and flicking them on the narrow canal of grime and filth which separated them. 'He finished his sentence two years ago.' Miguel took off his shirt and lay on the blanket. 'They lost his papers. Officially, he doesn't exist.'

Agustín thought of the night in the cell in Huarmey with Gabriel, an age ago now. Gabriel told him he would survive, but now Agustín did not think he would. He closed his eyes and looked for some picture from his past to sustain him. He saw his mother when she was young, his father on the day he took him to the zoo and carried him on his shoulders; he saw the pink church overlooking Huanchaco; he saw the stolen car. He saw Polo in Las Delicias, saw him and Pepe on the bus; saw the PIP, the lieutenant, the hooded men, Gabriel.

The pictures were going the wrong way, leading him where he did not want to be.

Someone hit him and he shot up, almost jumping off the blanket.

It was Miguel. He was smiling. He was holding out his hand, offering him something. A segment of orange. Agustín realized no one had struck him after all, and, feeling foolish, he eased. The sliver of orange tasted bitter and the grains of dirt it had picked up from Miguel's hands scratched his teeth, but the act of generosity warmed him, and, incredibly for so small a thing, turned his thoughts back to pleasant, comforting images. Pepe and Polo and Gabriel withdrew, displaced by Silvia, by Nita. The orange was a hallucinogen, helping to create and sustain images in his head. Agustín crushed the segment against the roof of his mouth and let the juice spread over the tongue to be trapped below and beside it. He ground the fibres between his molars and pushed the pulp around his mouth, letting every nerve-end feed on its sharpness. When the mash was on the point of dissolving, he held it at the back of his mouth for as long as he could until it slid into his throat and down to his stomach. He ran his tongue over his front teeth and found a shred wedged there. He worked at it until it came free and gently manipulated it between his incisors. The shred still contained some fraction of juice, and slowly he crushed it. He fell asleep and dreamed of oranges piled up on a cart.

The dream's course took a crude change. A naked girl was peeling the oranges. Agustín knew he was dreaming and knew, too, he could wake up at the moment of his choosing. He decided instead to pursue the dream, aware he could orchestrate its direction. He made the oranges vanish; he made himself naked and on top of the girl; she was making sounds like shivers, which excited him and he paused to savour them. He felt her take hold of his penis and he moved on to his side to give her more freedom. Her shivering moans became deeper, deeper, real and disturbing. Agustín realized what was happening. He jerked upright and awake.

Miguel was kneeling beside him, pants around his ankles, one hand on Agustín's genitals, the other making quick, vibrating movements just below the glans of his own penis. Angry and disgusted, Agustín rolled away. Miguel ejaculated: it appeared to give him no pleasure. The bursts of semen trailed across Agustín's blanket.

'Filthy *maricón*,' Agustín yelled. The other men chuckled.

Miguel was working the last of the come from his penis, tugging at it, coaxing it out.

'Fuck you. Get away from me,' Agustín said.

Miguel was not disturbed. He said, continuing slowly to rub his hand along the penis, 'You don't want it?'

'*Maricón!*'

Slowly, Miguel rolled over to his own blanket. 'You don't want it now,' he said into the night, his voice sleepy, 'next week you will, and if not then, the week after that.'

From then on, whenever Agustín saw Miguel in the exercise yard, he kept away, and, though he could not escape his company at night, he avoided his eyes and stayed on guard in a kind of half-sleep. From time to time he caught Miguel, standing in the exercise yard with his cronies, staring at him, and when Agustín glanced in their direction, they shared a joke that made him feel angry and maligned.

Agustín would occasionally see the terrorists passing from the *pabellón industrial* to their own exercise yards. He often heard them singing *huayno* tunes, revolutionary words supplanting the old lyrics, to the accompaniment of guitar, *charango, quena* and *zampoña*. He would hear the stamping of parade-ground feet, speeches, clapping, cheering, more revolutionary songs. From time to time he glimpsed their banners proclaiming the virtue of the 'Popular War', saw their red flags – huge, so that it needed two men to carry the poles. When he saw these things, he could not help wondering about Nita, and about Gabriel; and the more he saw them, the more he came to think of Nita and Gabriel as always together, so that he could not picture them except as side by side, thinking they belonged together, thinking that because they had hope they should always be together, and that he, believing in nothing, would always be outside them and alone.

One night Miguel put out his hand and Agustín was ready for him. He struck the man across the mouth and knocked him away. Sprawled on his back, threadbare trousers about his knees, Miguel wiped a hand across his mouth, examined the blood and smiled. His other hand was hardly disturbed in its masturbating rhythm. Agustín turned his back and heard Miguel moan as he came.

A man named Domingo Chávez arrived in the block. His right eyebrow had been separated by a machete blow that had also left a two-inch scar at the side of his nose and a vertical furrow in his brow. His crimes were many, and it was not his first time in Lurigancho. He was a friend, a jail-friend, of Miguel's, and they renewed their acquaintance by sharing a roll-up – a treasure Chávez had brought with him from the world outside. Then, to make room for Chávez, they evicted from the cell one of the prisoners, a scared-looking, half-witted *serrano* boy. At night they lay on their blankets and discussed money and sex. They dropped into whispers and took sidelong looks at Agustín, exchanging more whispers. Miguel bucked his hips suggestively and made short, breathless grunting sounds, and Chávez, with his eye fixed on Agustín, laughed raucously. Over the following days Chávez eyed him everywhere he went. Agustín asked the other prisoners what was going on. They replied by making small circles with fingers pointed at their temples: crazy man.

It was getting colder: the *neblina* hung in the air, moist and chilling, so wet Agustín could see pinheads of sea-rain suspended in the air. On some mornings the neblina was so thick that, on entering the exercise yard, Agustín thought that if he stepped forward and walked on far enough, the mist would accept him and hide him as it had hidden the old ghosts from Ayacucho his mother used to see when she first came to Lima. But when he stepped forward, a volunteer to the *neblina*'s cold and damp, the walls of mist retreated a step to elude him; and he looked around at the gun towers and walls and lights and he knew he was here, in prison, to remain seen, for ever.

Returning from the yard, as Agustín was passing an open cell, he heard something unusual: an echoey jangle followed by a split-second of a dancing, quivering sound: metal clattering on concrete. He heard a stifled curse that was a rebuke for clumsiness; then shuffling noises. Agustín glanced in and saw a man busy about a mattress, patting it down, taking a step back to scrutinize it, patting it again. Agustín moved on and took up position half a dozen doorways along. He watched the man leave the cell. Five minutes later two other prisoners entered. Agustín waited until dinner was called. The two men were among the first out with their plastic plates and spoons. Others entered the cell for their implements and emerged heading for the food line. Although there were still prisoners moving around the corridor, this was his best opportunity. He made for the cell, found it empty, pushed the door to behind him and searched the mattress, which was new and relatively unsoiled. The seam at the top had been unstitched leaving an opening of about half an inch. Agustín, one eye on the door, ran his hand along the horsehair which had bunched at the top, and felt something hard. He worked it down to the opening and kneaded it through. It was a five-inch long shiv, honed from metal tubing. Agustín put it inside his shirt and went to the door.

Two men carrying plates of thin stew and rice were on their way in.

'Who the fuck are you?' one shouted.

Agustín pushed past them without a word, thinking it had to be done immediately because these men had seen him. Chávez and Miguel would get word. He made his way to the food line and saw them standing in a corner, their food already consumed, talking together.

Chávez did not notice until it was too late. Agustín had the shiv in his hand. He brought it up and felt an instant's resistance as the knife pierced the man's side, then felt it change course as it connected with bone, forcing his hand up and the blade down. Chávez twisted suddenly and forcefully and Agustín lost his grip. Chávez was falling and to help him on his way Agustín got in two good punches to the side of the head. He turned to defend himself against Miguel but saw that the man had already fled. Chávez was on the ground, lying over the blade. Agustín stepped back to mingle with the bystanders, several of whom were chuckling. He heard a man call to someone, 'Get Dr Inconvenience.'

Dr Inconvenience was a gringo and the only man in the block more solitary than Agustín. Agustín had seen him in the yard, a man with an unhealthy, pitted complexion, long, spidery legs and a curious, loping walk. The other prisoners said he was a doctor, and they called him Dr Inconvenience because, although he spoke Spanish, he retained North

American expressions, dropping them randomly into his speech, his favourite being, 'That's inconvenient right now.'

Dr Inconvenience arrived and administered first-aid as the guards cleared a space around the fallen man. Agustín watched the gringo at work. To him, the doctor looked pained, as if *he* had received the wound. He watched as Dr Inconvenience soothed Chávez until the wounded man was removed to the prison hospital.

Later that day, in the misty exercise yard, the gringo greeted Agustín. '*Hola. Cómo estás?*'

Agustín said, '*Cómodo.*'

Dr Inconvenience was not a doctor. His name was Roy Jones, and, before his capture, he had been in the employ of a man from Shreveport named Lennie. Four or five times a month he piloted a Cessna freighting drugs and dollars between Peru and Colombia in the company of Antonio, a nineteen-year-old heroin addict and killer who made childish *wheee* and *whoosh* noises when they swooped low over the treetops.

Roy soon began to curse his bad judgement in having got involved. He traced his wrong move back to his year in Vietnam, where he had served, with credit, as a combat medical technician. A good year, a bad year? He still was not sure, but certainly a time that had changed him, and the way he thought about things.

Roy's parents, who owned a ranch in Oregon, had prepared for his return by reading about veterans and their experiences of readjustment. They were sensitive people and had been close to Roy before he had been drafted. They expected Roy to be difficult, moody and withdrawn, but hoped that with patience and understanding they could get back to the way things had been.

When Roy got in to Portland, his father, Bill, hugged him and said he knew Roy had been through hell, that he and his comrades must have suffered, but now they were home and it was all over. Roy immediately became angry.

He said no, he and his comrades had not suffered, that what had happened to them was nothing compared with what the poor miserable fuckers who lived out there were going through, that *they* were the ones who were doing the suffering, that if he had known what it was going to be like he would have skipped to Canada. 'None of this lonely hero suffering shit. I have not been traumatized,' Roy insisted loudly. '*We* traumatized *them*.'

Confused and hurt, Bill offered to find Roy's duffel bag; his mother picked lint from his tunic.

A heavy, sorrowful atmosphere hung over the house, and Roy's mother began to stay in bed late. After some weeks Roy left. He started to mix with people adrift. He got a job unloading crates at a food plant in New Orleans, and had a hundred more jobs like that.

He travelled to Mexico, lived cheaply and got involved with a woman. When she left him for another, better-looking, gringo, he moved on, ending up on a beach near Puerto Angel. For a year he paid a dollar a night for a hammock in a shack. He would remember that year as a time of many love affairs with the tourists who passed through, all of them made mysterious by being shrunk into four or five or six days. The affairs went through the conventions of more normal relationships, but condensed: the courting, the finding out, the resentments as adjustments are made, the jealousies, break-ups, recriminations and reconciliations, and, inevitably, the leave-takings. His greatest love was a schoolteacher from Stockholm who part-timed as a bus driver. She was large-breasted, a little overweight, pretty, not too tall, and gentle. After she left, the beach became oppressive. Three days later Roy walked the three miles to town and caught the bus to Oaxaca.

It was in a bar in Oaxaca that Roy met Lennie. Lennie had had a few drinks and was looking for a North American to talk to while his four-wheel-drive, at that moment broken down on the Pan-American, was being fixed. Lennie drank a lot. He worked out of Bogotá and Miami, and was in Mexico to tend to some business. The breakdown was costing him time and money. Roy said he hated driving, Lennie said yes, he felt the same. Roy said given the chance he would fly everywhere, flying was as easy as driving. You got in the seat, turned over the engine and took off. Lennie was all ears. They drank a lot more, Lennie buying. Lennie made Roy a proposal. There seemed nothing else for Roy to do.

Roy landed the Cessna at a strip he had been to several times before. Antonio, a Galil between his knees, had been whooping as they made their approach. As he taxied in, Roy looked over their accomplices on the ground: youths in baseball caps, vests and jeans, M16s, Galils and Uzis slung carelessly over their shoulders. One – his attitude made him the head man – sat on an empty oil drum nursing an M16 and watched as Roy cut the engine and climbed down. Roy did not recognize the man; someone new.

'Hi,' Roy said.

The man hoisted his rifle and fired. The bullet stuck the Perspex of the cockpit and hit Antonio in the middle of the forehead. Roy could have sworn he heard the boy go *wheee!*

'Hi,' the man replied, with a smile, lowering the gun.

'Hi,' Roy said, again; he could think of nothing else.

Men rushed to the plane. They wore the uniform of the Peruvian army. Someone knocked Roy to the ground, kicked his legs apart, and smashed a rifle butt into his upper back. A boot struck him on the side of the head.

When Roy got to Lurigancho, the narcos invited him into their block. Roy declined. They asked if he was crazy. Roy declined again, glad to have had the opportunity to get some distance between him and his former employers. They did not look well on his decision, and marked him down as a probable informer. The two senior men in the narcos block decided that, in due course, Roy would die.

It took time and a lot of thinking, but in the end Roy could see no alternative. He wrote to his father and mother. The letter came hard, but Roy did not want his parents finding out from whispers or newspapers. He said he was sorry for putting them through what he knew they must be feeling.

A month later, an hour after he had treated Domingo Chávez's knife wound, Roy received a thirteen-page letter in his father's hand, signed, again by his father, 'Mom and Dad'. 'Dear Roy,' it began, 'we are sad to hear of the trouble you are in.' It progressed, tortuously, into little items of news about the ranch. Roy had lost his parents somewhere, he did not know exactly when or how or why, and he had not been trying to find them with his letter. But he picked up on their sorrow and love for him, and he read on with a heaviness in his heart. The letter ended with his father saying that he had wired the American embassy in Lima five hundred dollars with the request that the consul see to it that Roy had whatever he needed and was entitled to. 'I have spoken by telephone with the consul, who seems like a good man, and he has assured me that the establishment you are presently confined in is of satisfactory standard and that prisoners are not maltreated which comforted your mother.' At first, Roy was annoyed by the consul's lie, then relieved.

Roy read: 'We are terribly sad and heartbroken that you are there at all, and we are doing what we can to find out if there is a way your trial might be hurried along or that you might get released on bail. Being all this distance away it's hard for us to get real concrete information but we want you to know that we are doing the best we can to help.' At the bottom of the letter was a postscript in his mother's hand. 'Dear Roy, I see your face everywhere here. Although I do not understand what has happened, what they say you did, I do not care. Whatever you do, whatever you have done, you are my son and always will be and I will always be your mother.'

Roy bit his lip, folded the letter and put it in his shirt. Then he went out into the yard, where he saw Agustín, walking, as always, alone. Roy Jones needed to talk.

The season of the *neblina* ended, the summer came and went. Then it was winter again, misty and wet.

In each other, Roy and Agustín had recognized parts of themselves, the part that had taken a wrong turning, the part adrift, looking for something. And they recognized in each other the things they did not possess: Agustín liked the thoughtfulness behind Roy's slow way of talking, was touched by his concern for others, which expressed itself quietly and in small kindnesses; and he liked Roy's patience and good humour. Roy admired Agustín's alertness and courage, felt safe with him, saw him as someone capable of making decisions. He was unsettled when Agustín was not around. Roy started to teach Agustín English, and Agustín learnt quickly. At night they would lie side by side and talk of things from the past.

One morning Agustín felt so bad he could not get up. Roy said he was a running a fever and went to get fresh water. While he was away, three gringos came into the cell. The gringos wore white shirts, short-sleeved and starched, on which each had clipped a plastic-covered ID card. Agustín, sweat running into his eyes, recognized two of them: Hal and Jerry, the New Era missionaries the Guardia captain had introduced and who had been active in the prison with their Bible classes and preaching.

'*Hola*,' Hal said, leaning over Agustín and sniffing the air discreetly. 'A little touch of the Inca two-step, huh?'

Agustín had no idea what he was talking about, but nodded anyway.

'I'm Hal. Jerry you know, and this here . . .' – he stretched a hand to indicate the third man – 'this here is Andrew Jank. Andrew is visiting us from the *Estados*.'

Agustín saw a young man with a fresh and eager look about him. He was tall, broad-shouldered, confident.

'*Hola*,' Andrew said, pronouncing the *h*. 'Would you like a piece of fruit? Got an apple here.' Andrew beamed at him and held out the apple while Hal translated. When Andrew realized Agustín had not the strength to take it, he said, 'I'll leave it right here for you. We'll look in again soon. Meanwhile, we'd like to leave this with you. Do you read?'

Agustín nodded.

'Right.' Andrew seemed pleased. He dropped a pamphlet beside the apple just as Roy came back with the water. Andrew and Roy looked into each other's eyes.

'American?' Andrew said.

'Yes,' Roy said bluntly, pushing past him. The North Americans left.

'Jeez,' Roy said, looking over the pamphlet. He read: ' "If you have a problem, God can help." Who says Americans don't have a sense of irony? They came to the right place, the evil bastards.'

'Why evil?' Agustín's voice was a whisper.

'Paraguay, Brazil, Salvador, Chile: wherever some fucking asshole is *pacifying* the people, the Mission is there to lend a hand. Guatemala, too. You know, the last couple of years the army there has wiped out 30,000 people – Indians, labour and opposition people. Shitstorm, and nobody gives a fuck. Here, drink this.'

Agustín did not drink. He had fallen into a fevered stupor. Dreams, of Roy not being able to cure him, of dying in prison, floated in and around his mind. He was hot, cold, thirsty, parched . . . sick. He did not know where he was, was convinced he was back in the cell with Gabriel and, like him, about to be shot. Every noise that came to him came as gunfire. He saw himself hunched in a corner of the cell in Huarmey, and he saw another of himself come in at the door, and he watched as the two others of himself exchanged words, one telling the other that he was going to kill him. It was too much and he decided to get out of it.

Everything cleared. He opened his eyes, feeling perfectly normal. Roy was leaning over him. He said to Roy, 'I've just been talking to myself,' and Roy, misunderstanding, said, 'And how. All last night and all of today.' Before Agustín could explain the obvious, that he had been talking to *himself*, that two parts of him had conversed, some treacherous support gave way and he was falling a long way down, spinning so much he was getting sick. He burped up vomit and bile and continued his fall. He was falling, falling, a long time on the way down. An age.

Roy was shaking him. 'Oh, man. Man, wake up.'

A dream? Roy looked worried, his face an inch away from Agustín's, eyes popping out of his head, his long hair dishevelled and falling in front of his face; he flicked it out of the way in that curious manner of men with long hair.

'Please wake up. Oh shit.'

'Roy?'

'It's Chávez. He's back. He wants you, and the narcos want me.'

Agustín drifted back into the cocoon of his fever. Roy shook him urgently. 'We gotta do something. Now!' He pulled Agustín to his feet. The other prisoners in the cell decided it was time for prudence and left. Roy went to the door and looked into the corridor. He saw prisoners staring at him. Knowing that Roy's life was over, they hurried to get out of the way. There were no guards. They had been told. From one of the other blocks came the sounds of an evangelical hymn.

Back in the cell, Roy said, 'We have to get to the admin, get protection. Can you make it?'

Agustín nodded weakly. Roy took his arm across his shoulder. Some little strength returned to Agustín, and he was able to walk with Roy's support. Roy peered from the door into the corridor. There was no one in sight. The two men emerged from the cell and, and as fast as he could manage, Roy hauled Agustín along. As they passed, cell doors slammed on either side to make an aisle of steel.

At the end of the corridor, Roy unhooked Agustín, planted a long fine hand against his chest and pinioned him to the wall while he craned to check the yard.

'No one,' Roy whispered. 'You okay?'

Agustín nodded.

'Yeah?' Roy asked.

'Yes.'

'Okay. We gotta get across the yard, down those steps and over to the control area. Gotta be some guards there.'

Roy hoisted Agustín to him, grabbed the wrist that came over his shoulder and put his other arm around Agustín's waist. Their bony hips bashed together.

Roy said, 'Let's go.'

They stumbled into the deserted yard like a pair of drunks. Summoning all his strength, Agustín found Roy's rhythm and they were able to pick up speed. No one came after them, no one rushed at them with knives, and Roy said, 'We are going to make it. Quick as you can.' He jerked his chin up to indicate the flight of steps leading down to the ante-room leading to the control area. Agustín took hold of the iron railing and followed Roy, who had gone ahead to push open the door. Wedging it open with his foot, Roy stretched out his hands for Agustín and caught him. They stumbled through the doorway.

Domingo Chávez was waiting for them; Miguel lurked just behind. Chávez slashed the air an inch in front of their faces, then brought the knife up for a second try, slicing, left to right, a horizontal line. Roy snapped back. The knife caught the long hair in front of his face and left a delicate border of blood on his forehead. Instinctively, Roy lifted one of his long legs and kicked out. The movement was so absurdly inelegant, so improbable, that Agustín could not help but laugh. Roy shot him a glance to say, 'I'm doing the best I can, damn it,' simultaneously using his high kicks to keep Chávez at bay. Roy was not a physical man, did not know how to fight. The Mission's hymn sounded nearer, louder.

Chávez doubled over. Roy, unable to believe his kick had connected, froze. Then he began yelling, in English, to the guards, still nowhere in sight, but who, he knew, must be watching from somewhere. Before Chávez could get straight, Roy danced forward and sank a foot into his crotch. Chávez went down on one knee and gasped. Miguel stayed where he was, behind his leader; he showed no enthusiasm for the job.

Roy pushed Agustín back towards the door and together they stumbled out on to the stairs. Agustín gripped the railing and started to pull himself up, Roy pushing him from behind, back the way they had come.

'I got him in the balls, right in the balls,' Roy jabbered. When Agustín paused to find strength, Roy grabbed him and half-lifted him up the remainder of the steps and into the open yard. 'Move, man. Move.'

But there was no escape. They were going back to the block, where they would be cornered, and now Roy was tiring. When they were still ten yards from the gate to the block, he turned and saw Chávez, the knife in his hands, emerge on to the stairs from the basement. Terror gave Roy strength to lift Agustín off the ground and get to the gate. Chávez sprinted after them; he was yelling and screaming in rage.

Roy and Agustín burst into the cell block and would have collapsed in a heap had they not been intercepted. Agustín felt someone grab the front of his clothes, pull him upright and slam him into the wall to one side of the gate. He saw another man doing the same to Roy, who had hunched his shoulders, and, in a hopeless, cowering defence, crossed his hands, palms out, in front of the lower part of his face.

Chávez burst through the gate. In the distance, the hymn-singing ended, replaced by a man's voice, weak and high, and the start of his preaching.

Chávez was in shock, open-mouthed, white-faced. From behind, two men grabbed his arms while a third twisted the knife from his hands. Chávez began to stutter a plea. A grim-looking man took a fistful of Chávez's greasy hair and pulled his head back. Agustín recognized the man: it was Dulio.

In the other block the preacher had paused. Someone shouted, '*Gloria al Señor!*' and the response came in an uneven chorus: '*Gloria!*', and again, louder, '*Gloria!*'

The knife came from behind and drew a line of crimson across Chávez's throat. The blood was frothy. Chávez's gaze was on the ceiling, so far back was his head. He gurgled briefly, and collapsed.

Dulio signalled his men, and, hauling Agustín and Roy with them, they strode into the yard and made for the ante-room, where Miguel, having nowhere to hide, stood in a corner.

'Miguel Antonio Peña,' Dulio said, 'we know who you are. Modify your behaviour or join that piece of shit, Chávez.'

The escort fanned out as they reached the gate which led from the ante-room into the central control area. The guards stepped back as the terrorists emerged and made their way calmly towards the *pabellón industrial*. Agustín could see Roy, held by the elbows, blinking and trying to shake the blood from his eyes. Agustín's legs had given out. He was being half-supported, half-carried along, yet he experienced sensations of strength, of invulnerability and invincibility. He was aware of prisoners and guards staring at them, could sense that they, too, recognized a power, could sense the haughtiness of the escort, its assertion of control; and he thought, this is what I have been waiting for.

Agustín's head was swimming, but he was conscious of standing at the opening of a long, narrow ante-room. On the walls were murals and revolutionary slogans painted in vivid, primary colours. There was complete silence.

As Agustín focused, he saw before him an aisle, like a wedding aisle, of two ranks of men. They wore red tunic-like jackets and stared at the new arrivals. On a command from someone unseen, they raised their right hands, in which they held red flags, so as to form an arc.

'Go on,' Dulio said to Agustín. He nodded to Roy to help him, and together the pair stepped into the arc and were received. As they did so, from the far end of the room came a burst of applause that continued and gathered in volume until they emerged at the other end of the arc. Sixty or seventy men waited for them, all clapping. From the yard came the swirling sounds of 'Flor de Cactus', the strumming of guitars and *charangos* and the hoarse, breathy sounds of the *zampoña*. The music and singing became higher and faster, and it connected with the fevered pictures in Agustín's head. He saw delicate patterns of intertwining circles and diamonds; he saw flowers in a field of long grass sliced by the wind.

One after another, the men came over to Agustín and Roy, shook their hands and said they were welcome. Tears welled up behind Agustín's eyes, his giddiness and joy were in danger of overtaking him. The music swirled and coiled up into the sky, drowning out the Mission's hymn.

The gathering moved into the yard, though Agustín was not sure whether it was the yard moving to them: he had the impression of being in a train waiting to leave the station, another train alongside, so that when the movement started he could not tell if his train or the other one had begun its journey. Roy was separated from him and Agustín led to a bench, where a young man laid a cool hand on his forehead, took his pulse, examined his tongue, and prised his eyelids open.

Agustín saw men holding hands to form a circle around the musicians; they began to dance, round and round, faster and faster as the tempo increased, until they became a blur and it hurt Agustín's eyes to watch, and he imagined himself going up, following the music up into the air.

A tall, thin man walked towards Agustín, silhouetted by the sun behind him.

'How is he?' the man asked.

'He'll live,' the man with the cool hands replied.

The new arrival squatted, dipping out of the sunlight. He was fair-skinned, green-eyed; the face smiling, generous.

'You lived,' Agustín said.

'As you did,' Gabriel replied.

NINE

S ince the day Rex had sacked him, pain had been building up behind Pascualito's eyes. Now it was alive. It was
crawling back into his head, burrowing into him with dull
malevolence. He had been thinking about the pain for some
time. It had to *be* something. The cause of this much pain
had to be discrete, an entity, wishing him harm. He decided
it was an insect. He had seen magazine pictures of insects
under the microscope. Close up, you could see they had
mandibles like serrated knife blades. The insect behind his
eyes was using these things to saw into him, and where it
went it left in its wake an acid slime. It was like fire in
Pascualito.

The bus hit a rib of tarmac and jolted a wave of nausea up
from Pascualito's stomach. He had to swallow hard to get it
back down; it left a taste of corruption in his throat.

The pain. The insect had bisected some sensitive membrane, had breached a perimeter into a yet more tender
place. Pascualito cringed. After a few moments, the pain
eased. He rubbed his temples and felt the veins tauten.

The bus pulled up at a set of traffic lights, and the
skyscrapers laid down a mantle of shade. He felt the tightness in his head ease a fraction. The bus started forward, at
great speed it seemed to Pascualito. The skyscrapers receded
with the velocity of traffic travelling in the opposite direction. Confused and alarmed, Pascualito turned to look at
them; they appeared to be falling out of the sky while he was
shooting upwards. The sun ambushed him and sliced into
his eyes. He fumbled for his Ray-Bans and pulled them on.

He noticed how slowly people were moving. From the

window he watched the people in the streets and saw them move as though under water; a woman raised her arm and pointed and another woman turned her face to follow the line – asking directions, Pascualito saw it at once; he was covering the same ground at the speed of light. Time had spread over these people and slowed them up. Pascualito was seeing things they could not see; he was understanding things they could not know.

Pascualito's eyes and brain were working fast. Normally, only the eyes work fast and they don't give the brain time to decode the messages. Pascualito was getting the message now, loud and clear.

Except for colours. Something was fucking up the colour messages. Pascualito tried to concentrate on colour. He had trouble getting language to co-operate. He could not put words to the colours he saw, except for red. There was a lot of red about: a woman's shopping bag; a man's shirt; a line of piping on a jacket worn by a girl across the aisle. Lots of red. There had to be a reason for it.

He remembered what he was doing on the bus, where he was going. *Wrong.* He was getting into the wrong thing. He was not ready for this. He wanted to get up and run to the front of the bus, tell the driver to turn back. He grabbed hold of the seat in front and made to stand up.

The woman in the seat beside him looked over, waiting. The thought crossed Pascualito's mind that she knew he was afraid. Her perception momentarily disconcerted him. He had to go through with this. He dropped back into his seat and tried to pull himself together. The insect was crawling further back into his head. The acid was oozing out and defying gravity: like rain on a windshield, it spread up into the roof of his brains. Pascualito glanced at the woman. She was no longer watching him. She stared ahead, purse clutched to her breast, elbows jammed into her sides, knees pressed together.

The colour messages were fucked up, but the smell messages were clear. There was something unpleasant beside him, the smell of slow decay, of prolonged and shameful illness endured in darkness, of furtive recuperation in closed rooms behind drawn curtains. Pascualito looked at the woman. She was old – fifty at least – but her mouth and jaw were firm, the nose fine and straight. She must have been good-looking as a girl. Pascualito moved his eyes down the length of her torso. Trim. What he could see of her legs seemed in good shape.

Something about the woman put Pascualito on alert. It took him a minute to put his finger on it. It was her clothes. She was dressed wrong. What she wore was not right for work, not for shopping, not for a party, not for travelling; an unsettling concoction of faded finery and gaudy cheapness. A scarlet silk scarf twisted around her neck. The shoes were cracked and dusty.

The red unsettled Pascualito, but the message from her strange clothes aroused his interest. There was some opportunity here.

He stared at her, deliberately. She would feel his stare and glance at him. Then he would go to work.

After five minutes, however, she had still not looked at him, and Pascualito changed tactics.

'Hi,' he said, grinning at her. Nothing.

Pascualito closed his eyes. He thought about the Angel Dust and Cross Tops, tequila and beer he and his girlfriend Sonia had been living on for the last few days since Rex had fired him. He did not know, could not imagine, how much money it had cost. It had been okay. Then it had stopped. He had borrowed, now he had to get some serious money. Either that or stop dead. He closed his eyes to go over his options.

'I have been to Tacoma.'

Pascualito opened his eyes. The sunlight, even through the Ray-Bans, distressed him.

'In the north.'

The woman was talking to him. Opportunity. What was she saying?

'Not like in Tennessee.' She spoke in heavily accented English. Pascualito had assumed she was white. It surprised him that she should turn out to be *latina.*

'Is that right?' he answered in Spanish.

'In Tennessee there is nothing.' She stuck with English.

'Yes?' Pascualito said in English. She did not look at him when she spoke, but continued staring ahead, her purse still clasped in both hands just below her chin. She looked like a little girl peeping from behind a protective shield: a child, except her face and eyes were old, and there were touches of grey in her hair.

'That's right,' she said.

'Is that where you're from?'

'Yes.'

'Tennessee?'

'I travel.'

'You travel a lot?'

'On buses.' The woman nodded seriously.

'Why? Is it your work?'

'All over. Florida, Mississippi, Alabama, Texas. Nothing in Tennessee.'

'You've been travelling around on buses?'

'Yes.'

'What do you do in LA?' Pascualito needed specific information.

'I ride on the buses.'

'No. I mean apart from the buses. You work, you got a job?'

'I ride the buses.'

'What?' Pascualito suspected she was making fun of him and straightened in his seat. He turned his face full on her to let the sunglasses do the work of unsettling her into sense.

She scarcely seemed aware of the Ray-Bans, or him.

Pascualito tried again. 'You must have a job – you got a job, you know, for money?' Nothing. Pascualito's suspicion that she was mocking him grew. In an edgy tone he asked, 'Where do you live?'

'Miami.'

She *was* doing it to him. Pascualito thought about hitting

her. But that would be the end of the opportunity. He had to be cunning, and patient.

He tried again. 'In LA, here, where do you live? You got some place – a room, an apartment?'

She did not answer. Suspicious bitch. She did not trust him. The insect was still cutting, still trailing its acid mucus. He waited for her answer and forced a grin.

'Where do you live?'

'Miami.'

'No. In LA. You must have some place to stay.'

The woman's face was blank. She seemed to understand something more was required of her. She said, 'I just came because they told me.'

'To LA?'

'To Miami.'

'Where from?'

'Cuba. They said everyone had to escape.'

'Well,' Pascualito said, 'that's good advice.'

'Yes?'

'Sure.'

'I ride the buses now,' the woman said, nodding gravely as at a profound truth.

Pascualito saw the opportunity diminish, fall away from him down a dark, bottomless hole. No point in following. He shut his eyes. After a few moments he heard the woman say, 'Do you think I did right to come to the United States?'

'How the fuck do I know?' he muttered. He slid down in his seat.

'Because my brother came too, and he got killed. At Tacoma, in the north.'

Pascualito was almost asleep.

'I haven't seen my sister for twenty-three years. She lives in New York.'

Pascualito did not hear.

The driver was shaking Pascualito's shoulder, it was causing his head intense pain.

Pascualito said, 'What?'

'This is the end of the road.'

Pascualito thought the man was threatening him and he jerked up, then grasped the driver's meaning. The driver was watching him in a funny way, as at an unpredictable dog. The woman had gone.

'Yeah,' Pascualito said, 'I know that.'

He got off the bus. The sun was high and strong, there were no colours here, not even reds. The glare seared his eyes. Pascualito touched the top of his head for the sunglasses. They were not there. He patted his shirt pocket, the front and back pockets of his jeans. He looked back at the bus. The driver had popped the doors and was strolling over to the cheap cafeteria across the road, where the other drivers were drinking coffee and eating doughnuts. The *cubana*. The bitch had robbed him. Seventy dollars' worth of sunglasses.

Pascualito remembered his money. Forgetting the pain, he quickly knelt down and pulled the side of his boot away from the ankle. The money at least was safe; but the Ray-Bans, the thought of their loss made him feel sick.

Yesterday it had seemed simple. In bed with Sonia, the bed damp from sweat and seepages and spilled drink, the sheets in stubborn tangles, Sonia trying to sort them out, Pascualito had taken the last two Cross Tops and emptied the tequila. Sonia had complained and said he was greedy. She wanted some. He looked at her sitting naked there, sweat beads round her throat and under her breasts, her hair tangled like the sheets. The fucking thing was, he explained to her as patiently as he could, that he didn't have any more money. The night Rex had fired him, he had borrowed money from Sabino and stolen thirty dollars from his aunt. Then he went to Dulio and borrowed money from him. Even Dulio, who loathed him but who had to practise what he preached, had given him money. Pascualito had professed himself grateful and said he would pay Dulio back. He would pay Dulio back all right. He would see to it that Dulio got what he deserved.

And now they had nothing left. Sonia was getting hysterical and he slapped her. She tore at him and caught him with a long nail under the eye, a crescent tear that had turned yellow and brown. When he had her under control, on her back, him on top, his knees on her skinny upper arms, he said, 'You're so fucking smart, where'd you get the fucking money?'

And she had said, 'From the fucking factory. What do you suppose they keep in the safe you told me about? Furniture?'

Pascualito's mind had raced ahead and bumped into Rex, and stopped.

Sonia said her brother Michael in Santa Ana could get him a gun, for money.

Pascualito had called Michael. Sonia went out and came back three hours later with forty dollars, a bottle of rum and some Crystal Meth. She acted as if she were far away from him. Later, she said, 'Just don't think I'm going to do *that* every time you fuck up.'

The stucco of Michael's house had once been painted pink. The front lawn held the imprint of one car – the patch was so distinct it was like where a picture had been removed from a wall – and the rotting remains of a second, a rusty white Oldsmobile with no wheels. There was a chain-link compound to the side of the front yard. Pascualito paid it no mind as he made his way up the steps to the front door. From the back of this cage a dog sprang up and launched itself forward, its claws scraping on the concrete floor. It hurled itself against the wire, rattling the fence.

Michael was at the open door. He was short, solid, more Indian-looking than his sister. Michael and Sonia probably had different fathers. Michael had a moustache of long, silky black hairs, and a few hairs sprouted from his chin. He was in *cholo* garb and wore a hair net.

'Yeah?' Michael said.

'I am Pascual Hernández.'

'So?'

'I spoke with you yesterday, on the phone.'

Michael said nothing.

'Right,' Pascualito muttered. There was a silence.

Michael said at last, 'Say what it is that you want.'

Pascualito had already told him. This was the annoying thing, but he had no choice. He said, 'What I want, man, what I want is a rod.'

'Is that right?' Michael said with amusement. 'What for?'

The question was humiliating, Pascualito was being put down. 'For some work I have in mind,' he said, just keeping his temper.

Michael took time to consider, a look of amused contempt on his face.

Pascualito's anger was rising. He said, 'Man, do you have it, or do you not have it?'

'Yeah,' Michael said slowly. 'I have it. This piece of work, when is it happening?'

Pascualito said, 'Saturday's tomorrow, right? Tomorrow night.'

'Tomorrow?' Michael was calculating. After a few moments, he asked, 'What exactly do you want?'

'Pistol – revolver, automatic, don't matter, long as it's big.'

'It's yours,' Michael said easily.

'Right.'

'Hundred and fifty. It's worth two hundred, but what the fuck are friends for.'

'That's too much.'

'That's cheap.'

Pascualito turned to watch the street and give himself time to think. He rubbed his temples. The veins were standing out, they felt like wire cables.

Michael said, 'How much you got?'

'Forty.'

Michael snorted. 'That gets you nothing.'

'I can get another forty.'

'How much this work going to make you?'

Pascualito had thought about this. There had to be at least a couple of thousand dollars in the office.

'Three thousand, maybe five.'

Michael nodded seriously. 'Okay. I tell you what. For a hundred, you get the piece. Then, when it's over, you come to me with fifty per cent of what you get. Right?'

The dog launched itself at the wire fence and, for the first time, barked.

Michael stared at Pascualito, contempt growing in his eyes. Pascualito tried to conduct his thoughts, get them working along the lines he needed. Instead, he found himself thinking of the *cubana*, riding around, not knowing why she was there, not knowing what she was doing, a crow, stealing shiny things like a crow that wouldn't know the value of what it was taking. He could end up like that, they all could.

Michael was saying, 'Fifty per cent seem like a lot to you? Figure it out. I don't know you. We never done business before. You want to give me eighty for something worth twice that, which I can't do for you. What I can do is help you, if you help me. I'm taking a chance. I'm taking a risk, if you get caught I don't get the rest of my money, and maybe you give my name to the cops.'

'Never.'

Michael shrugged. 'These things happen. These are the risks. You say there is three thousand, maybe five. Okay, I'm not greedy. There's three thousand, you bring me fifteen hundred the same day it's done. If there's more, if there's five, I still only want fifteen. That's the best I can do.'

Michael was looking at him. 'I do hope you're not wasting my time, man.'

Pascualito said, mustering his nerve, 'I didn't come here to waste time. Fifteen hundred is too much. I'll do it for three-fifty. Eight for the rod, the rest after the work is done.'

Michael said, 'Sounds good. Give me what you got.'

'You have the piece here?'

'What are you, crazy? I wouldn't stay in business long if I did that.'

Pascualito did not like it, but he handed over the money.

'Now what you want?' Michael said.

'What you got?'

Michael snorted and put a crooked smile on his face, like the manager of a supermarket asked if he stocks milk. 'A nice 9mm Ruger, or I can get you a Jericho.'

'What's that?'

'A Jewish automatic. Israeli army uses it. With .44 magnum ammunition, too.'

'That's the one.'

'The Jericho? Come back tomorrow with the other forty and it's yours. But don't forget what you owe, that's two-seventy right after the deed is done.'

'Right. What time tomorrow?'

'Noon.'

Pascualito was thinking about the *cubana*. She had stolen his sunglasses, but she was going nowhere. She was riding around on buses going nowhere. He was going to get a Jericho with .44 magnum rounds and five thousand dollars.

From the bed, Quinn looked around the small room as the light faded. He saw a cracked sink on the opposite wall, beside it a kettle on a makeshift shelf. There was an easy chair next to the window and a cheap box with two drawers. He saw a few books on the floor, most of them with titles in Spanish, and a religious magazine, *Simple Truth*. The floor was covered with broken lino, in places worn through in a way that reminded Quinn of the sole of an old shoe. The minutes passed and night entered the room, and, apart from the flickering on the wall from the red neon outside, Quinn was alone.

Quinn was from a place where there was no such thing as not knowing anyone, and loneliness was to him as mysterious as it was shameful.

After the shooting, after the seventeen weeks in hospital that followed, Quinn had passed days in Dublin, always meaning to do something and doing nothing, talking to no one. He ignored both clock and calendar, so that the seams separating the days came apart, and time stretched out around him flat and featureless. He flew from Shannon to New York on an Irish passport with a visitor's visa marked 'multiple entry' and 'indefinite stay'. The photograph was his own, the name was not.

It was only when he got to New York, the streets black with freezing rain, that he realized what it meant to know no one. He found a hotel, paid ninety-five dollars for a room, and moved the next day to a building which had drunks sleeping in the doorway. He spent a week looking for Jim Kerr, whom he knew from prison and remembered was living in New

York after jumping bail on a murder charge. He had no address for Jim, but someone at home had mentioned Jim favoured a bar call Cajun, which he found on Eighth Avenue and West 16th. No one he asked knew Jim, and the men were unfriendly. Someone suggested he try another bar, where someone else suggested another. Quinn spent the day getting drunker, colder. On the way back to his hotel room he thought he saw Jim on the subway, at the far end of the carriage, and he started to struggle through the passengers. People complained and one big man stood in his way to make the point that Quinn should be more polite. Quinn tried to push past, but the man held him with a grip of great force. Quinn could not move. The train pulled into a station and out again. By the time the big man had finished making his point, Jim Kerr, if it had been Jim Kerr, had gone. Humiliated, Quinn got off the train at the next station. He punched the wall until his fists bled.

He got a job washing dishes in a bar and restaurant in Greenwich Village. His first night on the job was the anniversary of the night of the shooting, the night Denis and he had got drunk. The doctors had told him that the chest wound had been the greater threat to his life. But, they went on, the chest wound was the easier to mend; the bullet he took in the head had caused serious damage to the bone structure, and would require further surgery, perhaps a dozen operations over the next two years. Still, he had been lucky to survive at all. The bullet had hit his right cheekbone, but, instead of going through to his brain, travelled in a semi-circle between the scalp and the skull, scoring the bone, before exiting an inch behind his left ear. The doctors did a good job patching up his broken face, and the painkillers got him through the headaches.

During that time Quinn refused all visits, except one from Seamus, whom he persuaded to do nothing. 'I'll deal with it,' Quinn had said. It was three weeks after Seamus's visit before he felt well enough to get out of bed by himself. The next day he discharged himself. Before they would let him go he had to sign a form stating his reason for leaving. He wrote, 'I feel well.'

In Greenwich Village, a year on, he asked himself why he had left home to come to this grim place, and answered himself, *To keep hold of Monica*, that only by putting distance between them could he hang on to her. It was hard to say why he should want to do that: there had been times when his anger at her had been so intense he had conducted fantasies of revenge through compartments in his mind, each yielding to a darker, more violent place; bitter words of reproach, shouting, a slap of the face, throwing her on the floor, a punch, a kick; rape, even rape, worse than murder. He still wanted to hold on.

In Greenwich Village, the cook, the waitresses and the barmen were all younger than Quinn and were part-timing at the bar to earn money to do other things. They talked among themselves about what they planned to do with their lives. No one asked Quinn what he was planning: they could sense the way his life was, and were edgy with him. After a couple of weeks, the manager got the same sense and Quinn lost his job.

It was cold in New York, and wet, and what he remembered of that time, whenever he thought of it, was not the people but small things, like the condensation on the windows of cheap cafés, the smell of damp in his room, the heavy coats of passengers on the subway trains, the rings of spilt beer on bars. He owed nine days' rent and the manager had his passport. He took a bus to Miami.

Miami was warmer, but no friendlier. In the spring Quinn moved back to New York, then on to Boston. He went to Chicago before deciding to go to the South. He spent time in Jackson. But still he could not find his way in to people and he came to feel that he was prowling the edges of people's lives, homes, happiness. And he came to believe that they could see this, that his eyes and demeanour proclaimed it, and this shamed him all the more. He, who had been brought up among brothers, sisters, cousins, aunts and uncles, who had lived with a wife, was alone. Alone, he was frightened, for the future and for himself.

He moved on. In Montana, near Glasgow, within sight of the lake, he worked in the frozen snow. Stoop labour, the men called it. No Americans, except the foreman, would work for hours bent in the snow. He shared a room with a man named Brian, who was from Montserrat and had until recently been living in Baton Rouge. Brian did not talk much. He drank whisky, though rum was his preferred drink; the quality of the rum in these parts, he would say, was *insufficient*.

Quinn and Brian spent two months together. It was the longest Quinn had spent in one place since leaving home. Brian was not aware of it, but Quinn was depending on him, drawing from him. One Friday night, Brian suggested to Quinn they go for a drink, and they found two women who were with two men, in a casual way, it seemed. The women ditched the men and went back to the room, where they drank whisky. Brian took his woman to bed and the other woman looked at Quinn. By then it had been nearly two years since he had seen Monica. He had not been with another woman, for he always had it in his mind that when he got back to Monica he could tell her that he had not been with anyone else. That would be an important part of the reconciliation, for, he knew, it would touch Monica, who understood the true value of gestures.

Brian was expert at what he was doing and mixed his pleasure noises with murmurs and encouragements, to which the woman responded. Her legs twitched. Quinn's woman looked at her friend, then at Quinn. Quinn knew she was thinking she had ended up with the disaster. She said, 'Well?'

Quinn said, 'Look . . .'

'Yeah?'

Quinn said nothing.

'What?' There was anger in her voice. 'You brought me back here. What is it, the whisky?'

'I suppose so.'

'What?' the woman repeated in a challenge. 'What are you? Some kind of fruit?'

He took her to his bed, not because of the gibe, but because the idiocy of his dream of Monica was screaming out to all around and he did not want this hard woman to hear. It was still a form of cowardice, of course; he knew that: he had been challenged and had surrendered. He fucked the woman – now, in Agustín's room, he could remember nothing about her, not her name nor the colour of her hair and eyes – and after it was over he never let himself think about what had happened; for it had happened, and there was no point in attaching words to it. They said nothing to each other during the act, and Quinn knew she was glad when it was over. She got dressed, lit a cigarette and told her friend to hurry up. 'There isn't even a phone,' she said to her friend, who could hardly be seen under Brian, a big man, 'to call a cab. You believe it?' She let out a jet of smoke and picked a flake of paint from one of her nails.

There was ice on the windows. As Brian slept, Quinn tried to wash himself clean. The cold water trickled in the sink. Brian woke up, looked at Quinn and said, 'Jesus Christ,' and went back to sleep.

Some days later, as they were about to leave for work, two men arrived at the room. Quinn was at the sink and did not hear them come in. He had shaved his cheeks and had lifted his chin to get at the hairs on his throat when he heard a calm voice say, 'Kindly don't move.' At the other end of the voice was a gun, which was pointed at Quinn's temple. 'Would you be so good as to get dressed?' another voice said. When Quinn reached for his shirt, the voice behind him said, 'Not you, sir. You just stay as you are, though you might consider putting down that there razor.' The men with the guns said they were police and had an extradition warrant to Louisiana, where Brian was wanted on charges of manslaughter and interstate flight.

The officers asked Quinn who he was and Quinn gave them a false name. They asked a few questions about what he was doing and where he had been. Quinn got the impression that they did not believe his answers but were not interested enough to do anything about it.

'You see what happens?' Brian said to Quinn when the policemen were handcuffing him. Brian's eyes were popping and Quinn could see he was frightened. 'Nothing's worth shit in this life.'

As the detectives pushed him through the door, Brian turned to Quinn and said, 'Be prepared to pay all the same.'

Brian was gone and Quinn looked around the room they had shared. He had been in someone's life, someone's story. Then Brian disappeared. The next day, Quinn bought the newspapers to look for news of him, but there was nothing. Someone's life just went away from him, instantly it had gone.

He left Montana on a Friday night after he had collected his pay. He did not go back to the room to pick up his clothes. He and Brian owed two weeks' rent and the manager had his watch.

For Quinn it was back to prowling the edges. A bus took him through mountainous country to the south and he came to spend time in Flagstaff. He worked washing dishes, drank when he had money, then became sick and stopped drinking. He got a little better, got worse and left town to see if it had something to do with where he was living. As the bus pulled into Los Angeles, he told himself he had improved, that he would start to sort things out. He began by ordering a greasy breakfast, which made him sick. He found a room for eighteen dollars a night, was told to pay one night in advance and went to a bar. Loneliness squeezed him. As he got drunker, he looked resentfully at those in company. He tried to talk to the barman, who only grunted. He spent the rest of his money on drink, found a phone and placed a reverse-charge call to Monica Quinn. The ringing tone, ringing, ringing. There were electronic bleeps and blimps of the connection being made, and a man's voice. The operator spoke. Quinn pulled the receiver away from his ear. The voice at the other end belonged to Denis. He hung up.

He could not remember where the hotel was and stopped a man on the street. 'Which way to the centre?' Quinn asked, thinking he could work out his way from there. The man pushed past him without replying, and Quinn spent his first night on the street. Ten days later Agustín found him.

In Agustín's room, with the red neon for company, Quinn waited to be let into another life.

It was Saturday and already past midday, and Pascualito had a lot to do. Things were behind. Sonia had started complaining at a bad time, so he hit her, hard, several times. By the time he had finished with her, it was almost one, and he still had to get to Santa Ana to pick up the Jericho. He didn't like all the hurry, but at least Sonia had got him sixty dollars, and some more Crystal Meth. He caught the bus to 18th Street to start looking for Wilson, a fifteen-year-old *chicano* he knew drove a car.

It was two-thirty by the time Pascualito found Wilson, in MacArthur Park. Wilson was selling a dimer to two white college boys. They hurried off once they had the bag, and Pascualito watched them resentfully as they pulled away in a waxed-up black Toyota truck.

'Hey, Wilson. What do you say?'

'Don Pascual, *qué tal?*'

'Yeah, great,' Pascualito said. 'Hey. Can you get me a car for tonight?'

Pascualito thought Wilson was looking at him in a strange way, but Wilson smiled and said, 'Man, this is the can-do society. Everything *can* be done.'

In spite of Wilson's smile, there was a definite glint of suspicion in his eye. Pascualito decided that once this was over, he was going to settle things with a few people. If Wilson didn't stop acting funny soon, he was going to be top of the list. Dulio would be next, then Rex, then Michael.

'I have to pick something up in Santa Ana, right now, in fact. Then, tonight, I want a lift to somewhere.'

'Where?'

'Near here. I'll give you thirty dollars.'

'How long's it all going to take?'

'What's it?' Pascualito checked the time. 'Four, five hours. Nothing to it.'

'I'll do it for fifty. I got a meet with some business associates in Pasadena at ten.'

'You got a car now?'

'This is the mobile society. Can't be mobile without wheels. Got the fifty?'

'Here's ten. I'll give you the rest tonight.'

Pascualito thought for a moment Wilson might not accept it, but he did.

They had to go back to 18th Street, where Wilson talked to his cousins Paco and José and got the keys to a 1974 maroon Pinto. Wilson told Pascualito he would have to give José twenty for the car. Pascualito cursed at Wilson. 'Here's a ten. He can have another ten when it's over.'

In the car Wilson was jabbering about the opportunity society. Pascualito told him to shut up and let him concentrate. He caught Wilson looking strangely at him again, like he was weighing things up. Another tricky one, like Sonia. Pascualito would outsmart him, too. Then he wondered what Michael would do if he found out what he had done to Sonia. Would she have called Michael? He hadn't thought of that. Still, when he left, Sonia was in no state to talk to anyone.

'So what's the big deal tonight?' Wilson asked innocently. The lights were red.

Pascualito started to tell him without being sure why.

'Why they keep that much in the safe?'

'What?'

'Ten thousand. That's a lot to keep laying around.'

'What are you saying?' Pascualito asked suspiciously.

'Nothing.'

'Then don't.'

'Jesus.'

'Hey, I come to you. I give this to you, an opportunity – all your bullshit about the opportunity society – and now what are you saying?'

'Nothing. I'm not saying anything.'

'Saying, questioning what I said to you? Is that what you're saying?'

'No.'

'There's ten grand, right?'

'Right,' Wilson said. 'I assume you got a gun. This is a violent society.'

'The best. A Jericho. You ever seen one before?'

'No.'

'Okay. The lights are green.'

The dog sprang at the fence as the car slowed in front of Michael's house. Pascualito made his way up the steps to the door, passing the white Olds wreck on the lawn; someone was sleeping in it, stretched out across the back seat.

Pascualito rang the bell and went down to rattle the dog. The dog leapt at him and he laughed and shook the fence.

Michael, who was smiling, appeared at the door. 'You like dogs?' he said.

'Love them,' Pascualito said, growling at the dog and starting nonchalantly for the steps. He wasn't afraid of Michael any more.

'Good,' Michael said. 'People that like dogs are good people.'

'Love them. I love dogs.'

'Come in. I got something to show you. Who's that?' He pointed to Wilson.

'That is my driver, works for me.'

'Got a business going already. That's good. Come in. You need a dog for your business, a guard dog, something like that, let me know. I can get you one cheap.'

They passed into the house.

'Turn the sound down, Rich,' Michael instructed a man watching the television. To Pascualito he said, 'Take a seat. You're a little late, by the way.'

Pascualito sat. he said, 'Yeah, it's my driver. Like he's down there in MacArthur Park, you know, forgets what time I told him to come for me.'

'No problem,' Michael said generously. 'Have a beer.' Pascualito popped the ring and put a third of the can inside him. Michael said, 'Show him what we got, Rich.'

Rich was slow shifting his gaze from the television to Pascualito. He smiled. Pascualito did not like it.

'Go ahead, Rich. Show the man.'

Slowly, Rich got to his feet. He went behind where Pascualito was sitting. Pascualito took a swig from the can.

Then, suddenly, Rich grabbed a fistful of Pascualito's hair, pulled his face back, and stuck the gun into his temple. Pascualito spluttered and the can fell on his lap and spilt over his jeans.

'The fuck!' Pascualito shouted in alarm.

Michael was standing in front of him, smiling, supporting one elbow in the palm of his hand and stroking the thin hairs around the corners of his mouth with his right. Maybe Sonia had got to a phone after all.

'Hey,' Pascualito said, gulping, 'what's this?'

'It's a gun and it's going to go off in your head, is what it is,' Michael said. 'Unless you got the rest of the money.'

'I got it.' Pascualito put a hand on his pocket. Rich brushed it away and checked himself. He removed four tens.

'You would kill me for forty bucks?'

Michael said, 'Who's talking about forty? Where's the rest?'

'What rest?'

'I don't like that you've forgotten already. Makes me suspicious to trust you.'

Pascualito realized what he was talking about. 'The two-seventy. I haven't forgotten.'

'When am I going to see it?'

'Right after it.'

'When's that?'

'Tonight.'

Michael stayed silent for long seconds. He nodded to Rich, who withdrew the gun from Pascualito's head.

'Have another beer,' Michael said, lifting the spilt can from Pascualito's lap. When Pascualito had opened the second can, Michael said, 'Now look what I got you.' He snapped his fingers. 'Rich.'

Rich handed Pascualito the gun he had been holding to his head.

The gun was a monstrosity. It had a barrel eight inches long and the grip was walnut with deep finger grooves. The thing must weigh ten pounds, Pascualito thought.

'Is this a Jericho?' Pascualito asked.

'Better.'

'What?'

'Way better. What you got here is a .22 target pistol, which all the pros use. Even if you never held a gun in your life before, Pascual . . .' – Michael paused to let him know that he knew Pascualito never had – 'you can hit a man at a hundred yards. Believe it. Jericho just makes a lot of noise.'

'It's not the same when you need it to frighten somebody.' Pascualito said petulantly, peering at the gun from different angles.

Michael smiled indulgently. 'Rich did not seem to have a problem with you.'

Rich snorted.

'Where's the magazine go?'

'Rich, get him the other rounds.' Rich moved to the settee. 'No extra charge. Spare rounds. I'll give you fifty, case you want to start your own war.'

'Where's the mag go?'

Rich was standing above him, holding out a plastic bag with the bullets. Michael came over and put an arm across his shoulder. Pascualito was on his feet, examining the base of the grip, looking for the magazine housing.

'*Hasta muy pronto entonces,*' Michael said, steering him to the door.

'Tonight, yeah.'

It was only as he was about to get in the car that Pascualito began to feel he had been tricked.

'Put that fucking thing away,' Wilson said as Pascualito settled in the passenger seat. Michael's dog was barking, paws up against the fence. 'That the Jericho?' Wilson asked, glancing at the gun.

'Can't find the magazine.' Pascualito said.

'That ain't got no magazine, it's single shot.' Wilson put the car in gear and pulled away.

'Mother.' Pascualito found the breech and pulled it back.

'You put the bullet in there,' Wilson said.

Pascualito fumbled a round in and pushed the mechanism home. He balanced the gun in his hand. The dog's barking continued in his head.

'Turn round. I forgot something,' he said. When Wilson sighed, Pascualito said, with more force, 'Do it, man. Don't make me angry.'

They drew up outside Michael's house. 'Whoa, whoa,' Pascualito said. He rolled the window all the way down, took aim and fired. The dog reacted as if it had been kicked, and it turned in circles, yelping. Then its back went and it had to drag itself by the front legs. The yelping diminished into whimpering. Pascualito ejected the spent cartridge and inserted another round. Wilson was jabbering again. Pascualito told him to shut up. He took aim at the white Olds and fired. He caught sight of Michael and Rich crouching at the window; they looked scared. Pascualito was laughing when he said, 'Okay. Let's go.'

They took the Five north. Wilson was still muttering complaints as they passed through Anaheim and into Buena Park.

'Hey,' Pascualito said. 'I told you, didn't I, to shut up.'

Wilson kept quiet. They were in Bell Gardens before he spoke again. 'Listen, man, I gotta see someone before tonight. Take me maybe an hour. It's a business meet I can't miss. What I'll do, I'll drop you and pick you up later. Just say where and when.'

'No, there won't be time.' Pascualito's eyes were taking everything in; his brain was rushing ahead: he saw through Wilson.

'I'm assuming this is night work you're thinking about?' Wilson said. 'There's time, man. I'll pick you up at, say, eight?'

Pascualito could see the suspicion in Wilson's eyes clearly now. Wilson was smiling very hard but was really sick. The shooting had done Pascualito a lot of good; he had got a rush from that better than the Crystal Meth.

'Tell you what,' Pascualito said, 'pull over here.'

'What?'

'Do it.' He pointed the gun into Wilson's face and Wilson did what he was told.

'Get out,' Pascualito said.

Wilson said, 'Man, will you at least leave the car back with José? You'll see him on 18th Street. Either him or Paco.'

'Sure.'

As he pulled away, Pascualito was suddenly disturbed by the *cubana*, who, without warning, intruded into his thoughts. The crazy Ray-Bans thief. Her face was before him, weirdly smiling. Something about her had unsettled him from the moment he first noticed her: the confection of peculiarities, each contradicting the other – a face that was old but unlined, eyes that were young but malicious, clothes that were not right for where she was. Pascualito shivered. He blocked out the *cubana*'s face and drove on; but the memory of the woman, her life reduced to bus rides without destinations, stayed with him.

He found he was instinctively heading back to the hotel and Sonia, which, when he realized what he was doing, he decided was a bad idea: he would only have to apologize to her and do things to please her. But he did need somewhere to go. He needed somewhere to stay for a couple of hours, until the time was right.

Then he thought of Sabino.

Fred Feddersen told Andrew about his glory days in Korea, where he had served with Andrew's uncle Victor. Andrew listened appreciatively, making a good play at looking like he was being let into some secrets of history that this old man, whom muscular dystrophy had bound to a wheelchair five years ago, had in his store.

'Victor was the youngest of the gang we all hung around

in. I don't mean a gang like the kind of ruffians you see on the streets these days. I mean a gang of *men*,' Feddersen said.

Andrew nodded.

'Victor was younger than the rest of us by more than ten years.' Feddersen paused. 'I knew your husband in Korea, too, Mrs Dorfmann.' Feddersen's tone had altered only slightly with the mention of Martin, but enough to let Mrs Dorfmann know that Feddersen held her husband in much less esteem than Victor Jank. Mrs Dorfmann smiled politely. She loathed Feddersen.

'Even back then,' he continued, 'it was evident to me that Victor Jank would be a highly important personage one day.'

'You aren't without your own reputation, Mr Feddersen,' Andrew said.

Feddersen appreciated the compliment and chuckled. 'Oh, I made money. But any fool can do that.'

He glanced at Mrs Dorfmann to let her know this was intended as a gibe at her and Martin. She looked out the window and saw a Mexican gardener at work on the hedges, another Mexican was polishing the Mercedes on the gravel drive. There was a boat on a trailer in the second garage. By Feddersen's standards, she and her husband had not made money. Feddersen's maid poured some more coffee. She smiled at Mrs Dorfmann as she did so. One of us, the maid was thinking. Mrs Dorfmann gave her a frosty glare to correct the impression, then examined her own forearm. It was very white. She smiled to herself.

Andrew brought Feddersen up to date with the Mission's work abroad, starting in the Philippines, where Andrew had been just before Christmas.

'You get all over, don't you, Andrew?' Fred had said.

'I guess I do at that.'

'All that running around, though, must tire you out?'

'No, sir. To be frank, I enjoy it. I guess I'm kind of a born troubleshooter. I go see how the missionaries in the field are coping. Then I come back and make my reports, so that the Board know where's best to target resources.'

'Where were you before the Philippines?' Feddersen

asked. Feddersen had made his money selling packing crates to US companies with operations in Latin America. His company also supplied Dorfmann Furnishings.

'Chile.'

'It's a shame what's happening down there, after the sacrifices.'

The maid interrupted. She spoke English with an accent so strong that Feddersen failed to understand what she had said. He addressed her impatiently, 'Tell it to the señora,' indicating Mrs Dorfmann with a patrician wave of the hand, 'she understands Spanish.'

Mrs Dorfmann was furious, her lips quivered. She barely heard the maid's words and was only able to contain her anger by remembering Andrew was present; she did not want to do anything that might spoil her plans. She translated, 'The girl says Saturday is her night off and that if you don't need anything else, she'll be going.'

'She's new,' Feddersen said. 'Only had her a week. Last one walked out without a word the minute she got her first pay.'

Andrew nodded sympathetically. The girl looked anxious. Feddersen said, 'Is there anything else you'd like, Andrew? Mrs Dorfmann?' They shook their heads. 'Have another coffee.' He addressed the girl. 'Bring some fresh coffee and make up some more sandwiches.'

The girl left, glancing anxiously at her watch.

Feddersen said, looking after the girl, 'Nineteen years old and two kids. Unmarried of course.'

'That's always the way with those people,' Mrs Dorfmann said.

There was a long pause before Feddersen said, with a glance at Andrew and a chill in his voice, 'Quite so.'

Andrew broke the silence which followed by leading Feddersen back to Korea, and Mrs Dorfmann drifted into her own thoughts. Things had changed in the last few days, since the prayer meeting in the mission hall. There was a tension between her and Andrew now, unspoken; and, of course, both pretended nothing had happened. Several times during the meeting, she had caught Andrew snatching glances at her. And then, when it was all over and she and Martin were leaving, she twisted her ankle and Andrew had to help her to the car. He had put a hand around her waist and just as Maritza got into the car she turned into him. He took his hand away as though it had been burned, which alarmed Mrs Dorfmann, for everything else had gone so well. But then Andrew had said through the car window, as she was pulling away, 'Don't forget Saturday afternoon. Fred Feddersen. Can you pick me up?'

The message had been sent, and he had received it.

As she drove Martin home after the meeting, she told herself Andrew was inexperienced in these things, easily frightened. That accounted for his reaction as he had helped her into the car. She would have to be careful.

Martin, her husband of twenty years, snored in bed. She looked at the boils on his red neck and turned over and thought about Andrew, needing her, wounded, being comforted by her, her having to remove his clothes, stopping, breathlessly, just before it was too late.

Now, with Feddersen rambling on, she knew that the time had come. She had in mind her fantasy of looking after Andrew. That would be enough for her. Would it be enough for him? The thought that he might want more crossed her mind for the first time. She liked the idea. Her first husband had been a womanizing bastard, but at least he had wanted her. In her head, she listened to Martin's snores.

Feddersen was telling Andrew about the nightmares of trading with Latin American companies, and Andrew was making more sympathetic and subservient noises. Mrs Dorfmann excused herself and went to the bathroom on the first floor. The sun was setting and it was very beautiful.

She inspected herself in the mirror and was pleasantly surprised. She was whiter than usual, but since it was better to be safe than sorry, she made her face up with her favourite paste. When she had finished, she sucked in her belly and leaned into the mirror. She was wearing an orange-coloured open-necked blouse that, from certain angles, allowed glimpses of her cleavage. She sprayed her mouth with a freshener and ran her grey tongue across her teeth.

In the car Andrew talked excitedly, animated as much by Feddersen's compliments as by the cheque. He moved around in the seat like a child, twisting this way and that. 'You're going to outdo your uncle, I would say, and believe me, I know talent when I see it' had been Feddersen's parting words, while the maid, in a sullen silence, helped Mrs Dorfmann on with her coat. 'You're a young man with a future. Come and see me again soon.' Andrew glowed. Andrew's pleasure reached over to her. As she drove back along the Pacific Coast Highway, she stared at the gathering dark. In the car? Should she turn off the highway?

Mrs Dorfmann could not concentrate on the driving. She was going at thirty miles an hour, partly to give herself time to think, and drivers glared at her as they passed.

She said, 'You know when Mr Feddersen was talking about all the time you spend travelling for the Mission?'

'Uh-huh?'

'With all the travelling and field work you do, I suppose it must be difficult to think about settling down with a wife.'

'I haven't thought much about it, Maritza.'

Her name. She turned to give him a direct smile, which he received.

'I suppose,' he continued, 'I just haven't met the right girl yet.'

The cliché encouraged her. She said, 'You must have met a lot of nice young girls who would just love to marry you.'

'Oh, none that I've met so far,' he said modestly.

She gave him a coquettish smile. 'You could have your pick.'

He answered in a serious tone. 'There's something about modern girls,' he began. She was all ears.

'Yes?' she prompted when he seemed to have lost his way.

'It's real hard to put your finger right on it. When it comes down to it . . .' He ran out of words.

'I know,' Mrs Dorfmann said. He twisted in his seat,

agitated. She put her hand on his knee and patted him. 'Yes, yes,' she said consolingly.

Andrew looked at her hand, then into her face. She smiled, turned back to the road and moved her hand up his thigh, gently patting him. She could hear her own breathing, and his. She felt him shift slightly in the seat, bringing his crotch a fraction further down. She gave his thigh a gentle squeeze and withdrew her hand. He caught his breath.

She said, 'I have to pick up something from the factory. Do you mind?'

TWELVE

On Saturdays the Chi-Chi Club did not start to fill until after ten, and when, at a little after six, Agustín and Quinn walked in, they were the only customers. The walls and doors were painted matt black and the ceiling was low. The air already smelt of cigarettes, beer and sweat. Behind the horseshoe bar two waitresses perched on high stools. Quinn went to a table in a dim alcove while Agustín ordered.

Quinn had on clothes Agustín had given him: a worn blue shirt, a battered brown suede jacket and a pair of work jeans. The jeans were wider in the waist than he had waist for, and longer in the leg. The shirt sleeves came down to his fingertips.

'You sure you feel okay?' Agustín asked as he came up with the beers. 'We didn't walk too much?'

'No. I'm okay.'

Agustín scrutinized the man. He would have looked pathetic sitting there in the over-sized clothes were it not for the eyes. Agustín had noticed how they flicked as they moved from person to person, thing to thing; they were light blue and quite large, but not innocent: they were alert, in spite of the tiredness in them, almost to the point of being distrustful. Still, there *was* an air of innocence about him: the baggy clothes, perhaps, or the fair hair recently washed and brushed, the freshly shaven chin. He looked better than he did when Agustín had found him in the alley, but not by much. There was no guessing his age, a badly worn twenty-five, a wiry forty, anywhere in between. His face was very pale. As Quinn sipped his beer, Agustín looked at the livid scars and stretched skin around the crushed bone in his cheek. His hands were long and fine, the fingers delicate.

'How do you like LA?' Agustín asked.

Quinn drank before answering. 'I don't know,' he said. 'I think it's missing something.'

'What?'

Quinn paused to think, 'There's no centre of things. Anywhere I arrive I always want to know where the centre is' – he sipped his drink and shrugged – 'so I can find my way.'

Quinn looked over to the waitresses. One of them was very pretty. She had dark brown hair, straight and thick, and it was held up in a bun with what looked to Quinn like a pencil without a lead. Some strands had come loose and lay on the nape of her neck, making her look vulnerable and lovely. She turned abruptly and caught Quinn watching her. She gave him a severe look that made him feel as if he had been doing something dirty. He lifted his glass to hide behind.

'LA's like hundreds of miles of suburbs pushed together,' Agustín said, 'and no reason for their existence.'

'I've never lived anywhere,' Quinn said, trying to push the girl's rebuke from his mind and pick up the thread of the conversation, 'where there wasn't a river. When I first got here, I walked for miles, looking for a river. After a time, someone pointed me to a concrete ditch. Inside was a thin line of water.'

Another customer had entered. He carried a glass of beer to a fruit machine a few feet away from Quinn and Agustín. The coins sounded like trickling water.

Agustín said, 'Roy will come soon.'

It was not Quinn's first time in the Chi-Chi. He had spent a couple of hours in the club the night before, after Agustín had returned from work. Quinn had improved, was feeling stronger, but the beer had still hit him hard. After three glasses his head ached and he began to feel faint. He went back to the room, leaving Agustín at the table. He got into bed and was almost asleep when he needed to vomit. He pulled on the jeans Agustín had given him and made for the toilet on the landing below, where he spent half an hour spluttering green phlegm and throwing up. The following

161

day he woke expecting the worst and was surprised to find he felt good, apart from some aching muscles around the ribs. He told Agustín he would be able to go on his way soon. Agustín received the news without comment. He made some coffee, which Quinn had in bed, then made up a vitamin drink Roy had brought for Quinn. Quinn gave an embarrassed laugh when Agustín handed it to him because he always thought it funny when men looked after men.

'Drink it,' Agustín said. 'Vitamins to make you strong again.'

'You don't work on Saturdays?' Quinn asked. The drink had a metallic taste.

'No,' Agustín said sleepily; he felt very tired. 'I'm going to take a shower.'

Agustín pulled a thin, grey-white towel from the box under the window and left his watch on the edge of the sink. He went to the shower room next to the toilet on the floor below.

Agustín's body felt hot and swollen. The shirt, in which he had slept, stuck to his shoulders. The dregs of an unpleasant dream from a few nights before were still in his system, and they mingled with other feelings – fear, foreboding, anger; above all, frustration. Since the Mission's prayer meeting, Agustín's thoughts had turned with renewed intensity to Andrew Jank. They got to him and stopped. Every time Agustín tried to push them forward in search of a way to resolve things he became stuck, and the effort would exhaust and anger him. Perhaps, he began to think, Dulio was right: killing Andrew Jank held no meaning. But he had to do it, he had to do something. Not to do it would be to make a confession of the sort he could not contemplate.

Yet, in spite of all this, Agustín experienced a sensation of lightness, even of optimism. While he showered he tried to locate its source. He gazed vacantly around the shower room: there were pools of water, grey with washed-out dirt and soap; torn sachets of shampoo littered the floor; on the ceiling and upper parts of the walls a furry dark green mould spread to make islands and continents; there was the smell of sitting water. But Agustín, the lightness still with him, did not mind. The water was hot and he let himself drift back to the verge of his sleep. It was so unusual for him to feel this way that he refused to wake, to give himself time, conscious time, to work out reasons and causes. Better just to enjoy it, unthinking. That, he had realized long ago, was the secret of other people's happiness.

Someone banged on the door and yelled for him to hurry up and let others take their turn. He could ignore it. He refused to open his eyes. He stretched two arms in front and leaned against the wall, letting the steaming water fall on his crown and run down his neck, shoulders and back. It was then he found her: she had brought the lightness.

He had liked her aggressiveness, the way she carried herself, more like a man than a woman. She was the source, but he did not want to examine it closely. The more he thought about her, the more he realized that this feeling had no foundation. He became suddenly angry and shut off the water: the memory of her and the feeling she had brought him began to dissolve, running out of the drain with the water.

Back in the room, Agustín said to Quinn, 'Stay as long as you want. You are in your house.'

Quinn had a flash of Brian and the room they had shared, a life he had almost entered. Before he could say anything, Agustín asked, 'Do you want to go for a walk? I will show you the treasures of Los Angeles.'

They took buses in a roundabout route for Griffith Park. On the way Agustín pointed out the Dodgers' Stadium, the Hall of Justice, the Federal Building and Universal Studios. In the park they looked around the bird sanctuary, then walked up the hills, still green after late rains, through the pine and sycamore and into the chaparral. The air was sweet with sage; the manzanita bark was a beautiful reddish brown; and in the distance green petals snaked out of century plants, tongues of green against the thin, rocky desert soil. Quinn had never seen anything like it.

When Quinn began to tire, they descended and went to eat at Fat Boy's, then caught more buses to the Museum of Natural History, where Agustín showed Quinn the exhibits from pre-Columbian civilizations.

'You know Cortés, the Spanish conquistador, and his lieutenant, Pedro de Alvarado?'

'No.'

'What exists in Mexico now, exists because of those men. But in all of Mexico it's nearly impossible to find a statue to Cortés, nor either to Alvarado, who was more bloody even than his master. Do you know Pizarro?'

'No.'

'It's the same with Pizarro. Cajamarca in Peru is where Pizarro defeated the Incas. He captured the Inca emperor, Atahualpa, and had him strangled. Yet in Cajamarca there is no statue to Pizarro. On top of the hill is a statue to Atahualpa, built by the descendants of Pizarro and his men.'

'Why?'

'Because Cortés, Alvarado, Pizarro ruined a whole continent and their descendants have never been able to rebuild what the conquistadors destroyed. They can only look to the past, before the continent was overthrown.'

'It sounds like you don't think it has a future?'

'How can you have a future without a present? Are you hungry? We should eat.'

They caught a bus and ate at a taco stand on Whittier, then Agustín suggested they go to the Chi-Chi Club.

Roy joined them at seven-thirty and ordered beer for the table. The pretty waitress brought it over and Quinn avoided looking at her.

'How's my patient?' Roy asked.

'A lot better,' Quinn said.

'Still coughing up phlegm?'

'Not so much.'

'What about the pleuritic pain?'

'What?'

'Does it hurt when you breathe?'

'A little.'

'That's the inflamed lining. But the antibiotics'll take care of that. You're still taking the Amoxil?'

'The capsules? Yes. Thanks for everything.'

'Three times a day, Sean,' Roy said seriously. He pronounced the name oddly. Quinn liked the sound of his name spoken in this foreign accent. 'Hey, Agustín, how's Dulio keeping?'

Quinn soon fell behind Agustín and Roy in the drinks, mindful of the advice and what had happened the previous night. But he had already reached that stage where things began to look and sound better. The tinkle of the coins; the crashes, beeps and sirens of the slot machine; the muttering of the men around the bar; the splashing of drinks poured and consumed: all came to him pleasantly, gently. Though Roy and Agustín were engaged in private talk that had to do with their shared past, Quinn did not feel excluded. He felt he had been invited to listen. Roy started to talk about his girlfriend, a Texan named Alice. A good woman, he said, but strange in some ways. She lay around the house and never paid anything towards the costs. She said she had no money, but she went out regularly to buy clothes. Roy had no idea where she got the money, or where she kept it. She had no credit cards or cheque book and he had never seen her with so much as a dollar bill. Still she went – with a girlfriend Roy had never met – on shopping expeditions to buy expensive clothes.

'Also she has some strange ideas,' Roy said. 'Texan ideas. Thinks that taxes are too high and that it is in violation of the American constitution for the government to put them up. I said, "Well, they are going to raise them, baby. So what are you going to do about it, take the President to court?" She said, and she wasn't kidding, "I will bear arms." I swear she meant it. "I will bear arms," she said. I can see it, too, her running down there to Houston to take part in the assault on City Hall. She's that kind of woman.'

'Does she pay any taxes?' Quinn asked.

'How would I know? I've lived with her six months and I

don't know the first thing about her. Just that she's very well dressed, when she goes out at least, and doesn't pay for anything round the house.' He emptied his beer. 'Don't say it, I already know I'm being taken for a ride. But what can I do?' Roy scratched his acne-scarred chin and licked the froth of beer from his bandit moustache. His eyes were bleary and reddened. 'I love the woman, and you won't find anyone that doesn't have her faults.'

Quinn drifted out of the conversation and found himself watching the pretty waitress, looking at the nape of her neck where the loose strands of hair fell. She was leaning across the bar and joking with a customer, a playful smile on her face. After a while she caught sight of Quinn and her expression changed abruptly. She gave him such a look of contempt that Quinn felt he had been ejected from the company. Prowling, stalking the edges of other people's lives. Quinn realized how precarious was his connection with the two men at the table, now the only people he knew. He was suddenly desperate, a kind of panic took hold of him.

He moved back into the conversation of the two men. They were talking, in a broken way, about an organization called the Mission, neither bringing his sentences to any conclusion, each – Quinn sensed – waiting for the other to finish the statements left hanging. After a time, they fell silent and Roy said he wanted to eat. There was a hamburger place half a block away, he said. They finished their drinks and stepped out into the night.

Someone shouted Agustín's name. They stopped and looked around for the source. Judy Mendoza called again from the walkway of the hotel across the street.

'Wait,' she shouted. 'Wait for me.' There was an urgency in her voice. The three men watched her hurry down the stairway.

'Who's that?' Roy asked.

'She was at the Mission the other night,' Agustín said.

'Is she one of them?' Roy asked, suspicion in his voice.

'I don't know anything about her.'

'One of who?' Quinn asked.

Neither Roy nor Agustín answered. They stood and waited until Judy came up. She was panting hard, her hair was tousled and her eyes were wide.

'Do you know Sabino?' she said.

'What's happening?' Agustín said.

'You have to come with me.'

'Tell me what's going on.'

'A boy came to Sabino's house. He had a gun. Please hurry.' Judy had Agustín by the arm and was pulling him to her car.

'Who had a gun?' Agustín asked as he went along.

'Some boy. He's on something. I'm telling you, he's dangerous. He came to the house and was trying to get Sabino to go with him. Sabino's wife got me out and told me to get you.'

They were in the car. Judy selected a key.

'What were you doing there?'

She turned the key in the ignition, the car did not start. 'Shit,' she said between her teeth; she turned the key again and her face twisted as though it involved physical effort and concentration.

The engine caught. Judy was putting the car in gear when the back door opened; she jumped with fright. It was Quinn.

'Who are you? What do you want?' Judy said.

'It's okay,' Agustín answered her. To Quinn he said, 'Get in.' Agustín saw a resoluteness in Quinn that he had not seen before, but was not surprised to find: he behaved in a way that reminded Agustín of people who have an unexpected expertise.

Judy raced the engine and they moved away. As they turned the corner Agustín could see Roy, looking worried as ever. Roy gave a small wave, like a gesture sad women make during leave-taking; Agustín did not scorn it in Roy.

'This boy came to the house. I'm positive he was doped up. He told Sabino to get his coat and go with him. Sabino's wife said he couldn't go and the boy took out this gun and waved it around.' Judy spoke fast and stumbled over her words. 'Jesus,' she said, shaking her head in disbelief.

'Who was it? Did Sabino's wife say?'

'No. She just told me to get you. I went to your room and banged on the door. Then I saw you and those other guys. Can you direct me?'

Agustín checked to see where they were. 'Take the second right. What were you doing talking to Sabino?'

'I knew he had worked for the Dorfmann woman. I wanted to find out what he knows about the Mission.'

'Sabino doesn't know anything.'

'I had to try.'

'Why are you so interested in the Mission?'

She kept her eyes on the road and did not answer at once. 'I'm trying to find my sister.'

'Is she a missionary?'

Judy laughed sourly.

'Take a left here. Then – you see that theatre? – turn right there. Is she a missionary or not?'

'No,' she said; her voice had anger in it.

Quinn caught snatches of Judy's eyes in the mirror. They were brown, but not soft.

'What happened to your sister?'

'I don't know. Not for sure. But the Mission does.'

Agustín gave her more directions. He said, 'You told me you were a student at UCLA.'

'I used to work in San Francisco, in the Public Defender's office.'

'You're a lawyer?' Agustín asked.

'An investigator. I find witnesses for the defence, check reports, get background information, that kind of stuff.

When my sister went missing. I did some research on the Mission and found out they were setting something up in LA. I quit the job and came down here.'

'You're not a student?'

'Jesus, no. I was trying to get to talk to Victor Jank and Nick Zenga by pretending to be a theology post-grad at UCLA. But it was no go.'

'It's over there,' Agustín said.

*

The house was a two-room bungalow, one family in each room. A semi-transparent shower curtain that divided the room was the family's attempt to create some privacy. The paint was dark green and peeling, the light bulb was bare and there was no ceiling fixture; the crumbling plaster had been plugged in places with damp tissue paper that had dried and hardened. On the walls were a portrait of the Pope and a calendar with a view of an oil refinery, below which the days belonged to August 1986. There was a photograph of Sabino and the children: Sabino stood, narrow-shouldered, hunched shyly, hands at his sides, arms rigid; he was thin and his clothes hung loosely: a *serrano*, humble, intimidated by the world of *los mistis*, the whites.

In the corner of the room, three children, two girls and a boy, clustered for safety. The boy, barely a toddler, took an uncertain step forward and gazed at Quinn, the *misti*; the girls held back in open-mouthed uncertainty. An older boy sat with his mother, who was crying. The woman was Indian-looking, more so even than Sabino. She was dressed in a shapeless black jumper and a sleeveless blue housecoat. Agustín addressed her as Hilda and spoke to her in Quechua. The woman dabbed tears from her eyes and spoke slowly. Agustín asked a series of rapid questions and the woman nodded.

'We have to go,' Agustín said to Judy.

'Go where?'

'The boy who came here was Pascualito Hernández. I think he is going to rob the Dorfmann factory and he's taken Sabino with him.'

Judy looked at the woman, still crying, and at the children, who stared at her in the silent, bewildered way of children when they see something is wrong but do not know what it is. The woman stared at her through her tears and Judy felt guilty and out of place, as if it had been she who had brought them disaster. Judy knew she had intimidated Hilda when she had arrived to talk to Sabino. Hilda was only a few years older than Judy, but they came from and belonged to different worlds. When Agustín pulled her arm to hurry her along, Judy was glad to be gone.

At the cyclone fence, Mrs Dorfmann got out of the car and unlocked the gate. She drove through and parked behind the extension so no one driving past would know she was there. Better safe than sorry. She walked back and shut the gate.

Andrew had talked all the way from Feddersen's house. He talked about his uncle, about Nick Zenga, about New Guinea, the Philippines, Peru, Chile; about how he would have to learn Spanish because of the Home Programme and because after it he would probably be sent to a Latin American country for an extended period; about the Mission's 'boot camp' where he had studied linguistics and semiotics, though he had to admit that really he was not good at languages. He talked about Feddersen, what an insightful man he was, saying that if there were more like him, prepared to put his money where his mouth was, the Mission's work would be a lot easier. Mrs Dorfmann listened patiently and smiled to herself: he was trying to pretend nothing was happening. She herself was surprised at how in control she felt. She knew that it was going to happen, and in a way Andrew's nervousness, as well as making her look forward to it all the more, made her feel more secure.

The car parked and the gate shut, she and Andrew walked to the factory's back door, secured by a single lock. They passed into the factory and went to the office, where Mrs Dorfmann stopped to turn off the burglar alarm.

'I'm glad you are with me,' Mrs Dorfmann said. 'I would not like to be here alone.' She smiled at him. 'You can protect me,' she said and squeezed his biceps. He smiled back weakly.

'You know, Mr Feddersen's got a lot of influence with the Board.' Andrew's voice was in whispers.

Mrs Dorfmann opened the office door and the two went inside. She did not turn on the light and they were in half-darkness.

'It's obvious that Mr Feddersen admires you,' Mrs

Dorfmann said. Her voice had dropped to match Andrew's; they were part of the same conspiracy. 'You are really a very admirable person.'

'No,' Andrew said in a rush.

'Everyone says so.'

'What do you want from here?' Andrew asked.

'I just need an invoice. Now,' she said, moving some things about on the desk, 'where did I leave it?'

'What does it look like?'

'Green.'

Andrew bent over the desk and picked up some papers. Although Mrs Dorfmann's heart was thumping, it did not disrupt her sense of control or her confidence. She knew she could not wait for Andrew, knew that she would have to be the one to act. All the same, she needed a sign from him.

'Just as well Martin's not here,' she said coquettishly.

'What?'

'If Martin was here,' she answered, slightly disappointed, 'he'd be suspicious.' She looked at him while he continued to search the papers on the desk. He said nothing. 'He wouldn't like it,' she continued, 'if he found the two of us here, alone, in the dark.'

He looked up. There was fright in his eyes.

'I was joking,' she said quickly. 'Just a joke.' He still did not move. Mrs Dorfmann put her hand on his arm. He looked at it strangely, but did not move away. 'Don't worry,' Mrs Dorfmann said, closing on him. Without thinking about what to do next, she kissed him on the mouth, dragging her tongue across his clamped teeth. He swallowed and opened his mouth. She pushed her tongue inside and pressed into him. She tried to encourage his tongue into her mouth; it would not come. She pulled back and pinched his cheek as though he were a naughty boy.

'Don't you like kissing?' she said.

He held his head as far back from her as he could. He whispered, 'I was thinking of your husband.'

'Think of me,' she said. She kissed him again. She took his hand and put it on her breast. She moaned to encourage

171

him, sensed instead panic and quietened down. He tried to pull his head away and she had to struggle to keep their mouths together. When it seemed that he would win, she gambled everything and put her hand between his legs and pressed the heel of her hand into him. He sighed and she felt his body relax. She allowed him to take away his mouth. 'You like that, hmm?' she said. She started to undo his belt. He was letting her do whatever she wanted. She unbuttoned his trousers and got her hand into his underpants. He moaned and dropped his head to her shoulder. She pushed her tongue into his ear. He flopped forward into her, almost unbalancing her.

She said, 'I have to go pee pee.' She drew back and looked at him, gloriously undone. He was breathing as if after a hard race. 'Don't go away,' she said with a smile. He looked appealingly stupid and confused.

She closed the door behind her. There was enough light from the moon and the street for her to check her reflection in the mirror and fix her hair. She looked at the smudged lipstick in triumph. She undid the top button of her blouse and flicked the collar to open it further. Then she heard something.

Pascualito had not seen Mrs Dorfmann's car after he and Sabino had scaled the cyclone fence, and he had broken the lock on the back door with a crowbar without, in the process, noticing the door was unlocked. He dropped the crowbar and it hit the ground with a clatter. Sabino, who was just behind him, jumped with fright, and Pascualito, who had already decided he wished he had not taken him along, told him to get hold of himself. Pascualito took out the .22 target pistol; he was trembling and did not feel at all good.

As he stepped inside, he saw that Sabino was running back to the fence. He pointed the gun at the retreating shadow and almost fired. More trouble than he was worth, so he let him go.

When Pascualito reached the office door, he inspected the lock. The wood frame was flimsy and would require little more than a shove with his shoulder. He charged, the door gave way and Pascualito tumbled inside.

From the bathroom Mrs Dorfmann heard the crash and her first thought was that Martin, or Nick Zenga or Victor Jank or someone had seen the couple and followed them here. She mumbled something, the beginnings of an excuse. She stayed still, clutching the sink in front of her, and held her breath. The anxiety made her stomach heave.

Pascualito was on the floor. He found himself looking up at a white man who was gazing at him dumbly. Pascualito realized he was still holding the .22 and, without thinking, he fired. It made a louder noise than he had expected. It was only then that he saw that the white man had his shirt undone and his trousers open and around his knees. He was convinced it was only after the noise had cleared that he saw the man flinch and heard him say, 'Ow,' as if stung by a wasp.

When the man did not fall down, Pascualito scrambled to his feet and fled.

Mrs Dorfmann, on hearing the shot, crouched down and crawled under the sink, put her arms and hands over her head and started her excuses for real.

As Pascualito burst from the back door, he saw two men running towards him. He waved his gun at them and they stopped abruptly. Headlights from the other side of the fence shone directly at him. He put one hand up to shield his eyes and stretched the gun out.

'Get out of the way,' Pascualito shouted in Spanish.

'Sabino. Where's Sabino?' Agustín demanded.

Pascualito was manoeuvring himself, his back against the wall, to get to the fence.

'Where is he?'

'Don't get in my way or I'll kill you. I already killed someone' – Pascualito nodded to indicate the factory – 'and I don't mind if I make it two.'

Agustín ignored the gun and dashed inside. The movement startled Pascualito and he lunged at Quinn with the gun, striking him on the head. Quinn went down. Pascualito sprinted to the fence, climbed up and dropped to the other side, landing beside Judy's car. When he got to his feet, he found Judy looking at him.

Instinctively, he raised the target pistol, only to discover the woman was pointing a gun, a big gun, at his head. Pascualito froze, then backed off slowly, turned and fled to his car. He reversed out into the street and sped away.

Judy put her gun away, got out of the car and called to Quinn, who was slowly getting up.

'I'm okay,' Quinn said between splutters.

Agustín found the office door hanging on one hinge across the threshold. He pushed it out of the way and it fell to the floor with a slam.

The noise came as Mrs Dorfmann was crawling to the door of the bathroom. She had opened it a fraction, after the moments of silence had convinced her that the gunman had gone, and was peering into the office. She could see Andrew, who was leaning against the desk, clutching his right side and trying to hoist up his trousers.

At first Agustín was unable to believe what he saw. Andrew's eyes were wide with shock and he was mumbling. 'Please contact my uncle, Pastor Jank. Please, I'm hurt.'

'Do you remember me?' Agustín asked.

'Help me, please. Can you call my uncle? I'm hurt. I think I'm shot.'

'You don't remember me?'

Andrew nodded. He said, a little breathlessly, 'Mr Ar-say, of course. Please, the phone is there, on the desk.'

Agustín reached over to the telephone. Andrew looked on expectantly and sighed with relief.

Agustín swept it to the floor. He took a switch-blade from his pocket.

'I'm hurt,' Andrew said, gazing at the knife.

Agustín started for him. As Andrew dashed for the door, Agustín slashed his back. The missionary shrieked but managed to blunder out of the office and into the main part of the factory. Agustín followed, calmly, the knife at his side, pointing down. Andrew tried to steady himself by putting a hand out to the wall. Agustín brought the knife up and stuck it into his arm. Andrew received a short burst of strength from the pain and stumbled on. He tried to get to the back door, but Agustín got there before him and slammed it closed with his foot. He swung the knife out and caught Andrew in the face. Andrew moaned, limped backwards and fell into a workbench. Agustín moved in on him. When Andrew struggled to his feet, Agustín stabbed him in the thigh. Andrew saw the blood squirt out and said, 'Is this it?' He fell down, landing on his back.

Agustín watched his victim for a moment. He stooped and took a handful of Andrew's hair, pulled his head up.

He said, 'More weight?' Andrew's face was blank.

Agustín slit his throat with a movement of the hand so fine he could have been adding a final stroke of the brush to a masterpiece. He let go of Andrew's hair, straightened, folded the knife and put it in his pocket.

Quinn was staring at him. They looked at each other in silence for some moments.

'Let's get out of here,' Agustín said.

Judy was sitting quite calmly in the car. When Agustín and Quinn emerged from the back of the building, she got out and shouted to them, 'Did you find Sabino?'

'Let's go,' Agustín hissed urgently. He and Quinn scaled the fence and jumped into the car.

'What happened?' Judy asked, alarm in her voice after catching their tension. 'Is Sabino all right?'

'Let's hope so,' Agustín said. 'Where are you living?'

'Me?' Judy said. 'Lakewood.'

'Drive there.'

Mrs Dorfmann did not move for five minutes. Even after she heard the second car drive off she stayed where she was, on her hands and knees, cowering behind the door of the bathroom. When finally she emerged, she saw that Andrew was not in the office. She paused and listened, but could hear nothing. The silence was extraordinary. Muttering a prayer, she raised herself to her feet and stepped over the broken door of the office.

She noticed at once the wreckage of the workbenches. They were knocked over in a way that suggested a trail or flight. She trod carefully.

Andrew was still alive. She did not feel horror at seeing him, though he was horrible to look at, smeared with blood and helpless in the way of the dying. She pitied him and said, without realizing it, 'Oh poor baby.' His eyes were wide and he was gasping for breath.

She held his head and rocked him as the soft gurgling sounds grew further apart in time. She did not like to see his naked chest, thought it somehow indecent, and began to button his shirt. Then she tried to rearrange his trousers. His gurgling turned to wheezing. Mrs Dorfmann could not get the trousers properly up. She saw that she had mismatched the buttons and holes of the shirt, so that it looked twisted; but it did not matter. She decided that he looked better for her efforts, more decent.

She concentrated on comforting him in her arms, stroking his head and face. The wheezing grew fainter. She bent to his mouth and listened for breath. Gradually, it slipped away. When there was none, she gently lowered his head to the floor. There were tears in her eyes when she went to the phone.

When Mrs Dorfmann phoned Victor Jank, she was quite coherent. The shock of Andrew's murder and the fears for her own safety had not confused her mind; had, rather, clarified the situation. She should phone the police, but something told her not to.

'Pastor Jank,' she said, 'something terrible's happened.'

'Maritza, is that you? What is it?'

A pause. 'They've murdered Andrew.'

There was a whisper, silence, then at last, 'What are you saying?'

'They killed him,' Mrs Dorfmann said.

'Where are you?'

'At the factory.'

'The factory?'

'We had to stop to pick something up after we saw Mr Feddersen when we—'

'When? When did it happen? Have you called the police?'

'It just happened.'

'Oh my God.' Another silence, longer this time. She heard him clearing his throat. 'Okay, wait for me to come. You're sure . . . you're sure he's dead?'

The question touched off tears and she found herself without a voice.

'Maritza? Maritza? Are you there?'

'I saw them.'

'You know who it was?'

'Yes.'

Jank paused to think. 'Maritza, I want you to call Rex right away. Tell him to go to the factory and wait for me. I'll get Nick Zenga. Don't do anything else, don't call the police yet. We'll take care of everything. Okay?'

There was no answer.

'Maritza? Do you understand?'

'Yes. I'm sorry. I'm so sorry. They came to rob me and they murdered him.'

'Call Rex. Have him come over. I'll be there in twenty minutes.'

'Victor, I'm sorry.'

'Call Rex.'

'Yes.'

'Maritza?'

'Yes?'

'You're sure he's dead?'

Mrs Dorfmann's tears answered him.

At the factory Nick Zenga watched Jank weep beside his nephew's body, while in the bathroom Rex helped Mrs Dorfmann clean the blood off her face and hands.

Jank finished a prayer and stood up. He addressed Zenga, without taking his eyes from the body. 'What did Maritza say? Did she say who it was?'

'Someone who works here apparently. A man she thinks is called Agustín Romero.'

'Does she know where he lives?'

'No. He might be hard to find. Shall I call the police?'

Jank continued to gaze at the body.

'Get Rex out here,' he said.

Zenga went to the office and Jank bent down to kiss Andrew's forehead.

Rex and Zenga stood waiting.

Jank breathed in deeply and stood up. 'Is she all right?' he asked Rex.

'I think so, señor.'

'Do you know Agustín Romero?' Jank asked.

'Yes. I hired him a couple of weeks ago to work on the extension.'

'Do you know how we can find him?'

Rex thought about it. 'I think we can find him.'

'I'm going to call the police from here,' Jank said, 'but I'm not going to tell them what we know. We will settle this ourselves.' He looked at Andrew's body. 'Maritza says that it was a robbery, but this' – he indicated the trail of blood – 'this was not for a robbery. This is something else.'

'You think so?' Zenga said; he seemed unconvinced. 'These people are psychotic. They butcher for just a few dollars.'

Jank nodded. 'Maybe.'

'What are you going to explain to the police about not calling them earlier?' Zenga said.

'I'll handle it. Mrs Dorfmann was in shock, something like that. Nick, can you go with Rex and find Romero?'

'Sure.'

Rex went to the back door. Zenga held back, eager to talk to Jank in private. He looked down at the body, at the tangled shirt and opened trousers, at the fingerprints of blood around the flies.

'What does she say she was doing here with him?' Zenga asked.

Jank turned to him but did not speak. After a few

moments he brushed past on his way to the office. 'Find Romero, Nick, and settle this for me,' he said as he went inside.

Zenga left with Rex.

In the office Mrs Dorfmann was sitting in her swivel chair.

'I'm sorry,' she said, wiping her tears.

Jank went to the phone. The receiver was sticky with blood and he held it in a pincer of two fingers. He dialled the policy emergency number and spoke briefly to a woman on the other end of the line. He put down the phone and looked at Mrs Dorfmann. She dabbed her eyes with a handkerchief, then blew her nose.

'I'm sorry,' she said again.

Though, years before in a Paraguayan rain forest, in an act of self-defence, he had shot and killed two women, Victor Jank had never struck one before. Only when Mrs Dorfmann was on the floor, humiliated, did he feel any regret, and then not enough to stop him lifting her by the hair and throwing her into the chair.

part three

Silver into Dross

Tijuana always brought back a memory. Judy was not sure how she remembered it – with bitterness or with some mixture of regret. But then, she would tell herself, all love affairs leave after-tastes which are never all one nor the other, just infuriatingly contradictory trails that, at best, lead nowhere, or, at worst, lead to fury and reproach. She did not want to think about it, but, although she tried hard, she could not avoid the memory, above all in Tijuana.

Driving with Quinn through San Diego, stopping at a late-night store to get him some better-fitting clothes so that the border patrol would think he was North American and wave him through without asking questions, she had been concerned less with their actual difficulties, with fleeing the scene of a murder, than with the memory the approach of Tijuana always produced in her. It made her angry with herself, because that incident, that man, that time were all so trivial.

His name was Mike. He was an attorney in a big San Francisco law firm, though he had started out in the Public Defender's office, where they met, before going into private practice and dropping his criminal work for corporate clients. He was a Stanford graduate and used to call himself a socialist. When Mercedes met him and Judy later asked what she thought, Mercedes avoided giving a direct answer. All she would say was, why was it that the word *socialism* in the mouths of North Americans always sounded so glib?

It had not struck Judy that way, perhaps, Judy thought afterwards, because she herself was glib. When Mike had first asked her out to dinner, she thought to herself, Why not?

And after dinner, when he suggested coffee she looked him over, confirmed her earlier impressions of his good looks, and thought again, Why not? Three months later he suggested she move in.

Mercedes had never once criticized her, yet ever since she was very young Judy had the feeling Mercedes was only just succeeding in withholding her disapproval; or disappointment, which was worse. As she grew up, Judy came increasingly to look to her sister for approval. Mercedes was outside everything Judy knew. She was tall and beautiful, though not in a way that men always appreciated. Judy was the one most men chose. Mercedes disturbed a lot of men. Mike, for instance, although he tried hard to hide it. Mercedes had pale blue eyes, the gift of their Italian mother, and she had their mother's thick black hair. Judy used to comb it until Mercedes cut it off, which almost made Judy cry. Mercedes just laughed.

One time, when Mercedes was visiting Judy in San Francisco, Mike suggested they go, with two other lawyer friends – Peter and his girlfriend Sue – to San Diego for the weekend to stay with Mike's brother David. Mercedes said she had to stay in San Francisco to see a friend and said goodbye to Judy.

In San Diego Mike said, 'Hey, why don't we take in Tee-u-wana? Do some shopping down in Me-hee-co?'

They drove David's BMW across the border, and parked off Revolución, where the two couples split up to do their shopping. 'Meet you back here at the Denny's at three, right?' Mike had said.

Mike returned to the restaurant with an armful of things. Judy was feeling tired, having spent four hours jostling with the tourists and listening to Mike talking about how cheap thing were.

Peter and Sue were admiring each other's buys.

'I got this' – Peter held up an embroidered shirt – 'for ten bucks. You believe it? What would that cost in the States?'

Mike said, 'We got a pair of—'

'*You,*' Judy corrected him, 'you got.' She lit a cigarette.

Mike gave her a worn-down look. 'Yeah,' he said. '*I* got a pair of Nikes. Wait, twenty-five dollars.' He pronounced each syllable of the sum with exquisite pleasure.

'No!' Sue said. 'They're the real thing?'

'Twenty-five. I'll show you the shop.'

'I'll bet you got a few dollars knocked off because Judy speaks Spanish,' Sue said.

'No,' Mike said with a glance at Judy, 'she wouldn't do any bargaining. But I speak enough anyway, to get by.'

'Twenty-five dollars,' Sue said, marvelling at it.

'That's Tee-u-wana for you,' Peter said.

The waitress was by them.

'Honey, what do you want?' Peter asked Sue.

'It's pronounced Tijuana,' Judy said.

Peter said, 'What?' He looked nonplussed.

'I said, it's not Tee-u-wana, it's Tijuana.'

'Is that right?' Peter said, mildly surprised. 'We've been mispronouncing it all this time?'

Mike gave Judy an angry glare, mixed with *Please don't start, these are my friends.* She mouthed back *Fuck off.*

'Please, miss,' Mike said to the waitress. 'I'll have enchiladas. Is that how it's pronounced, Judy?'

'Miss,' Peter said. 'Make that two more enchiladas.'

Judy ordered the same.

'Jesus,' Peter said, poring over the menu. 'What does that work out at, including the beer? Twelve bucks for four?'

'Eleven and some change,' Mike said, studying the menu.

'No wonder Mexico's so poor,' Peter said.

The waitress brought the beers and retreated, smiling, with the menus. Judy could not look her in the face. She thought of Mercedes and was thankful her sister had not come.

Mike was recounting a case from his days as hero of the Public Defender's Office, in which he cast himself in the role of the sardonic onlooker with biting wit and insights into everyone else's motives.

'Justice,' Mike said at the conclusion, 'has nothing to do with it. It's winning and losing.'

'Right,' Peter said. 'I always think of it, doesn't matter what the case is, I always think of it as winning or losing.'

'You got to,' Sue said. 'That's what an adversarial system is. In any fight, it doesn't matter if it's markets or courts, there's got to be winners and losers.'

'If I win,' Peter said, 'I've won something. Say they want to give my guy a hundred years, and I get him ninety, I've won.'

'Right,' Mike said. 'You've won him ten years off.'

'If *we* win, the client is going to feel happier,' Peter said.

'And if *we* lose, are *we* going to do the time?' Judy asked him.

'Honey,' Mike started.

'No, Mike,' Peter said, 'she's right. We have to remember that, you know, that . . . like there's someone else involved.'

'Someone else *involved*?' Judy asked incredulously.

'Right,' Peter said with supreme innocence. 'That's why it's important to win. Go in there and kick ass, because, Judy, if you don't win, your client's gonna be pissed. It's in both your interests.'

'God,' Judy said.

'I had a client. Jack. You would not believe this guy,' Sue said, turning Peter away from a fall he did not know he was heading for. And she told the story of her client, a born loser who ended up pulling life in Folsom. When she finished, Mike and peter had their own stories. They both started, 'I had this one guy . . .'

At last, Judy said, 'Why do doctors have this code of confidentiality but lawyers don't? How would you like it if at the next table we overheard a bunch of doctors discussing their patients?'

'Could be interesting,' Peter, who was ahead on drinks, snorted.

'Specially if it was *your* doctor discussing *your* flatulence.'

'Hey, Judy,' Mike said.

'Well,' Sue said under her breath, dabbing her mouth with a paper napkin.

'Fuck you,' Judy said, to Mike and to them all.

Judy got up and walked out into Revolución. A tourist

luxury coach was parked in the street before a concrete rubbish bin the size of a wide barrel. An old woman was leaning in to pick out the gringos' discarded treasures; a young man was scrabbling so deep in the bin his legs were up in the air like a victory sign.

'Jesus Christ,' Mike said from the door. 'What did you think you were doing?' He was red with rage.

Onlookers started to snigger at the angry gringo. A man with a sombrero holding a donkey painted like a zebra shouted to Mike, 'Picture? Have your picture taken, sir. A memento from Tee-u-wana.'

Mike dismissed him with a wave of the hand as he would a fly. The man said something in Spanish and the people around laughed.

Judy was storming up the street. Mike caught up with her and pulled her around.

'What the fuck was that all about? We were having a perfectly civilized conversation.'

'Civilized?'

'Yes, civilized. When people who work hard get to relax, people who all do the same thing, it's natural they talk about what they do. That's civilized.'

A shoeshine boy said to Mike, 'Shine, sir?'

'No, grassy-ass,' Mike said impatiently.

'Ah, come on, you need it,' the boy said. His English could have been learned on the streets of San Diego or Los Angeles.

'No,' Mike insisted, just keeping his temper. 'Look, go way. No shine, grassy-ass.'

'*Chinga tu madre*,' the boy said.

Mike was staring hard at Judy when the boy's words sank in. 'What did he say?' he asked Judy. 'Was that rude?'

'He said, "Have a nice day", ' Judy replied.

The boy grinned at Mike.

'It sounded rude.'

'Mike,' Judy said, '*Chinga tu madre*.'

The boy laughed and went on his way. Mike shouted after her, 'Don't be like this. You haven't got a car.'

'I'll walk.'

'Always holier than thou, Judy, aren't you? You know you're getting more like that cunt of a sister of yours every day.'

Judy stopped and faced him. 'What did you say?'

'Jesus Christ. You're trying to be like her. Isn't that obvious to you? Because it is to everyone else. What do you do? Practise in the mirror so you can try and get more like her?'

'You bastard.' She strode towards him. 'You bastard.'

'You try and make me and my friends feel bad. What's so fucking special about you? That fucking sister of yours – she should've been born a man, that way she could pretend to be Jesus fucking Christ.'

Judy glared at him. It occurred to her to hit him or spit at him. Instead she said calmly, 'You're pathetic,' and turned away.

Judy took a bus to the border, crossed the footbridge, caught a bus to San Diego and an overnight Greyhound to San Francisco. She tried to find Mercedes when she got back, but Mercedes had already gone. Judy packed one suitcase and left Mike's keys on the table.

Whenever she reviewed the scene in Tijuana she felt satisfied enough, although she knew that how you thought of your own performance in such confrontations was never the way the other party saw it. However, part of her felt uneasy, because Mike was not a bad man and there were things she missed about him. That was why Tijuana always made her gloomy. She would not have come with Quinn had it not been the natural place to run to after a murder.

The brown and grey United States Border Inspection Station straddled sixteen lanes of highway. It stood low, on short, centipede legs through which the cars passed: hundreds, hundreds of cars, even at this time of night, queuing for entry to the US, each to be scrutinized, the drivers and passengers questioned, their papers inspected, their status challenged, their identities confirmed.

There were no lines for those heading south; the cars were

waved on by bored men in uniform.

Judy, however, was waved down. She wound down the window and the guard stooped to peer inside.

'Are you American, miss?' The guard himself was *chicano*.

'Yes, I am.'

'You, sir?'

Quinn said, 'Sure am,' in the accent he had practised with Judy during the drive. He thought he saw Judy flinch and concentrated on working a smile into his expression. At the same time, he tried to stay as much as he could in the shadows to conceal where Pascualito had cut him on the forehead.

'We're both from San Francisco,' Judy said quickly. 'We're taking a short vacation in Mexico.'

'Uh-huh,' the guard said lazily. 'Do you have any ID, miss?'

Judy showed him her driver's licence. 'This okay?' she asked. The guard looked it over, paused before handing it back and said, 'Have a nice trip.'

Judy moved off.

'Why didn't he want to see my papers?' Quinn asked.

'You're white.'

'What about Mexican customs? Won't they want a passport?'

'There's no problem here.'

'Further on?'

'Just pretend you're American,' Judy said impatiently.

'How do I do that?'

'You have two choices: you can either act gross or stupid.'

'Stupid?' Quinn said. 'I won't have to act.'

What did he mean by that? Judy thought. The accent, the inflexions were strange to her.

'What about Agustín? Will he get across okay?' Quinn asked.

'Probably,' she said. 'They don't try to stop illegals crossing *into* Mexico.'

They had dropped Agustín in San Diego. Judy and Quinn could pass the border without problems, but with him in the car it would be difficult. He said he would cross on foot, in his own way, and meet them at the Hotel Rey in Tijuana: with luck he would see them some time the following day.

'Do you think anyone's after us?' Quinn asked.

'How would I know?' Judy snapped. She did not welcome the reminder of what had happened. Yet she felt oddly ambiguous about it. In the chaotic drive away from the Dorfmann factory, she had wrung from Quinn and Agustín, in bursts of ill-tempered demands and shouted responses, the fact of Andrew Jank's murder. She took a wrong turning, reversed at speed, swung the car around. 'Jesus. Andrew Jank is dead?' 'Yes.' 'How?' 'I killed him with this,' Agustín had said, holding the knife in his hand. He wound down the window and tossed the weapon into the doorway of an abandoned building they were passing. Judy visualized it, the murder of Andrew Jank, saw a life seeping out in red, and had been shocked. Her work in the Public Defender's Office had brought her into direct contact with violent death, but only five or six times in as many years and she did not consider herself truly hardened. The shock was real, but as they proceeded to the border, driven by the instinct for refuge, somehow the deed did not seem so terrible; she could almost persuade herself that if they were stopped and explained who Andrew Jank was, what he and the Mission represented, the authorities would understand. The idea stayed with her as they drove to the border; there was no need for panic, it was not that serious.

During the drive Judy realized that she welcomed Andrew Jank's death and her part in it: it meant something was happening now. Judy was an investigator, that was her work. But uncovering things was as far as it went. She followed trails and, when she got to the end, she told someone else, and that person, always a man, would see it through. So it had been after Mercedes's last letter, after the falling of her silence. Judy had uncovered clues, followed trails: they led to the Mission. But, though she had a gun, still she could do nothing further, her imagination had failed. She had to wait for something to happen through the act of someone else.

The act was Agustín's. Their flight would bring her to Mercedes.

'You're right,' Quinn said finally, jolting Judy out of her thoughts and back to their present difficulties. 'How would you know if someone was after us?'

Judy glanced at him to try to assess how he intended the words. It was hard with this man; not only because she had only met him for the first time three or four hours earlier, but because his manner and intonations were ironic, of a species of irony she had not encountered before. There was no stress on any of the words to indicate their meaning, nor any indication in his face. Dead, she thought, glancing at him. She saw the scars and smashed bone. The face dead from its wounds. You can't tell anything from the dead.

They saw a low, pink building with an Asemex sign. Judy pulled over to the right. 'I'm going to get insurance here for the car,' she explained. 'No sense in getting stopped for not having it.'

Quinn waited in the car while Judy sorted out the documentation. It took about twenty minutes. She did not say anything when she reappeared, but started the engine and moved out into the traffic. Quinn felt he might as well not be there.

Ten minutes later they were in the town. Judy parked in front of a bar. 'I need a drink,' she said.

Inside were half a dozen or so Mexican men, and a middle-aged American couple, out of place and nervous. The couple smiled on seeing Quinn, an ally, another gringo. The man held his smile longer than the woman, who, once she saw Quinn's bashed-up face and head, returned to her drink as though Quinn smelt bad.

'First time in Tee-u-wana?' the man said to Quinn.

'Yes.'

'Ours too.'

'First and last time,' the woman added, chancing a glance at Quinn.

Judy ordered two whiskies.

'You don't like it here?' Quinn asked.

They paused on hearing his accent. The man gathered his wits and said, 'Some people can stand the poverty, maybe. Not us. Our car broke down. Engine overheated while we were waiting in line to cross back home.' The man glanced at his watch. 'It's sure taking them a long time to fix it.'

'Really,' the woman said. She added, 'I'll never come back.' She did not look at Quinn when she spoke. 'Our daughter loves Mexico. She's travelled all over. Acapulco, down to Oaxaca and the Yucatán, all over. She loves it. She said we should come down here. We sure didn't expect this.'

'How did you expect it?' Judy asked, her voice brittle.

'Not so much poverty, I guess,' the man said. 'The people here should do something about it.'

'The children . . . how do they eat? I'll never come back,' the woman said.

'Right,' Judy said. 'Come on.' She nodded Quinn to a table in the far corner.

'Goodbye,' Quinn said. 'It was nice to meet you. I hope the car is fixed soon.' The politeness in his manner got through to the woman. For the first time since he had entered the bar she looked him directly in the eyes. 'Thank you,' she said.

At the table Judy said, 'She'll go home to her friends and say that the children are dirty and starving and Mexico is terrible. She'll never come back and that way she can pretend it doesn't exist and that she's not responsible.'

'You think she's responsible?'

'Of course she is. You think people like that don't benefit from Mexico? You better believe it. Cheap maids, gardeners, oil, fruit, coffee, markets for American goods. We all benefit.'

Quinn looked over at the couple and felt sorry for them. They did not know what they were in.

'When we've finished here, we'll go to the hotel and wait for Agustín,' Judy said. 'How much money have you got?'

'Nothing,' Quinn said.

'Nothing?'

'Look,' he said. 'I'm not asking you for anything.' He

became conscious of the drink in front of him. He thought of pushing it towards her, but decided it would have been a pointless gesture. 'Please don't feel responsible,' he said quietly.

'I don't,' she assured him in a loud voice, and Quinn felt stupid. The Mexicans glanced at them and some of them smirked unpleasantly. 'Finish your drink. It's late and I'm tired,' Judy said.

The Hotel Rey was on 4th Street, half a block down from Revolución. There was an old man behind the desk. He sat below a glossy poster of a gleaming black car and a near-naked white woman embracing it: underneath the image was the word *Success*, the *S* a dollar sign.

Judy spoke to the old man in Spanish. The man shrugged before replying, indicating the pigeonholes behind him, in which three keys dangled. Judy, an exasperated expression on her face, spoke again, her voice more insistent. Again the man shrugged.

Quinn did not like it, not knowing what was going on. 'What's the problem?' he asked Judy.

Judy ignored him and continued to argue with the old man. It went on for some minutes. At last the man took one of the remaining keys and moved out from behind the desk. He beckoned them to a stairway. The rooms were arranged around a central courtyard closed in from the sky by sheets of pebble glass.

As they climbed the stairs, Judy said, 'Look, this is the only room they've got. I asked for two separates, which they didn't have. I asked for twin beds, which also they didn't have. We're going to have to share a bed, but, just so you understand, it doesn't mean anything, okay?'

Quinn nodded too quickly. He felt chided for some dirty thought he was not guilty of having; he remembered the waitress in the Chi-Chi Club and blushed.

The old man opened the door for them and turned on the dim light, said something, to which Judy replied curtly, and departed. She inspected the room, painted a cream colour gone to light brown, and sighed with weariness and disapproval. The window was screened, a corner of one curtain had come away from the hooks on the rail. The bed was large and soft. A door in the far wall from the window opened on to the bathroom and shower.

Judy spent some minutes washing and brushing her teeth, and she turned the light out before undressing. She kept on her pants and she fished out a T-shirt from the small case she had packed in Lakewood. She smoked in the darkness while Quinn undressed. The last words that had passed between them had been on the stairs, Judy's warning to him. She stubbed out the cigarette and turned away from Quinn, pulling the covers around her shoulders.

Quinn did not fall asleep for some time. He wondered what Judy was thinking, whether she had been frightened by what had happened. Had she been this close to a killing before? His mind slipped him back to the factory where he had seen the wounded man's blind stumblings around the workbenches and tools, to Agustín's cat-like stalking of him. Doe-eyed the young man had faced death: fear and surprise and innocence all there in his features. Quinn had seen it before. He imagined it on his own face as he sat in the alley and waited for Denis to kill him.

He heard Judy shift in her sleep, the slow movement of limbs rustling linen, the breathing of sleep, heavy like a child's; and he thought of Monica. She always invaded his thoughts at this time of night. Sometimes she laughed at him; sometimes she said she was sorry; sometimes she came to him and loved him. Those were the worst times. She was loving him now, now sweeter than she knew, her lovely sad face pressed into his, her mouth leaving kisses on his face and lips.

Quinn shut his eyes.

Judy was in the shower when he came awake. He heard sounds that he had not heard for a long time and they were strange to him. He listened: the running water with a woman's noises, not the hawking and hoarse grunts of men;

even the sound of skin and hair being towelled dry was different, as were the footsteps, the noise of a comb going through long hair, a zip of a toilet bag, a squirt, a spray. He lay in the bed transfixed by the sounds.

The door to the bathroom opened. Judy, wrapped in a thin white towel, barely looked at him. I want to get dressed,' she said.

He reached for a towel and got up. 'I'll have a shower.' He passed close to Judy and their skin almost touched. As he stepped into the shower, she said, 'Where did you get the scars?'

'At home.'

'You must have been very careless around the house.'

'Yes,' he answered. 'The trouble was, I didn't look where I was going.'

'That can be dangerous.'

While he was under the water, Judy shouted to him that she would wait in the lobby. He had a coughing fit and spat bile into the basin. It left him weak, but at least the pain in his chest was less severe.

As he dressed, Quinn looked at the clothes Judy had discarded on the bed. They were small and different to what he knew. The sight of them, like the sounds of her moving in the bathroom, made him uneasy. He crunched them out of his mind, hurriedly finished dressing and went downstairs.

'Let's eat,' Judy said.

They went to the Denny's on Revolución. 'This is where the gringos come,' Judy said. 'Mexican food American-style.'

It was too early for the tourists, and the only customers apart from Judy and Quinn were a handful of Mexican men and women dressed in business suits. Quinn ordered coffee, rolls and eggs. Judy had tea and toast. She ate with gusto and ordered more.

'Tijuana is a duty-free zone,' she said between mouthfuls. 'Americans come for the low-price goods. All down this avenue, Revolución, there are shops for them. Then there are bars for kids who aren't old enough to drink in the US. So the town is always full of gringos. The whores are down on Coahuila. It costs twenty bucks, ten if you know how to bargain. You want one?'

'No,' Quinn said, 'I don't.' He had been smiling as Judy talked, pleasantly surprised by her manner, which seemed more relaxed and friendly, until she mentioned whores.

'Anyway,' she said, 'that's *Tijuana la fea*. The gringos love it.'

'Aren't you a gringo?'

'I'm neither one nor the other. The guard last night asked me for my ID because I'm brown, according to his standards. Here they dislike me because I'm a *chola* who's got above herself, who speaks English, who's got US citizenship, passport, clothes, the works. Plus I have trouble with Spanish. They think I'm putting that on, pretending I don't speak it too well, pretending I'm not one of them.'

'You seem to be doing okay to me.'

'Yes, but not to them.'

'Do you think Agustín will arrive today?'

'I hope so. I left a message at the hotel for him to wait for us there. When he gets here maybe we can sort out what we should do.' She called to the waitress for more coffee.

'What do you want to do?' Quinn asked.

'It's not a good idea to go back, not yet anyway.' The waitress arrived with the coffee, filled their cups and departed. 'Perhaps I'm making excuses. The fact is, I don't want to go back.'

'Never?'

'I don't know about that. I want to go on, find my sister.'

'What's your sister's name?'

'Mercedes.' Judy lit a cigarette. 'This had happened,' she said, expelling smoke from pursed lips, 'this . . . thing. I have a feeling about it, that it's leading somewhere.'

'To Mercedes?'

'I suppose so. Finish your coffee, I'm going to show you Tijuana.'

While Judy paid with her credit card, Quinn went outside to wait in the street. A little further down, a man stood beside one of the donkeys painted with black and white stripes. The man tilted his sombrero and said in English, 'Photograph, sir? You can have it taken with the zebra.'

'Where's the centre?' Quinn asked.

'This is the centre. You're in downtown Tijuana.'

'Is there a river?'

'*Depende*,' the man replied.

Quinn frowned. 'What does that mean?'

'It means, depends.'

'What does *that* mean?'

'This is your first time in Mexico?'

'Yes.'

'It's something you are going to hear a lot in my country. You ask, "What time does the bus leave?" The reply is, *"Depende."* Or, "Is there a room in this hotel?" *"Depende."* Does that make sense to you?'

'Not about the river, no.'

'Ah, that's because we are in the desert. Sometimes there's a river, sometimes not.'

'*Depende?*' Quinn asked.

'You are learning, señor. Right now, yes, there's a river, but only a very little one.'

'Thank you,' Quinn said.

'*A sus ordenes, señor,*' the man said, with a bow.

Judy emerged from the restaurant. When she saw the man with the make-believe zebra, she burst into laughter.

'What's the matter?' Quinn asked her.

'Nothing,' she said, and laughed again, so hard she almost doubled over. 'I'm sorry. I was thinking about a friend of mine. The last time I saw him was here.' She took hold of Quinn's arms and said, 'Let's go see the sights.'

They walked the length of Revolución. There were more Americans on the streets now, fat, middle-aged couples, men dressed in canary-yellow pullovers and checked trousers, their cameras resting on paunches, women in nylon track suits pulled tight around their lumpy thighs and hips.

Judy led Quinn down 2nd Street, on to Niños Héroes and Coahuila. It was eleven-thirty in the morning and the prostitutes were gathering on the corners. Lounging around them were men with scars, cigarettes in the corners of their mouths, a studied sleepiness in their eyes, waiting for a chance. They and the girls turned to stare at the strangers as they passed. Quinn felt Judy clutch his arm more tightly, and liked it.

A couple of blocks further on they turned right. At the end of the street was a main road, which they crossed. Up an embankment there was a chain-link fence, about nine or ten feet high. Quinn smelt water.

'This is *la línea*,' Judy said, 'the border fence.'

Quinn pointed to a line of men sitting on a low wall at the top of the embankment. 'What's the show?' he asked.

'They're waiting to cross,' Judy said.

They walked up the embankment, people staring at them.

'A river,' Quinn said. It was more like isolated bits of rotting cardboard. Still, Quinn liked it. He sniffed in its smell.

'The Río Tijuana. Across there,' Judy pointed, 'that's the US. You see the K-Mart sign?' The *K* was red, the only dash of colour in the landscape of sand and shades of light brown. 'That's what these people want, they want to get to the K-Mart. They'll wait till night, then try to cross.'

They sat on the wall. Across the river a squat US Border Patrol vehicle was like a spider waiting for its prey. The sight depressed Quinn. He and Judy gazed across the border in silence.

After a time Quinn said, 'What happened to your sister?'

Judy was rummaging through her shoulder bag. She took out a pack of cigarettes and offered Quinn one. He told her he did not smoke.

'I was born in Guatemala,' Judy said, lighting up. 'Have you ever been there?'

Quinn shook his head.

'My father was a lawyer in Guatemala City, but he had to leave in '65. He had been a supporter of Arbenz, who got thrown out in the '54 coup. We settled in New York. My father got into practice there and encouraged me and my sister to take up law, which we didn't do.' Judy stopped. Her voice had begun to tighten. After a minute she continued, 'Mercedes was radical, like my father. She got involved in all kinds of things. Then she decided to go back to Guatemala, this was about eighteen months ago, to work there. My parents did not want her to go. She wouldn't listen. She never did.'

Judy came to a stop.

'What happened then?'

'Like I said, Mercedes went to Guatemala. She wrote. Occasionally she telephoned. Sometimes she talked about what was going on there, the political situation, that kind of thing, but mostly her letters were about family and personal stuff. She wrote that she met a man in Antigua Guatemala, someone called Salvador, which made me laugh.'

'Why?'

Judy chuckled. 'Mercedes is pretty intolerant of men.' She laughed at some memory. 'She thought men weren't as brave as women, I suppose. Were kind of weak. That was her point of view. Anyway, after a while Mercedes wrote me that some trouble had started in the area she was in.'

'Where was she?'

'In a small town called Patzún, between the capital and Panajachel, where all the tourists go.'

'There was trouble there?'

'There's trouble all over the country. In the highlands, the Indian areas. Tens of thousands of people have been killed by the army. Did you know that?'

'No.'

'Hardly anyone does. But it's true. It goes on, day after day.' She drew deeply on the cigarette before continuing. 'Mercedes wrote me about two gringos who had arrived in Patzún. She said they were from the New Era Mission of Christ, an evangelical organization based in Florida. She implied they threatened her. That was the last I heard, but she wrote my parents a couple more times after that. Then the letters stopped.'

'Did your parents make inquiries?' Quinn asked.

'They contacted the US embassy in Guatemala City. The

embassy said the zone Mercedes was working in was one they advised nationals not to enter. Like it was her own fault. They basically didn't give a shit.'

'Is this New Era Mission the one you and Agustín were talking about in the car on the way to Sabino's house?'

'Yes.'

'I heard Agustín talking about the Mission earlier. Has he some connection with it?'

'He hasn't told me.'

'Why do you think the Mission has something to do with your sister?'

'Last month, we got word from Americas Watch that someone who had gotten out of Guatemala had given a deposition which mentioned Mercedes. I got a copy. This guy implicated the Mission in everything. The Mission, he called it, just the Mission. It was the Mission this, the Mission that, like it was some kind of *power*. The missionaries go around the villagers saying, "God wants you to tell the army who all the communists are." The man who gave the deposition was part of a death squad. He and two other men were taken to Patzún to meet an army officer and a civilian. The civilian was a gringo from the Mission. During the meeting he was told that certain people in Patzún were communists who had to be got rid of. Mercedes was one of them.'

'What happened?'

'This man deserted. He claims he fled to Mexico before the death squad picked up these people. Probably he had some run-in with his bosses or something like that and feared for his life. He's no saint, that's for sure.'

'Do you believe him?'

'I haven't met him or questioned him, so I can't say. But it doesn't matter whether I believe him or not. Mercedes is missing. She was last seen in Patzún. She mentioned in her letters the Mission was in Patzún. For me that's enough to establish a connection. This deserter's deposition adds more weight to that idea.'

They gazed out over the river. More people had gathered to sit on the low wall and stare, like them, across to the

United States. A second Border Patrol vehicle pulled up: both sides were getting ready.

'I have to find Mercedes,' Judy said. 'I can't not know what happened to her. Do you understand me?' She did not look at Quinn when she spoke; she was addressing herself, not him.

After a while Judy asked Quinn, 'So how do you like Tijuana?'

'Better than Los Angeles,' Quinn said.

'You're kidding? The people here think LA is paradise on earth, the big K-Mart in the sky.'

'Tijuana has a centre.'

'What?'

'And a river.'

'Ah, that depends,' she said, smiling at him. 'I'm thirsty. Let's get an orange juice.'

A toothless old woman in a shack across the road squeezed oranges for them. She addressed Quinn in Spanish.

'I'm sorry,' he said. 'I don't understand.'

She spoke in heavily accented English, 'Is this your first time in Tijuana?'

'Yes.'

'Is she your woman?' The woman was looking at Judy, who was out of earshot, with the particular mischievousness the ancient are permitted.

'No.'

'Ah. That's good. Not enough meat.' The woman slapped her rump. 'Do you know where the whores live?'

'No,' Quinn said.

'You don't know where is paradise?'

'No.'

'How old are you?'

'Thirty-four.'

Judy put down her glass. 'Come on,' she said.

The toothless woman said to Quinn, 'You are not so young. But there is still time. Maybe.'

On their way back to the hotel, Quinn and Judy passed the Centro Evangélico, a narrow, one-storey building painted

white with a double-door entrance and long, barred windows
on either side.

Quinn was surprised at his reaction when they found Agustín
at the hotel. Without thinking he embraced him, and then
withdrew quickly, embarrassed.

'Let's get something to eat,' Judy said.

They found a small restaurant where there were no tourists.

'I had to cross the line further down,' Agustín said. 'About
ten miles east of here.'

'No problems?' Quinn asked.

'No. It's not so hard coming this way.'

'What are we going to do?' Judy asked.

'There was no news of it in the *Los Angeles Times* this
morning. Which might mean that they haven't found him
yet.'

'They're bound to have found him by now,' Judy said. 'It
probably just didn't make that edition.'

The word *him* was being spoken tentatively; they were all
aware of it.

'The question is whether there is anything to link us to it,'
Quinn said.

'What could there be?' Agustín asked.

'Witnesses?' Judy suggested.

'Who?'

'Someone might have seen the car waiting outside the
factory.'

'That is not very likely,' Agustín countered.

'Then there's the boy, Hernández.'

'Pascualito is unpredictable. Maybe he will talk, but then
he would get in trouble.'

'You'd be surprised at how many people talk their way into
shit. The lobby of the Public Defender's Office is full of
them.'

Agustín scooped up some rice and beans.

'It's fifty-fifty, I would say. You could chance going back,'
Judy said.

'Perhaps,' Agustín replied. 'You can go back, even if I cannot. No one would connect you with it.'

'I suppose you're right,' Judy said without enthusiasm. She sipped a mineral water and ate some salad.

'What was he doing there?' Quinn asked. 'By himself at that time of night?'

'Who knows,' Agustín said vaguely.

'What about the car?' Quinn asked.

'You mean Hernández's car?' Judy said.

'The one, a big one, parked by the half-finished part of the factory.'

'What make was it?' she said.

'I don't know what make it was. The red one. It had a white top part, the roof and the parts at the sides of the windows.'

'That's Mrs Dorfmann's car,' Agustín said slowly. 'She drives a red and white Chevy.'

'She was there?' Judy asked. She and Agustín exchanged glances.

Agustín remembered the disarrangement of Jank's clothes and understood. He lowered the glass he had in his hand. 'She was there all the time. They went there together.'

They fell silent, each considering where this took them.

'What about him? They wouldn't know who he is,' Judy said, looking at Quinn. And with that one word, *him*, the morning's closeness was blown apart. Another *him*.

Quinn looked away from Judy Mendoza because it hurt him to be reminded of her and the whispers of Monica that breathed within her.

They stayed in the restaurant until the last light of the day, then moved to a bar on Revolución. On their way they passed the border fence. A helicopter with a searchlight circled above the men and boys clinging to the barrier. Waiting to cross a border, waiting to cross. At first Quinn thought the refugees were merely desperate; then he grasped that, for all their desperation, they had at least taken a decision. They were going to cross. He admired that. They were looking for something better: the fence and the helicopter with the searchlight stood in their way, but they were still going to cross. Borders, barriers, fences, walls. Quinn was going to have to cross. If he was going to find something better.

Judy disappeared for half an hour and when she returned she announced to Quinn that he now had a separate room.

That night Judy slept with Agustín, thinking, Why not? He's good-looking, and in the morning it will be over and forgotten.

When Quinn saw they would sleep together, he drank faster so as to obliterate the awkwardness that had come over the company, each pretending that the thing that had been settled between the man and the woman had not been settled. He drank to change his feelings, which, if he had had the honesty and courage to talk to himself, he would have conceded were feelings of sadness and regret; these he altered so that he could pretend he did not care.

In the morning, as Judy had foreseen, it was as if it had never been. If it should pass that they were in each other's company for any length of time, perhaps she and Agustín would sleep together again, saying almost nothing to each other and exchanging no words that expressed pleasure, affection, consideration or thanks. That was how it was with Judy, who knew about the coming and going of love.

It was not that way with Agustín.

FOURTEEN

A few desultory changes apart, neither Quinn nor Agustín spoke to the other the following day; and, apart from a visit to the money-changing office, Judy stayed in her room. The sense of relief they had experienced after getting out of Los Angeles and across the border had melted; reality was falling hard on them and the only shelter was in their own silence. It was not until the night came in that they found each other again, and, almost wordlessly, made their way to a restaurant. Agustín had with him a copy of the *Los Angeles Times*. It was a busy news day and the murder was reported, below, a one-column photograph captioned 'Andrew V. Jank, slain missionary', in four paragraphs on page three: the apparent motive was robbery and there were no witnesses.

'Maybe he was there alone, after all,' Quinn ventured.

'We don't know if it's true,' Judy said quickly. 'The police may be trying to trick us back.' She waited impatiently for the two men to signal their agreement: she wanted there to be no choice, for her there had to be no alternative. She was irritated by the report, by the ambiguity it had introduced to their situation. She would have challenged the men with direct looks, but could not. She never knew how to take Quinn, and she had been avoiding Agustín, who she sensed wanted to talk about the night before. She did not want that. All she wanted was his help to find Mercedes. So far he had refused to say anything about the future, which angered and frustrated Judy. She began to suspect he was like Quinn, a man simply letting things happen, biding his time until the moment when he could at last give up.

'It doesn't make any difference,' Agustín said flatly, and inside Judy eased. 'It's time for us to move.'

'When?' Judy asked quickly.

'Tomorrow.'

She waited for him to go on. Her hopes had risen, she thought that perhaps she had got him wrong.

'We should try and get started early,' Judy said when it was clear Agustín had nothing more to add. She was drinking tequila neat and had already had three glasses. She swallowed the remains of the fourth and got to her feet. 'I need some sleep.' There was a chill in her voice.

When they were alone, Quinn waited to see if Agustín would talk to him. Agustín gulped down the last of his drink and stood up. 'I have to try to talk to Dulio,' he said.

'Who?'

'A friend. He may be in danger.'

'Wait,' Quinn said. 'Stay and talk.'

'I have to warn Dulio,' Agustín said and he walked out of the restaurant.

Had he had the money, Quinn would have stayed in the restaurant and got drunk. Instead, he walked the streets. On Revolución he passed the Denny's, where he and Judy had had breakfast the day before. It was closed now and dimly lit. Quinn went to the plate-glass door, peaked his hand over his eyes and peered inside. He looked at the deserted seats and cleared tables, and found he was looking at himself and Judy. He could hear them talking, their voices coming to him above a rising level of kitchen noises. A waitress appeared at their table, then another; customers started to arrive. The background noise was getting higher and only with difficulty could he make out what he and Judy were saying to each other. He saw himself say something; he saw Judy laugh. He was encouraged and said more things that made her laugh. Her hand was on the table, fiddling with a box of matches. He put his hand over hers. He saw Judy lower her head slightly; under the table she crossed her legs, began tapping her foot. Then Agustín appeared before them.

Quinn jerked back from the window and hurried away.

Anger filled him up. He cursed out loud. He tried to summon up Monica, whispering her name over and over. No image of her would appear. He went on blindly, not aware of where he was going. A couple of blocks further on he stumbled into a group of American teenagers about to enter a bar. A fair-haired boy who was clowning for his friends flipped over to do a handstand and almost knocked Quinn over. The boy jumped back to his feet. 'You all right?' he said. He had collected a wide, silly smile from his night out and was slightly drunk.

'Yes,' Quinn said.

'I'm really sorry. I always just get kind of crazy down here, you know? That's Tee-u-wana, isn't it? Crazy place.'

Quinn, still unsettled by what he had seen in the window, said breathlessly, 'Listen, could you lend me some money?'

The boy's expression changed abruptly.

'Just a couple of dollars?' Quinn said; he heard some of the boy's companions mutter, 'Jeez.'

Quinn cleared his throat to try to muster whatever dignity was possible in such a situation. 'Please,' he said.

The boy regarded Quinn contemptuously for a moment. He said, 'Get lost,' and turned away.

Quinn walked on quickly, aware of what the teenagers were saying to each other. How have I come to this? He thought. You bastard, you stupid bastard. Coughing, and welcoming the pain in his chest as a distraction, he made his way again to the border fence to watch the nightly ritual. The helicopter with the searchlight clattered in the still air above. I've got to cross, Quinn said to himself.

When he woke in the morning, he could not remember how he had got back to the hotel.

It was ten o'clock before they left Tijuana on the road south. At Ensenada they took Federal Highway One, thinking to drive non-stop to La Paz at the foot of the peninsula. Quinn was in the back seat, shut out of what conversation there was. He had a heavy heart and he concentrated on the desert scenery and imagined that he was wandering away into the hazy distance, away from people.

The fantasy made no sense, he knew. When he and Judy and Agustín had discussed what they should do, he had said he would go with them. 'I have no option,' he had told them. They did not ask what he meant, for of the three he was the one who at least appeared to have an option: no one knew who Quinn was; he was a shadow in a continent. When it came to the moment of choosing – between staying alone and being part of something, part of someone's life again – Quinn had only one choice to make. In Dorfmann Furnishings, witness to murder, he had made it for Agustín and Judy. He stared harder at the monotonous and silent desert. He had had his opportunity to walk away, and had not taken it. Somewhere within him, resentment against Judy and Agustín sparked, for they had shown no appreciation of what he had done: the thought was cynical and selfish, he realized. He was doing this for himself.

They stopped in Rosario for soft drinks and for Judy to stretch her legs. She strolled down the street, under the sagging, untidy telephone wires, attracting the attention of men who lounged against walls or leaned in the doorways of shops and bars.

'Did you talk to Dulio last night?' Quinn asked Agustín.

'No. I have to try again, to warn him.'

'What about Sabino?'

'Dulio will know how to take care of him.'

They were both watching Judy. She was walking towards them, the stares of the men clinging to her. She had a disdainful look on her face.

'I hate towns like this,' she said when she came up. 'I hate those half-finished boxes of concrete the people live in and the way the heat makes everything heavy.'

The road was good, there was little traffic. Judy drove fast and with confidence.

'Where is it we are going again?' Quinn asked.

'La Paz. We can get a ferry to Mazatlán on the mainland from there,' Agustín said.

'Why are we going that way?'

'It is not the most direct way. If anyone is coming after us, they would not think we would go to La Paz.'

'How long before we get there?'

Agustín checked his watch. It was ten past two. 'Probably more or less at eight tomorrow morning.'

'If there was a witness,' Quinn said, 'they might have seen this car.'

'Could be,' Judy said.

'So we should dump it.'

'We will when we get to La Paz. From there we can take the ferry to the mainland and disappear.'

'Maybe we should dump the car now.'

'And do what?' Judy said. Her voice carried some irritation. 'Look where we are.'

They had passed through mountains and were now in a plain where the cactuses were so numerous they could have been sowed by men for harvest. A hunting buzzard hung in the thermals, its head twisting every few moments as it scanned the earth for prey. A crushed Coke can lay beside a cluster of little wooden crosses where the road took an unexpected bend.

'The important thing is to get as far from where it happened as fast as it is possible,' Agustín said.

Night fell early and as it fell the buzzards deserted the sky. The clouds turned black, and the cactuses became rows of frozen spectators who emerged at dusk to watch the moving people of the real world.

Judy began to talk about Mercedes, about where they would start to look for her. They would go to Antigua Guatemala and find Mercede's lover, Salvador. He must know something. 'I know she's alive,' Judy said.

Neither Agustín nor Quinn said anything. Quinn was sure Mercedes was dead. A woman he had never met, whose story, apart from some small details, he did not know, and he was sure she was dead. Agustín glanced at him over his shoulder and Quinn knew he was thinking the same.

'What would you do?' Judy asked, addressing neither of them directly, sensing what they were thinking.

'I would look for her,' Quinn replied. He felt sorry for her; her hardness and disdain were so brittle. 'How did your parents take it?' he asked.

'My father took it worse than my mother.' She was silent for a time, then said in a vague way, 'Before it happened, I always thought I was my father's favourite.'

She paused again, then continued, this time with greater force in her voice. 'My mother has taken it better. Maybe because of her family. They're from Ferrara in Italy. During the war they hid people, like who were on the run from the authorities. My mother spent the last three months of the war in prison in Ferrara after they found someone in the house. You know, my mother says that if she had that time to live over, she would do the exact same thing. The family had to help this man, didn't matter what. I used to hear my mother always saying, "You have to do the right thing."

'When I was a child, that kind of talk was old-fashioned – embarrassing – and I never took any notice. Mercedes did. Maybe because of her age, she's eleven years older than me. She was always involved in something. Protesting the Vietnam War, always out there on the street.'

'Why did she go to Guatemala?' Quinn asked.

'She said that there was nothing for her to do in the States any more.'

After a time Quinn asked, 'Who was this man you mentioned?'

'Salvador?'

'*Salvador? Nada más?*' Agustín looked at her.

'*No sé su apellido ni su dirección, sólo que vive en Antigua.*'

'What?' Quinn said, irritated by their lunge into Spanish. He had never been in a country where the people did not speak English, and he had not appreciated how belittling the failure to understand could be.

'I don't know anything else about him,' Judy said. 'Just his first name, Salvador, and that Mercedes met him in a hotel in Antigua.'

*

Dusk had passed into black night and stars stood out in the sky. The talking faded away.

Judy had been brought up a Catholic. She was used to the idea that her life, and every moment in it, was being watched. The idea had never disturbed her, for the God she had grown up with had been tolerant and forgiving. When she stopped believing in God, the notion that she was under a kind of benign scrutiny persisted. Alone, at work, at home, she would from time to time say something out loud, as if to excuse an unworthy thought or deed. In time she realized that Mercedes was the onlooker. The idea was not disturbing: Mercedes was as tolerant as God had been – intimidating, the way the powerful always are, but seeking to direct rather than reproach her. Mercedes was one of those people against whom one instinctively measures one's own life and worth, though she never set herself up for that.

Judy's thoughts switched to the two men in the car: the man behind her, coming apart, who had come apart once before and whose stitched scars could not stop him coming apart again. Both men were running not from something, but into something they hoped would swallow them. She could not stop being angry, at them, at herself for being with them and for not being able to go on without them.

Oh, Mercedes, Mercedes. How could I have missed you? You were my sister and still I missed you.

She thought of her own life. How could she record it? If she were to fall in love with one of these two men and go through the exchange of lives in bits and pieces, what would she have to say? A failed academic career, a job that any broken-down cop could do. A series of lovers, none of whom she ever really cared for. A doctor, she remembered from when she was sixteen: he had said, when she resisted, 'Why not?' And so it had gone on. A college teacher, a lawyer, another teacher, a self-obsessed sculptor, a tennis instructor: all of them so bland she asked herself how she could have been so fickle. And yet these were her *serious* relationships. She wanted to hit herself for having been so stupid.

Then another lawyer: Mike. What was there to say about

the year they had lived together? Why had Mercedes not said something to straighten her out? Judy had missed her sister, overlooked the value in her. They had lived together under the roof of their parents' house and somehow Judy had missed the opportunity Mercedes carried within her.

Mercedes, when she was living in New York, had invited Judy to a New Year's party when Judy was visiting her parents. When was that? Eight, seven years ago? Judy, always used to the attention of men, got attention, but saw Mercedes was getting something else: Mercedes standing in a group of men and women, laughing, the crinkle of skin gathering around her blue eyes. The other women at the party did not like Judy and she knew why: pretty, flighty, not serious; they had her figured. And they paid attention to Mercedes, the men as well as the women. They listened to her easy way. Mercedes had a frankness that bordered on the wondrous and still she was taken seriously. A woman in a tight black dress kept hanging around Mercedes and, when Judy finally got her sister alone, she said, 'That woman, is she a dyke?' Mercedes, slightly drunk, looked at her very seriously, put a hand on Judy's cheek and spluttered into raucous laughter. Later in the night Judy saw her sister with her arms around the woman. A man offered Judy a lift home and for the first time in her life when she asked herself 'Why not?', she could think of several reasons, or so it seemed. She said no, firmly, rather impolitely, and the man had enough grace not to pursue it. Judy, standing alone at the dying party, watching her sister's slow dance, tried to isolate the reasons behind her 'Why not?' and found there was only one: Mercedes.

In the car panic suddenly loomed up on Judy. Oh Mercedes, help me. I don't know what to do. She swallowed and concentrated on the road ahead.

She recalled the last letter Mercedes had sent. It was to their parents, and Judy felt jealousy pinch at her. After Mercedes's disappearance, after the approaches to the embassy and the State Department, her mother decided it was time to talk to the media. A television crew came to the house and interviewed her father and mother. Judy had never seen her father so upset and incapacitated. It was then she realized he had become old. Judy kept in the background, resenting the presence of strangers in their house, indignant at the imperious way they had shifted the furniture and drawn curtains and rearranged lamps. The interviewer asked about Mercedes's history of 'political activism', and her father, haltingly, talked about the daughter he loved. He showed photographs of Mercedes on demonstrations and sit-ins, of the house she and her friends squatted and turned into a refuge for battered women, of Mercedes with her cousins during a demonstration in Turin. In all the photographs Mercedes was smiling her gorgeous smile. Then the interviewer asked if Mercedes had been a communist. Her father could say nothing more, he was choking with emotion. Her mother leaned forward and explained that Mercedes had always been concerned about the lives and conditions of poor people, people who were denied their human rights, that she had been taught to stick up for people who could not stick up for themselves.

The interviewer cut it there and, without taking any notice of her father's condition, as if the pain could be turned off with the cameras, asked him to read out parts of Mercedes's last letter. Her mother had put her hand on her father's shoulder – the gesture conveyed so many things Judy recognized as the secrets of their family and from which strangers were excluded, and it hurt her to know that it had been made for her father, the one who was strong. Without a word her mother rose to get the letter. Silently, she handed it to her father, who wiped his eyes and put on his reading glasses.

The camerawoman focused, the sound man checked the levels. 'Dr Mendoza,' the interviewer said in his television voice, 'in your daughter's last letter before her disappearance she had a premonition that something was wrong.'

Judy found she was clenching her fists: how dare this clown put it like that, how dare he? Her father, the elegant *criollo*, took off his glasses and pretended to wipe them clean. His eyes were red-rimmed and moist and he tried to rub them without calling attention to what he was doing. He cleared his throat and, with fingers trembling, replaced his glasses. He read so slowly and in such a way that Judy, who had dropped her head and shut her eyes not to see her father's pain, was easily persuaded that Mercedes was in the same room, standing behind him with her hand on his shoulder, repeating the words with him. His voice faltered, became croaks; the words were by turns high-pitched and throaty. When he could go on no more, her mother took the letter and, in a resolute voice, finished reading while her husband sobbed. That afternoon, while her father slept, Judy kissed her mother goodbye, returned to San Francisco and gave up her job.

Agustín was asleep, but the man in the back was not. Judy knew he was looking at her.

'I like being driven,' he said to her gently. 'Especially at night.'

It was quiet. They had not passed a car for an hour. The car's headlights swept the road ahead and the tarmac rushed at them. Some tumbleweed blew across the road.

'Are you all right?' Quinn asked her. 'Do you want me to drive?'

'It's okay,' Judy replied. 'I was thinking about my sister.'

Quinn said nothing.

'Have you ever been in this kind of trouble before?' Judy said. 'Do you mind me asking?' She had made her voice soft in response to Quinn's. He was thinking that it was the first time she had asked him anything about himself. He was gratified, but he wished it had not been on this subject. Then, he thought, what else could it have been on? There was nothing he could discuss with her that was lighter, happier.

'I've had some trouble,' he said.

'Serious?'

'I suppose so.'

'How did you handle it?'

Quinn thought a while before saying, 'You have to live

through your time of trouble. It's all you can do.'

'I suppose you do.'

Judy asked nothing else, and Quinn regretted that he had been unable to say anything to keep her interest. Agustín straightened in his seat, mumbled, opened his eyes and looked into the oncoming tarmac. Then he closed them again and settled back into the seat without waking up.

'Are you tired, Judy?' Quinn asked.

'I should be,' she said softly.

'What time is it?'

'Three-twenty. Maybe another five or six hours to go before La Paz.'

'If you find Mercedes, what will you do then?'

'I don't know. Right now I don't seem able to plan beyond that.'

'Is this a main road we're on?' he asked.

'Yes,' she said.

'If someone was after us, would they take this road?'

'It's the only road.'

Quinn said nothing.

'Does that concern you?' Judy asked after a while.

'Yes.'

'Anything else?'

'You've been paying for everything with credit cards and cheques.'

'What are we supposed to pay with? You haven't got any money, neither has he. It'll take a while for them to find out where the bills are coming in from. As long as we make good time, we can keep a step ahead of them. That's if anyone is after us. We don't know that they are. Don't worry.'

'I'm not worried,' Quinn said. He looked out into the night and added: 'This is not going to last long.'

'What do you mean?' Judy asked querulously, the softness in her voice gone.

'These things never do.'

He was sleeping in cars now. The third night he spent in the Pinto, Pascualito dreamt he was back on the bus that had taken him out to Santa Ana to see Michael. Although it was daytime and the sun was shining, everything in the dream was dark, and the people were looking at him strangely. When he got on the bus, the driver held the coins in his open palm for a long time, poking them with the index finger of his free hand. 'It's good money,' Pascualito told him. He said it in a way that was politer than he wanted to be, for the driver was big and was looking at him to let him know he could handle himself. 'It's good money,' he repeated, adjusting his tone further. The driver said slowly, 'It never is. It's just that people like you always think it is.' The man frightened him and Pascualito did not dare move. After an age, Pascualito said, 'Well, is it good money? Can I take my seat?' 'Go ahead,' the driver said as if he had not cared all along. The bus moved off and Pascualito started down the aisle. The passengers were gazing at him as if they knew something about him. Pascualito stared from face to face and saw suspicion and hostility. He was too intimidated to get angry. He went to sit beside an elderly, inoffensive-looking man, but the man shuffled over in the seat to stop him. Pascualito spotted another empty seat and made for it, but the same thing happened. Everyone was watching and it was very embarrassing. He started to move quicker, practically dashing to the empty seats, but the passengers kept leaping into the space before him. At the end of the bus he saw a huge mirror, a driving mirror, with the eyes of the bus driver as big as footballs watching him, studying his progress, waiting for him to give up. The eyes wished him harm. He turned around and saw that the bus had somehow reversed itself, that what had been the back was the front and the front the back. The driver was driving the bus from the back and was looking down the aisle. They were going the way they had come. 'Hey,' Pascualito said. 'This isn't what I want. I'm going to Santa Ana.' 'There's a seat,' the driver said with an unkind smirk. He pointed and as he did so the passengers raised their fingers in unison in the direction of an empty seat. Relief, then excitement welled up in Pascualito as he slumped into the seat, for there was a young woman beside him. She wore dark glasses and had a good body. She turned to him and smiled. He shifted closer. The woman leaned into him and pulled up the sunglasses.

Her eyes were mad. He saw now the face was old, it was lined, fallen and hard. 'You've joined me at last,' the woman said, taking his hand in her lap and stroking it. 'We can ride the buses together now.' The *cubana* leaned over and kissed him. Her skin was cold and hard. Pascualito started to scream.

Pascualito stumbled out of the Pinto and retched into the gutter. Exhausted and breathless, he was unable to straighten for some minutes. His head was dizzy and treacherous. At last he pulled himself together and started to walk. His limbs and joints were stiff.

The sun had not come over the second horizon of the Los Angeles skyline, and it was cold. He pulled his jacket around him and blew into his hands. He crossed the waste ground and passed the crumbling buildings and burnt-out cars, and found a corner that hosted a small rectangle of weak sunlight. He stood in it and waited for the rising sun to heal him. A wino in rags staggered past; the sight and the smell alarmed Pascualito.

The insect in his brain had been busy all night, forcing Pascualito to shift in his sleep every few minutes to find a position that would make it harder for the insect to continue its work, but it was asleep now. Pascualito shut his eyes in thanks. He felt in his pocket for the bottle of Cross Tops he had bought after he had sold the .22 target pistol. He shook out two tablets and swallowed them, breathing in deeply as he did so. He wiped his leaking nose. The sun was warmer now. He could think.

So many people were after him: Michael because he had shot the dog and Olds and owed him money, and maybe also because of what he had done to Sonia; Wilson's cousins because he had not returned the car and owed them money; Agustín because of Sabino, and that meant Dulio as well; and probably the police because of what had happened at the Dorfmann factory. Pascualito had read that a man had been murdered during a robbery at the factory, and had thought of escaping to Tijuana. Then he looked closer and saw that the dead man had been shot *and* stabbed. Pascualito grasped it at once. Agustín had gone in there looking for Sabino and for his own reasons had killed the white man, Pascualito looked at the man's picture in the newspaper and at the name beneath it. They meant nothing to him. Pascualito was confused. In movies outlaws always knew if they were wanted and would leave town if they could; or, if they were in the clear, they would stay until the next piece of work. Pascualito was annoyed because he did not know whether he was a suspect or not; he did not know what to do. He unscrewed the bottle and took two more pills: he could feel the blood speed, jolting through him. He stood in the sun and tried to think things through.

He did not notice a man approaching from behind until it was too late. He felt both arms locked behind him in a powerful grip and the shock thumped once powerfully at his heart, merging into a blow he felt to the back of his neck, as if two powerful waves had broken over him at the same time.

He did not lose consciousness, although he was close to it and his knees had given way. Another man approached him from the front.

'What are you doing to me?' Pascualito mumbled.

'Relax,' Nick Zenga said. 'We'd like a little talk with you. Rex, put him in the pick-up.'

Zenga had a pen between his teeth and was clutching several scraps of paper. On the fourth ring Victor Jank answered. Zenga pushed the receiver up with his shoulder and got the pen out of his mouth.

'It's Nick.'

'Yes, Nick?'

'Well, our friends in the Department just now came through. It looks like the people we want are down there in Tijuana.'

'Is that so?'

218

'I think we should take a trip to Mexico ourselves to sort it out.'

'As you see fit, Nick. I'm leaving it to your discretion. Anything else?'

'We located Señor Hernández this morning and talked with him.'

'Does he know anything?'

'No. He acted suspicious when we picked him up and he can't remember where he was Saturday night, but he's drug-addicted, so that's no surprise. There's nothing to tie him to Andrew.'

'Get rid of him, then.'

'Well,' Zenga said slowly, 'I was thinking he might come in useful.'

'How?'

'He hates Agustín.'

'Uh-huh?'

'I was thinking,' Zenga went on, 'maybe we should take him with us to Mexico. You know, if anything is going to happen down there, involving *anything* that is, it might be useful to have someone like Señor Hernández. He's unstable, that's for sure, but directable, if you understand me.' There was silence on the other end of the line. Zenga continued, 'Hernández is like – how would you say – a natural suspect. If anything does happen, well, Rex and me, we could leave with our hands clean, so to speak.'

'Sounds like a good idea, Nick. Will he go?'

'I would say so. Just one problem. Rex hates his guts.'

'Rex knows how to keep his feelings under control when the situation demands it.'

'How's Maritza?'

'The doctors say she needs rest. She's still sedated.'

'You think she'll get over it?'

Jank paused before replying. He said, 'You know, I wonder if someone like Maritza – she's very highly strung – will survive this. But we can talk about that later.'

Zenga said nothing.

'The funeral's tomorrow,' Jank said.

'I'm going to miss it. I'm real sorry.'
'Can't be helped. Call me from Tijuana, or wherever.'
'This is a sick world,' Zenga said.
'God bless you, Nick.'

FIFTEEN

They arrived in La Paz later than they had expected. It was just before midday, and the windows, front and back, were rolled down, so that the car appeared to share its occupants' exhaustion. Judy stopped on Obregón opposite La Perla Hotel and cut the engine. She felt as though she were dreaming, and in a way she was for she should have been asleep after so long on the road. The sun was scorching white, the brightness searing; colour had gone from the sky and sea and all their surroundings. Sounds were wrong: shopkeepers were locking up, but the jangle of keys and rattle of the shutters were muffled for Judy, or came to her like echoes, as did the hushes of the low waves and the creaking squawks of a gull. A pelican skimmed a wave and Judy fancied she heard the noise of the water parted by the beak. A boy on a shrieking motor scooter jumped a red light. There was no other traffic.

Quinn got out to stretch his legs. He looked at the lamp-posts on the pier, three on either side. A pelican stood ornamentally on each. There was a light breeze, but not enough to dissipate the sun and its heat. Sweat stains under his arms reached almost to his waist.

'Let's go,' Judy said. Quinn climbed back into the car.

They drove a few hundred yards and parked opposite a restaurant on the seafront. They were the only customers and took a table by a window that looked back on the pier. Judy ordered three beers.

'What now?' Quinn asked.

'We'll go to the ferry office and get tickets to the mainland,' Judy said.

The waiter returned and set out the glasses, napkins and bottles, poured, then retreated to join a friend at the bar.

'There are three ways to get to the mainland,' Judy began. 'There's the airport, there's the ferry from here, then there's Cabo San Lucas down the coast a little more, where we could also take the ferry.'

'I don't like the idea of flying,' Quinn said. 'Airports are always tight. If we're getting the ferry, we might as well get it from here and save time. When does the ferry leave?'

'We'll have to ask,' Judy said.

'It's time to ditch the car,' Quinn said. 'And the credit cards.'

'What are we going to do for money?' Judy asked.

'Sell the car.'

'Why not?'

'Can we do it quick?'

'Better if I do it,' Agustín said. 'I can find someone who will keep it off the streets for a while.'

They were thirsty and drank quickly.

'What's the word for beer?' Quinn asked.

'*Cerveza*,' Judy said impatiently.

'Sir-what?'

'*Cerveza*,' she repeated harshly.

Quinn lifted his glass and sloshed the remaining beer around. He held up three fingers and said, 'Three sirvies.' He was grinning in a very stupid way, even he knew that, the supplicant tourist. The waiter's friend chuckled unpleasantly. The waiter deposited three more beers. Quinn thanked him.

'Are you always so polite?' Judy said; it was not intended as a compliment.

'Let's eat,' Agustín said.

They left Quinn with Judy's suitcase on the beach by the pier. Agustín told Judy to drive around town.

'What are we looking for?' she asked.

'I'll know when I see it.'

At a garage he told her to slow down as he scanned the

forecourt. He looked carefully over the two men working there, then told her to drive on. Judy drove for more than half an hour before Agustín said he thought he had found a promising place and told her to pull over.

'Go back to Quinn,' he said. 'I'll meet you in the bar of La Perla after I sell the car. I might take some time. Have you got enough cash for the ferry tickets?'

'I've got about twenty dollars and a few thousand pesos.'

'If the tickets cost more, reserve for tomorrow three places. You can pay the deposit today.'

'Okay.'

'How much is the car worth?' he asked.

'Three, four thousand dollars, I guess.'

'We are not going to get so much, but I will do what I can,' Agustín said. 'Give me the keys.'

As Judy handed them over, their fingers touched.

'Are you afraid?' Agustín asked her.

'Of you?'

'I meant, are you afraid with the situation?'

'Sometimes,' she said. 'What about you?'

'No,' he said.

Judy pursed her lips and stared straight ahead. 'You know, I don't regret what happened.'

'That's because you think what happened is the start of something that will take you to your sister.'

'Yes,' she said defensively.

'What I did was hopeless,' he said. 'I did it . . . I can't even say why I did it.'

'You've had some connection with the Mission. You know about them. That's why you did it.'

'I had a motive,' he said, 'but that's not what I mean.'

'What do you mean?'

He thought for a moment. 'Dulio told me that the act of one person, alone, changes nothing, satisfies no one, only deludes you into thinking you *can* do something.'

Confusion rose in Judy. 'What are you saying?'

'I've already said it. What I did was hopeless. And looking for Mercedes, that's just as hopeless.'

She slapped him across the face. Before she could get out of the car, he had reached across and taken hold of the handle. She was crying. When he tried to hold her, she fought him off with elbows and small fists.

'Mercedes is dead,' he said. Judy screamed, and Agustín saw passers-by turning their heads to the car. He said quickly, 'Don't you see? Don't you see what Mercedes was doing when she went back to Guatemala? She wasn't acting alone any more. She would tell you what you are doing has no meaning.' Judy screamed, louder than before. Agustín released her and said, 'I'm sorry, I'm sorry.'

Judy composed herself as best she could. She wiped her eyes and gave her voice time to steady itself.

'You and Quinn, you're both pitiful. You have already given up. Maybe you think you've got reasons, but to me it's pathetic. I'm going to find my sister.'

She brushed his hand from her arm and got out of the car.

Judy took a taxi to the pier. She found Quinn sitting in the shade with his back to the wall. Two young girls, seventeen or eighteen, Judy guessed, were sitting next to him, one on either side.

'You're a fast worker, Quinn,' Judy said.

'No,' Quinn replied evenly. 'In fact, I'm very slow.'

Each girl looked at Judy with the expression of a woman at a party who had been disturbed by the arrival of the wife of the man she had assumed to be unattached. They got to their feet and said goodbye in English to Quinn, who stood up to shake hands with them. The girls giggled and went off.

'You look pleased with yourself,' Judy said.

'I enjoyed the company.'

'Don't take it as a compliment that young girls come round you. It's the white skin and blue eyes, nothing else. You see fat, ugly men down here in Mexico with beautiful young girls. It's because they're white, and here white equals money, options – the things they don't have.'

'Oh. I thought I was something special.'

She regarded him severely. 'You have everything it takes to

be a big success in Mexico, Quinn. Maybe you should stay.'

Quinn dusted sand from his jeans. The sun had reddened his face, the scars were white and delicate.

'No,' he said. 'I'm not part of this world.'

His refusal to acknowledge her sarcasm made her feel a little guilty. 'Let's dump the suitcase in La Perla and get the ferry tickets,' Judy said, regretting what she had said to him and the way she had said it.

'Those girls thought I was your wife,' she chuckled as they walked along.

'That explains it, then.'

'What?'

'Why they were sorry for me.'

She had to ask several times before they found the office. It was on Cinco de Mayo, near the garage Agustín had surveyed earlier when looking for likely buyers for the car.

'There's a big queue,' Quinn said as they approached.

'A what?'

'A queue.'

Judy looked blank.

'A queue of people, waiting to buy tickets.'

'We call that a *line*,' Judy said.

'Well,' Quinn said, 'it's big.'

Behind them a woman with an infant pressed to her breast complained to Judy about the slowness of the clerks. When one of the clerks abandoned his window and disappeared into the office behind the counter, it provoked a chorus of grumbling, as if the volume on a radio or television had suddenly been turned up.

'What's going on?' Quinn asked.

'The clerk's gone for dinner.'

'Do you mind if I stand over there, out of the sun?' Quinn said.

'Always so polite. Go ahead.'

The woman with the infant started talking to Judy. After a while she indicated Quinn, who was leaning against the wall and appeared half asleep.

'How did your husband get those terrible scars?' she asked Judy.

'A road accident,' Judy said.

'Poor thing.' The woman put her hand consolingly on Judy's arm. 'But he's made a good recovery?'

'Not completely,' Judy replied, with a glance at Quinn. She remembered him ordering the 'sirvies' in the restaurant and laughed inwardly. 'He's gone a little simple,' she confided to the woman.

'No?' the woman said, shocked; 'He looks quite handsome,' she added, with a covert peep at Quinn.

'It's very sad,' Judy said; then, in English, she said to Quinn, 'Isn't that so?'

Quinn looked over. Judy smiled to encourage a smile from him. He returned it with a confused look.

'See?' Judy said.

'Poor thing,' the woman said, putting a hand to her mouth.

It was almost four by the time Judy got to the cashier's window, too late for that day's sailing. She paid a deposit on three tickets to Mazatlán for the following afternoon.

'Let's get a drink,' she said to Quinn, putting the papers into her purse.

They did not go to La Perla. Judy did not want to see Agustín yet. She replied to her question of the night in Tijuana. The answer to the 'Why not?' was now obvious. She had been in similar situations before and the way she dealt with it was always to pretend that nothing had happened: nothing in her words, nor even in the inflexions of her voice, nothing in her manner would indicate that there had ever been anything between them. They were man and woman, not boyfriend and girlfriend. If the man was prepared to be reasonable, behave correctly, then she would. If he tried to get closer, start conversations she did not want to be part of, she would put up barriers between them. It was easier to do, in Judy's experience, with men who fell in love easily; harder when it was someone like Agustín. It was appropriate, when Judy thought it over, that it had happened in Tijuana, a transient town, where everything is on the surface: so the joining of Agustín and Judy had been just as ephemeral.

'How do you like La Paz?' Judy asked.

They were sitting in a quiet restaurant on Obregón, one of the town's more expensive places, overlooking the sea. There was no glass in the windows and a cool breeze periodically came in and touched the people.

'I liked Tijuana better,' Quinn said.

'I forgot. Because of the river,' Judy said, remembering.

'No.' Quinn looked directly at her. 'I liked the morning we spent together.'

He did not take his eyes from her and it was she who had to break off by turning away.

'How close are you to Agustín?' she asked after some moments.

'I hardly know him,' Quinn said, 'but I sense something about him. I think that once we had a similar experience.'

'What?'

'I think we got put back together after something,' he said.

'You've been put back together?'

'It's a manner of speaking.'

'Are you married, Quinn?'

The question kicked at his heart. He nodded.

'Where is she?'

He did not know what to say; eventually, 'She lives in another country.'

They ordered seafood and more drinks and watched the night come in from the mist on the sea. The restaurant filled up with affluent-looking tourists and locals. Teenage girls and boys promenaded on the seafront, gathered under the palm trees, cruised in cars and jeeps. Quinn watched two fireflies – flashing silver, lightning blue, gold and amber – make loops around the light of a lamp-post on the pier, chasing, but never catching each other. He and Judy did not talk, and from time to time when Quinn broke away from the fireflies' figures and patterns, he saw that she was watching him. They were both slightly drunk.

She put her hand up and touched the bruise Pascualito had given him.

'Is it okay?' she asked gently.

'Yes,' Quinn said, looking at her.

She took her hand away. 'Not the first knock you've taken,' she said. 'Did you like the *ceviche*, the seafood?'

'It was fine.'

He had eaten delicately, chewing every morsel before swallowing, and did not finish until well after Judy had pushed her plate away. Judy had noticed in Tijuana how little he ate. The last scraps were an obstacle for him and his chewing slowed still more. At last he finished and stretched luxuriously in his chair.

They talked about small things. She told Quinn about Mike and his friends Peter and Sue. Quinn thought the story was funny, but did not want Judy to see him laughing at Mike's expense: his interest in her, and the conventions of courtship, in Quinn's imperfect understanding of them, forbade it.

'He was such a jerk,' she said, wiping tears of laughter from her eyes. 'Tell me a story,' she demanded. She felt happy with him and did not want it to stop. He started to tell her a story, slowly, humorously, in which he featured as the last character to catch on to what was happening. She laughed often in the telling of it. She asked herself why she was softening towards him. Of the two men, she had thought Agustín was the one in motion, who could do things. Now she was not so sure.

Then Judy realized that she was doing with Quinn what she always did with men. In another hour she would be asking herself 'Why not?' and would be unable to think of any reason. Quinn was talking, smiling, looking at her, but she heard him as though he were on the other end of a bad telephone line. She took hold of herself.

She interrupted Quinn sharply. 'I better go to La Perla and see if Agustín's back. We're going to need rooms there tonight.'

Quinn showed no signs of hurt at Judy's tone. He hurried to finish his drink, but she put a hand on his arm.

'Wait for me here,' Judy said, suddenly feeling guilty for the way she was behaving. 'I want to come back.' Her voice was serious.

'I'll be here,' Quinn said.

She stood behind him and put a hand on his shoulder. He brought up his hand and touched her fingers, then she was gone.

Quinn ordered a drink and watched the fireflies. He thought about Agustín and felt uneasy. He downed a whisky and ordered another, then turned back to the fireflies.

'What time is it?'

Someone was talking to him in English.

'Excuse me?'

A Mexican, about forty years old, wearing an open-necked white shirt, leaned over his table to Quinn.

'What time have you got?'

'Sorry. I don't have a watch.'

The man called to a waiter and spoke in Spanish, then said to Quinn, 'It's ten-fifteen. Are you from the States?'

'That's where I've just come from.'

'I would like to join you.'

Quinn was trying to work out how long it had been since Judy had left. There flashed into his mind the looks Agustín and Judy had exchanged in the bar in Tijuana as they made their silent agreement, and he grew alarmed. He became aware of the Mexican, waiting for a response.

'Please,' Quinn said.

The Mexican took a chair opposite and put down the executive briefcase he carried. He stretched out his hand.

'I am Rafael,' he said.

'Sean,' Quinn said.

'Vacation?'

'Yes.'

'How do you like Mexico?'

'It's nice.'

The man laughed. He clicked his fingers to get the

attention of the waiter and ordered whiskies for Quinn and himself.

'I think you say that because you are a discreet person. No one can believe Mexico is "nice", especially someone who has lived in the United States. Mexico is a poor country.'

'Have you lived there?'

'The US? Of course. Me and my brother, we are twins. When we were twelve years old, we went over at Tee-jay. My father was already living in Los Angeles and he sent for us. My family is from Chihuahua. Do you know San Clemente?'

'No.'

'You don't know San Clemente? It's near LA. My brother was killed there. He was in the United States two hours. We were in the trunk of a car, five people. Come the San Anofre border stop on the Interstate we had to get out and go on foot, cross the hills, all that shit. You know the Interstate?'

'Does it go from Los Angeles to Tijuana?'

'That's the one. The Five.'

'I was on it.'

'Then you know it's very dangerous. We had to cross to get into the hills. We hid in the bushes and waited for the traffic to like make room for us. Must have been twenty, thirty other people. An INS truck came, we ran. I lost sight of my brother. It turned out he got hit by a car. Later, they told me it was a big red Caddy. You ever see animals caught in the brights? That's what it is like on the Five, except it's people, Mexicans. He didn't die or anything at once. He crawled to a bush beside the road.'

Rafael hailed the waiter and ordered two more drinks. There was still no sign of Judy.

'My brother Santiago, he stayed in that bush two days. You see, he was afraid to come out because he knew they would send him back to Mexico. People saw him – you know, the people driving in their cars? – but they thought, it's another beaner waiting to get across the road. In the end someone took him to hospital. He died that night.'

'It's a true story, and you know what I learned from it?'

Quinn shook his head.

'It's obvious. It's better to live in the United States than here in Mexico. My brother *died* to stay in the United States. No, Mexico is not "nice", Central America is not "nice". People die trying to get away from it.'

Rafael was smiling. There was gold in his teeth, on his fingers and his wrists. He said, 'I like to talk to tourists, you get a different point of view. You know what else I learned from the death of my twin?'

'What?'

'That everyone must have revenge. It's an instinct, like sex. But stupid people think only one form of revenge is possible. You know, to kill? Let me tell you, when I found out my brother was killed by a Cadillac, I swore I would get revenge. And I did, but in my own way. Look into the street.'

Quinn did as he was told. 'What am I looking for?'

'You don't see?'

'See what?'

'The Caddy? You see it's red, like the one killed Santiago. I asked what colour was the Caddy killed Santiago. I am happy it was red. Red is the colour of a lot of things. Anyway, that's my revenge. Santiago, he would have appreciated it. What do you think of the Cadillac as a car?'

'I don't know about cars. Why don't you still live in the States?'

'It's hard for us. To be truthful, I got caught dealing drugs and after I did three years they deported me. Prison wasn't so bad. You get three squares a day, somewhere to stay, learn to speak good English, which is a big advantage. Plus you get connected. So now I do some business from Mexico.' He indicated the briefcase, as if by way of explanation. 'It suits me for the time being. I can be rich here.'

'I thought you said Mexico was a poor country.'

Rafael took out a slim cigar and offered it to Quinn, who declined. Rafael lit it. 'Not always,' he said. 'Before the Spanish came, Mexico had riches. You know San Luis Potosí?'

'No.'

'It's a rich area of mines. When the Spanish discovered it,

they took all the gold, the precious stones, and now nothing, almost nothing, remains. The richness of Mexico is gone, stolen. Like in Peru and Bolivia. There is another Potosí in Bolivia, did you know that? They say it was the richest mountain in the world. Millions of slaves died in the mines there, millions. The Spanish, they brought slaves from Africa to work in the mines. But in Potosí there are no black people. Once I was there on a business trip and I asked, where are the black people? They said, they died. That is what happened.

'The strangers came and turned our silver into dross, they turned the lives of the people into dross. This continent, when it was overthrown, became one vast plantation of slaves. Some people say that it's still the same, only the Spanish have gone and now we have the gringos. You think I am exaggerating?'

'No.'

'I am not. You should go to see the mines in Mexico and Bolivia. Take the time to do it. You will see people in the twentieth century who look like from five centuries ago. They dress in rags, they freeze in the cold and rain, they are dirty, like beasts. They work and live in misery, and then they die. That is their life.'

Rafael stopped to order another round.

'Now, of course,' he continued, 'there is another richness. *La droga*. It makes me smile when I think of it.'

'Why?'

'Because we have reversed this principle of the conquistadors.'

'Which one?'

'Of turning our silver into dross. Now we turn dross, a worthless plant, into silver. Is that not amusing?'

'Yes,' Quinn conceded.

Rafael slapped him on the back and laughed heartily, as though Quinn had said something very funny. 'Where is that waiter?' he said, and snapped his fingers, but it was Judy who appeared.

'Is this your wife, Sean? She is a charming young woman.'

He got to his feet and introduced himself to Judy.

'Let's go, Quinn,' Judy said, ignoring Rafael.

Quinn finished his whisky and stood up.

'Thank you, Rafael. It was a pleasure to meet you.'

'My pleasure. It's always interesting for me to talk with people from different places. Perhaps we'll see each other again.'

As they were about to leave, Judy noticed a copy of the *Los Angeles Times* on the chair by Rafael.

'Is that today's?' she asked.

'Yes. Please take it. I buy it every day to look for news of my business associates in the United States. In this paper there is nothing about them, I'm happy to say.'

Rafael shook hands with Quinn.

In the street Quinn asked why she had taken so long.

'I had to talk to Agustín.'

Quinn looked at Judy to see if she was going to say more; perhaps he should say something.

'He sold the car,' she said, and he knew she was diverting him.

'How much did he get?'

'Five hundred.'

'Is that good?'

'Where do you come from?' she asked, and when he said nothing she continued, 'No, it's not good. It's not going to last long.'

'Maybe we haven't got long.'

She stopped and gave him a hard look.

'I've booked rooms in La Perla for tonight. You and Agustín can share. Tomorrow we'll pick up the ferry tickets and the day after we'll be in Mexico City. From there we can go to Oaxaca, cross into Guatemala and find Salvador. Or you can do what you want, it's up to you.'

The rooms were on the second floor and they went up in the lift.

'You're in twelve. Agustín's already there,' she said.

'What happened, Judy?' Quinn said as they stepped out of

the lift. The talk with Rafael had pumped optimism into him and he felt ready to tackle her. 'Before, in the bar, it was like in Tijuana that morning. I keep wanting to try to keep it like that between us.'

'You're drunk and I don't know what you're talking about.' She turned away from him but he took hold of her arm.

'Yes you do,' he said.

'Let go of me.'

'Judy,' he said.

'Let go of me. Haven't you got a wife somewhere?'

'My wife is living with the man who shot me and left me for dead,' Quinn said quickly, without stopping to think.

'Don't tell me, and now you've met me you can forget her. I'm not going to hold you up.'

Quinn released her and she drew back. He had wasted so much time and believed he had sensed the same about her. He said, 'We could change. We could make up for it.'

'You're talking in riddles,' she said. 'You're just a man who wants fucked.'

Quinn only just kept himself from striking her. He turned and left her on the landing.

The room overlooked Obregón and, beyond the road, the sea. Agustín was in bed but not asleep.

'Are you okay?' Agustín asked.

'Yes,' Quinn replied. 'You?'

'Yes.'

Quinn sat on the edge of the bed and stared out into the night. The sky and sea were dark. The night loomed dismally and he was able to see no way forward.

'I'm not going with you to Mazatlán,' he said to Agustín.

Before Agustín could say anything, there was a sharp rap at the door, followed by Judy's voice calling out urgently. Quinn let her in. She clutched the copy of the *Times*. She slumped into a chair by the window next to a small writing table.

'What was Sabino's second name?' she asked quietly.

'Gutiérrez,' Agustín said.

'Oh Christ.' Judy put the paper on the table and hung her head.

Quinn lifted the paper. He saw the story at once.

'What is it?' Agustín said.

Quinn said, 'Sabino and Dulio, they're dead.'

SIXTEEN

What ground there was between Quinn and Agustín had not been established through words but intuitively, as Quinn had told Judy, through the sense they had of each other. But that night, after Judy had returned to her bed, after the lines in the newspaper had been read and exhausted, both men wanted the beat and murmur of words: not to *describe*, not to confess motives or emotions. Both men shrank from talking directly about what they felt. It was not that they were embarrassed. They understood that feelings addressed openly convey neither depth nor extent nor reality; the more candid the confession, the more contrived. Instead, the words they chose went to make stories; for only stories, told with all their artifices and protective feints, let the listener and the questioner into another life.

The thing of which Agustín had felt himself a part had lasted only a short time. But it was intense, like the music of the place – the swirling, winding *huayno* songs, the shrill, dissonant notes of the *zampoña* that called to his attention like screams and made the hairs on his neck stand up before their discordance segued into melody. The instruments would begin a swell that would lead to the climax he knew was coming. He could predict the precise moment of its coming: it would fall over him like a wave and he would stand drenched and shivering in the music and voices of his comrades, his emotions sparking, smarting, swarming.

> *The people's blood has a delicious perfume,*
> *It smells like jasmine and violets,*
> *And like gunpowder and dynamite.*

He lived beyond surviving in Lurigancho. Gabriel had, in the cell in Huarmey, told him he would survive, and at that time, with the trailing rifle shots streaking into the sky to scar the face of the moon, that was enough for Agustín: he wanted no more, merely to survive. But once within the dismally stained concrete walls of the prison, he understood that physical survival was an end attained with comparative ease: lice-ridden, scabby, the ragged men survived – at a cost. The cost was to themselves and it was as total as it was unrelenting. Payment was in the acts and attitudes that counted towards independence, integrity, control; most of all it was the surrender, torn from a few but yielded willingly enough by the rest, of the thing that mattered most. An acknowledgement was required from those who inhabited this world by those who controlled it: that one's hanging on to life took priority over all, including even the lives of friends and brothers.

Listening to the music spiralling up into the grim sky, the chant-singing echoing off the walls, watching the red flags unfurled for parades and marches, or even the numerous comedies of their situation. Agustín understood what Gabriel had told him, that physical survival was not enough.

It was with less frequency now that Agustín – car-thief, robber, prisoner – heard his own footfalls, as he had heard them that day he walked the Carretera Central in search of his mother and his sister. To be aware of one's footfalls, to hear them, was a painful isolation. He associated them with the room his family had shared in the *callejón* in Lima when he waited for his mother to return with her tray of sweets and cigarettes, her footfalls empty on the wooden stairs, a forewarning of the sadness and failure that came with her.

And through the hours and days he spent talking to Gabriel, the sound of his footfalls receded further and further, trailing away almost to the point of dying out; they became the faintest whisper, until for a moment there was no sound at all. Then, suddenly, they returned, not alone this time, but in the stamp of a hundred pairs of marching feet, accompanied by the chant-singing and the snaps of the wind striking the banners and flags.

Swept up in the march, carried along by it, Agustín survived.

His only sadness was that the more he lived in this march, the further he left Roy behind. Roy – a foreigner, a gringo, a man sullied by his connection with the narcos – was treated well enough, but with a formality that no one could pretend did not mark distance.

One day Roy said to Agustín, 'It's infringing me, man, all this marching and shit. I have to leave the block.'

Agustín was horrified, unable to understand. They argued, for the first time, each disappointed at the other's failure to comprehend. Agustín appealed to Roy. Roy said, 'I'm not saying it's wrong here. It's right for you, just not for me.'

As he spoke, Agustín became heated and he said vicious things. Roy became miserable. He had the appearance of a man who somehow managed to look perpetually soaked, as if he had his own private downpour permanently above his head. He said, 'The lectures, all the organization and discipline. Man, this is the kind of thing I've been trying to get away from all my life. I didn't expect to find it in a Peruvian prison.' Agustín walked away and did not talk again to Roy Jones.

Gabriel agreed to Roy's request to leave the block and he sent word to the other blocks that the gringo Roy Jones was not to be molested. Roy looked wetter than ever the morning he left the *pabellón industrial*, tears streamed down his face. The prisoners lined up on either side of the narrow ante-room that connected the block and the central control area, and each man shook hands with Roy as he left. Roy knew it was not spontaneous, for little passed here that was not planned, and he detected barely concealed hostility in the eyes of some of the men who took his hand, and suspicion in the eyes of others; more than a few were glad to see the gringo go. But there were others who hugged him warmly and whispered their farewells in choked voices. He sniffed back the tears, took a last look to see if Agustín had relented, saw he had not, and left.

Some days later Gabriel came to find Agustín. He was not harsh, for that was not Gabriel's way. So, quietly and without implying rebuke, he made Agustín understand that his behaviour had been petty and unworthy. Sullenly Agustín reminded him that Roy had turned his back on his comrades. Gabriel took a long time to say anything.

'Perhaps,' he mused. 'But we do so many stupid things. Thankfully, in most circumstances, our latest piece of stupidity does not have to be the last act of our lives.'

'I'll talk to Roy,' Agustín said.

'You can't talk to him,' Gabriel said, and Agustín stiffened in alarm. 'Nothing has happened to him. Nothing bad. He is in Oregon with his family.'

'How?'

'How did he get out? Money, of course. Dollars' – Gabriel was smiling – 'in our poor country can work miracles. Are you pleased?'

He was, though he was nagged by a sense of injustice, that the gringo could buy his way out of trouble.

Gabriel read his thoughts. 'Don't tell me you begrudge him his freedom?'

'No,' Agustín said.

'Yes you do, for your own reasons. Let's see if we can make you feel more generously towards the gringo. Soon,' Gabriel said, changing his tone, 'within a week, we will say goodbye to this place. Not one or two comrades. All of us are leaving.'

A worried engineer named Leopoldo had thought of it. They had dug in the heat and dark, anxious to avoid detection not only by the guards but by other prisoners. When the darkness became so intense that even Gabriel became frightened, an electrician rigged up lights. The dark was halved but the lights brought other problems. In the tunnel the heat was such that men scraped out the earth naked and wreathed in sweat. The bulbs gave off more heat, they burned the flesh, the sweat conducted the electricity.

Agustín had suspected nothing and felt an initial surge of anger at his exclusion. But he fought his anger down and reminded himself that he, a thief, had yet to earn trust.

'I have no doubts about you,' Gabriel said, and he said more things. The words and phrases he used to include Agustín – used, it seemed, casually, as if it were already understood that Agustín was one of them – settled in Agustín, and in his mind he heard the fading away of his footfalls, heard swelling up the music and the stamping feet. He would make up all that he had done wrong.

Three days later, in the midmorning, Gabriel came to him again.

'Come with me.'

At the far end of the cell block, the point furthest from the fence at the guarded entrance, was a locked door beyond which the prisoners kept their food supplies in a communal store. A flagstone in the floor, normally covered with sacks of rice or crates of vegetables, was prised open, and warm air, mixed with the smell of earth, came out to meet them.

Gabriel and Agustín stripped and entered the tunnel.

They crawled its length. Wooden supports, inserted above them, creaked with threats. The tunnel was not uniform: in some places it was wide enough for two, in others the sandy earth pressed on the shoulders; in some places it was just possible to crouch, in others the ceiling was so low that Agustín thought his back was all there was to prevent the earth falling in. Earth and dust sprinkled his hair and eyes, Gabriel twice kicked him in the nose with the bare soles of his feet as he struggled through the grip of the walls; the current from the light jolted and panicked him and he muttered curses, not in pain but in fear. He was glad when there were no more bulbs to burn and shock him; but then the darkness became complete.

After twenty minutes Gabriel said, 'We're here.' The tunnel had been excavated into what seemed like a nest, where it was just possible for two men to crouch. Gabriel took Agustín's arm and guided it above them: he felt a roughly circular opening and, to the side, wood hammered together in a crude ladder.

Both men were panting heavily, the atmosphere was mixed with poisons.

'I wanted you to see this,' Gabriel said, 'because when the time comes it is better to have experience, so that you won't be afraid.'

'I won't be.'

Even in the solid dark Agustín knew Gabriel would be looking at him with his amiable, ironic smile. Now Agustín welcomed the dark: it covered his unease. More than ever he felt he had defrauded this man. The tunnel belonged to Gabriel and the others, and he, Agustín, had no place in it. If there had been light, Gabriel would have seen through him.

They sat in the dark, wedged together in the tiny nest. The air was sour with their sweat, rank with the poisons. At length Gabriel said it was time for them to go.

'I want to ask you something,' Agustín said as Gabriel manoeuvred. 'In the cell in Huarmey I thought they were going to kill you, and you said something to me when I asked you if you thought your life had been wasted. You said you had no alternative but to say "more weight".'

Gabriel laughed softly. 'I read it. They were the words a writer gave to a man under torture who could not save himself and keep his name and his face. So he asked for death, "weight".'

'I'd rather live.'

'Don't say that. It disappoints me. I feel sorry – or is it contempt? I don't know – for those that live cautiously, always anxious, protecting themselves. The kind of people who would never end up in a place like this.'

'Why sorry?'

'They will never know what we know.'

Agustín said nothing, and let the silence ask, What? What do we know?

And Gabriel understood the question formed by the silence. He said slowly, 'Sacrifice, and the things that come from that.'

In the storeroom Dulio and Leopoldo were waiting for

them. They hoisted Gabriel and Agustín out. Two basins of steaming water had been prepared.

'Wash here,' Gabriel told Agustín.

Leopoldo wore gold-rimmed spectacles that made his big eyes look bulbous. He was thin and balding, though still young, and he spoke as he moved, asking Gabriel questions in rapid, nervous bursts, his lips barely moving. Gabriel calmly assured him of the tunnel's integrity.

Leopoldo did not seem wholly satisfied, but he did not pursue the matter further. He came over to Agustín, who had just finished dressing, and clapped him on the back. 'Well done,' he said; he turned and left the storeroom. Once again Agustín felt ashamed. Dulio removed his basin; it was like having a servant wait on him. Agustín tried to stop him. Dulio said taciturnly, 'This is my job today.'

After lunch Agustín played chess with Dulio. The Party prisoners had, long ago, torn the doors from their cells and given themselves freedom to move around the block at will. They had banished the guards from the block and kept them to the fence at the entrance. Some prisoners had used the material from the doors to construct shelving. Dulio, a carpenter, had used his to make a chessboard. He had stained the squares a rich, deep red and a parchment yellow, and decorated the edges with tiny portraits of the Leader in his different guises of underground fighter, political thinker, peasant worker.

The two men played without talking. The patterns and intricacies of the game diverted Agustín, as he had wished, from the worries and excitements struggling to call to his consciousness. But the feeling of loneliness which had sprung up and invaded him in the last few days was too strong to throw off. The warmth of those around had done nothing to lessen it, in fact had increased it. When he was a boy in the *callejón* in Lima Agustín had sometimes woken up in a state of anxiety or sadness, sometimes with a feeling of dread, which stayed with him the whole day and occasionally developed into real depression. When he was older, he searched for the source of these feelings, and he found it:

the causes of his vague dread were, when stripped to their core, small things – sad words of his mother overheard before he went to sleep; an argument with Pepe or Polo in which some slighting thing had been said to him; his father irritably chasing him away. Once he had located the source of the dread, he could banish it. But now it was different: he did not have to look for the cause of his sadness and renewed feelings of isolation. He did not deserve to be in the *pabellón industrial*, to be taken in by Gabriel and Dulio and the others, he did not deserve to be clapped on the back by Leopoldo. Like Roy, he should have left. His nature was not to be part of this.

It was three o'clock when Andrew Jank, Hal and three armed guards came through the fence, walked through the ante-room and out into the yard. Agustín heard someone shouting, 'The Repression is here.' He heard the scuffle of feet, men running, bumping into each other. Dulio sprang up and ran into the corridor. 'Come,' he shouted.

In the yard the prisoners had formed a circle around the missionaries and their guards to check their advance. Jank was smiling beatifically. He and Hal were attempting to distribute leaflets. The three guards, their rifles at port arms, looked nervous and muttered to each other while glancing back towards the ante-room.

The prisoners' anger did not seem to bother Jank. Hal appeared more concerned.

Agustín saw Gabriel striding towards them. Gabriel beckoned to a group of men, who rushed over and formed an escort for him. The shouting subsided as Gabriel pushed his way through the circle to address the missionaries.

'You should know, señores, that no one enters this block without the Party's permission.'

Jank answered in English. Hal translated.

'We only want to talk and distribute our leaflets.'

'You may now leave.' Gabriel waved and the men separated to make a clear line to the ante-room. The guards were anxious to go.

Hal looked to Jank and whispered to him in English. Jank

kept his eyes on Gabriel. He said, 'Perhaps another time.'

'Never,' Gabriel replied. He stretched out his hand in the direction of the ante-room.

Dulio, hanging back from the crowd, whispered to Agustín, 'The last thing we need now is a confrontation.'

Sullenly and slowly, the missionaries and their escort began to make their way to the ante-room. As they moved forward, the crowd of prisoners pressed them from behind. A guard tussled with a couple of prisoners who were snatching at his rifle.

'We'll be back,' Jank shouted to Gabriel.

'Be under no illusion,' Gabriel said, 'if you try to come in here again I will cut out your tongue and feed it to the dogs.'

Jank laughed. Agustín could see that he did not believe Gabriel. 'You are a stupid man,' Agustín said under his breath.

As the swarm reached the steps leading down to the ante-room, one of the guards tumbled. A great cheer went up and men in the crowd lunged forward. Agustín caught the expression of terror on the guards' faces. Gabriel shouted for calm, but his voice was not heard above the din. There was more jostling. Hal and Jank were being man-handled. Gabriel fought his way to the thick of it.

A rifle shot rang out. Men scattered this way and that, some running bent over, some sprinting. A few dived to the ground and were crawling out of the way. There was another shot, another. Cracks and pops, too many to count. Agustín found himself on the ground, unable to remember how he had got there. He raised his head and saw Leopoldo kneeling beside him fixing his spectacles. He saw a scuffle going on at the steps to the ante-room. He made out Gabriel, taller than the rest, in his vest and red baseball cap. He saw him raise his fist and swing. There was another shot. Agustín ducked. When he lifted his head, he saw Leopoldo stretched out face down on the ground, his gold-rimmed glasses lying smashed just beyond his head. He reached over to the stricken man and tried to turn him over. He was heavier than Agustín had imagined.

Agustín looked back to the stairs. A group of prisoners –
among them he made out Dulio as well as Gabriel – were
fighting with the missionaries and the guards. There was a
volley of shots from the fence. Men fell down. Those still in
the yard scattered for shelter. Agustín ran.

For several seconds, before the guards knew where to aim
their bullets and before the officers had found voices to
command them, the silence was complete. Agustín found
himself on the ground floor of the cell block; he had no idea
of how he had got there.

He became aware of movement further down the corridor. He saw Dulio carrying a rifle, Gabriel and two or three
other prisoners manhandling two guards and Andrew Jank.
Jank was bleeding from the nose and mouth and both
guards had head injuries. Gabriel shouted orders to barri-
cade the entrance to the block while he led their prisoners
to a cell at the far end, next to the storeroom. Gabriel
noticed Agustín, and beckoned him to follow.

Agustín took a quick look from the window. Leopoldo was
stretched hopelessly where he had left him. Further back in
the yard another prisoner was splayed out. By the steps to
the ante-room lay the body of Hal, spread head down on the
stairs; beside him, a crumpled guard.

'Stay here,' Gabriel instructed Agustín at the doorway to
the cell.

Gabriel went inside. Agustín heard Andrew Jank say, 'Are
you going to kill us?'

Jank's voice betrayed anxiety but it did not have real fear
in it. Agustín stole a glance at him and to his intense
disappointment saw the man was under control.

Gabriel spoke, but Agustín could not make out what he
was saying. He turned his attention to the defences Dulio
had organized. He was telling two men with captured rifles
to go to the third floor, from where they would have a clear
line of sight across the yard. The others armed themselves
with what sticks or lengths of iron they could find. Someone
gave Agustín a short tube taken from a bedstead across
which a sharp stone had been fastened to make it a primitive

axe. Three men who had been wounded by the guards' gunfire were taken to a cell for attention.

Later Gabriel emerged from the cell. He saw Agustín clutching the axe. 'Keep your weapon,' Gabriel said, 'and use it. We are not saints to be martyred. Kill them. Kill as many as you can. You know the words of the song, "The people's blood has a delicious perfume"? Remember that when you kill them.'

Just then Agustín felt the ground shudder beneath him. He looked to Gabriel, as if for explanation, and was about to say something when the roar overtook him and threw him against the wall. A strange clatter had started, which he took a long time to grasp was gunfire, though he, who had always known he would hear fire of this intensity, would experience and live in it, had it fixed in his mind that it would be a tempest of bullets, that the sound would be so overwhelming it would gather in one great, irresistible storm: this was not like that. He heard the bullets, the single bullets, one by one, explode in the chambers and launch forth in jagged volleys.

He saw Gabriel get to his feet, heard him say, 'So, they wouldn't wait.' Gabriel rushed out into the corridor and Agustín called after him, shouting that he would stay with him for ever.

And it begins. The slaughter. Have you seen a massacre? Watch. A man with a hole in his chest staggers as though under a weight, arms crooked at the elbows, knees slightly bent, the burden pressing him down. He comes to a stop and topples, landing among the other dead. Two soldiers corner a group of about a dozen in the yard below a painting of the Leader, whose giant face appears above the people marching together. The men scatter, some to the left, some to the right, others cross their hands in front as though the flesh and bone in their hands will shield their faces. The soldiers do not have to hurry, they fire in bursts of three or four and the prisoners jerk and pitch, dead on their feet. A splatter of blood hits the Leader's glasses and trails down his face; the marching people are soaked. One of the dozen is still running, spared because the numbers of prey are so great; like a pigeon in the flock which the hunters have fallen on, he soars away capriciously unharmed because so many are already dead. The man runs with the wind under his feet. He sprints along and when there is distance between them, when he can see the opening into which he will run and hide, he turns his head to look at the executioners, and as he does so he sees the rifle's muzzle and the shot that will kill him come tumbling slowly at him, white hot, gathering momentum until it slaps his forehead and throws him into the opening. An officer with a pistol stalks the piled dead and dying, bending over to inspect the bodies, firing now and again, his face betraying no more than as if he were a casual shopper at a market picking over some fruit. The report of his pistol is tinny, the crack of the bone profound. A man is hit in the thigh and staggers back but does not fall. He feels no pain and has the surprised and embarrassed expression of a man who has tripped on some broken pavement as he has been walking along with his friends. He sits down, bewildered. He calls to a friend and points to his thigh, already drenched in blood. He grins; he smiles, even. Two minutes later he is unconscious, a minute after that he is dead; he is still sitting, he is sitting in a throne of his own blood. A man is thrown from a window on the third floor. At first he is suspended in the air and will not fall; then, as though someone has cut an invisible rope, he plummets. The crash is dull for he has landed on the dead. Above, a helicopter beats the air, it is the icon of death and war and surveillance. Water is on the floor and running down the walls, the explosions have shattered the pipes, they pierce the ground as snapped bone the flesh: there are shoes lying waterlogged in gathering pools. A prisoner they have made prisoner lies face down and puts his hands behind his head. The soldiers take aim. The impacts are so powerful and so many that for a moment it seems as if the dead man is performing a trick, jumping to his feet from the prone position. He collapses at last. Two prisoners are dragging a third, who has taken refuge from his pain; his trousers are in tatters, his left leg has a line of gouged bullet wounds, fifteen or twenty-five; the leg has no bone and the mashed limb flaps heavily. Do you see that running man? Arms and legs flying. A soldier fires and the bullet enters the man's back with a thump and bursts through his chest. And because he does not know he is dead he still runs. He is running to get away, he covers ten, twenty, thirty feet and drops. The bullets fly above you, all around you. You cannot tell where they are going; you cannot jump out of the way. To jump here is madness, it is to jump into bullets. Dig, bury yourself, lie there. A man jerks and his arm unfolds and comes to rest across your face. You hear the boots on the ground, the man who will kill you is standing over your dead body.

> *The people's blood has a delicious perfume,*
> *It smells like jasmine and violets,*
> *And like gunpowder and dynamite.*

The soldiers are in the cells at the far end of the corridor. They give each other covering fire and advance cell by cell. Plaster dust and gun smoke swirl up and gather in clouds in the air. And then the noises fade: there are no screams, no shouts, only one rifle shot in a hundred has sound. Agustín watches in his trance. He can hear the crack, it has invaded the swirl of the music and resounds like the crash of the drum. A voice calls and he does not know if it is his voice. A face is bloody and he does not know if it is his face. Have you seen a hundred and seventy men killed in twenty minutes? You must tell me about it, for I believe it must be a terrible sight. Gabriel and Dulio are both bloody and their progress along the corridor is by throwing themselves recklessly from shelter to shelter. They scuttle into the cell where Agustín is crouching, clutching his stone-age axe. The American and the guards are wide-eyed. Gabriel is smiling through his blood. He takes the rifle from Dulio and edges to the doorway. There is an explosion and the fine plaster dust is sucked into the vacuum, then blown back the way it came in a great, violent sneeze. Gabriel pulls Agustín to his feet. 'Go now.' He fires into the corridor. The moment calls for an exchange, something that declares debt and love, but there is no time, and whatever word could be said in that moment would have failed: what word could match the moment? Agustín is hesitating, Dulio bursts out before him and scurries through the dust and water and debris and shoes into the storeroom. 'Go now.' Gabriel is firing at the soldiers. Agustín is in the mouth of the storeroom, behind the low cover of a sack of rice. Behind, Dulio is clearing the boxes from the flagstone: he heaves the tablet, it crashes down and shatters. Dulio enters the tunnel. 'Come,' he hisses at Agustín. 'Come, now.' Agustín looks at his left hand and sees a line burn, the kind you get when you let out rope and there is a sudden pull. Clatter. The soldiers are firing, working their way from cell door to cell door, firing and rolling, crouching and firing. Agustín enters the tunnel. The soldiers cannot see him. He watches Gabriel's rifle spend itself and the Captain of Fifty throw down the useless weapon. The soldiers are upon Gabriel. The officer who has picked fruit, choosily pawing it for signs of life, is upon him. Andrew Jank is freed from his bonds and comes forward. The officer is smiling as he welcomes the American. In the officer's outstretched hand is the gun, and Andrew walks towards it. Gabriel is crying but Agustín knows it is not for himself, not for his life and death, but for a hundred thousand things the American will never know. The gun is taken. The weak hand that grips it is surprised by the weight and the gun lurches down before it is corrected as Jank adjusts to its heft. He brings the gun up to the head of the crying man and pulls the trigger. The body folds and a triumphant cheer goes up. Shots are loosed into the air to tell of the victory. Clatter and clatter.

A year later, in the chilly winds of El Alto, the town of tin and cardboard overlooking Bolivia's La Paz, the overnight rain had frozen before dawn and the town was of a silver the conquistadors never desired. Agustín lay in bed beside the taciturn and bearded man. Somewhere in the months since the massacre, a change had fallen over them, a reversal. Dulio needed him and looked to him. It was easy to explain: Dulio had never before been alone, had never before betrayed. This was Agustín's special territory. Here, he was the expert.

As Dulio slept, Agustín watched over him. He now understood that all men and women believe themselves capable of heroic self-sacrifice, understood that many among them have readied themselves for such a sacrifice with a lifetime's preparation. Most are never given the opportunity and they die either frustrated or certain about what they would have done. I needed more time, Agustín said to himself, I needed more time. He glanced at Dulio and looked away, ashamed.

He became aware that Dulio was cold and brought the blanket up around the man.

Rex was driving and Zenga was talking, as usual. Pascual gazed at the countryside, a brittle and flaky parchment that had an exhausted air to it, as if it had long since come to terms with having its contours arbitrarily crumpled and torn. The sight – its desolation, the poverty within it – repelled Pascual and he turned to study himself in the wing mirror.

Until recently he had been avoiding mirrors. In Tijuana, in the Centro Evangélico, he had looked in one and, startled, had spun round into a crouch to defend himself. Then he understood and crept back to the mirror, keeping his eyes down, and, glancing quickly into the glass, testing it, readying himself for it, he moved square before his reflection. The whole cast of his face had altered. On first glance the impression was scary: there were hollows under his cheekbones and lines drawn through the taut, grey skin; the mouth had narrowed and tightened, the lips had become thinner: he puffed them up, trying to make them thicker, trying to get more life into them. It did not work. He studied his eyes because everyone who suspected a dopehead looked at the eyes. What the fuck could they see? He could recognize nothing different. He leaned into the mirror. Nothing. He gazed at his image.

Yes, he conceded, the face was different, but less disturbing on closer examination. The longer he stared, the more satisfied he became with the alteration: hard, not crazed.

It was as it should be. It had been easier than he could have imagined. In the last five days he had shot a dog, wounded a man who later got killed, and maybe even hit another one, if the bullet he had fired into the Olds on

251

Michael's lawn had struck lucky.

And he had killed two more. He was impressed. He was no longer Pascualito, little Pascual, who had been working around men since he was twelve years old after he had come from Sonora with his sister and his cousin, and, because of his pretty looks and his enthusiastic ways, had never really been one of the men, had always been treated as a kind of mascot. He was now Pascual Hernández, and he had been recognized. Zenga had seen his value.

Zenga was a smart man, and Pascual felt something approaching gratitude towards him, though it was mixed with other, more confused feelings. Pascual glanced at the Italian. He was talking easily, the glassy smile fixed on his face. The smile was always there. He had yet to see Zenga betray impatience or irritation. The man hid his feelings behind a permanent cover of good humour, and Pascual never knew what he was really thinking. He found that scary: somehow Zenga's even keel should make him predictable, but it didn't; the opposite, in fact. The man had to be watched.

Rex, too, though Rex *was* predictable. On the drive down from Tijuana, through El Rosario and then to La Paz, across in the ferry to Mazatlán and on to Mexico City, he had caught Rex looking at him a thousand times with his wrenched eyes. It was as if Rex had constantly to check on Pascual, bring himself up to date every few minutes in case there had been some change. Pascual was ahead of Rex, so far it made him laugh inwardly because Rex did not even begin to suspect how far behind he was.

Rex, at the wheel of the pick-up, was staring at him again, thinking Pascual had not noticed. After a time, Rex turned back to the road and Pascual took his turn to stare.

There was a laugh from Zenga. 'You know, if the evil eye could kill, I'd be driving myself to Oaxaca.'

Pascual hoped things would work out with Zenga. The Italian reminded Pascual, uncomfortably, of his father. The child Pascualito had always got his way with his mother and aunts, could charm them into anything. But, when he looked into his father's eyes, he saw his own motives written out, stripped and reduced to their shameful core.

Zenga had said he could use someone like Pascual – called him *Pascual.* Pascual liked that, recognition of the change, of the new him. But there were times when he thought Zenga was plotting against him, with Rex, times when he thought they must *know* what happened at the Dorfmann factory. On a couple of occasions, alone with Zenga, Pascual had tried to put some distance between the Italian and Rex by commenting on something Rex had done. Zenga stared at him the way his father used to and smiled in a way that made Pascual feel transparent. On other occasions he had tried throwing Zenga collusive glances after Rex had said something particularly stupid, but Zenga had repelled them with his painted smile.

This hurt Pascual because he liked the Italian, though he did not trust him. What he liked about the man was how he never doubted the outcome. Agustín and the Mendoza woman were dead, the white man too, though no one knew his name yet. Zenga would stretch out on the seat of the pick-up while Rex was driving and comment on things. He did it with a kind of tolerance and distance from the subject that convinced you he was wise, that he knew a lot about a lot of things. Human nature, in particular. Zenga was the one person Pascual had met that he did not mind having to listen to. It was a new experience. He thought about all the fools – the Michaels, Richies and Wilsons – and about how they were turning their tiny deals. They all thought they were king of the castle, and they were, he supposed, but of castles so small no one else knew they existed. Zenga and his organization were different. With them, Pascual knew things were going to get done; he knew he was on the winning side. The first time in his life.

Three days getting to Mexico City, closing in on Agustín, the *puta* and the white man, Zenga kept up a running commentary on everything: the state of world politics, the Soviets, the Arabs, Latin Americans; the state of Mexico, why the people were so poor; the moral philosophy of the United

States and its economy; recessions and booms; decadence and liberals; about why some people got ahead and not others. Though he was careful not to show it, Pascual was impressed because a squatter of its meaning eluded him; any more and he would just have been confused.

It was when Zenga talked about religion that Pascual made his mistake. Confusing Zenga's monologues for conversation in which his opinion counted for something, Pascual joked about religion being a good business to be in, that recessions never seemed to hit the God business. Zenga went cold on him and did not answer for some minutes. Rex turned his twisted eyes on Pascual to let him know he was enjoying his mistake.

After a while Zenga said, the habitual good humour and tolerance straining to keep a presence in his voice, 'You know why I am Christian? There's a God. It's been proved. So the question is how you serve God. Did God put us on earth, create us in His image, for us to fool around in caves and stuff? Huh? No. He made us so we could progress ourselves. The more highly developed the man, the more pleased God is, like you're pleased when your kids do well, get on in life.

'To progress you need material things. You don't develop sitting in a tin and cardboard shack in the *barrio*. When you got material things you have to defend them from other people that don't have them and want to take what you got away from you.

'Christianity allows man to serve and worship his creator, which is only right. It allows people who deserve, and who want, to progress, and it gives them the motivation to do that, because it recognizes the moral value of private property.'

Zenga smiled at Pascual with his hard, small brown eyes, then continued, 'God has a plan for us. Like any plan it's no good if you don't stick to it. So you stick to it all the way, no questions. Then everything comes all right in the end.'

Zenga smiled directly at him. Rex was smirking.

*

They were two hours out of Mexico City, though it was hard to tell where the city stopped and where the countryside around it began. LA was a big city, spread out, but this was worse. It had no lines, no boundaries, nothing that conferred definition. They passed shacks and half-finished, squat concrete buildings with skeletal steel rods poking from them. The buildings were not in order, not in blocks, but scattered.

Zenga was talking about human nature. When he said that most people do not realize their potential until someone comes along and unlocks what they have inside, it hit something in Pascual. Zenga had unlocked his potential and he wanted Zenga to know that he understood that. It would create the bond Pascual wanted, that he was sure he could create if only Rex were not with them.

He knew Zenga liked him. After Pascual had recovered from his shock at being picked up by Rex and Zenga, he realized they had already decided Agustín was the killer, and he became calmer. Sitting in a back room of the mission hall in Los Angeles, Pascual realized that they were talking to him only to tie up some loose ends. All he had to do was keep quiet and go along with them. As they talked, Pascual became aware that Zenga was weighing him up. After a few hours, during which time Zenga was in and out, making and taking phone calls, arranging and checking on things, Zenga put the proposition to him. It solved all Pascual's problems. Rex and Zenga left him alone in the hall and said they would be back in a couple of hours and that he should be ready to go to Tijuana.

They did not think he would find it, but he did. There was a big stainless-steel oven in the back room, the kind they have in fast-food places to keep the junk warm. Pascual saw the oven and knew it was there. He pulled the oven out from the wall and saw a plasterboard square that had been jammed into the wall where the brick had been removed. He prised the plasterboard out. The attaché case was wedged into the cavity behind it.

It contained three handguns of different makes and

calibres, several boxes of ammunition and $3,755. Pascual counted it. He was not stupid enough to run off with the money. The thought did not even enter his head.

Instead, Pascual concentrated on the guns. He did not know anything about guns, but he was like a natural artist. He felt confident with them, though at first he could not match the shells with the weapons. He crushed two Cross Tops in his mouth and washed them down with water from the tap. Seconds later the speed hit him and he was ready to sort them out. He inspected the engraving. He was not a good reader, but the names were easy. One was an Astra Terminator, another a Cold Delta Elite. The people who made these things knew good names.

He settled for the Colt Commander. He liked its weight, not heavy, but solid. He found the .45 ammunition and loaded it. He took two twenty-dollar bills and replaced the rest of the money. He went for the door. It was locked, and the windows were barred. He got out through the roof. He was feeling so confident, he did not even try to keep himself out of sight as he shimmied down to the street. He carried himself boldly, meeting the gaze of anyone who cared to look at him. This was the way to do it. He was on the winning side.

It was not until he was out in the street that he decided that he was going to kill Michael. It was late afternoon and Pascual had trouble getting a taxi. When he got one to stop, the driver refused to take him to Santa Ana, so Pascual decided to do Dulio instead. Ten minutes later, he paid off the cab, broke into Dulio's shabby room and settled in the gloom to wait.

It turned out better than he had expected. Dulio *and* Sabino arrived. They were in work clothes and Dulio was getting out of a dusty jacket, when Pascual stepped forward with the gun. He had planned some kind of victory speech, but the look of surprise and terror on Dulio's face was so satisfying he needed nothing else. He pulled the trigger and Dulio disappeared from view. Sabino stood blinking, then he, too, disappeared.

Sabino had seven dollars hidden in his sock. Dulio had two fives and some change. He noticed Dulio was still alive. Pascual thought about hitting him again. But, when he put the gun to his head, he saw that Dulio's face was broken. The man would not live and with luck would die in a lot of pain. Dulio's eyes focused for a second, Pascual kicked the man hard in the ribs.

By the time Zenga and Rex returned, Pascual had replaced the gun and the money. He did not care whether Zenga and Rex knew he had been out, because he felt like a different man now, whole, capable. It is an amazing thing, the giving and taking of life. Think about it, he was telling them silently, as they moved around collecting things for the journey, finishing someone's life, stepping in and taking over life itself. The enormity of the power he had discovered astounded him.

Zenga said they were leaving for Tijuana. Then, in the pick-up, the Italian pretended he had forgotten something. He went into the mission hall and came out five minutes later carrying the attaché case. Pascual smiled to himself.

On arriving in Tijuana, they went straight to the Centro Evangélico to talk to the pastor there, a friend of the Mission's. Rex went to buy supplies, and Zenga and the pastor disappeared into an office to talk. Pascual stood in front of the mirror. He felt different, very strong.

Zenga was watching him. They were alone.

'What do you see?' Zenga asked him.

'What do you mean?'

'You see something different now, don't you?'

Pascual said nothing. He was looking at Zenga's reflection in the mirror. Zenga's eyes went up and down his body, there was a smile on his face that held amusement that disturbed him. Zenga put his hand on Pascual's shoulder, his fingers dug into the muscle and gripped him. Zenga had a powerful hold, he swayed Pascual gently back and forth. 'You made the right decision, Pascual,' Zenga was saying. 'You've never been on a team before, have you?'

'No.'

'There are a lot of advantages being on a team.'

'Only the winning team.'

Zenga laughed and shook Pascual and massaged the muscles in his neck. 'The winning team can protect you, right?'

'Right.'

'But only if you play by the coach's rules. You know that, don't you?' Zenga's grip was tightening and relaxing ominously. The touch both excited and unnerved Pascual.

'Yes,' Pascual said into the mirror.

'Good,' Zenga said. He let go of Pascual's neck and slipped his arm around his shoulder. 'Good.' Zenga leaned into the mirror and when he spoke it was with his eyes on his own eyes.

'You got to have the team spirit, so that the team can win. You understand me?'

'Yes.'

'Because, Pascual, I'm not disappointed. What you did last night confirmed what I already knew about you. That's good. Nothing wrong with that. Initiative is a good thing. Just remember the team spirit and don't do something like that without asking first.'

Zenga left him. When Pascual looked in the mirror again he saw a hole at the side where Zenga had been.

In his hotel room in Antigua, Quinn tried to separate the days, one from the other. They had melded, the dawns turning into dusks and back to dawns, the light remaining always blue-grey. Without days he could not separate events or see how they were related. It had rained heavily that afternoon, and in the hour before night the air was chilled. The cool came as a relief to Quinn, who had been sick and taking Lomotil since the beginning of the bus ride from Mazatlán to Mexico City. Now he felt strong enough, just, to have a stab at making sense of the last few days.

On the bus from Mazatlán, after they left the ferry, he had wrapped his arms around his stomach and hunched up in the corner of the seat, his temple shuddering against the window. They had arrived in the capital in the early after-noon and the heat and fumes of the streets reminded him of the times he had, as a child, stood impatiently beside ice-cream vans waiting to be served, the smell of diesel streaming up into the summer air. He went to the toilet in the bus station and stayed there for three-quarters of an hour. Agustín came looking for him, to tell him they had seats for Oaxaca. He took hold of Quinn's arm and pulled him up. The movement was rough and Quinn felt the power in Agustín's grip as he came to his feet, and he sensed his own frailty.

Agustín took him to the little cafeteria in the terminal, where Judy was waiting, and made him drink mineral water and camomile tea. Cramps rippled Quinn's stomach.

On the bus to Oaxaca, Quinn and Agustín sat together, with Judy in front. They did not talk. The ground between them now was littered with words and stories. Quinn's as well as Agustín's, but the distance had grown. It was as if what had been established intuitively had been ruined by the words, as if the words had been, among other things, a sign of weaknesses, of which, now they had been confessed, both men were deeply ashamed. They had miscalculated. They had told their stories because they believed the time had come for their exchange. But afterwards they felt denuded, and regrets had already grown into resentments.

Since the night they learned of the deaths of Dulio and Sabino, the night of the stories, Agustín had separated himself from Quinn and Judy. A bitterness was in him, his silences were long and gloomy. Quinn tried several times to coax him out with gentle questions, but these elicited no response, and Quinn felt he understood the humiliation of the women whose fate it is to animate moody husbands and sons with inane conversation. He was embarrassed at the triteness of his words, but could not stop himself.

Agustín consented to answer only one question. During the darkness of the early hours when the people on the bus were in that grimy, tiring, fully clothed sleep that belongs to overnight travellers, Agustín told, in a mechanical and careless way, of what happened after he and Dulio reached Bolivia.

In El Alto, the decision had been made, without it having been spoken, that Agustín and Dulio would not go back to Peru. They would escape to Mexico. A travel agent sold them false documents and tickets.

Dulio and Agustín were two years in Mexico City, working, for the most part, in foreign-owned factories. They moved on to Guadalajara, Aguascalientes, Chihuahua, Nogales. Sometimes they earned as much as six dollars a day. In Tijuana, they ran into Sabino, who had been in Mexico for seven years after jumping ship in Vera Cruz. Sabino had worked around the port and had saved enough during the boom years to get his wife and children from Ayacucho to Lima to Mexico. When the oil years went sour, Sabino decided the time had come to move his family to the United States. He had already been fleeced once by a *pollero* – the man had taken three hundred dollars to get him over the border, then disappeared. Dulio and Agustín had already decided to cross, and when they went they took Sabino and his family.

From Los Angeles, Agustín wrote to Roy Jones in Oregon. The letter was forwarded by Roy's parents and one day Agustín came back to his hotel to find Roy waiting for him. Four years had passed since they had last seen each other, and the meeting was not easy. It was as if they realized that they had nothing in common, did not really like each other, but were stuck together through some quirk of fate. To share the burden, Agustín brought Roy to meet Dulio. The three men spent a long evening together, drinking, saying very little, until a complete silence fell over them. They met three or four times after that, unwilling to admit there was so little that joined them after such an experience. But the meetings became too painful. They stopped seeing each other, and for a time Agustín did not know where Roy had moved. Dulio spent some months working on a mansion in Santa Barbara and Agustín was left alone. Somehow, a year further on, they converged again. Roy was dealing small amounts of dope and fixing up knife and gunshot wounds for people who did not want to go to hospital. Dulio and Agustín went with Sabino each day to the corner of Pino and Main to wait for someone to hire them. They were taken on by a Guatemalan foreman to work for a woman named Dorfmann. One morning, when the foreman picked Agustín and the other labourers up, he passed out some leaflets. They read: 'It is Revival Time. Come and join us once more in Praising of the Lord. The Lord has Something Special for you. If you are sick, depressed or have any kind of Problem, God can sort It out for You.' At the top of the leaflet, in bold capitals, was, THE NEW ERA MISSION OF CHRIST, and among the names of the preachers was that of Andrew Jank.

Agustín had drifted too far and too long to believe in fate, but here was the proof, and here was the opportunity.

In Oaxaca, Quinn had rested in the cool of the late afternoon. Because he was sick, Judy had insisted on staying in a decent hotel, one with clean bathrooms and room service. It overlooked the zócalo, and from his window Quinn saw a blind guitarist sit with his back against a wall and sing what he took to be love songs. He saw a shoeshine man clear leaves and litter from in front of the metal-framed chair his clients sat in, the black imitation-leather upholstery and the chrome tubing lending it an ominous look, something from a hospital. A small boy sold candyfloss in cellophane bags – pink and blue – tied to a pole three times his height. A woman with a red sweater, red shoes and handbag talked into a telephone at the corner near the post office; a man beside her made her laugh and she hit him playfully and tried to stretch the cord of the phone around the corner where she could get away from him. Near by, a black Chrysler Shadow was up for lottery and a man with a megaphone called people to admire it. There were clusters of balloons, some were silver, some had been inserted inside larger ones and reminded Quinn of frog spawn. Quinn left the window and went to the bathroom. His coughing led him into vomiting, and, when there was nothing left, he went back to bed.

He brought Judy into his mind. She was beautiful: it was the first time he had conceded this, and he did so reluctantly. She was aware of the attention she got, liked it, he could see, took it for granted in a haughty kind of way. For some reason her beauty irritated him and he started an argument with her about it, in his mind. He told her things about herself that she knew but had buried and did not acknowledge, but that he, of course, could see: that she was just another girl with good looks and there were plenty of those around, that all she had was her attractiveness to men, her beauty, and that it was only skin deep, that it did not last, that it was not as important as . . . as . . . what? Clichés. He moaned at how obvious his thoughts were. He was, Judy had said, just another man who wanted fucked. He hated the words: Judy knew too much about the coming and going of love. She was beautiful, he was jealous. It was that simple.

The next morning Quinn was still sick, but they could waste no more time. Judy hired a car using her credit card and Quinn was too weak to protest. They drove on Highway 190 at Tapanatepec and took the coast road to the border at Talismán, where Judy changed some dollars and their remaining pesos into quetzals. She gave Agustín some money and Agustín went to cross the border on foot to meet them later on the roadside. Judy negotiated with the border guards while Quinn stayed in the car going in and out of fitful, fevered dozes. The bargaining took three hours and twenty minutes and Judy paid more than she wanted.

They crossed into Guatemala and even in his fever Quinn saw and sensed enough to know they had passed into a different place. It was not just the soldiers, in their mirror sunglasses and peaked caps pulled low; nor was it even the dead silence that shrouded the people and the countryside: it was something bleak and cruel which said that here the risks were of a different order and life was lived along different lines.

They picked up Agustín some kilometres over the border

and drove to Quetzaltenango. Judy stopped at a big hotel on the main square, where she and Agustín ate while Quinn used the toilet. An hour later, they were back in the car heading east for Los Encuentros and Antigua. 'Patzún, is near here,' Judy said when they came in sight of Lake Atitlán, 'where Mercedes was.'

After the desert and dust of Mexico, the green of the forests here struck Quinn as beautiful and intriguing. He gazed at the scenery, its magic touching him all the more because he sensed it through delirium. The desert had no secrets, he saw now. It laid its story out, candid and shallow. Yet the forest also unsettled him. Disturbing images invaded him, vivid, though he knew they could not possibly come from first-hand experience: he saw armed men tramping with prisoners to a clearing, and could smell damp, newly turned soil; he heard shots and the soft thud of shovelled clumps of earth. He groaned and shook his head to clear his mind. Judy and Agustín glanced at him over their shoulders.

Judy turned off the Pan-American at Chimaltenango. The road was deeply rutted in places and in others climbed so sharply that the engine sometimes seemed on the point of giving up before just making it, the roar subsiding in gratitude.

Agustín was now silent more than before. He stared at the scenery, and would not speak even when directly addressed.

Quinn fell asleep in the car. It was dark when he woke. The car was shuddering on cobblestones, and thunder rolled in the distance. The hotel Judy chose was a colonial building with a large main courtyard leading on to smaller patios, around which the rooms were arranged, shaded and protected by cloister-like passages tiled in red. Quinn had only a vague recollection of getting into bed.

He woke to find Judy sitting on the bed. She was holding his hand. She smelt of soap, and her hair was between wet and dry, and she looked as if she had been weeping; the dirty pearl of a tear hung stubbornly to her cheek, refusing to fall.

'Is this Antigua?' he asked.

'Yes.'

'Have you found Salvador?'

Judy shook her head. 'How do you feel?' she said softly.

'Better, I think,' Quinn said. 'Where's Agustín?'

'I don't know. Gone . . .' Her voice trailed off.

She still had hold of his hand. Quinn brought his eyes down, slowly, not wanting to draw her attention to their fingers in case she pulled apart. But only if he saw them touching would he believe it.

'What are you thinking?' Quinn asked her.

'About Mercedes.' Judy looked at their fingers. She used her free hand to trace lines across his trapped fingertips. 'I found someone who said that a man who might be Salvador is sometimes in a hotel near here in the evenings. It's four o'clock now. We'll go about nine.' She looked at Quinn and without saying anything curled on to the bed and put her face on his chest. She was sobbing and Quinn stroked her hair. Her thin shoulders shook and Quinn put an arm around her to pull her more on to the bed. She cried for many minutes before falling silent. Gradually the light changed into orange and made its slow slide across the ceiling, further and further before slipping away out the window, until they were lying in darkness. The rain came down heavily and there was a rumble of thunder that would not break. Quinn felt Judy's hot breath on his chest, and then he, too, fell asleep.

In the rain of the early evening Quinn dreamt he was in the desert talking about revenge to Rafael, who stood clutching his briefcase. Stupid people, Rafael said, think there is only one kind of revenge: to kill. In his dream, Quinn said, defensively, No, no, I know that, this is something I know about; and, laughing, Rafael drifted back into a forest behind him, back, back and away. The forest disappeared with him, and Quinn was left alone and naked in the desert.

Judy was gone when he woke. He sat up and looked for her in the semi-darkness. The wall of his stomach became cramped and nausea rose into his mouth. He searched for the Lomotil pills and found them on the floor beside the bed. He swallowed two. There was a knock on the door.

'I can't find Agustín,' Judy said. 'Are you well enough to come with me to find Salvador?'

'Yes. Wait a minute.'

Quinn spent fifteen minutes in the bathroom, vomiting and showering. It was nine-fifteen when they left to make the short walk to the hotel.

Judy said, 'We don't even know if anyone's after us. Don't you find that odd? To be running away, and not know if you really have to be running. It's almost as if, if we wanted, we could just go to the airport, buy tickets and fly home.'

They were outside a colonial building painted a red the shade of rich clay. The brickwork around the windows was painted white, and behind the ornate bars terracotta pots held musty-smelling red geraniums. They entered into a courtyard through a wide doorway. Underfoot the lines of the cobblestones made an interlocking pattern that was intricate and endless, and Quinn was reminded of a kaleidoscope he had been given for a birthday long ago.

Above the first door on the right was a sign: RECEPTIÓN. A thin man of medium height, his hair swept back to reveal a long, fine widow's peak, bowed slightly and said in Spanish, 'Good evening. How may we be of service?'

The man's manner took them both slightly by surprise. It was watchful and formally polite, but there was also a disarming elegance to it.

'We're here to meet someone,' Judy said.

'Of course,' the man replied. He was tidily dressed in a suit which was neither fashionable nor out of date, and his tie was carefully knotted. He extended a hand to the left. 'You will be more comfortable in the restaurant. Please.'

'Thank you,' Quinn said.

'*A sus ordenes,*' the man said gravely, inclining his head.

There was no one in the small restaurant except an Indian barman dressed in black trousers, white shirt, red bow-tie and cream linen jacket. Judy ordered a glass of wine for herself and a mineral water for Quinn.

'Does Salvador definitely come here?' Quinn asked after a time.

'I don't know,' Judy said in a dispirited voice. 'I asked all over town. No one seemed to know him. Then a woman in another hotel said she knew a Salvador who comes here.' Judy paused. She said in a weary voice, 'It's pretty thin. Maybe I should just forget the whole thing, go back to San Francisco, or New York.'

Quinn said nothing.

After a while Judy said, 'When I talked to Victor Jank, back in LA, I could see him as a loving husband, a father, a good neighbour. You could imagine him helping to change the wheel on your car, or unblocking your drains, fixing burst pipes, doing stuff like that. He seems so normal. If we had to argue our case in front of some passer-by, who do you think he would side with? Us? He wouldn't. We are the outsiders in this. Jank is the one on the inside.'

She looked at Quinn seriously, as if for reassurance.

'I don't know what to say,' Quinn replied with a sorry smile. The truth was he knew this ground; it was his. Judy was just discovering its bitterness, but he had tramped it for a long time. Its contours and paths were familiar to him, and did not surprise him any more.

Judy turned to the barman. 'Do you know Salvador?' she asked in Spanish.

The barman was drying a wine glass with a white towel. He slowed and looked at the wall beside him, then back at Judy. He said, shaking his head, 'No, señorita. I am sorry.'

'He comes here regularly.'

'I don't know anyone of that name.' He inspected the glass, put it down and picked up another.

Half an hour later the man from reception entered carrying a sheaf of papers. He inclined his head towards Judy and Quinn. 'Your friend has not arrived?'

'Not yet,' Judy said. 'Maybe you know him? His name is Salvador.'

'Lamentably, I do not know the gentleman,' he said in his gravely polite manner. 'Perhaps you would like to dine here while you wait for him?'

'No thanks,' Judy said, 'we've eaten.'

The man smiled and bowed. 'With your permission.'

'Please,' Judy said.

The man sat down at a table opposite them and laid out his papers. He ordered a glass of wine, which the barman brought to him. 'Your wine, Don Saturnino.'

'Thank you, Jorge.'

The barman retreated and Don Saturnino took a fountain pen from an inside pocket. Carefully, he unscrewed the top and began going over the papers.

'How long will we wait?' Quinn asked.

'I don't know,' Judy said, then added: 'How are you feeling?'

'Better.'

Quinn and Judy were nursing their drinks when two men entered. Don Saturnino was on his feet at once and took their hands enthusiastically.

'Come and see the song. I think it is ready now. Not perfect, you understand, but we'll see. Jorge, fetch my guitar.'

The men nodded politely to Quinn and Judy before settling at the table. Don Saturnino's manner had changed, an excitable side to him had emerged with the arrival of his two friends. He said, pressing the box of the guitar high up against his chest, 'I don't know if I can sing this song. It may be too high for my voice.'

Jorge set drinks for the men on the table.

Both Quinn and Judy were astonished by Don Saturnino's singing. His voice was clear and high, and perfectly pitched. At the end of the song his companions applauded the singer, who bowed with grace.

Both Quinn and Judy clapped and Don Saturnino acknowledged them. 'The next song,' he said to them, 'comes from the pampas of Argentina and you must imagine that certain notes represent the high whistling of the wind in the grass, which is one of the great constants of that place.'

Don Saturnino was accompanied by the elder of the two

267

men with him. The man had a rich baritone voice, and his chin and the spare flesh on his throat quivered whenever he held a note. They sang alternate verses and for the last combined in a duet. Quinn watched the two men and noted how little their appearances hinted at the richness of their voices.

They sang more, and later the other man sang to the accompaniment of Don Saturnino's guitar. No one else came into the restaurant.

At midnight, Judy, dragging herself away from the spell of the music, said they should go. Don Saturnino got to his feet.

'Our friend has not come,' Judy said to him.

'I am sorry.'

'You're sure you don't know him? Salvador?'

Don Saturnino shook his head sadly. 'You do not know anything else about him?'

'He was a friend of my sister's, Mercedes Mendoza. They met here in Antigua. I don't know anything else about him.'

Don Saturnino seemed to be considering something. 'How long will you be staying in Antigua?' he asked slowly.

'We want to move on to Patzún as soon as possible.'

'Patzún is a dangerous place,' Don Saturnino said.

'It's where my sister stayed.'

'Tomorrow, will you be in Antigua?'

'I don't know.'

'Tomorrow is the feast day of San Antonio. There is a village named after the saint near here. You should go there. There will be a fiesta.'

'I don't think we'll have time,' Judy said apologetically.

'I think you should go,' Don Saturnino said; he added: 'I will meet you there at one o'clock.'

Judy said, 'Do you know Salvador?'

Don Saturnino was shepherding Judy from the restaurant into the courtyard, cutting off her attempts to ask more. 'It may be the same man. Until tomorrow at one. Goodnight,' he said, once more inclining his head.

'Goodnight.'

Don Saturnino shook hands with Quinn and bowed again.

'He knows Salvador,' Judy said as they got to the main square. It was almost deserted. Only a few tourists sat out at the tables in front of the bars and restaurants.

'I think you're right,' Quinn said.

Judy was brisker now. The good news, the trickle of hope Don Saturnino had started, had enlivened her. She seemed only half aware of Quinn and he began to feel angry. Only when she was sad and made lonely by her situation did she come to him.

'We'll go to San Antonio,' she said quickly. He stared at her in silence and she picked up on his mood. 'I'm going to bed,' she said.

Quinn's sleeplessness and stomach pains had made him childish and irritable, but Judy's behaviour would probably have been enough to provoke a burst of temper from him in any case. He turned away from her and banged his fist into a wall.

She stared at him in silence for some moments before saying, 'Quinn, that's pathetic.'

'I don't give a fuck.' He smashed his fist into the wall again; the skin came off the knuckles and a bead of blood slipped down the side of his finger.

'Someone as fine as you behaving like that,' she said, 'it makes me sad.'

Quinn waited until she had gone. He did not want her to see that his anger had disintegrated, that she had dispersed it. He held his hand and cursed himself under his breath.

'My friend,' someone hailed Quinn from one of the tables near by. Quinn saw a man stand up and pull out a chair of white plastic and aluminium from a table and indicate it to Quinn. 'Please. Join me for a nightcap.'

It was Rafael; he was smiling collusively. 'With women there are always tensions,' he said. 'For true friendship we must stay men to men and women to women, that's what I say. Do you agree?'

Quinn took the seat. 'What are you doing in Antigua?'

'Antigua is more or less the centre of the business I am in.' He indicated his briefcase under the table with a brief gesture. 'So I come here often. I miss my family, but it's a nice town, no? Have you visited the ruins?'

'Not yet.'

'You must see them. You will understand better what I told you about the destruction of the continent. You remember what I told you?'

'Of course.'

'Good. I think that the ruins tell us something more.'

'What?'

'As I told you, Antigua is in some ways the centre of *La droga*. Here, on one hand, the ruins signify the decay of one empire and the drugs signify the existence of another. But what is important is that the relationship between the north and the south stay as it is. You see, the north overthrew the south and became dominant and rich. Naturally, I believe that is a catastrophe because I am *latino*. But the United States, because it's so rich, makes possible the existence of a new empire here in the south. Thus I am not like the communists or the terrorists. I do not want the yankees overthrown. They are making possible my empire. That's why I can call myself a nationalist and support, and I mean sincerely, the status quo. Do you agree?'

'I don't know what you're asking me to agree to.'

'That my position is the only realistic one, given the circumstances.'

Quinn shrugged. 'I suppose so.'

'Good. I am happy you understand. Now, we drink and you can tell me your impressions of Mexico and Guatemala. Then we will discuss women.'

When the phone rang, Alice, who had been lying on the couch watching television, got such a fright she let the glass drop. It broke on the floor and the liquid spread into the carpet like ink on blotting paper. She looked at Roy wide-eyed as Roy made his way to the instrument, approaching it as if it held danger. Roy lifted the receiver. He pressed it to his ear for several seconds before saying, 'Yes?'

'Roy. It's me,' Agustín said in Spanish.

'Man, oh man. Where are you?'

'Antigua.'

'Where?'

'Antigua, in Guatemala.'

'Is everything okay? Are you okay? Man' – Roy had trouble getting his voice to work – 'you know what they done? Did you hear?'

'I read it in the *Times*.'

They were silent.

'What are you going to do?' Roy asked.

'It's going to end here.'

'Shit, man.' There was silence from the other end. 'Agustín?'

'Roy?'

'I'm here.'

Roy glanced at Alice and turned away. He was trembling.

'Do you think if you leave revenge too long the act becomes meaningless?' Agustín asked.

'Maybe,' Roy said uncertainly.

'Dulio never believed in revenge, *the* act of the individual, only in people doing things together.'

'Man, that's philosophy. I can't handle that stuff. All I know is saving yourself . . .'

'That was Dulio's point. Don't you see? We can't save ourselves, only each other.'

'Save yourself, man.'

'There's nothing left for me to do, except to keep others from sinking. This is to say goodbye and to thank you for everything.'

The line went dead.

'Agustín? Agustín?'

Roy put the phone down.

'What's happening?' Alice asked. She was shaking, and Roy went over to hold her.

'Don't worry, baby. It was Agustín. He's in Guatemala, in Antigua. Oh man, is he in trouble.'

'What about us? Are we in trouble?'

Roy shook his head. 'No, honey.' He pulled her head forward and kissed her hair. He started to pace the floor, but the pacing did not relieve his agitation. He smacked his fist into his hand over and over as he walked. 'Baby,' he said, 'I just need some air. Do you mind?'

'No, honey,' Alice said from the sofa. 'You go right ahead.'

Roy got his jacket, bent down to kiss Alice and went outside. Alice listened until she was sure he had gone, then rushed into the bedroom. She emerged a couple of minutes later with a travelling case and an armful of clothes. She stuffed the clothes into the case and sat on it to get it shut. She dialled the airport and got the time of the next flight to Houston. She lit a cigarette and dialled again, this time calling a cab. 'Make it fast,' she said. She looked at her watch, stubbed out the cigarette and lit another one. She got up and walked to the window, chewing the inside of her mouth. She picked up her purse and found a scrap of paper, which she took to the phone.

'This is Alice Marie Washington,' she said when the man on the other end answered. 'Mr Zenga gave me this number and said I should call if I had anything to tell him.'

'Yes?' Victor Jank said.

'Well, I do. That Agustín fellow, he's in Antigua. It's down there in Guatemala. He just called right now.'

Outside a car horn sounded. Alice took the phone to the window and saw the taxi.

'I got to go now. Will you make sure and tell Mr Zenga what I said? It's real important.'

'Thank you for calling.'

The driver was pressing on the horn. Alice grabbed her case and ran out. She did not close the door behind her.

EIGHTEEN

When Judy knocked, Quinn was still in bed, though it was late and he had been awake for some time. He covered himself with a towel and let her in.

Judy looked at him for some seconds. She said, 'I shouldn't have walked off like that last night.'

'It's okay,' Quinn answered hurriedly, embarrassed at the note of conciliation in her voice and at the memory of what he had done. The knuckles of his right hand ached. He bunched his fist and felt the skin tauten and break.

'I'll get dressed,' Quinn said.

Judy pursed her lips and nodded.

'Did Agustín come back?'

'No,' Quinn shouted from the bathroom.

'What's happened to him? Where is he?'

Quinn did not reply at once. At last he said, 'I think he believes that, for him, it's over.'

When he emerged from the bathroom, Judy asked, 'What do you mean? What's over?'

'I don't know, Judy,' Quinn said with an emphasis Judy took to mean the topic was closed, and she felt Quinn was punishing her for failing to understand something that was obvious; punishing her, too, for the part she had played in Agustín's disappearance.

Quinn finished dressing and when they stepped out into the cloister, Judy took his arm and pressed herself against him, chuckling softly. They walked on together. Quinn was surprised and delighted by her mood this morning. He started to laugh.

'I've never seen anyone beat up on a wall before,' she said.

'We're old enemies.'

On a street west of the plaza, they ate in a restaurant run by a Dutch woman who served fruit salad, orange juice, strong coffee, eggs and toast with a variety of jams and marmalades. Quinn picked at the food and wondered if his stomach would accept the coffee. He decided to chance it. He had not vomited since the previous afternoon, and, besides, his head needed it. He had drunk a great deal with Rafael. Judy ate everything on her plate and ordered more.

'How long will it take to get to San Antonio?' Quinn asked.

'Twenty minutes. Are you in the mood to party?' She looked at him with a grin.

'I've been partying. I bumped into that fellow Rafael – do you remember him? – from La Paz.'

'He's here?'

'On business, he says. We had a few drinks.'

She studied him for a moment, until he had to say, 'What?'

'Why have you come with me?'

'A lot of reasons.'

'Like?'

Quinn sipped his coffee. 'Things haven't been going right for me for some time. I want to help you.'

'Helping me won't make things go right for you.'

'I think it might help put things back together.'

'I want to apologize to you for something,' Judy said.

'Don't. You have no apology to make to me.'

'That night in the hotel in La Paz, on the landing. I didn't mean the things I said. I behave badly when people try to tell me they care for me. Perhaps I've had it too easy.'

They spoke no more until they finished the coffee and food and were outside in the street. Judy looked at her watch.

'I left the car keys at the hotel,' she said. They set off across the plaza and down Quinta Calle. As they neared the hotel, Judy said, 'I'm worried about Agustín. I treated him badly.' She heard her words and felt ashamed: I sound trite,

274

she thought, I sound desperately trite. 'What is your wife's name?' she asked.

'Monica.'

She was surprised that Quinn had answered her. Emboldened, she continued with another question. 'Do you still think about her?'

Quinn did not reply.

'Will you tell me – not now, later – what happened between you?'

Quinn nodded. 'Yes.'

They collected the key from the reception clerk and crossed the patio to Judy's room.

'Now, where's my bag?' Judy said. She found it beside the bed and picked it up. 'Have you ever . . .'

'What's wrong?' Quinn asked when she stopped.

Judy said nothing, but sat down on the bed with the bag on her knees. She pulled out bits and pieces – a compact, an address book, a purse, lipsticks, a small perfume spray – and tossed them on the bed.

'What is it?' Quinn asked again.

'My gun,' Judy said. She got up and looked around the room. Her eyes fell on a shirt draped over a chair before a full-length mirror. She went over and picked it up. 'Someone's been in here. I didn't leave this shirt on the chair, I know I didn't.' She dropped the shirt and pushed her hand through her hair.

'You had a gun?' Quinn said.

'I had a licence because of the work I did in the Public Defender's Office.'

'When did you last see it?'

She thought for a moment. 'Last night.'

Quinn was examining the lock on the door. It was not broken, but it could easily have been prised open without leaving marks.

'Pack your stuff,' Quinn said.

Judy paid the bill for the two rooms with her credit card. As Quinn watched her, he heard someone greet him from behind. It was Rafael.

'Are you leaving?' Rafael asked.

Quinn said, 'Just changing hotels. How's business?'

'Not so good. You have read the paper this morning?'

'I don't read Spanish,' Quinn said.

'It's very depressing. A village near here was taken over by the communists during the night. There was shooting, bombs, everything. Terrible. Some people are dead. All this means it's harder for me to do my business. More police, more soldiers. You have seen the helicopters?'

'No.'

'There are two. I saw them this morning. Military ones.'

Judy came away from the desk. Rafael greeted her formally, then patted Quinn on the arm. 'Well, excuse me, I must collect some things.'

'Let's go,' Quinn said to Judy.

A few minutes out of town, they passed a military checkpoint. A bus had been stopped. Two jeeps were parked nose to nose across the road, and squatting in the cover of the trees and scrub to either side Quinn saw a dozen or so young soldiers in camouflage fatigues. One soldier trained his rifle sight on a group of the bus's passengers, most of them Indian women, who were standing by the door of the vehicle. The other soldiers had their rifles across their knees or pointing up to the sky. An NCO was checking the passengers' papers, one by one, while his men went through their baggage. Only the NCO spoke, and when he addressed the passengers he did so curtly, without looking at them. Above, the blades of a circling helicopter thumped the air.

An army truck pulled up alongside the car. In the back two soldiers, neither of whom appeared to be more than sixteen years old, sat with their weapons across their knees. Between them was a young Indian dressed in a dirty, open-necked blue shirt and jeans; he was barefoot, and his hands were bound. His hair was thick and raven, roughly cut so that it stood up in tufts on his crown. There was a large, dark smudge on his left temple.

An officer leaned into the driver's side, startling Judy and Quinn.

'Tourists?' the officer asked in English. He wore jungle fatigues, a visored cap pulled down low so that his brow was completely covered, reflector sunglasses that covered the middle band of his broad face; in his wide mouth he clamped a cigar. He stretched an arm across the roof of the car and bent his body at the hips to look in at them. He had a gut. Quinn put his age at over fifty.

'Yes,' Judy answered in English. 'We're from the States.' She put effort into the smile for the officer, whose face remained studiedly impassive.

'What is your name?'

'Judith Mendoza.'

'Where are you going?'

'San Antonio, for the fiesta.' Judy was hoping he would not ask for their papers. 'I'm told it's very colourful.'

The officer grunted. 'For Indians, maybe.' He looked at Judy's case in the back seat. 'What hotel are you staying at?'

'We just checked out of La Posada Don Rodrigo in Antigua.'

'Any other luggage?'

'No,' Judy said.

'You're travelling light.'

'We left most of our stuff in San Cristóbal in Mexico. We thought we'd spend a couple of days down here in Guatemala. We did it kind of on impulse.'

'How do you like our country?' the officer asked.

'Beautiful.'

'The land of eternal spring. Is this man your husband?'

'No.'

'Boyfriend?' For the first time the officer's face showed some sign of animation; he was grinning to show his understanding of the ways of the young.

'Yes,' Judy said with a coy smile to show she was willing to be the recipient of the officer's indulgence.

'What do you do in the United States?'

'I teach at NYU.'

The officer's grin widened. He took a long drag from the cigar and blew the smoke upwards.

'My son is at NYU. He is studying business administration.'
'Really? I'm in the law school.'
'Yes. His name is Efraín García. Maybe you know him?'
'I don't believe so. The U is really big.'
'So he tells me.' The officer was smiling broadly. 'Some coincidence, huh?'
'Really.'
'I am General Efraín García.' The general took a printed card from his top pocket and handed it to Judy. The smell of the cigar smoke filled the car.
'I'll look up your son when we get back and tell him I met you. Business administration, right?'
'Business.' The general said the word with admiration. 'Please do so. He will be happy to meet you. What a coincidence,' the general said again, shaking his head. 'NYU.'
'Yes,' Judy said, 'isn't it?'
From the driver's cab of the truck, another official called to the general, who grunted a reply. Quinn and Judy saw the soldiers in the truck raise the Indian to his feet. The man's hands had been tied behind him. The soldiers hoisted him down.
'People say this country has many problems,' the general said to Judy and Quinn. 'In truth it has only one.' He glanced at the Indian prisoner. 'Well,' he said, 'I hope you enjoy the fiesta at San Antonio. Myself, I find such celebrations uncivilized.' His face had set again, the points of contact, for what they were worth, obliterated.
The general did not wait for a reply, but straightened and shouted a command to the drivers of the two jeeps. The men put the vehicles in reverse and the jeeps parted. The general banged the car roof with the palm of his hand twice and waved Judy on.
The road to San Antonio had started well, but, almost immediately after the checkpoint, turned into a narrow track with tall, thin trees on either side. The mist lingered about the higher branches like cords of cigarette smoke. Birds cawed and the noises were echoic; the flapping of their

wings was heavy, like blankets beaten from windows. Rain-drops, the advance guard of a storm, splashed on leaves and hit the car like a handful of pebbles. There was a sudden crack and Quinn and Judy turned to each other.

'Was that a shot?' Judy said.

'I don't know,' Quinn said, though he was sure it was. He remembered the images that had come into his mind as they had driven into Guatemala, of forests and clearings and the tramp of the executioners' feet. He concentrated on the rain. It was falling torrentially and the wipers were unable to keep the windscreen clear.

'Who would have taken the gun?' Judy said.

'Someone in the hotel?'

'Agustín?'

'How's he going to find us?'

'Shit,' Judy said. 'This is so messy.'

They saw a roadside shack and pulled over. The shack's roof, sheets of plastic held down by car tyres, was taking a terrible beating and looked as though it would buckle at any moment; the spray was like a corona. An Indian woman with a child at her breast stared at the strangers in the car; beside her a young boy stared dumbly out at the rain.

After a quarter of an hour the rain gave way. The wind picked up and sent its song and hiss around the trees. Then it, too, died away; the clouds moved on and the sun came out.

The plaza before the church had been converted into a bull ring by a crude fence. Several hundred men and women circled the ring, the women almost all in Indian dress, the men barefoot in rough work trousers and shirts. Many had climbed on to the fence and the tin roofs of the shacks around the plaza from which beer and soft drinks were sold. Quinn and Judy joined the press. The smell of the bodies was sour and of earth.

Inside the ring a dozen or so men were at different stages of drunkenness. Most of them were young, but one or two had grey hairs. They carried beer bottles, and one held before him a bright blue plastic cape that had once been a sack for weedkiller; another held a black bin liner. The bull glared at the men, but did not charge. After five minutes the animal snorted, turned around and looked for a way back to the refuge of its pen. The crowd tossed rubbish and pieces of wood at the bull, which eventually charged, more in exasperation than anger.

Judy and Quinn walked away from the ring and along the rutted street. The villagers' homes were of cane and thatch with compacted earth floors, and they ran off the street in narrow alleys that petered out within a couple of hundred feet. Shrines to the baby Jesus and the Madonna were set out like sentinels at the alley mouths; the papal colours were everywhere. Judy took Quinn's arm and hugged him as they walked in silence, inspecting the faces of the people they passed for that of Saturnino.

They heard music and followed the sound. It took them behind the church and into a muddy clearing where there was a huge shrine, the biggest they had seen, and, beside it, a marimba band. A couple of dozen villagers stood about and watched the musicians, poor men dressed in their best clothes. The music was melodic and between happy and sad, as if it were saying to the listener, You choose. Judy leaned into Quinn, holding his arm with both hands.

From behind the shrine four *gigantes* appeared and the people gasped and laughed. They were fabulously painted and attired papier-mâché figures, ten foot high; the men inside them were on stilts. The first was a French colonial officer in a sky-blue tunic and kepi; the second was a Spanish grandee in gold and black, his face painted a colour that was the perfect imitation of Judy's: both men were thin-lipped and proper. The other two figures were black women, the kind Quinn assumed came from Haiti or some such place: they wore their hair in a handkerchief and had dangling earrings of gold. Their breasts were enormous and comic, and their hips wide, and the smiles painted on their faces were coquettish and, from some angles, scornful, knowing and mocking. The female *gigantes* danced with the solemn men. The music quickened. Judy took Quinn's hand and coaxed him into the clearing. They danced breast to breast. Some of the Indian women giggled behind their hands.

Quinn heard the thunder toll and felt a bloated raindrop land on his temple and trickle down the side of his face. The thunder sounded again. The light changed, and then came the rain. The *gigantes* waddled into the church for shelter, and the musicians lifted their instruments and scurried after them. The Indian women laughed as they ran. Judy reached up and put her hand on the side of Quinn's face. He bent and kissed her. When their mouths parted, Judy clung to him. The rain lashed them.

'We should get out of this,' Judy said.

They ran to the church. The people were standing silently, glumly looking out at the clash of the rainfall on the ground.

'I wonder if he will come,' Judy said.

'I'm sure he will.'

'Do you know,' Judy said slowly, 'I don't know if I care any more.'

'What about Mercedes?'

After a moment she said quietly, 'Maybe it's because everything has been so chaotic. Agustín's disappeared, the gun's vanished, just one thing after another going wrong.'

When the downpour stopped, the people began chattering and laughing, as if the rain had changed their moods and with its passing something had been lifted from them. They poured out of the church, the younger ones running ahead to get good positions.

Judy had turned to walk further into the now near-deserted church and Quinn followed her. The altar was gilt, and in the chapels to the sides shrines surrounded by candles and flowers had been set up. A few old Indian women prayed, whispering their prayers and supplications in a drone that rose and fell in rhythms more ancient than the things the building and its artefacts had been inspired by. Judy stopped at an alcove. Dozens of crutches were suspended from the ceiling above the head of an alabaster figure of a monk. An old woman rose and found Quinn and

281

Judy gazing up at them. She smiled and said, 'Hermano Pedro will answer all your prayers.' She looked up at the crutches. 'His speciality is to make the lame walk. He can also make the one you love love you in return, a much harder feat.'

'Then he must be very popular here,' Judy said.

'We have many happy marriages,' the woman replied.

The woman left them, and Quinn and Judy went outside. They spent an hour walking around the village, and only when the dark approached did they give up on Saturnino. Quinn could not tell whether Judy was disappointed or relieved. They walked back to the car, past fires on which Indian women cooked. People stood around in small groups. The light was eerie and belonged to another place.

In a shack across from where the car was parked some men sat on rough benches and drank beer and rum. Agustín was among them, but neither Quinn nor Judy saw him. Agustín watched as Judy kissed Quinn and got into the car.

Judy drove slowly and with her headlights on full.

'What are we going to do?' she said.

'We'll find another hotel in Antigua, then go and see Saturnino again.'

'I'm not sure I want to,' Judy said. 'I want to get out of here. Tomorrow morning we'll go to the airport in Guatemala City. I was never going to find Mercedes.'

'What about Agustín?'

'This is his world, Quinn. We're the strangers here.' Her voice was thick and unsteady. Abruptly, she pulled over to the side of the road. 'Will you drive?'

For the rest of the journey Judy cried.

In Antigua they found an expensive hotel north of the plaza, a former convent. Judy spoke to the clerk in Spanish while Quinn looked at the garden courtyard.

'Come,' she said when she had the key.

The room had a wooden floor and elaborate dark wood-panelled furniture. Steps led up to a bathroom. The bed was wide, and an ornately barred window gave out on to the street. Judy took off her jacket and closed the shutters. She was watching Quinn as she kicked off her shoes. She leaned back against the wall and waited for him.

She was a small woman, and light, and Quinn had not expected to find hips and breasts so round, or the curve on her stomach that hinted at weight to come; the flesh of her pleased him. When she was lying on her back, he lay beside her with his hand on her breast, kissing her. Her knees were bent and drawn up together and it took time for her to let him reach her. He brought his thigh up between her legs and opened his eyes. She was watching him. She gave a small laugh because she knew what he had felt, and that his discovery of her softness and wetness had opened his eyes. She traced a finger around his lips, looking at his mouth with serious eyes, her breathing becoming harder, her look growing more serious. She gave a little cry and pushed her fingers into Quinn's mouth. She took him on top of her and locked her ankles around his legs just below his knees.

Stories. Stories bind, though Quinn felt ashamed of telling his because he was retelling it, and he knew what effect his story would have. Its drama was too manipulative and he tried to reduce it, but that made it worse because Judy misinterpreted him, thinking he was being noble. Judy asked and Quinn told. She listened and from time to time kissed him, on the face, the eyes, the neck. She put her head on his chest although it was uncomfortable because he was so bony; she liked listening to the beat of his heart as he spoke, the accompaniment to the lyrics. He told her about Denis and Monica, about Seamus, about looking for Jim Kerr, about the misted windows and beer-ringed tables in New York, about Jackson and Glasgow, about Brian and the woman he made love to. He felt Judy's shoulder was cold and asked her if she wanted to get under the sheets and she said no and hugged him. During his story her hug grew into a fold so that she folded herself over him, found him, and moving on top of him as he kissed her brown nipples, moved until her muscles gave out and she said, 'No, I can't do that any more. He rolled her on to her back and finished it with her, and she lay for a long time without moving. He told her Agustín's story and she listened silently, and although she had already been quiet, the silence after he mentioned the name of Agustín seemed deeper, more complete, so that both Quinn and Judy knew that all this had to be worked out, and that it would cause pain. There was pain to come.

Stories. Stories bind, Quinn knew; and they separate. When Agustín and Quinn had counted on words, the experience left them feeling naked in front of each other; but here, naked in front of Judy, he felt protected by them. He loved her and he told her so. When he rose from her, their breasts separating, a bead of sweat trickled quickly from her nipple and then hung, growing fatter and heavier; as it was about to burst forward with the weight, Quinn put his head down and licked it up. She put both hands in his hair and gripped him with her legs.

Quinn was awake, Judy asleep on her side, her back to him. He ran his hand down her back, on to her buttock and between her legs. She was soft. She stirred and mumbled into the pillow. Quinn moved against her, and she accepted him that way.

They fell asleep.

Outside, in the darkness, a man was walking. He stopped at the door. Quinn rolled off the bed and crawled to the door while Judy continued to sleep. He looked around for a weapon. The only thing near by was Judy's handbag. He gathered the strap in his fist and, his back against the wall, rose. He was not going to wait for him, was not going to be surprised. He put his hand on the door knob and pulled it open. A man tumbled inside.

Quinn lashed out with the handbag. Judy awoke and cried out in fright. The bag's contents rattled on the tiles. Quinn drew himself up for a second swing when he saw Saturnino in a half-crouch, one arm raised in protection.

'I didn't mean to frighten you,' Saturnino said in English. He was looking at Quinn's nakedness. His eyes went to the handbag, as did Quinn's.

'What do you want?' Quinn said, closing the door.

Judy was up. She had a sheet pressed to her front.

'It's all right,' Quinn said to her. 'It's Saturnino.'

'I want you to come with me now. You have a car, don't you?'

'Yes,' Judy said.

'Follow me.'

'Why didn't you turn up at San Antonio today?'

'There has been trouble. I want you to come now. There is someone who will tell you about Mercedes. It will be a long journey.'

'I'm sorry to be calling so late, but communications here are problematic,' Nick Zenga was saying. 'You cannot believe it. You know you can't even make international calls from the hotels in this town? You got to go to the Guatel office and wait in line till they book your call.'

'Alice rang. They're right with you in Antigua,' Victor Jank said.

'We've seen them. At least the Mendoza woman and the white man. His name, by the way, is Sean Quinn.'

'Who is he?'

'Just a loser got mixed up with the Mendoza woman.'

'What about Agustín?'

'No sign of him so far. I know they drove together from the border to Antigua. My man followed them from Mexico. He says Agustín disappeared some time yesterday and hasn't showed up since. We got in this afternoon. So, what should we do?'

'I think they've had enough time to enjoy themselves at our expense.'

'It's done, Victor.'

'What about Hernández?'

'Pascual is coming along well. He knows what he's got to do.'

'So everything is working out?'

'Beautiful.'

'I've been praying for you, for all of us,' Jank said.

'I feel that, Victor. I know why things go so well for us.'

'You think you'll have any trouble with the authorities down there?'

'I can give you a categoric no on that. Don't worry about us.'

'You can call on our people there if you need them.'

'The authorities here have been totally understanding of our situation. Plus we have Rex, who has a lot of friends here.'

'Nick, give Rex and Hernández a free hand on this.'

Zenga paused before saying, 'I will.'

'God bless.'

Zenga stepped out of the booth and made his way to the desk, where he paid the clerk. As he stepped outside, he saw Rex running towards him.

'They're leaving,' Rex said a little breathlessly. 'In the hire car. They took the road to Chimaltenango.'

'Damn,' Zenga said. 'Damn it.' He scratched his head.

'There's no problem. There's only one road and we can catch them.'

'Okay. Where's my man?'

'He's outside the hotel.'

'Tell him to wait here in case Agustín shows up. After that he can join us at the mission in Santiago. Meet us at the pick-up in five minutes.'

Zenga jogged the two blocks to the pick-up. He burst into song. It was 'You Can't Always Get What You Want'. He was not sure why the song was appropriate, but felt sure it was.

'The winning team is about to touch down,' Zenga said, as he climbed into the driver's seat. He leaned over and kissed Pascual on the mouth.

NINETEEN

H alf an hour from Antigua, Judy and Quinn came to the military base just before Chimaltenango. The two guards had let Saturnino's car through, but, as Judy and Quinn approached, a soldier stepped into the road and waved them down. The soldier stooped and shone a torch through the driver's window. Judy flinched when the beam struck, as though her face had been slapped, and, blinded, she submitted to the inspection. Whatever the soldier saw did not interest him, and he motioned them on impatiently before turning back to his friend, who said something that provoked crude laughter from them both.

At intervals they passed more military bases. Some were purpose-built and heavily fortified, others were no more than primitive stockades guarded by men and boys in torn civilian clothes and sweat-stained baseball hats; these poor soldiers carried machetes or old bolt-action rifles, and they stared glumly as the cars passed; all had the same look of suspicion and resentment mixed with sadness.

Judy drove and Quinn stared out into the blackness. It was a dark he did not know or understand. He was from the city, and, like all city people, he knew the dark as half-light, never the pitch of the countryside: a dark without points of light, tangled and congested, silent, with no guides.

He shivered and turned for reassurance to look at Judy. She had a frown of concentration, and the *V* of veins in her forehead stood out in ridges. Her small chin was forward in a way that could have suggested determination, but which Quinn, because he knew her now, understood was Judy trying to hold herself together. She was frightened, and did not talk.

They had been driving for about an hour and a half, hanging on to the tail-lights of Saturnino's car, when they left the highway for a secondary road. Within minutes the road gave out and they were driving on a track. It was so rutted that for much of the time the cars were in second gear, and they lurched uncertainly this way and that. At one place they went down a steep gradient and Judy, without meaning to, put the clutch in and lost control of the car. The trees were marching into the road and their branches scraped along the car's roof as it picked up speed down the slope. Judy shouted 'Shit' and Quinn clutched the dashboard with both hands and made his arms rigid. The gradient unexpectedly gave out and they rolled to a stop in a shallow stream. Ahead they heard the trapped wheels of Saturnino's car spin in the mud, then break free. The red lights showed there was a steep incline before them. Judy put the car in first and roared forward, skidding several times before they made the hill.

Another hour along the tail-lights of Saturnino's car were extinguished. The trees formed an arc over the road and the effect was that of a tunnel.

'Put out the lights,' Quinn said.

Judy switched them off. 'What is it?'

Quinn leaned out the window. 'Slow down,' he whispered. Judy dropped her speed. In the sky was a beating noise that started as a whisper and grew louder in steady progression. The rhythm was broken by a muffled whoosh which sounded like a child's imitation of an explosion. The noise drifted away and there was silence.

'What is it?' Judy asked again.

Before Quinn could answer, the clatter was on them. It had come out of the silence and was deafening. Directly above, the air was being punched, and in a thousand places the canopy's holes let through points of pale light, as if a weak sun had swooped down to within inches of the tree-tops. The light itself trickled down as in a shower and flashed away almost instantly in a kind of strobe effect. After the machine passed, there was a noise in the air like the crashing of waves.

'Helicopters,' Quinn said, 'with searchlights. I think they're firing rockets, or maybe dropping grenades.'

Judy crashed the car.

Quinn found himself on the floor, squeezed into an impossible space. As he pulled himself up, he saw Saturnino at Judy's window.

'Are you okay?' he asked Judy in English.

'Yes, yes,' she said impatiently. She opened the door. 'I want to get out.' Her voice was urgent with a barely suppressed panic. Quinn watched as she broke free from the car, watched her as she tried to bring her nerve under control.

'Have they seen us?' Quinn asked. He could barely make Saturnino out, though he was only a couple of feet away.

'I don't think so,' Saturnino replied.

The cars were dented, Judy's more than Saturnino's, but not immobilized.

'What's happening?' Quinn asked.

'It's a raid by the army,' Saturnino told him. 'There is a village about eight kilometres from here. The army attacked it earlier today. This is their way of keeping up the terror.'

'Are there soldiers in the area, the ones who attacked the villages?'

'No. They come in, do what they do and leave.'

'Are we going to go on?' Quinn said.

'Someone will come and take us by foot. The village is very isolated.' Saturnino paused before adding, 'I should warn you.'

Quinn was not sure what Saturnino meant, whether his warning referred to the village's isolation, implying a walk, or whether he had left unfinished another, darker warning.

'How long before this person comes?' Judy intervened. Quinn could not see her clearly, just her silhouette, but her voice told him she was more in control.

'We must wait,' Saturnino replied.

'Is Mercedes there? Is she alive?' Judy asked.

'Please. Be patient.'

The voices came out of the dark, disembodied. Quinn longed for daylight.

Quinn did not hear them approach. He and Saturnino had put the cars as far into the verge as possible, and he was locking the doors when he heard Saturnino, off in the darkness, speak in Spanish in a way that he knew was not to Judy. He saw, or rather sensed before he saw, three or four figures come out of the shadows. They carried weapons at their hips. Saturnino spoke to him in English, telling him to be calm. There were some rapid exchanges in Spanish. He heard Judy's voice and heard her speak her sister's name. But what answer she received he could not tell.

Within seconds they were walking in single file along a trail; Judy and Quinn went in that curious manner of those who are half guests, half prisoners, with only something very small dividing the two states. Quinn saw that there were young women among the armed figures and, when he got closer, that the weapons they carried were crude, home-made sub-machine guns.

The trail became so narrow that the line along which they walked soon lost the last of its definition, and Quinn found himself ducking, stretching, craning and weaving to make his way forward. In places the ground became rocky and broken, and as the displaced stones tumbled they made sounds that were metallic and almost musical.

They crossed streams and gullies, climbed and descended. There was light in the distance, dawn coming. As if the retreat of the dark had freed his thoughts, Quinn began to reflect on what had happened between him and Judy, and on what was going to happen. Mercedes was dead, of that there was no doubt. It was good, Quinn decided, that Judy was going to find out. Their lives had kept them both imprisoned. What had passed with Monica and Denis had kept Quinn locked in for too long now. He had tramped around – endlessly, pointlessly – waiting, looking for an excuse to give up. He thought of his time in New York when he looked for Jim Kerr, when loneliness and the shame that came with it first settled on him and he had started to stalk the edges of other people's lives. That was all over. He was coming back, he was being released from the thing that kept his life dead.

Judy, too, when she was freed from Mercedes, would feel what he now felt. He could not ask her now, would not be able to ask her when she found out about Mercedes, but he would, at some near-future time, ask her to continue her escape with him. And she would accept.

Quinn could make out Judy now in the pre-dawn light. She was walking ahead of him, small, neat, pushing branches out of her way. He felt terribly sad for a moment, and protective of her. He would do all he could to soften the blow of Mercedes's death.

He thought about Agustín, but those thoughts led nowhere, created only an anger, a defensive anger, in him. There built up in his mind an imaginary scene, a confrontation between him and Agustín. Agustín was shouting at him, accusing him of betrayal, of taking Judy away from him, and Quinn replied in a voice full of rage that he took what he wanted. The lines had been drawn, the sides had taken their stand. There was nothing left now except the confrontation. Let it come.

The armed man in front of Quinn stopped. He turned and motioned Quinn into a crouch, and the whole line followed suit. They stayed that way for ten minutes before they rose and continued on their way.

Fifteen minutes later the same thing happened again. No one spoke. Quinn squatted and waited. The black, closed clouds were opening, thinning out. The light was growing stronger. Quinn smelt something and his stomach rumbled. He realized he was hungry. A good sign. He had not vomited or been thrown into a coughing fit for some time, the smell was of cooked meat; pork, he decided. It mixed with the smell of wood smoke, and his stomach gurgled again, a long rumble of demand and expectation. He shifted his position

291

to ease the strain in his thighs; holding the squat for so long was exhausting. Where would he and Judy settle? It was the smell of food and its association with home life that made him think of this. Before he could answer his own question, the column rose on some silent order and moved off.

The trail widened out dramatically as they came into a field of trampled grass; it was like emerging from the tunnel into a football stadium.

The smell of roast meat was stronger now, and deliciously sweet. Quinn saw a cluster of buildings in the distance, and, a hundred yards before them, a knot of people in olive fatigues. Among them were three or four civilians, one a woman, her gleaming black hair in plaits, dressed in the mauves and purples and blues of Indian dress in this country. The woman and the other civilians were crying. A young girl in a combat jacket, tight blue jeans and red baseball hat, and carrying one of the home-made, blocky-looking sub-machine guns, looked at the new arrivals and spat; she worked the spittle into the ground with her foot.

Quinn did not know why he had not noticed it at once, but now he saw the thatched huts of the village were charred and smoking. He hesitated before moving on.

'Go on,' Saturnino whispered from behind. Quinn turned to look at him. The man retained the elegance and charm he had first noticed that night in Antigua, but now there was something mingled with it that was quite disturbing: an edge, a hardness that was harder because of what had gone before. Quinn realized he had underestimated the man.

Quinn stepped forward. His foot struck something and he almost tripped up. He looked down and saw it was the torso of a woman, charred down the left side. He spluttered and almost lost his balance. Saturnino put a hand out to keep him up. Quinn regained his footing. Saturnino indicated the group at the entrance to the village, and Quinn went on.

As he and Judy approached, the group separated. They parted like curtains drawn back to reveal a stage and its drama. Quinn and Judy walked through, and sensed eyes follow them.

They walked as in a sleep, and as if there were no choice but to go on. On either side of the path into the village, stakes, seven or eight feet high, had been driven into the ground. On top of each stake was a human head, badly charred but not burnt beyond recognition; behind the rictus each face retained its expression, it was still possible to see what had made it individual. Quinn looked to the ground, convinced that, like candles, the heads would have melted spots of flesh, but he saw nothing. He looked back up at one of the heads: at the side where the ear had been was a brittle nest of singed hair. He moved on.

In the doorway of a hut they saw a woman kneeling over a body. The woman was wailing soundlessly, and she rocked back and forth, her eyes fixed on the body. The scalp was peeled back and the top of the head was smouldering, wisps of smoke rising from it.

Quinn and Judy wandered on in their own terrible trance. A dog skipped across the mud street followed by an infant, naked except for a torn T-shirt. The child stopped to look at them, squatted to piss, ran after the dog.

They reached a clearing, a primitive square at one corner of which was a concrete well. Around the well were the bodies of a dozen or more people. A small group of Indians looked on silently. They stirred when they saw the strangers, but apart from that everything was still.

Suddenly, at the other end of the square, a hut burst into flame and the child they had seen reappeared, running to the site of the fire and standing before it, mesmerized. No one else moved, no one tried to quench the flames.

An elderly man detached himself from those beside the well. He beckoned to Quinn and Judy, and they went forward at his insistence. They passed the sprawl of bodies, and he led them to another clearing. Smoke rose from the ground and Quinn smelt something sharp and synthetic that caught in his nostrils: paraffin or petrol. Quinn could feel the heat of the ground come up through his shoes and he shifted uncomfortably. The old man, his bare feet as gnarled and scaly as deformed claws, stopped and pointed. It was a pyre of bodies, charred like pigs. Quinn looked away. His eyes fell on two men about to lift a dead woman; one took her arms, the other her ankles, and they lifted: the head rolled away.

They saw Saturnino approach. Judy began to cry, and Quinn went to comfort her. At his touch she pushed him violently away. He took hold of her again and held her tight.

'She's dead,' Judy said. 'That's what this is all about, isn't it?'

'We'll get away,' Quinn said. 'We're going home.'

She broke free. Saturnino was beside them.

'Why?' Judy demanded. 'Why are we here? You could have told me in Antigua that Mercedes was dead.'

Saturnino said nothing.

'She is dead,' Judy said in a way that was half-question, half-affirmation.

Saturnino nodded. Judy let out a sob, but recovered herself at once.

'Then why?'

'So that you would understand.'

'Understand what?' Judy said angrily.

Saturnino looked at her a long time and did not answer.

Judy screeched, 'No!' Quinn went to her, but she pushed him out of the way with surprising force. She strode off, back the way they had come.

When she had gone, Quinn said to Saturnino, 'Why didn't you tell her who you are, Salvador?'

'It would have made Mercedes's death too' – he paused in order to select the word – 'personal.' He added: 'For both of us.'

'Was her body found?'

'A body was found. I am sure it was Mercedes.' Saturnino looked away. The old man was standing before the pyre, gazing at it. 'You must understand that this, like what happened to Mercedes, is nothing out of the ordinary. But it has a meaning.'

'That's hard to believe.'

'We have to believe it. You can go back to the United States—'

'I'm not American,' Quinn interrupted.

Saturnino gazed at him for a moment. 'It makes no difference,' he said with a finality that made Quinn feel ashamed, as if he had tried to wriggle out of something on a technicality. 'You can go back to wherever you come from and shake your head at the arbitrary horrors of this place. For you and for Judy, it is a nightmare. But for us, who live here, it is our daily experience and we must find meaning in it. That old man' – Saturnino pointed at the barefoot figure before the pyre – 'will recover better than Judy, even though he has lost five members of his family. He knows this has a meaning, that it is part of his history and his future, whereas Judy sees the death of Mercedes only as a personal tragedy.'

'She has a right to do that, don't you think?' Quinn realized his question sounded naïve, but he felt he had been manipulated and it made him angry.

'Of course,' Saturnino said evenly. 'But I wanted to give her a choice about how she recovers from Mercedes's murder.'

'She'll recover without your help.'

'Perhaps. Though not by finding a meaning in the death of Mercedes, but by forgetting it.'

'What about you? You were Mercedes's lover? Have you forgotten her?' Quinn's tone was tight, just below anger.

Saturnino shook his head. 'I did not know Mercedes long before they murdered her. But I loved her, and I believe she loved me. I cannot say if the future would have sorted itself out for us. I miss her. But I cannot think of her death as a waste. I brought you here so you would understand that.'

Quinn said nothing.

'What will you do now?' Saturnino asked.

'Take her home.'

'To the states?'

'If I can.'

'She belongs there.'

Quinn started after Judy, followed, silently and at a distance, by Saturnino.

When they had cleared the village, Saturnino said, 'They

will take you back to your car. Go to Panajachel, it's the place for you. From there you can arrange things. Or you can drive to the Mexican border. You will be safe there.'

'Are you coming?'

'No,' Saturnino said. 'I'll leave you here.'

Because of his past, a belief had grown up in Quinn that he shared something with people like those he saw around him. But he now felt alien, a stranger among them – clumsy, crude, smug, self-important, the bringer of sadness and misery. There was no softness in Saturnino's farewell, such as it was: there was the hotelier's formal politeness, there was a stiff concern for his and Judy's well-being, but most of all there was reproach, implicit, unstated yet relentless. You do not belong here, Saturnino was saying, and you are not one of us. Quinn imagined Mercedes and Salvador together and felt envy twist within him. He was shut out of the secret, brilliant thing they had.

When Judy drove into Panajachel, it was just after ten o'clock, and the tourists were starting to come out of their hotels in search of the day's treasures. Quinn experienced a sensation he had not had for many years – of having seen and done momentous things during the night and then rejoining the ordinary world, moving among people whose day had just begun and who were unaware of what had gone on while they were asleep. He felt awake, alive; things were happening.

Judy had not spoken and had rebuffed with irritation Quinn's attempt to discuss what they had seen and learned. It was because she had lost her feelings, Quinn told himself, because she could not reach inside for them. He understood and did not press her.

She got them separate rooms in a modern, expensive hotel of grey concrete overlooking the Lake Atitlán and the volcanoes behind it. She said she was going to make some phone calls to the States and wanted to clean up and rest. Quinn nodded.

He stood under the shower and its lukewarm dribble for

half an hour, then lay down on the bed. There was a tiredness behind his eyes and somewhere in the middle of him. His head ached and his mind was racing. He wished he had money so that he could book two plane tickets, for himself and Judy; and then he wished he had a passport and he began thinking about how he could go about getting one. He did not like the idea of having to do it from Guatemala City. They could slip over the Mexican border, he was sure, and he could organize one from there. He had a sudden rush of temper. It was the unfairness of the need for money and papers after what they had just seen. He imagined going into a consulate and telling the clerk of the charred bodies and the decapitated heads and saying, 'Give me a passport,' and the clerk understanding, saying 'Yes, you must have a new passport at once.' Quinn got quite excited, but then, his mood suddenly changing, reviewed the scene more realistically and saw the clerk shrugging his shoulders and holding up his hands to demonstrate the impermeable nature of bureaucracy, and saying, 'I can't give you a passport unless you have the necessary documents. I'm afraid there's nothing I can do.' Well, it would take time; so what? Where would they go, he and Judy? New York? San Francisco? Back to Ireland? Dublin, perhaps? Why not? Judy would like Dublin, would, he was sure, be charmed by it. They could not go to Belfast, of course. He pushed the city – Denis, Monica, the house he had once lived in – out of his thoughts, and realized that for the first time they no longer held any power over him.

Dublin. He had a friend who lived in a beautiful, spacious flat in Fitzwilliam Square. They could stay with him. They could go for walks around St Stephen's Green, and he could get a car and drive her up into the Wicklow Mountains. He wanted to be with her in Dublin. He wished she was with him now. He found himself going over their love-making of the previous day. He wanted to excite himself by it as a way of making her nearer to him. He shut his eyes to concentrate, but it did not work as well as he had hoped: he would remember them together and remember the expression on her face, and then, looking into her face, seeing its changes, his thoughts went off in other, unwanted directions and, no matter how hard he tried to point their way, they ended up at Agustín. He felt fear and anger. It was irrational, he told himself. Agustín had gone, vanished, and in any case, if they were to meet, what would Agustín do? There was no need for the confrontation. He had dreamt it up, made it out of nothing.

He supposed he had fallen asleep. The light was fading. He suspected he might vomit and he tried to cast away the feelings of sickness and foreboding that came with him out of his sleep. He started coughing and could not stop. At last he managed to swallow some pills.

He knocked on Judy's door. The room was identical to his, featureless in the way of modern hotels, a rectangle without recesses, everything ordered and uninteresting. Judy sat on the bed and lit a cigarette.

'Are you okay?' he asked.

'Yes,' she said irritably.

'How long will we stay here?' Quinn was aware that his voice had gone quieter, had taken on the tone of someone not wishing to cause annoyance through asking stupid questions. He felt weak.

Judy drew on the cigarette and inhaled the smoke. There was something elusive in her manner that Quinn, without knowing what it was, recognized as carrying the possibility of disappointment. She consented to his taking her hand, but he let it go at once because it was cold. When she blew out the smoke, she turned her head away from him. She did not look at him when she spoke.

'I've booked a flight to New York from Guatemala City. It leaves tomorrow afternoon at three.'

Quinn felt something give way inside.

She continued, 'I'll book you a flight to wherever you want, or, if you want to stay here, I'll leave what money there is. If I can get some money with my credit card, you can have it.' She turned to him and stared at him in a hard way. He thought she was preparing to say 'Sorry,' but instead she said, 'Okay?' Her eyes were on his in a challenge. They were very hard.

'Yes,' Quinn said. He wanted to get out of the room, but found himself hanging on.

'Oh for God's sake,' Judy said. She got up and went to the window and stared out over the lake.

Quinn thought about speaking, but any words would have collided and done damage. He left the room, and Judy.

The boats and launches were coming in, and on the hillsides overlooking the lake men worked in patches of fields which were almost perpendicular. The sky was darkening.

Quinn crossed the road and stepped into a restaurant. It was almost empty, too late for lunch, too early for dinner, and most of the tourists were still down at the lake, out on the boats, or browsing the stalls. Quinn mocked himself bitterly for the plans he had been making in his room. He checked his pockets and found he had a few dollars and some quetzals. He ordered a beer and a cuba libre, tossed them down and ordered the same again. When the waitress took away the empty glasses he noticed two rings on the table. He stared at them resentfully and then, with a violent sweep of his hand, wiped them out.

The restaurant's interior was a sprawl of rooms, one leading on to the next, others up steps and off to the left and right. The roof was supported by pillars, and the windows were small and let in little light. Seated at a table by a window that gave out on to the main street were Nick Zenga, Rex and Pascual. The light from the window fell across the table, and it seemed to suck in all the other light from the immediate vicinity, so that the three men were practically invisible from where Quinn sat.

'I would say the time approacheth,' Zenga said. He looked out the window and said, 'Another twenty minutes and it'll be dark.'

'The boat's ready,' Rex said.

Zenga nodded, the minutes passed and the night came in. At last Zenga said, 'Rex, why don't you and Pascual go on over to the hotel and pick up Señorita Mendoza so that we can get going. Take her down to the pier. I'll join you with our friend here.'

Rex and Pascual got to their feet.

'And remember,' Zenga said with his rictal smile, 'you're on the same team. So team spirit, right?'

Zenga felt almost sorry for the white man, who had not even raised his eyes to watch the strangers leave the restaurant, had no inkling of the nearness of his death. Zenga called the waitress and told her he wanted to pay his table's bill and that of his friend, the gringo over there sitting alone. The waitress made a quick calculation and went off with the notes Zenga gave her. While he waited for his change, Zenga leaned back in his chair and ran things over in his mind. They had come together more or less as he had foreseen. He had hoped to get all three in Antigua, but then they split up and he had almost lost the Mendoza woman and the white man during the night. But Rex knew the area and assured him that if they waited where the car had turned off the main road, they would have to come back. And sure enough the car reappeared, bashed in a little in the front, but with Mendoza and the white man. They followed them to Panajachel and Zenga chuckled as they pulled into town. Better here than in Antigua, as a matter of fact. More isolated, and, just across the lake, was the New Era mission at Santiago, where they could take them and talk to them in private. All that remained to do was to find Agustín, and he was on top of that.

The waitress returned with his change. He tipped her, neither generously nor meanly, but precisely.

Zenga watched Rex and Pascual emerge from the hotel with Judy. Rex had her by the wrist and the woman flounced petulantly. The scene looked, to the objective eye, like a father taking a wayward daughter in firm hand. Well, if you didn't look too hard. Because Pascual, in fact, looked nervous and suspicious.

Zenga waited until they had settled in the boat.

It was time.

He patted the handle of the Colt Commander and rose. He went up to Quinn, opened his jacket to show him the gun, which was stuck in his belt under his stomach, and spoke softly. 'Hello, Sean.'

Quinn looked up, but did not say anything.

'We have Judy, Sean. So why don't you come along?' Zenga indicated the glasses on the table. 'They're on me.'

Quinn hesitated.

'In case you're thinking of not coming,' Zenga said evenly, his smile stretching, 'I ought to let you know that I will kill you right here and now. Don't think I won't, because I will and, believe me, nothing untoward will happen to me. The police won't come and rescue you, or arrest me.'

TWENTY

The launch was small. Rex steered. Judy sat next to Pascual, who kept his head turned from her; but she had already recognized him. She calculated that Zenga did not know about Pascual and Jank's murder, and she almost blurted it out, before deciding it would do no good, not here, in the boat. She would have to hope for a chance to use the information to greater effect.

Judy would not look at Quinn, who sat facing her in the prow, Zenga perched behind him. The water was calm and the boat speared through it with a gentle swish. The dark clustered about them like a besieging foe, readying itself for the final push; in the distance Quinn could still make out the conical peaks of the volcanoes and the sharp, high hills. The lake was vast, Quinn realized, almost like a sea.

'I don't want an answer right now,' Zenga said in his reasonable tone; he waved the pistol from Quinn to Judy in an off-hand way; his eyes flitted from the prisoners to the darkening water and back. 'I'm willing to wait – say, ten minutes. If you tell me what I want to know, maybe we can work something out.

'So, where is Agustín Romero?'

'I . . .' Judy started at once, but stopped when Zenga held up a hand.

'Please. I want you to consider your answer. I have the feeling you were going to say something I wasn't interested in hearing. Right, Judy?' He smiled tolerantly at her, then put a hand on Quinn's shoulder and shook him playfully. 'Try harder.'

Quinn shivered. It was cold now; it was the thin, piercing

cold that settles on higher elevations when the sun goes down and takes with it whatever temporary warmth it has created. Warmth here is an intruder, this place is meant to be cold, Quinn thought. Above the noise of the outboard, he heard the engine of another boat. He saw lights. This boat, bigger and faster than the one they were in, caught them up and, for a short while, went in tandem with them. A spotlight danced on the water before it.

'The regular passenger boat, not the Seventh Cavalry,' Zenga said. The larger boat left them behind. 'So?'

It was Judy who spoke. Her voice was firm, which at first surprised Quinn. 'I don't know where Agustín is, and he' – she indicated Quinn – 'doesn't know either. The last . . .'

Zenga made clicking noises with his tongue and shook his head in theatrical disappointment.

Judy persisted – 'The last time we saw him was in Antigua the day before yesterday. He left the hotel and didn't come back.'

Zenga continued his clicking. Quinn saw the two other men smile.

'She's telling the truth,' Quinn put in. He did so half-heartedly.

Zenga studied him from behind for some moments. 'I believe you,' he said at last.

Quinn felt his shoulders relax a little, and hated himself for it. Even now, he told himself, after all you know, you persist in clutching at straws. It is a fact, he continued to himself, borne out by experience a thousand times a day, that men and women consent to be taken into the dark before them. In prison, years before, he had read the account an austere Russian writer had given of his arrest: the man had *agreed* to go with his captors, had done nothing to try to escape. It was not that the writer had been over-whelmed, it was worse than that: traitors inside him gave him up the instant his enemy approached. He delivered himself up. Only once had Quinn spontaneously attempted flight, the night he was shot by the soldiers. And that night he had been drunk.

In the distance Quinn could see the lights of a town.

'Santiago,' Zenga said, reading his thoughts. 'Nice town. Very colourful. The tourists like it.'

It was another thirty minutes before they reached Santiago. From about forty feet they could see a rickety wooden pier which went out through reeds into the water. The passenger boat had just been moored, and the people were disembarking. Quinn heard the laughter of children and the thump of baggage on the pier's slats.

Rex guided the boat to a smaller landing about a hundred yards to the east. He tied the boat up, and Zenga covered Quinn and Judy as they got out. Zenga took Judy by the wrist, and Rex held Quinn by the upper arm in a bruising grip. The town was quiet, and the passengers from the other boat, who were already making their way from the pier up the path into town, paid them no attention. The streets ahead were curiously empty and still, so that it became possible to believe the men and women from the two boats were the only inhabitants.

As they went on, they became aware of a distant murmur, rising in intensity as they approached. Zenga and Rex exchanged glances, and Pascual said, 'What the fuck is that?' They walked on, turning left at the top of the street from the pier into the town, and continued for four or five minutes more. The noise – a droning hum – was louder now, still more intense, and they were able to hear above it occasional voices. They turned a corner. Down a narrow flight of stone steps before them was the plaza.

At first sight, in the blackness of the night, the torches massed in the plaza gave them the impression of looking down from a mountainside on the lights of a huge city in a valley. The air smelt of wood smoke, paraffin and alcohol.

Quinn felt Rex's grip tighten as they descended. Their movements were not entirely their own, for from behind a press of men carrying more swarming lights pushed them on. It seemed to Quinn that they were being sucked into the crowd, as though the crowd were a sea and there were currents pulling them in. He saw a tight look edging out the smile fixed on Zenga's face as the Italian elbowed aside the small Indian men. Many of the men had a look of sullen, unfocused anger. They regarded the strangers warily and shuffled reluctantly to let them pass. Quinn heard Rex speak to someone in the crowd, staccato bursts of speech without inflexion or cadence. They pressed on into the sea, but made scanty progress. Little shifts from unseen people far beyond created waves to beat them back. After a few minutes they reached a solid wall of people and could neither advance nor retreat. Rex muttered something to one of the people and the man grunted some reply.

'What's going on?' Zenga demanded of Rex.

'The army disappeared someone from the town, took him down to the base. They want him back.'

'I don't believe it,' Zenga said, exasperated. 'Of all the times . . .'

Quinn looked around and saw that Pascual had become detached from the group. He was struggling, arms raised, like a swimmer out of his depth, ten or twelve feet away. Zenga, after struggling to free his arms, motioned to him impatiently.

The crowd surged forward with a sudden jolt. Quinn lost sight of Zenga and Judy. The crowd eddied back and, for a moment, cleared from around him and Rex. Muttering curses, Rex craned to find Pascual. His grip relaxed. Quinn swung his right fist around and caught Rex on the bridge of the nose. Rex did not fall down. Quinn hit him again, but was unable to get much force behind the punch. Simultaneously he strained to pull his arm out of Rex's grip. Rex, who was stunned, held on. Quinn hit him again and wrenched forward. His arm tugged out of his jacket. Rex was crouching, one hand covering his nose, the other gripping the empty sleeve. Quinn got out of the other sleeve and lunged into the crowd.

As he struggled on, he became aware of the heat of the torches. Blisters of sweat erupted in his hairline, a bead rolled down the side of his face and tickled him maddeningly; there was no room to lift his hand. The crowd went forward, against Quinn. He felt someone punch him from behind and, fear piercing him, he ducked down as far as he could. But it was just one of the Indians, and the men around him laughed at Quinn's over-reaction. He pushed and pulled through the crowd. Someone slapped him hard on the head. He did not bother to react, but pressed on.

Quinn was frightened, but something else tugged at his fear. It was exhilaration, the feeling that he was in a race, or rather watching one on which a great deal depended, but from which, either way, he was ultimately immune: the outcome was less important than the race itself. Perhaps, he thought, he had always been this way, detached, even from the most important events of his life and the lives of those around him. He pressed on, fighting against the people; but if he did not win, it would not matter.

The crowd came to an end in as defined a way as if there had been a fence or a hedge, and he burst through into an empty street. He stopped to gather his breath and to look back at the sea of people. It was moving forward slowly but he could see ripples that disturbed its patterns, and he knew that they were caused by his enemies. He said aloud, 'There's nothing I can do for you.' He thought he was addressing Judy and a low feeling entered him, of punishing her for her rejection of him. Then he understood he had been talking to himself. 'Oh Christ,' he said, 'oh Christ.'

The ripples were getting closer. He saw Rex, the man's twisted glare standing out, almost disembodied, a pair of eyes shining out of the dark mass. Quinn turned and ran blindly. The streets were narrow, and the only illumination came from candles and paraffin lamps in the windows of the hovels.

A sudden cheer went up behind him, and a clatter of shots. Another cheer. One shot, another. Shrieks, but not shrieks of panic: men baying.

Quinn turned a corner, saw it led into a courtyard, turned back, left and on. He came to a flight of steps, ran up them three at a time and found himself in another courtyard. He sprinted through it.

He found himself before a long wall of white sheets hung from a line which stretched between two low shacks; a corner of one of the sheets lifted in the breeze. He found a way through and discovered a second wall of sheets. He pushed through, under, round: a third wall. He got through to find another; panic rose in him. He imagined himself to be in some vast and weird encampment. He slowed down and strained to listen. He heard footsteps. He realized he was half shrouded by a sheet and he moved forward to get out of its trap, only to find himself more entangled.

Rex, his nose comically bloodied, appeared before him and raised a pistol.

The shooting came as wild popping. Even though he did not see anything – his eyes had closed to keep out the danger – Quinn knew the shooting had been undisciplined, ragged. He knew at once that he was not hit. It seemed only then that he heard the final explosion, but he knew that his senses were playing tricks, for Rex was already on the ground. Quinn fought off the sheet and got up. The body was three feet before him. There was no obvious wound, but Rex was dead.

Agustín stepped forward. A sheet trailed from his shoulder and reluctantly slid away.

Quinn could only gaze at him. He had the impression he was looking at someone he had never known, and he felt terribly, desperately sad. A dissonant, jarring music started up in the distance: the slow, dread beat of a drum and the high screeching of pipes. Agustín came forward. He was holding Judy's gun. He stood before Quinn.

Gradually, imperceptibly, sense built up in the music and a rhythm was established, meaning. Agustín let it reach him, as he had the music of Lurigancho. He understood then what had been so important to him about the music and the prison, when he had stood and let the voices drench him.

> *The people's blood has a delicious perfume,*
> *It smells like jasmine and violets,*
> *And like gunpowder and dynamite.*

In the music, in the prison, Agustín Cienfuegos de la Cruz, thief, had experienced the possibility of the heroic. A family in wreckage, his choices mean. Then he entered the *pabellón industrial*, not a prisoner but a refugee from a life of low and selfish acts. Here he came to glimpse the world of Gabriel, Nita, Dulio.

In the distance, mixed with the music, there were more shots, not the sharp piercing sounds of modern high-velocity weapons, but the booming of ancient shotguns. There were more cheers and shrieks.

'What are you going to do?' Quinn asked.

Agustín raised the gun and examined it. 'I don't know that there is anything left to do.'

The nature of Agustín's early life had encouraged in him the belief that if only he were bold and brave enough to grasp the opportunity, he would win out. It was not until he entered Lurigancho that he understood what it was to be in the midst of others, and to act with them. But still some part of him – an instinct more compelling than any other he recognized in himself – strained against what he had discovered. So powerful was it that it carried him along for all the years of his wandering with Dulio, from El Alto to Los Angeles. His craving for revenge came from the enormity of his loss. But, in killing Andrew Jank, he forfeited what he had learnt – for revenge is *the* act of the individual, as low, petty and mean as the robberies that had first inspired him. So there was only one thing left to do. Watch over Quinn and Judy, as he had, sensing things were coming to an end, through all the hours of their search, their talking, their finding each other, their love-making. *We walk on thin ice, there's no one keeps us from sinking, except each other.* Agustín had not recovered his forfeit by saving Quinn, but he had gone some way to appeasing the Captain of Fifty.

Quinn said urgently, 'We have to find Judy.'

Just then he saw a man in European dress come down the alley of sheets. His pace was unhurried and his quartertips clicked on the stone. It was Rafael. Agustín turned and raised his gun, but Quinn did not know if he fired. Agustín dropped the gun, bent over and put his hands to his stomach. Slowly, he lowered himself to the ground and held himself in a sitting position, rocking slightly. Rafael continued unhurried, walking towards him. In his right hand he held a pistol, in the left, improbably, his briefcase. Agustín hugged himself and rocked in time to the music. Abruptly, the drum beat ceased, and the wind instruments went off in squeals, and then were silent.

Agustín laughed to himself. The whole of his life was a deceit, like the music; his heroism and sacrifice had no more substance than the notes he had hung on; music is no more than trickery.

'I told you,' Rafael said to Quinn with a smile, 'I told you Central America is not "nice".' He worked at the smile, he liked the idea of killing with *élan*. Rafael noticed Agustín's rocking and finished him with a shot in the back of the head.

Quinn ducked and scuttled under the sheets. He did it without thinking, without fear; he was still in the race.

There was a shot, but he was not sure that Rafael had fired it, could not tell if it was near or far. It did not matter to him. He was fleeing, exhilarated, running on pure excitement. Down a flight of stone steps, across a dirt street into an alley, right, right, left, going on instinct, judgements made in split seconds, into a courtyard, into another street . . . into the night.

Pascual was lost and the town was in chaos. People streamed through the narrow streets, their torches gone, the anger frightened out of them. A helicopter with a searchlight circled above, and from time to time there was the heavy rattle of its gunfire. Sometimes it seemed close, sometimes far away; he was never certain when he should be taking cover.

An old woman grabbed his head in both her hands and addressed him in a language he did not understand. He told her in Spanish to leave him alone, and tried to prise her hands away. But she got more hysterical and found strength in her hysteria. She muttered in broken Spanish, 'They're killing the people. The soldiers are killing the people.' She frightened Pascual, and when he could not free himself he punched the woman in her toothless mouth. She moaned and fell down. Two men running past looked at Pascual, at the woman on the ground, but did not stop.

He asked for the mission and shook a man into directing him. He lost his way, asked again and wandered, wandered. There kept coming into his head the image of the *cubana*. He was like her, he was like her, only the thinnest membrane kept him from pitching into her world. Whenever things got this confused, the *cubana* and the bus ride to Santa Ana sprang unbidden into his mind. 'I got to keep myself together,' he muttered to himself repeatedly, as if in prayer. A boy ran past and Pascual grabbed him by the throat.

'Tell me where the New Era mission is, you little fucker. You know where it is, don't lie to me.'

The boy's face was expressionless with shock. Pascual shook him.

'All you fucking Indians, you're all liars,' he screamed into the boy's face. 'Now tell me where it is.' He put his gun to the boy's temple and shook him.

The boy pointed down the street, down the way he had come. There was an explosion near by. Flames snaked up above the shacks.

'Back there?' Pascualito said suspiciously. 'That way?'

The boy nodded. A group of four or five men ran past, jostling Pascual. There was another explosion somewhere and Pascual saw a glow of orange flare up in the sky.

'You come with me,' Pascual said to the boy, and he started off, his hand on the boy's shoulder, clutching him by the shirt. The boy turned and ran, ripping his shirt. Pascual turned and fired wildly after him. The people running towards him scattered into the doorways of the hovels on either side of the street; except for one man, who was carrying a large drum, too dazed to move. The man shrank back as Pascual passed, dropped the drum and pressed his palms into the wall. Pascual lifted the gun and fired into the man's face. The body fell with a speed that astonished Pascual, as if the dead man had been dropped from a height, and a hand fell on the drum to make a vibrating note. Then Pascual ran, muttering to himself, 'Shit this fucking country, shit this fucking country.' This, too, a prayer.

It was Zenga who found him. He had been standing by the window of the mission, looking out and shaking his head in disbelief, when he saw Pascual walk past, the mad speed look in his eyes, the gun at his side. Zenga shouted to the two missionaries in the building to keep an eye on Judy while he dashed out after Pascual.

When he had calmed Pascual down, Zenga dismissed the missionaries, a blond American boy from Kentucky and his Indian assistant. The shack they shared was near by, they assured Zenga, and they could reach it safely. They were glad to go.

Gradually the chaos outside subsided. The gunshots died away and the streets cleared. Pascual told Zenga that he had followed Rex after Quinn had broken free, that he had got lost, then saw Rex again and started running after him. He described seeing Rex killed, then described how a man carrying a briefcase appeared and shot Agustín. Quinn had got away again, but the man with the briefcase went after him. Pascual said he tried to follow them, but lost the trail.

Zenga rarely drank, but he decided that tonight he would make an exception. There was a bottle of rum in a cupboard, and he poured drinks for himself and Pascual.

'Where's the woman?' Pascual asked.

'In the back,' Zenga said with a smile that turned into a conspiratorial grin, encouraging some thoughts that Pascual liked, until he suspected he might have misread the Italian and that these thoughts were not the ones Zenga wanted. The idea that he was being set up for something pinched at him.

'Always suspicious Pascual, huh?' Zenga said humorously.

'No.'

'Nothing wrong with that.' Zenga poured them each another drink. 'Are you suspicious about women, or is it just men?'

'Women are worse.'

Zenga laughed and put his hand on Pascual's shoulder.

'Who was the guy with the briefcase?' Pascual asked.

'My man. I left him behind in Antigua to wait for Agustín to show up. My guess is that while we were following Judy and Quinn, Agustín was following us, and my man Rafael was following him. Or maybe Agustín came to Santiago on a hunch, because of the mission here, or maybe for his own reasons. Who knows? The point is my man saw to him.' He grinned at Pascual. 'I told you you were on the winning team, didn't I?'

'Yes.'

'You're tense,' Zenga said, and he began kneading the taut muscles in Pascual's neck and shoulder, the way he had done in the mission in Tijuana. His tone changed; it became more confidential. 'Why are women worse?'

'You can't trust them,' Pascual replied quickly. The massaging of his neck was absorbing him, exciting him.

'I agree,' Zenga said. 'Does that surprise you?'

'You're a smart man.'

Zenga laughed, a little hollowly. 'I have other reasons,' he said, and stared into Pascual's eyes. His hand was cupped round Pascual's neck and he brought Pascual's head forward so that their faces were only inches apart, Pascual's slightly lowered. 'Maybe they're the same as yours.' With his free hand he lifted his drink and drained the glass. Pascual remained still, his head bent forward, waiting. He heard Zenga's glass settle on the wood of the table, and felt Zenga's two hands, one on either shoulder, kneading the muscles. Zenga was breathing heavily, the breath filling his lungs and staying there for a long time and making no noise as it escaped; only the sound of his taking in air was heard.

'Do you want to please me?' Zenga whispered.

Pascual trembled. 'Yes.'

Zenga kissed Pascual's head. Pascual put a hand on

Zenga's waist. Zenga pushed him back suddenly to look into his eyes, then kissed him on the mouth. Before Pascual could join in the kiss, Zenga thrust him back again. Pascual was confused.

'First we have to talk to the Mendoza woman,' the Italian said in a business-like voice. 'Will you come with me?' He spoke in a way that was like a father asking a child to do something that would be a token of love and regard for its parent, though, of course, in reality, there was no element of choice involved.

'Yes,' Pascual said.

'Good.' Zenga got to his feet and directed Pascual to the back room.

They went inside. Judy was tied to a chair. She screamed when she saw them.

'Judy, Judy,' Zenga said, 'there's no need for that.' He made shushing sounds.

'Look, please,' she said.

'Judy, Judy,' Zenga said in a tone that implied disappointment.

'Please let me go. I only came to find out about my sister so I could tell my parents. Please. They're old. They just wanted to know. Please don't hurt me, please don't hurt me.'

'Oh Judy,' Zenga said. He stroked the side of her face. Her eyes were very big. 'Why did you come down here?'

'Just to find my sister.'

'No,' Zenga said. 'Tell me the truth.'

'Please.'

Zenga waited but Judy would say no more. 'Maybe,' he said, 'you don't know the truth. Or you won't admit it to yourself. Is that it?'

'I just wanted to find Mercedes.'

'No, no, no,' Zenga said. There was anger in his voice. 'You had some hair-brained idea, isn't that right? What were you thinking of? That you and those two dregs could right wrongs, something like that?'

Almost imperceptibly Judy nodded.

313

'Judy, you're an intelligent woman. How could you have even thought something so fantastic? What were you trying to prove?'

'I just wanted to find out what happened to my sister,' Judy said.

Zenga gave her a tired smile. 'But Mercedes was very, very bad. She had idealistic notions that were leading people into disaster. Look, Judy. You've seen this country and you've seen Mexico. You can't tell me those countries, or any Third World country, can be different than what they are. Communism is a utopia, it doesn't work. So that's out. These countries can't be like America because there just isn't room for that. There can only be one America.

'So what's left? I'll tell you. Calm the people down, make them forget about hopeless ambitions, fix their minds on God and reality. Some of them will make it – I'm talking economics – more if they truly take Jesus into their heart and live according to what the Bible lays down. We're helping them be realistic, to adjust to realism. Mercedes was doing the opposite.

'You know what she was doing? Let me put it in a way you'll understand. Take a cripple. Someone, say, can't walk. Now, you cannot go to that person and say, "Do what I tell you and you'll be an Olympic champion." That would be cruel, Judy, wouldn't it, hmm?'

'Yes.'

'But you can say to that person, "Accept the situation you're in and make the best of it. You can get around okay. You can get a job, somewhere to live, buy stuff, things like that. But you are never going to be Olympic champion."

'Judy, do you understand what I'm telling you?'

'I see that,' Judy said. She nodded earnestly. 'I see that.'

'Good,' Zenga said with his painted smile. 'Your sister Mercedes – and you can believe this or not – I don't know how she died. I haven't had time to find out. To be frank, I don't know if we, well, if we asked the authorities to speak to her and maybe the authorities went too far, as they sometimes do down here. I don't know, I really don't. That could have happened. I'm not denying it. But say it did happen that way, Judy, say it did. So what? I know she was your sister, but she's just one more idealist who was doing harm, though she may not have realized it. She was harming the people. She was telling the cripples they could be Olympic athletes.

'Now she's dead. And that's profoundly sad for you and for your family. I accept that. But really – and, Judy, you have to admit this – the people are better off without her. You think they miss her in Patzún, where she worked?' The idea was preposterous, Judy had to admit it. 'You think people that get up at four in the morning and work in the fields until night and don't have running water or electricity or doctors miss your sister? Judy, Judy.' He stroked her hair. 'Answer me, Judy.'

'No,' she said. She smiled at him weakly.

'That's right,' he said. He regarded her with the eyes of a stern but fair parent. 'You didn't come down here to look for your sister, Judy, did you? That wasn't the real reason.'

'No,' Judy said in a whisper.

'You came to prove something. Isn't that right?'

Judy nodded.

'What?' Zenga asked softly.

Judy hung her head. She said very quietly and slowly, in the manner of a confession, 'That I was as good as my sister.'

'Like when kids jump over rocks that their big sister has jumped over and look over to their dad, like to say, "Dad, look at me. I can do it, too." '

'Something like that, yes.'

'Except the daddy you want to please is inside yourself. Isn't that right?'

'Yes,' Judy said quietly.

'Like a game, right?' Zenga chuckled. 'But now you don't want to play any more.' Judy began to cry. 'You want to go home to your mom and your dad.' He patted her head. Judy was sobbing.

'Judy, what was killing Andrew all about?'

Judy did not reply.

'Judy, are you listening to me? Why did you and Quinn

and Agustín kill Andrew? Agustín's dead, by the way, so don't feel you have to protect him.'

'Dead?'

'Uh-huh.' Zenga smiled. 'You know I'm not trying to trick you, don't you?'

Judy nodded. She said, 'Agustín was in a prison in Peru some years back. There was a riot and his friend got killed. He said Andrew killed him.'

'Lurigancho? Agustín was in Lurigancho?'

'I think that was what he said.'

Zenga shook his head. He tugged at his lower lip and regarded Judy.

'Judy,' he said sincerely after some moments of thought, 'I always wanted to know something about women like you.'

'What?'

'Now, you have shared a bed with Agustín, we both know that. Agustín's dead. He's just been killed. Tell me, how do you feel about that? The reason I ask is, you didn't show any sign of sadness, nothing, when I told you. So let me tell you this. Quinn, he's also about to die. Now, you fucked him, too. So, tell me, how do you feel about that?'

'You filthy—'

'You're the filth,' Zenga shouted back with real hatred. 'You and your kind.'

Zenga stepped back and breathed in deeply to recover his composure. After some seconds he shook his head in amusement to show he was back under control. 'It's all just a game with you, Judy,' he said. 'Even fucking. You represent to me nothing but the dregs. You don't engage in anything. You fuck a man, it means nothing to you. His death means nothing to you. Your sister, she doesn't mean anything, either. You didn't come down here because of her, but because of you. Politics, religion, family, loyalty, *love*, sex – nothing. Agustín had a motive, that at least I can respect. Revenge is the act of the true man. Quinn? He's just living out the end of his days the only way he knows how. But you? You have nothing except your little game.'

Judy turned away from him.

'Well,' he said, bending down and taking her chin in his hand. 'I'm afraid you can't leave your little game just yet. That's not possible. You see, Pascual here wants to play now.'

He straightened, smiling fixedly. He put his hand out again to stroke her hair. Judy spat at him; the glob landed on his right eyebrow and he let it trickle into his eye before slowly wiping it away.

'Pascual,' Zenga said, indicating Judy. He took a knife from his pocket, unsheathed it and gave it to Pascual; then, without looking back, he left the room.

Without Zenga there, Judy's hopes rose. Now was the chance to use her information. 'Pascual, I won't tell him about Andrew, not if you let me go.'

Pascual stared at Judy. A tingle started in his mouth, spreading, like a dentist's anaesthetic, from the left side of his tongue into the lower gums and teeth. Dark spots and violent, broken streaks of light, like lightning flashes, came before his eyes; they seemed to be floating on a film and they jumped across his field of vision as he blinked in an effort to clear them. The whole lower left side of his mouth and face was numb, and a worrying loss of sensation had spread into his right hand. He gazed at the fingers wrapped around the knife and moved them, one by one; he felt he was looking at them from a distance and had the feeling they belonged to someone else. At that moment, the insect struck. It cut viciously into his brain and he groaned in agony.

He could hardly see the woman in front of him; his peripheral vision had gone. He had to bring the knife up to within an inch of his face to make it out: the blade fascinated him and he examined it wonderingly.

A voice was trying to get through, as if it came from the other side of a door at the end of a long corridor. He was in the corridor, sheltering in its soothing darkness, he could see the door, see himself hesitate. He did not know whether he should answer the voice or not. There was something about it he liked. It belonged to a woman, was that it? He took an uncertain step and stopped, straining for the voice; it came to him coaxingly, and he started off, still warily, but also with a faint kind of trust. The voice was soft, soft. The insect attacked again and he put his head in his hands and groaned in despair. At last the pain receded and he went on, his footfalls echoing, clipping on the stone. He came to the door and listened to the voice on the other side. It was addressed to him and it was saying nice things about him, though the words were irritatingly vague and he did not understand them all. He listened, fascinated; desperately he wanted to make them out. They were about him, telling him he was . . . what?

He wanted to hear.

He put his ear to the door and at last was able to hear plainly what the woman was saying: 'Don't hurt me, don't hurt me. He's using you. I won't tell him about Andrew.' The voice spoke inside his head and he heard himself say, 'Yes, yes. That's right.' 'Put the knife away.' 'You're right, he's using me.' 'Put the knife away.'

The door opened and at once destroyed the gentle darkness of the corridor. In piercing brightness he saw the woman framed. The light made him scream, and the insect, fed by the light, lacerated the insides of his head. He groaned, screwed his eyes shut against the brightness and held his head.

The woman spoke again and he recognized the voice. He brought his hands away from his face and carefully opened his eyes. Before him, sitting in the seat of the bus, was the *cubana*.

'Put away the knife, Pascual. He's using you. Put the knife away and I won't tell him about Andrew.'

'Where are my Ray-Bans?'

At one o'clock in the morning Zenga saw a patrol of soldiers pass along the deserted street outside the mission. They had two prisoners, a man and a woman, whose hands had been tied behind them. He watched the patrol as far as the corner and then it was lost from view. An hour passed. Nothing stirred on the streets. There was light in the east, but it came from fires; dawn was still hours away.

Judy had stopped screaming. Zenga was relieved. He had a headache caused by the rum and the tension. But it was not because Judy's screaming aggravated his headache that he was relieved it was over, it was because screaming was disorderly, and almost always unnecessary. It offended him and his sense of what was right. Still, this time it had been worth it. He sipped the rum and thought about the conversation he would have with Victor Jank, the man he admired more than any other living person. He had fulfilled Victor's orders, had traced and eliminated the murderers of Victor's nephew and had discovered the reason for Andrew's death. He felt sure Victor would find, as he had, some strange kind of relief in Agustín's motive. It made sense, he told himself. The enmity had been made in the course of Andrew's witness. These things happen; it was only to be expected. It was part of the war they waged against Evil.

Pascual was two hours with Judy. Zenga was sitting at the table nursing a glass of rum, his fifth by his reckoning, shuffling his plans to take into account Rex's death. He had planned to drive back to Los Angeles through Mexico, but had more or less convinced himself that he would instead go to Guatemala City and fly home from there. He could book into a nice hotel, shower, have his clothes cleaned, watch satellite TV, make his calls and spend the night in a clean bed. Then be back home in five or six hours. It was a more attractive prospect than three or four days' non-stop driving.

The door to the back room opened. Pascual stood, a little dazed, on the threshold. Behind him Zenga glimpsed things out of order – an overturned chair, a woman's shoe, a newspaper, a bare leg. Zenga lifted the glass to his lips, sipped from the drink and regarded Pascual over the rim.

'I do hope you didn't catch anything from Judy,' Zenga said seriously. 'You know her morals.' Pascual's suspicious look spread into his face until Zenga turned his smile on him and started to chuckle. 'Come here and have a drink.' He beckoned to him. 'And close the door. I don't want to see that stuff.'

Slowly Pascual trudged to the table. He dropped into the

chair across the table, opposite Zenga, who poured a drink from the near-empty bottle. Pascual raised his right hand to the glass but stopped when he saw that he was still holding the knife. The blood that covered the blade and handle as well as Pascual's fingers was thick and congealing, and it was hard to tell where the flesh and the metal met. Pascual gazed at the knife and made to put it on the table.

'No, no,' Zenga said. Pascual looked at him for explanation. 'No,' Zenga said again, wrinkling his nose as if he were correcting a mild error of etiquette on the part of a young son. 'It's just right. Really. Perfect.'

'Yes?' Pascual said. He smiled.

'You know, Pascual, that's the first time I have ever seen you smile.'

Zenga reached over and ruffled Pascual's hair with his left hand. With his right, he shot him dead.

TWENTY-ONE

B ehind Quinn, fires glowed orange and red in a line that seemed to him to be the horizon but, he knew, was too close to be that; still, the line was perfect, and beyond the dance of the flames it was impossible to think anything else could exist. So the notion of a near and terrible horizon pursued him as he ran.

He passed some stragglers, terrified men and women bent low, dithering about where to take cover. He was on a dirt track winding upwards, lined by trees; below was the lake, illuminated by the fires. Before too long there were no more stragglers, and he was alone, running, though not in a determined way, not for all his life was worth. He was exhausted, and caring less and less about the outcome. Agustín was dead, and death had not looked so bad.

The pain in his chest and side grew sharper as he went on. He found he was less able to run now and he leaned against a tree for a few moments, panting heavily, feeling sick. He dry-retched. His skin was hot and prickly. He thought of Agustín sitting down and rocking himself to sleep. It could not be so bad. The thought that he might survive struck him and caused him a sudden rush of panic and fear. When he had woken in the hospital after Denis had shot him and had grasped what had happened, he felt revulsion with himself, and had not cared about the future. He felt like that now. Let's not go on, let's get it over with, he said to himself. Then he thought again. But this is cowardice, fear of the suspense I am living through. Most feelings, most motives, all stories, are at bottom banal; strip away the layers of artifice and you come to mean things. His motives with Judy?

Fear of being alone, sexual attraction, what else? Monica? What about Monica? No answer came to him.

He vomited. The suspense had made him sick, he decided. He remembered the first time he had been interrogated by the police. He was one of fifty or more men taken in that night, and the interrogators, who had little time to spend on them, were going in heavy, hard and fast: the initial interrogations were brief, violent sessions, after which the detectives and intelligence officers went away to confer and pick out the weak for further treatment. In that first session a detective had put Quinn in a chair in an empty room, and cuffed his hands behind him. Quinn had nothing on his feet, and this, more than anything, made him feel vulnerable. It was a joke in his house that his mother had always teased him about, that he never went around barefoot or in anything except his boots, even in the middle of the night if he needed to piss. The detective before him slapped him across the face. It stung and frightened him, but he was more worried about them finding his bare feet, which seemed to him to be huge and obvious; they hit him in the shoulder, hit him in the back of the neck, but they had not noticed his feet. The tension was killing him. It was as if he had hidden a gun in his house and was watching the police search for it, getting closer and closer. After a while the detectives left, saying they would come back. He worried about his feet and was certain that when they came back they would stamp on them, break all the bones. He believed they had known all along about his secret vulnerability, but had not exploited it so as to stretch out his agony. He decided that when they returned he would sign: he could not take the suspense.

They did not come back, and Quinn, in the internment camp, became the owner of a reputation he did not then deserve – of someone who had held out. He had let this reputation grow into his very nature and shape it, though really it was a distortion of his nature. He had wanted to give up, to surrender responsibility.

He vomited again. 'I'm ready to give up,' he said out loud.

He was answered by a shot and he heard a thud, followed by a whizzing, a drone, that ended with a slap into something old and solid: the bullet burrowing into the tree he was leaning against. He found new strength and bounded on.

He ran off the dirt road and on to a track dividing a field of maize plants eight or ten feet high. It was darker here, for he was leaving the fires behind on the other side of the hill; it was more like the pitch he had seen on the way to the village when they were following Saturnino's car. He turned and was able to make out the figure of Rafael coming towards him. Rafael ran awkwardly for he still carried the briefcase.

Quinn plunged into the maize. There now was no light at all. There was a flicking noise, a patter, rain on the leaves.

The downpour started. Quinn pressed on, not frightened by the dark this time, but wanting to embrace it, and to be embraced by it. In Agustín's story to him, Agustín had spoken of the *neblina*, the sea mist, that came into the prison and hung there like a protective mantle, bidding him enter and be made safe.

As he burrowed into the dark, he understood that he had been a coward all along. He was going to live now, he realized, he was escaping and he did not want to give up. Only fear and suspense had made him think that there was some profound reason why he should let himself be killed. He pressed on, pushing the tall plants aside, going further into the vast field, but remembering to turn and weave so as not to leave a straight line for his pursuer to follow. The rain lashed him, he had never known it so heavy. He chuckled aloud. 'You fool,' he said. 'You fool. You were just frightened. You thought he was going to get you sooner or later and you couldn't stand it, so you gave up.' He thought of the Russian writer again, now with great contempt.

The ground gave way abruptly and he found himself thigh-deep in freezing water. The cold winded him and, when he pulled himself out of the ditch, he was shivering uncontrollably. He went on in as much of a run as the dense plants would allow, still turning and weaving to confuse Rafael. The dark was like ink, and he loved it.

For a second time the ground gave way and he was in another ditch. This time, when he crawled out, he lay on his back, exhausted, and listened. There were no footsteps. Apart from the rain, there was no noise he could hear. He crawled a little further on, away from the ditch. In a small clearing he curled up on his side. He was cold, but he told himself the cold was a small price to pay for his escape. He resolved to get to Mexico, find an Irish embassy or consulate and fly home as soon as it could be arranged. He would need money and, for a moment, he thought money would be an insuperable object. Then he thought about tele-phones. He was in another country, halfway around the world, but there were telephones. He would phone Seamus and get Seamus to send the money. He thought of phoning Monica. No, he said, no. Fuck Monica. Fuck Denis. That was all over. His life was starting again, without them or the burden he had created for himself out of his past with them. He put his hands between his legs and drew his knees up. The splashes of rain felt quite warm. The damp earth smelt sweet. The night wheeled above him. He was going to be all right.

He had escaped. He was going to live. He was going to live. He was going to live.

Rafael let the animal-feed bag he had worn as a cape drop from his shoulders. The rain had stopped an hour ago and the smudge of dawn light was spreading in the east: it would not rain again until midday.

He gazed down on his target, foetal and asleep, his back turned to him, but stirring now, coming out of it. Rafael's instinct had not proved wrong. He knew Santiago and its surroundings well, and though he did not know this field he had made a guess based on his general knowledge of the topography. After plunging into the maize after Quinn, he had decided that his best chance lay in not following his quarry, but withdrawing to the track, which he knew Quinn, in the end, would have to come out on. He started to follow the track and discovered it led sharply upwards and round in a curve to the left. As he went on, the suspicion grew within him that he was climbing a hillock overlooking the field. He continued until he sensed he had come to the summit. He found a plastic bag and slit it to make a shield against the rain. Then he settled in to wait for the dawn light to tell him his guess was right.

The field was pitifully small, half an acre at most and divided by a channel of brown water. As the light improved, Rafael could make out the lines of Quinn's flight. There was something quite sad about them, the way they crossed and recrossed, always turning back on themselves. The lines told him Quinn had crossed the channel twice, at two different points. For someone who had gone nowhere, Quinn had travelled a long way. And now Rafael saw him in the small clearing, a dozen yards from the channel.

Rafael opened the briefcase and took out the rifle's stock, then the barrel, which he inserted without difficulty. He tightened the locks, drew back the bolt, pushed a round into the chamber and flipped the bolt down. He tucked his right foot under his buttocks, and stretched his left leg out, bending the knee until he had formed a tripod with his limbs and torso. The torn plastic bag hung at his back and he pushed it out of the way with his elbows. It made a rippling, crinkling sound, quite gentle.

Quinn stirred, straightened his legs slowly and then drew them back up. Rafael raised the rifle and took aim. A bead of rainwater unfurled from the parting in his hair, ran down his forehead, paused at the tuft of his eyebrow, then dribbled the length of his nose, where, etiolated, it hung for several moments before dropping. A breeze picked up the plastic bag and took it down the hill in the direction of Quinn.

Quinn opened his eyes and at once they filled with the water that had gathered in his lashes. Slowly, he took his hand from between his legs and lay flat, gazing up into the sky. 'I have come back,' he said. He turned to look at the hill.

Rafael believed that Quinn, in the last second of his life, observed the sullen eye that saw him to his dark home. It needed only one shot.

In the end it took Zenga ten days to get out of Guatemala. The military imposed a twenty-four-hour curfew on Santiago and no amount of wheedling or name-dropping would persuade the garrison commander to make an exception. So Zenga had himself to remove the bodies of Judy and Pascual, which he did with the help of Rafael, who arrived shortly after dawn.

Some said thirty people had been killed that night, others a hundred. Whatever, Judy and Pascual were just two more. Agustín and Quinn? They counted for nothing.

The day the curfew was lifted, Zenga and Rafael travelled by launch together to Panajachel, where they found Rex's pick-up, and drove to the capital. They booked rooms in the Camino Real, and Zenga made his calls, the first to Victor Jank. Jank did not comment directly on what Zenga told him.

'The Home Programme has a new slogan,' Jank said. ' "Let's Retake Los Angeles". The mission hall is full every night, they line up in the street to get in. We've had TV, radio coverage, newspapers – the lot. Last night – you will hardly believe this, Nick – we had thirteen thousand people at a hall we specially hired.'

'That's outstanding, Victor. It means a lot.'

'It means Andrew didn't die for nothing.'

'No. No one could say that. He's left something behind, and he was greatly loved. I don't know who could say that about the people we dealt with here. That says something, doesn't it?'

'Really. I've been thinking a lot about this. I keep thinking that Agustín, the Mendoza woman and Quinn, that in a way they're like the disruptives that appear in society from time to time. And we, well, we're like the traditions, the continuity that maintains society, keeps it glued together. Looked at that way, because the disruptives are gone, Andrew's death was a positive-type thing. It helped strengthen us, brought our continuity into focus.'

'Power right to the end of the world,' Zenga said, suddenly put in mind of the prayer meeting in Los Angeles the night he had first talked to Judy. 'I don't know how they thought it could have had a different outcome,' he said. 'What about Maritza?'

Jank paused. 'I was going to tell you. I talked with Martin and, well, he's divorcing her.'

'Is that right?'

'She's not taking it too well. She's still on medication and now she's mixing it with liquor.'

'That's real dangerous.'

'It can be.'

Neither said anything for a time, leaving it at that.

'While you're there, Nick, maybe you could look in on some of our people. Would you have time to visit Pataxte? I had some reports of a little difficulty there.'

'I have as much time as it takes. Should I bring Rafael?'

'No. It's not his kind of work, more a morale-type thing.'

'No problem.'

'Anything you need, let me know. God bless you.'

Zenga dropped Rafael at the airport and headed out on to the road to Cobán, turning off at Tactic and driving as far as Río Zarquito, where he had to leave the pick-up and proceed by boat to Pataxte. The problem was not serious, a disagreement with the local Mormons and an unhelpful military commander who had sided with them. Zenga straightened things out and set off back to the capital.

He had been away five days. On his return to the Camino Real he caught up with the latest news. The big story was still the violence in Santiago. Foreign journalists were coming and going in droves. One result was that when he went to book his flight out he discovered he would have to wait two days.

Since the night he killed Pascual, Zenga had been drinking more than he really wanted to. It was an old temptation and no longer the problem it once was. Still, it depressed him that he needed to drink now. He went down to the hotel bar. He swallowed two vodka Martinis and moved into the restaurant. Later, he could not remember how, he got into conversation with two journalists, both British correspondents in El Salvador who had been sent by their newspapers to Santiago. Both men were good drinkers and good company. Both had a sense of perspective. They did not like what they had seen, but they had seen worse.

One of the men said, 'I told the foreign desk they could get it off the wires. But they insisted. I filed fifteen hundred words. They didn't even run it. Something happened in Latvia blew it off the page.'

'I think mine got in,' the other man said. 'But it was nothing they couldn't have got from the Reuters guy. Except for that weird thing with the corpse.'

Zenga was interested and asked what they were referring to.

'By the time we got there,' the journalist explained, 'there wasn't much to see. Burnt-out huts, some bullet marks on the stonework. So we spent a day tramping the hills above the town. We came across this group of soldiers and peasants in the field. The peasants were digging something up and the soldiers were watching them, guarding them, I suppose.

'Anyway, out comes this body. It had been in the ground two or three days and wasn't too badly decomposed. It was a white man.

'Now, you can kill as many Indians as you like, no one really gives a shit. But one white skin is worth interest. We asked the officer in charge what was going on.'

'Did he tell you?' Zenga asked quickly.

'Yes. He was extremely forthcoming. It appears that the military had a report that some peasants had found the gringo lying dead in their field. The peasants panicked, thinking they would get the blame, and buried the guy on the spot. But this rumour went round and the authorities heard. So they had him dug up. That's when we arrived.'

'Who was this white man?'

'There was no ID. But they were able to get fingerprints apparently, dental impressions, that sort of thing. I thought it might have been a journo, but there's none missing.'

'Was your paper interested?'

'Mine wasn't. I saw it got a par in the *Los Angeles Times* yesterday. "Mysterious unidentified corpse" sort of thing.'

'What if they can't find out who he was?'

The journalist shrugged. 'Is that vodka you're drinking?'

Back in his room Zenga called Jank and told him about his meeting with the two journalists.

'You think this might make problems for us?' Zenga asked.

'These reporters, they're like bees round honey. As soon as they smell something sweeter, they move on. Next week you ask them about Santiago and even the ones who were there won't be able to remember. Rest easy, Nick.'

It was a twenty-minute taxi ride from the Camino Real to the airport. When Zenga checked in, he discovered his flight to Los Angeles had been delayed two hours. He sighed and made for the cafeteria. There was little to do, and it was expensive, crowded and uncomfortable. After an hour, he got up and started to wander around the small airport. The time passed slowly. He checked again on his flight: it had been delayed another hour and a half. He wandered over to arrivals and watched passengers emerge from customs, most of them middle-class Guatemalans but quite a few young European and North American tourists. He was looking them over, inspecting them with vague interest, when his attention was caught by a man of abnormal height. It was Roy Jones.

Zenga followed him at a distance to the airport bank, watched him change some money and buy a newspaper. Roy turned the pages as if he were looking for something specific, found what he wanted and read. When he moved on from the stand, Zenga bought the same paper and, from the patterns of the newsprint, quickly found what Roy had been reading: the report on the massacre at Santiago. There were pictures of bodies, pictures of burnt-out huts, pictures of soldiers. According to the report the president of the Republic had ordered the garrison out of the area, had ordered an inquiry and said it was too early to comment on the denunciations in the international press. In a box, tacked on to an eyewitness account of the massacre, were two paragraphs about the discovery of the body of a white man whose identity had not yet been established. The body had been removed to the hospital at Sololá for examination. The police were investigating.

Zenga watched Roy Jones stride outside to the taxi rank and thought about following him. He decided instead to call Victor Jank. It took twenty minutes for his call to be put through.

'He's obviously read the reports in the *Los Angeles Times* about the white man's corpse, figures it's Quinn. He's probably come down to look for his buddy Agustín. What do you want me to do?'

Jank was silent, considering.

At last he said, 'If Jones finds his friends, he will find them dead. Then what's he going to do? I don't think that should bother us.'

'He'll know what happened, he'll guess.'

'Don't let it worry you.'

'You're sure you don't want me to take care of Jones?'

'He can't do anything to us, Nick. He's just like his friends – on the outside a disruptive. We know where to find him if we have to.'

'I suppose so.'

'Come home, Nick.'

Zenga put down the telephone and stooped to pick up his bag. As he passed through customs half an hour later, the words he had uttered in his trance at the prayer meeting came back to him: *Power right to the end of the world.* What chance did an individual like Roy Jones, like any of them, have against that? Against the fire and the hammer.

Epilogue

TWENTY-TWO

T he bar had been open for three hours and no longer smelt stale, as it had when Denis had entered, twenty minutes after opening time. Now it had that smoky, beery smell that he found so comforting. Oddly, the smell always made him think of the word *nook*. There used to be nooks in this bar, years before, when he had first started to come here, when the floor used to be sprinkled with sawdust. He could not decide if he associated the word with the smell because of the old nooks, or because he thought of nooks as being warm, and safe places.

He felt warm inside. It was not just the drink, it was being where he was, among people he knew. There were times when his reputation as a *character* annoyed him, when he felt belittled by it. But most of the time he was happy enough; he had affection and approval – though neither was ever stated – and that mattered to him almost as much as life itself, almost as much as Monica.

Brendan came up to the table and set his pint glass down; some beer slopped. Pat Coogan, who was not behind the bar that day, bantered with him a bit, and he, in his rough, affectionate way, teased Pat by calling him Shot-in-the-head, and Pat, for once, took it in good spirit. Brendan had a copy of the *Irish Times*, and Pat said Brendan was getting highbrow. Brendan, in good spirits too, laughed it off, and they fell to discussing the merits of the local paper. Fifteen years ago, Brendan recalled, the local paper was nothing more than ten pages of death notices with a page of news on the front and the football and racing on the back. No, they agreed, it had not been strong on news. They discussed the death notices and agreed that, although there used to be too many, they missed them now. It was important, Pat said, to be remembered.

At this, Brendan fell silent. Pat ordered more drinks. They were joined by others, some of whom stopped for one drink, some for three or four. Denis liked it that Brendan was with the company. Brendan was well-liked, he was the kind you wanted on your side in an argument, not because he was a brilliant arguer or knew a lot, but because he so rarely took sides; he was unopinionated and therefore people respected the opinions he delivered. Denis wished he was like that. But he was not. That was not his nature. He was up-front, on the surface, always ready with his opinion. He looked at Brendan, who had started talking about the death notices again, and, impulsively, reached out and chucked his cheek.

'Fuck's sake, put a sock in it,' he said to Brendan. And Pat and Brendan both laughed and gulped from their drinks.

Since his time of trouble, things had begun to sort themselves out, slowly and not conclusively, but then things, you realized as you got older, never did resolve themselves with any degree of finality; all you could realistically hope for, he now accepted, was some kind of small improvement; sometimes you had to put up with just keeping things as they were, and praying they did not get worse.

He was not sure how his troubles had petered out. One moment everything seemed to be closing in on him: the trouble over the gun; the trouble over the money; then Quinn's unexpected return. He was horrified at what he had done, but proud, too, for he had done something he had never known he had the courage for: he had wanted something so badly he had been prepared to do anything. Not many people can say that about the way they have lived their lives.

Had it been worth it? Things had not worked out with Monica. She said she believed him when he denied having anything to do with Quinn's shooting, and the way subsequent events turned out his denial seemed to have so much support he began to believe it himself. Men who had treated him warily at first, men who were awaiting the verdict of an unseen yet irresistible authority, resumed their normal attitude towards him: the authority had spoken, in secret, and had let it be known that he was not to blame. There were days when he could convince himself that he had not done it.

Still, Monica had retreated. She hardly went out, had trouble with her nerves. Her skin had gone bad and the doctor diagnosed eczema. Her eyes had a permanent, painful red crust around them; but she never cried. When she had been at her worst, he had taken her to Donegal and rented a cottage by the sea, but she seemed further away than ever, and it hurt him terribly to feel so excluded. On the day they arrived, she had stared out over the cold sands of the bay that stretched a mile or more to the sea, and would not speak. The next morning he woke to find her already up. He went to the window of the front room and found her again staring out at the sea. The tide was in. 'The sea,' she said, as if to herself, 'has taken all the sand away.' Then she looked at him in a scary, unfocused way, and said, 'Will it bring it back?'

They left the cottage that afternoon.

Brendan was still discussing the death notices. It began to depress Denis, and with the mention of a name he nudged the conversation into a shared past. They found themselves discussing the men from the cages. A couple were doing all right: the playwright in Dublin, the screenwriter now living in Melbourne. Most of the others were not doing too well: one a drunk, another a hood, others back inside; many, many dead. But the path to success was not always smooth, Pat reminded them. Did they not remember that the playwright had been captured on the Greek border some years back with AK-47s in the boot of his car. True, Denis said, very true. And the playwright went on to great things, had married a blonde actress whose body they had all seen and admired.

When they got hungry, they sent a kid for pastie and chips, and went to eat them in Pat's mother's house. And, while Pat's mother washed up after them, they drank the tea she had made. Then they went on to another bar.

Denis kidded Brendan about the *Irish Times*, and Brendan said, a little tersely, that there had been something in it he had wanted to read. A Reuter report, he said.

'A fucking what?' Pat said.

They drank, met more people, drank with them and moved on to a club where they drank some more. Later, they went to eat pizzas, then returned to the club. Friends and strangers stopped at their table, talked, shared drinks, slapped backs and moved away. The rounds mixed one into the other, the next one and the next one. In the toilet Denis had to put his hand against the tiles to keep on his feet, something he normally would not have done, for reasons of hygiene.

It was one o'clock in the morning when Brendan went to telephone for a taxi. Pat excused himself and lurched towards the toilet.

While Pat was away, Denis began to look through the newspaper. His eyes were dazed, but it was the usual fucking shit, and he exhaled heavily. The paper soaked up beer from the table; he folded it and put it on Brendan's chair.

'Did you see anything of interest?' Brendan said on his return, nodding to the paper.

'Just the usual bad fucking news.'

'Bad indeed.'

The taxi blew its horn and someone shouted for Brendan.

'Where's Pat?' Denis asked, vaguely remembering Pat had been with them, that he had been a long time in the toilets.

'Pat's not coming,' Brendan said. 'He has something else sorted.'

'Fucking Shot-in-the-head. Do you remember that time? Fucking so funny. The cunt.'

'Let's go.'

The car was nice-looking, Denis liked it. New and unblemished. He would be comfortable in the back seat, could close his eyes and forget about everything and be delivered home. Jesus Christ, he thought, wouldn't it be a fine thing always to be lifted and laid, like the well-to-do, and have people waiting on you? That was never going to happen, though, not to the likes of him. A taxi home, late at night, a smooth ride in the darkness, in a new car – that was his luxury.

Brendan opened the door for him, and, with some awkwardness, he climbed inside. There was someone already in the back seat.

'What the fuck?' he said, irritated, his luxury spoilt by having to share. The man was drunk, slumped against the window.

Brendan was in beside him, the car moved off.

A man in the front passenger seat turned round. It was Sammy.

'Did he see it?' Sammy said to Brendan.

'No. He looked, but he didn't see it.'

'That's just like Denis.' Sammy pointed to the man in the back seat. 'You remember Eddie Stilges, don't you, Denis? Say hello.'

Slowly, he turned to look at Eddie. Eddie was dead.

The sound was sharper because it was morning and the air had not had time to thicken and dull things. So Monica shivered when she heard the knock. She put on a dressing-gown, went down the stairs and opened the door.

'Are you Monica Quinn?' a very young man asked her. He stared at the *V* of nakedness from her breast to her throat. She pulled the gown around her.

'Yes.'

'Denis won't be coming back.'

'What are you saying?'

'They're waiting for me. Take this.' He handed her an envelope.

The young man walked to a car and got in. The car moved off smoothly, almost silently, and turned the corner out of view.

On the doorstep Monica opened the envelope. It contained a cutting from the *Irish Times*. Monica read it and went inside to the living room, locking the door behind her.

She pushed the gown off her shoulders and let it fall to the floor. She found her cigarettes, lit one and sank into the armchair. She looked down on herself. Her body was pale and thin. She stroked her arm and felt the flesh tight with cold. She stroked her belly and the coarse sponge of her pubic hair. Her gaze drifted around the room and came back to her own body. She felt quite calm and saw no reason to move from the chair.

Later in the afternoon the telephone rang: she regarded the instrument vaguely. She sat in the armchair, smoking, still naked, still cold. The curtains had not been opened. She had her first drink.

By nightfall she was running a bath. While it filled she went to her bedroom. The telephone rang again; she could not remember what she was supposed to do about it. She brushed the bottles of pills from the bed and lay down. She felt her body from top to bottom. She pulled out strands of her hair and examined them, she investigated each of her toes.

She went to the drawer where she kept her papers and found what she wanted.

She heard the water slop on the floor. It took her a long time to associate what she heard with what was happening. The bath overflowing. Imagine, she thought, imagine. Sounds are changing, nothing is true to its nature any more. Friends are strangers, strangers are strangers. No one knows anyone. The sea has stolen the beach and will never bring it back. She wandered to the bath, got in, the water still running. She placed the photograph of Denis and Quinn behind the cold tap and, staring at it, let it suggest the places she should go.

Time passed. Nothing was true to its nature any more, but something lingering in her ordered her out of the bath. The water was freezing. It was the moment to leave the bath. Towels and clothes had no nature she could see the point of, so she left the house without them. Dawn was not far off.

She walked, carrying the photograph of her husband and her lover, up the slope of the street. She looked over the lough. The sky was still dark and she knew it was not about to brighten. The red clouds gathering just above the horizon would soon spread all over the sky and take it away. She gazed at the clouds and saw the images of Denis and Quinn form in them. The clouds spread, their red deepening. Red, everything became red. She looked on abstractedly as the red continued its advance, until it dissolved and conquered the two men.

When they were gone, Monica started to laugh.

ACKNOWLEDGEMENTS

I would like to thank the following for their help in the preparation of this book: Leslie Beck, Stephen Burgen, Sara Chetin, the Archbishop's nephew 'Cox', Paul Cullinan, Dulio, John Feihl, John Fitzmaurice, Rosie Gilbey, Sean Hanna, Luis Hernández, Peter Leuner, Melanie McFadyean, Anita Moreno Peña, Mónica Mosquera Javier, Liz Murray, GP, Eric Resnick, José Romero Arce, Madeleine Rosales Campos, Sabino, Tessa Sayle, Leopoldo Silva Guevara, Irene Soriano, Vince Stevenson, Wilson Cabanillas, Sonia Yamula V. and, above all, Georgina. Special thanks to the prisoners of Block 4b, Canto Grande, Lima, who, by standing up for themselves and each other, have created a human environment out of inhuman conditions.

RONAN BENNETT

The Catastrophist

Shortlisted for the 1998 Whitbread Novel Award.

Gillespie, an Irishman, goes to the Congo in pursuit of his beautiful Italian lover Inès. Unlike her, Gillespie has no interest in the story of the deepening independence crisis, nor in the charismatic leader, Patrice Lumumba. He has other business: this is his last chance for love.

'Bennett's writing is as lush and sensual as ripe mangos . . . The tone, which is perfectly pitched, and the exotic setting collude to evoke an era of colonial decadence' *Financial Times*

'Glowing with psychological insight . . . I have not read such a good thriller in years . . . The prose is as sharp as a whip, though subtle and poetic' Ian Thomson, *Evening Standard*

'A great achievement, an impressive testament to the appeal of strong narrative and sympathetic characterisation' *Sunday Telegraph*

'A memorable book, with a ring of deeply felt authenticity' Hugo Hamilton, *Sunday Tribune*

0 7472 6033 8

review

DES DILLON

Itchycooblue

Derrick and Gal are best friends. When Derrick's Da falls sick, he and Gal set out to get him a moorhen's egg – which they believe will cure him. The two boys swerve through a landscape of slaggies and steelworks, encountering the full range of life's experiences in a day that seems as elastic as childhood itself.

All that stands in their way is their fears, and mad Mackenzie who's escaped from Borstal . . .

'The pages are stuffed full and spilling over with imagination, they are shiny with it, brightly coloured, and the whole book is a testimony to its transforming power in the grimmest of realities. A child hero is difficult to do, but Dillon succeeds marvellously' *Scotsman*

'A cracking read' *Big Issue*

'Brilliantly funny' *The Times*

'A heartwarming and exhilarating read' *Sunday Herald*

0 7472 6198 9

review

If you enjoyed this book here is a selection of other bestselling titles from Review